Love, Lies & Larceny

Another Terrible Romance Novel by
M.J. Fifield

Favorite Spoon Publishing

Printed in the United States of America
First Printing, 2026

ISBN: 979-8-9954137-0-7

Favorite Spoon Publishing, LLC
1720 Malabar Road #500509
Malabar, FL 32950

Cover Design by ebooklaunch.com

Also by M.J. Fifield

The Terrible Romance Series

Love & Other Lies

The Coileáin Chronicles

Effigy
Second Nature

Other Titles

Retail Rhapsody

For Maddy, of course

Acknowledgements

So, here's the thing: This book wasn't supposed to exist. It certainly wasn't supposed to be a part of a series because the first book—*Love & Other Lies*—was supposed to be a one-and-done kind of deal. Been there, wrote that, what's next?

But then my lovely goddaughter requested another book and, as I cannot say no to her, I set out to write her another book. It took a while—a *long* while—to figure out what this story would look like, and how it would come together, and even *if* it would come together (there were doubts), and there were many days (and weeks and maybe even months) where it honestly felt like it would just be easier (not to mention quicker) to give her a kidney than another book, but at long last, here we are.

Love you, hon. I hope you find this story worth the wait. (And yes, I am now working on the third book…)

And as for the rest of the usual suspects…You know who you are. I could not do this thing I do with your continuing help and encouragement. If I haven't mentioned it lately, you are the very best support team for which an author could ever ask. I am eternally grateful to have you on my side, and I love you all.

No lie.

Love, LIES & LARCENY

M.J. FIFIELD

1

THIS IS NOT HOW THIS job was supposed to go. It was supposed to be quick. It was supposed to be easy. It was supposed to be the exact opposite of what it's turned out to be. If I manage to pull this off, I just may kill Jay later.

But in order to do that—or anything else, for that matter—I first need to get out of here.

Which means I need to work the damn problem.

I close my eyes and breathe deep. Exhaling slowly, I open my eyes again and look at the safe in front of me.

Okay. Let's do this.

First, a check of the time. According to my watch, I have five minutes before security will be doing their walkthrough. Not ideal, but it could be worse. A lot worse. They could already be here. But they're not, and I have five minutes. Four minutes. When they do get here, I should really be somewhere else.

I can do this. God knows I've worked under worse conditions. This will be a cakewalk. Whatever the hell a cakewalk is.

I press my ear against the safe door and turn the dial to the right.

Drop.

I turn the dial to the left.

Drop.

A glance at my watch. Four minutes. Which means I have three.

All right. Back to it.

I'm not hearing anything. Why am I not hearing anything? Did I miss it? Shit. This would be easier if I had…*anything* to help me hear. Or any idea that there would be a goddamn safe standing between me and the target.

No. Focus on the problem now. Kick Jay's ass later. I mean, sure, it's his job to provide the intel I need to pull off a job successfully. It's definitely his job to tell me if I'll need to crack a damn safe to do it. I can crack a safe—well, most safes, anyway—but it would have been nice to have a heads-up about this one. This is a skill—an *art,* frankly—that requires time and concentration, and doing it on the fly is—

Drop.

Oh. There it is. Maybe Jay will live to see another day after all.

Opening the safe, I search the contents inside. Beneath a mess of paper is a small black ring box. I open that to see a blue sapphire surrounded by smaller diamonds, all sitting in a bed of gold. Not my taste, but it doesn't need to be. I'm not being paid to like it. Just steal it. Closing the box, I tuck it into my backpack, close the safe, and check the time.

Time to go.

I cross the room and use the bookcase to climb into the sub ceiling. After making sure the tiles are properly back in place, I crawl through the space until I reach the women's bathroom. It's just as empty as when I went in, so I slide out, replace the tile, and set to work on my next challenge: getting out of the building.

Not that it should be much of a problem. I should be able to go right out the front door with no one the wiser. The bulk of the security team should be on a walkthrough, leaving one lonely and bored guard sitting at the desk in the lobby. I act like I belong there, and he'll assume I'm just one of the many worker bees heading home. There's no way he knows them all.

Still, I take a moment to alter my appearance to look more like I've spent eight hours sitting at a desk complaining that a meeting should have been an email and less like I was just crawling through vents and breaking into safes. After slipping on a black wool overcoat, I stick my backpack into the black leather tote bag I carried on the way in and head for the bathroom door.

My hand is on the handle when I hear voices. Male voices. I freeze and reach for the knife stashed in my coat pocket. There shouldn't be anyone on the floor yet. Security should be at least one floor above me right now. Is this something else Jay got wrong? When a woman contributes to the conversation, I relax and leave the knife where it is. The entire security staff here is male. This is something else. This is a potential gift from the gods. Safety in numbers and all that.

I open the door just enough to get a glimpse at the group as they pass on their way to the elevator. Four men and two women, all dressed in their best businessperson outerwear. That'll do. It'll work nicely, as a matter of fact.

I time my exit so I step inside the elevator just before the doors close. I move to the back while they moan about having to work late and make plans to murder their boss. One of the men glances at me, then looks again. The shift in his demeanor suggests that he's decided I am someone with whom he should flirt. Lucky me. But as I plan to use him and his friends to get out of the building, I don't punch him in the throat.

He grins. His teeth are entirely too white. If we were outside, every plane for five miles would be changing course.

"Hey," he says. "Working late."

Pretty much always. I shrug. "It happens."

"Yeah," he agrees. "We're headed to O'Malley's for a drink, if you want to come along."

I shake my head. "I can't."

"Are you sure? First round's on me."

"Tempting, but I have somewhere else I need to be."

"Come on. Just one drink?"

I envision punching him in the throat. It's not as satisfying as the real experience would be, but I still smile. "Thanks, really, but no."

He shakes his head. "Your loss."

I'm sure. "Another time, maybe."

He perks up and smiles again. He really needs to cool it with the bleach. "Well, all right, then. I'll see you around."

Doubtful. I can't imagine I'll ever be in this building again. Bleach boy here certainly isn't reason enough for a return visit.

"Yeah," I say as the elevator doors open. "See you."

I stick with the group as they cross the lobby, making sure they stay between me and the lone man at the security desk. When they turn toward O'Malley's, I turn, too. I keep pace with them until we reach the first intersection. They go straight. I turn left and head for the nearest T station.

It's a quick trip along the red line to South Station where I leave the backpack with the man working the package storage desk. He gives me a claim ticket and tells me to have a nice evening. I thank him and store the ticket in my purse before exiting the station and heading toward Charlestown.

Time to see a man about a payday.

2

THE THIEVES' DEN IS PACKED, especially given the hour, but my booth in the back is empty. Knowing the owner has its perks. I sit with my back to the wall and look over the crowd. Where's Jay? It's not like him to be late. Well, no. It's very much like him. But *I'm* late. He shouldn't be. He should already be here, halfway through his second beer and wondering where the hell I've been.

"What can I get you?" a waitress asks.

I look at her. She's new. Otherwise, she'd already know.

I nod to the bartender. "Ask Robbie. He'll tell you."

My answer annoys her, but she returns to the bar. I return to people watching. Seriously—where the hell is Jay? He better not be trying to stiff me on this job. I really will kill him then. I look away when a plate is set in front of me. I don't recognize what's on it.

"Eat," Leo says.

I look at him. "What even is this?"

"Probably the first solid food that's been in front of you all day."

Yeah. I can't argue with that. "Fine, but what *is* it?"

"If I tell you, you won't eat it."

"I won't eat it anyway."

"Just eat the damn food."

I poke one of the things on the plate. "Don't you have any mozzarella sticks in this joint? Chicken fingers? Some kind of soft pretzel with a delightful dipping sauce, maybe?"

"This is a nice bar, Skye. Not a Buffalo Wild Wings." He nods at the plate. "Eat that, and I'll bring you dessert."

"Take it away, and I'll pay my tab," I counter.

"Yeah. Like you have that much money. Speaking of which…Anyone getting your drink?"

"Yeah. The new girl."

"Dolly."

"Dolly?" I echo. "Is that her real name?"

"You're one to talk about names." Leo looks away. "Your date's here. Don't let him eat your dinner."

Leo points a stern finger at me before walking away.

A moment later, Jay slides onto the seat across from me. "Magpie. How'd it go?"

"Where the hell have you been?" I ask.

Before he can answer, Dolly sets down my drink. She looks at Jay. "Anything for you, cutie?"

He smiles. "I'm good, sweetheart."

She winks at him and walks away. Jay leans back against the booth, looking pleased with himself.

"Still got it," he says.

I roll my eyes. "Yeah. The prospect of a tip has nothing to do with it."

Jay sobers. He straightens and pulls the plate closer to him. "You okay?"

"Don't I look it?"

He laughs and pops one of the whatevers in his mouth. As he chews, he says, "Mostly, you look pissed."

"Imagine that."

After he swallows, he holds up his hands in surrender. "Whatever happened, I didn't know."

"You never do," I say, bringing my glass to my lips.

Jay leans over and stops me. "What happened, Mags?"

I set down the glass. "Your simple job wasn't so simple."

"You in trouble?"

"I wouldn't be here if I was in trouble."

"No. You gotta protect your boy."

I immediately search for Leo. He's standing behind the bar with Robbie. "The boy can protect himself. You, on the other hand—"

"What did I do?" Jay asks.

I look at him. "Not your damn job."

"You said you're not in trouble."

"Yeah, well, I can handle myself."

"Then what's the problem?"

I sigh. "There isn't one."

"Then you got it?"

I slip the claim ticket out of my pocket and pass it to Jay under the table. He leans back to put it in his own pocket.

"Payment will be in your account tomorrow."

"It better be."

"So touchy," he says. "Does that mean it's too soon to talk about the next job?"

"Maybe a little."

"It's time sensitive."

"It always is. Still, I'm gonna need a minute." I nudge the plate closer to him. "See if you can find something else to do while I decompress."

Jay picks up another thing and eats it. I finish my drink. Where's Dolly? I look around for her. My gaze lands on the bar long enough for Leo to catch my attention. He gestures to Jay with a 'what the hell' expression on his face. I shrug and raise my glass. He won't want to bring me another one, but he will. That's what years of history gets me. The benefit of the doubt and unlimited refills.

Leo brings the new drink himself. He looks at the now-empty plate in front of Jay as he sets down the glass. "No more until you eat something."

Occasionally limited refills.

"Bring me some fries, and I'll think about it," I say. "Regular fries. None of that sweet potato or truffle oil crap."

"You try my patience," Leo says and walks away.

"They serve fries here?" Jay asks.

"No," I reply. "What's the job?"

"You sure?"

"Tell me before I change my mind."

Jay removes an envelope from an inside jacket pocket and slides it across the table. "Everything you need to know is in there. Target, day, time—"

"Day and time?" I frown. "I decide that."

"Told you it was time sensitive. It's a one-night-only kind of deal."

I shake my head. "I don't like that."

"The money's good."

All right. Maybe I like that. "How good?"

"Good enough that I'm bringing this to you when I know damn well you won't like the restrictions."

I glance at the envelope. "Good enough or pretty fucking amazing?"

"The latter, Magpie. I know you don't even crack a smile for good enough."

I definitely like the sound of that. I pull the envelope toward me. "Fine."

3

AFTER THE LAST CUSTOMER IS gone and the doors are locked, I move from my booth to a seat at the bar. I put Jay's envelope on the bar top and watch Leo sort receipts and cash. Robbie makes me another drink and winks as he sets it in front of me. I salute him as he walks toward the kitchen.

Leo glances up. "So much for me cutting you off."

I shrug. "Robbie likes me more than he likes you."

"Which is weird, considering I pay his salary and you don't even tip."

"What can I say? My presence is the gift that keeps on giving."

"Yeah, it is," Leo says. "So when are you going to tell me what happened tonight?"

"What makes you think something happened?"

"Years of experience. Spill."

"Just got some bad intel. I had to improvise."

Leo stops sorting. "Bad intel?"

I glance from side to side to make sure no employees are within earshot. "Surprise safe."

Leo presses his lips together and shakes his head. He goes back to his receipts.

I sigh. "Just say it."

"Okay." Leo looks at me. "Jay's gonna get you killed one of these days."

"It wasn't Jay's fault."

"He's responsible for getting you specs. He's responsible for getting you in and out—"

"I'm responsible for that."

"Well, he's supposed to make sure he's not setting you up to fail. He's supposed to make sure you have what you need to not get killed or arrested."

I spread my hands. "And here I am, not dead or in jail. Was it irritating? Yes. Did I manage to survive? Yes. It's not a big deal, Leo. It happens."

"It's happening too much. You should have left him years ago," Leo says. "And now you're gonna be all, 'you know why I didn't'—"

"You do know why I didn't."

"I don't, Skye. I really don't. At the beginning, it was different. You needed him—*we* needed him—but you're not that kid anymore," Leo says. "Everything you do for him, and he treats you like you're expendable."

"Well, to him, I am," I say.

Oh, I shouldn't have said that. Out of all the things I could have said, that is the absolute worst. I've always been the more pragmatic one—something else Leo hates—but being casual about my disposable existence is never the right choice in his company.

"I'm sorry," I say before he can break out the lecture. "I didn't mean that."

"Yes, you did."

Yes, I did. No matter how much he may hate it, that is the truth of the situation.

"I didn't mean to upset you," I say. That is also true. "I didn't think, and I'm sorry."

Leo sighs. "I'm just looking out for you."

"I know."

"The way you look out for me."

"I know."

"Because that is what we do. That is what we have *always* done. Friends to the end. Remember that?"

"I know, Leo. I remember," I say. "But you really don't have to worry about Jay. Or me. I can take care of myself."

"Don't remind me." He picks up his bank bag. "You coming upstairs?"

"Can't." I finish my drink and tap the envelope. "Got work to do."

"You can take a night off."

"Yes, I can. But I don't want to." I grab the envelope and slide off the stool. "I'll see you later."

He follows me to the doors and unlocks them. "Text me and tell me you made it home all right."

"I always do."

Leo opens the door and lets me go through. I don't look back, but I linger until the locks fall into place behind me.

He worries too much. It's habit. We've spent the majority of our lives worried about the other, and we'll spend the rest of our lives the same way. Some habits don't break. Some habits I wouldn't want to break.

Which is why, the moment I step through my front door, I text Leo. He knows exactly how long it takes to walk the three whole blocks between our places. If I'm late, he'll come rushing over in his pajamas and slippers just to make sure something didn't happen to me. After which, I will be treated to a loud lecture on how this wouldn't have happened if I hadn't gotten a place of my own.

Lectures and Leo's feelings aside, it still needed to be done. Leo has a life outside of work. Leo dates. As much as I love Leo, three's a crowd. Especially when that third wheel is me.

As a general rule, I do not play nicely with others. I am not built for relationships or crowds, and my apartment reflects that. It's made for one and just barely counts as having a separate bedroom that's just big enough for a bed just big enough for two. Not that I bring anyone home. I don't. Any and all hookups happen elsewhere. Leo's the only person with the address, and I intend to keep it that way. My own little Fortress of Solitude.

'Fortress' is the wrong word, though. 'Two-room shitbox' is probably more appropriate. The sight of it and its complete lack of creature comforts makes Leo cringe—in particular the kitchenette with its semi-functional two-burner cooktop and mini fridge. The loveseat was here when I moved in, and my table is a wooden crate liberated from The Thieves' Den. The television hanging on the wall is, by far, the nicest thing I own. The only reason no one's stolen it is probably because they look at the rest of the building and think nothing of worth could possibly be found inside. Which is, for the most part, true.

It may not be much, but it's mine.

After changing into yoga pants and a T-shirt, I sit on my couch and dump out the contents of the envelope on the wooden crate. An ID badge falls out last. I pick it up and turn it over. Tessa Martin, junior executive of the Pearson Pharmaceuticals sales team. She's a pretty close match to me, probably why Jay thought I would be a good fit for this job. If no one looks too closely at the photo, I should be able to pass for her without any trouble.

I set down the badge and look at the rest of the material. On a sticky note, Jay's written down the day and time. One night only. Tomorrow night. Not sure why that would be the case, but they don't pay me to ask questions. They pay me to retrieve the things they cannot retrieve themselves.

The target is a flash drive in a wall safe in Suite 7 of Pearson Pharmaceuticals, located on the ninth floor of the Skyreach Building in the Financial District. Not much security listed, but there could be more of which the client is unaware. The safe specs indicate that it shouldn't be a challenge to crack. How dull. The money must be to make up for the lack of challenge.

The real challenge will be the turnaround. A job tomorrow night doesn't leave me a lot of time for prep. I'll have to do some recon in the morning. Later in the morning.

I turn on the television. At this time of night, the only options are infomercials and sitcom reruns. I stop on an episode of *Friends*. It's the one where I spend thirty minutes wondering how a group of people who never seem to do any sort of work can afford to live in New York City. I know what I have done and continue to do in order to keep a crappy, tiny apartment in Boston.

I glance at Tessa Martin's badge. Where does she live? How does she live? Does she watch *Friends*? Maybe it's too lowbrow for her. Maybe she only watches *Masterpiece Theatre* or whatever they air on PBS. Maybe she doesn't have time for television at all because she has a family and a house in the suburbs and two kids and a golden retriever.

I don't even have a goldfish. Which is for the best. The goldfish community can rest easy at night. Or as easy as a goldfish ever rests. Maybe they don't rest at all. I thought I read that somewhere. They don't sleep and they have terribly short memories.

Lucky bastards.

The episode comes to an end, and I switch off the television and go to bed.

4

THE FINANCIAL DISTRICT IS A mixture of modern high rises and older brick-and-mortar buildings fighting for space and aesthetic. A lot of big companies with a lot of money. And security. It's all right, though. I like a challenge.

It's hard to tell from the outside whether the Skyreach will qualify as such. It's an older brick building, obviously named before skyscrapers were a thing. It won't be home to any of the bigger, wealthier companies, but that doesn't mean there isn't something inside worth stealing. I wouldn't be here otherwise.

Dressed in a pencil skirt, blouse, fitted blazer, and sensible pumps, I blend in with the other young professionals on the go, but instead of walking into the Skyreach, I go to a cafe across the street and order a coffee. I take my purchase and sit at a table with a view of the building. It doesn't look like much, and the intel Jay gave me suggests the same thing, but I would love to be able to confirm that for myself.

I dig my phone out of my black leather handbag and call Pearson's main number. The automated menu eventually leads to a human and I ask to be connected to Tessa Martin. The human puts me on hold, and I listen to classical music until they return.

"Thank you for holding," they say. "Miss Martin is out of the office this week. May I transfer you to another team member instead?"

"No, thank you," I say and end the call.

Tessa Martin's out of the office. Sounds like an invitation to take a look inside.

I finish my coffee and head across the street. A man in an expensive suit is coming out of the Skyreach as I approach, and he holds the door open for me. Smiling, I thank him as I walk past. Once in the lobby, I step to the side and pull my cell phone out of my bag. I tap the screen and bring the phone to my ear, pretending to have a conversation while checking out the building directory. Pearson Pharmaceuticals has the entire ninth floor. Only the law offices of Steele and Nash are above them.

"Uh-huh," I say, turning to survey the lobby.

Two security personnel sit behind a desk, chatting with one another, far more engaged in their conversation than anything happening around them. A third man is monitoring a row of turnstiles standing between me and the elevators. More accurately, he's working on a book of crossword puzzles or Sudoku or something, barely looking at anyone walking by. There's a wonderful lack of metal detectors and bag checks, which I appreciate. It might be difficult to explain the three-inch folding knife in my possession. Not only is it not *quite* street legal, but Tessa Martin's weapon of choice is probably more along the lines of pepper spray.

"Okay, I'll see you in a bit," I say, and then end my fake call.

I drop my phone in my bag and remove Tessa Martin's badge. I hold it up to the sensor on the turnstile base, and the light changes from red to green. The security guy doesn't even look up as I move on.

I get on the first elevator that's headed up and stand in the back. Everyone faces the doors but stares at their phones. I look around. Camera in the ceiling in the left corner, over the button panel. There could be a blind spot directly beneath it, but I'd have to see the security footage to be sure. It's at least the closest thing to a blind spot the elevator has to offer. The access panel is in the left back corner of the ceiling. I shouldn't need it, but it's nice to know it's there. If I can get in there, I can get to any floor I want.

I can't try it out today, though. People might notice if a woman in a pencil skirt and blazer decided to climb through the access panel in the ceiling. Then again, maybe they wouldn't. No one's paying attention to anything other than their phones. Smart phones and indifference are a thief's best friends.

When the elevator stops at the ninth floor, I step off with two other people. We walk past an empty receptionist desk and into the office itself. It's a pretty standard setup—cube farm in the center and a few offices and other rooms surrounding it. According to my intel, the safe is in Suite 7. Tessa Martin's office is Suite 3.

I walk through the office until I find the breakroom. A few employees sit around a table, drinking coffee and eating breakfast while talking about sales. They glance at me but don't seem either concerned or interested in my presence. I pour myself a cup of coffee and add some cream. I linger in the doorway, stirring my coffee with a little wooden stick, and study the rest of the office. It seems like a pretty normal place. Cubicles, bad coffee, and apathy. Being a thief is so much better.

I sip the coffee—it's worse than I expected it to be—and toss the stirrer into the trash before continuing my tour. Suite 7 is on the other side of the room. The walls and door are glass, so I can see a man sitting at the desk, head bent over whatever he's doing. Behind him is a framed aerial shot of Fenway Park at night. How original. Chances are, that's where I'll find the safe. There's an air vent in the wall, over a leather loveseat. My access point, I assume. Looks big enough that I shouldn't have any problems with it. As I pass the door, I note the presence of a card scanner. The air vent is definitely my way in.

Tessa Martin's office is farther down the hall. It, too, comes with a card scanner. So her badge does more than just get me in the building. The lights are off, but it's still bright enough to see the air vent behind her desk. This job may be almost too easy.

I think I've seen everything I can safely see, so I dump my coffee cup in the nearest trash can and head to the elevators. The receptionist is back behind her desk. She smiles at me in a reserved way. She doesn't want to be rude, but she's not certain I belong here. Probably because I don't.

I smile. "Maybe you can help me. I'm looking for Steele and Nash. Lawyers. They're lawyers, but I don't think this is the right place. Is it?"

The receptionist relaxes and points to the ceiling. "Next floor up."

"Thank you," I say. "I really appreciate it."

I take the elevator to the tenth floor. No one gets on, so I push the button for the ground floor. None of the security people notice me as I cross the lobby and walk out of the Skyreach.

I follow the sidewalk to the first intersection and stop on the corner, waiting for a break in traffic. I bounce a little. I don't want to go home yet, but where else can I go at this time of day? It's way too early for The Thieves' Den to be open, but Leo won't mind if I drop by. If I play my cards right, he'll even make me breakfast. Maybe even French toast.

The light changes. I dash across the street and head back to Charlestown.

5

I USUALLY ENTER LEO'S APARTMENT via the fire escape and the living room window. However, it's bright daylight, and I don't relish the idea of doing any of that climbing while wearing a skirt and heels when I don't have to. As strange as it is, I'll have to use the front door instead. Fortunately, Leo gave me a key. It doesn't get much use, but it has come in handy from time to time.

But even though my key unlocks everything it's supposed to, the door doesn't open all the way. The chain is on. I step back and grin. Fun.

Opening my bag, I remove a container of dental floss and get to work. Jay taught me to do this a million years ago, but I haven't had much need for it lately. Not a lot of safes concealed behind doors secured by flimsy chains. Still, it is a useful skill. I should thank Leo for the opportunity to practice.

A couple of minutes later, I walk into the apartment. The shower's running. Leo's already up *and* getting ready? Why is that? He's generally awake before me—most people are—but still, this is unusual. He closed the bar last night; he should still be asleep. I close the door behind me and slide the chain back into place before going to sit on the couch to wait.

"Someone's awake early," I say when he opens the bedroom door.

Leo scrubs his face with his hand. "What are you doing here? The sun's still up."

I jerk my thumb toward the window. "Yeah, what's the deal with that? Does this really do that all day? It's kind of annoying."

"You're kind of annoying." Leo drops his hand. "How many people saw you climbing in through the window?"

"No one," I say. He doesn't look convinced, so I add, "I'm wearing a skirt, dude. I used the front door."

He looks at the door. "Didn't I have the chain on?"

"And if I were a mere mortal, that might have been a problem."

"Wait…did you say *skirt*?" He looks at me and frowns. "What the hell are you wearing?"

"Work clothes."

"Not *your* work clothes."

"Maybe I got a new job. One in an office."

Leo laughs. "Maybe you were casing an office."

"Yeah. Maybe."

He shakes his head and goes into the kitchen. "I hate your job."

"I know." I move to one of the chairs at the counter. "But I'm good at it."

He opens the fridge and takes out a carton of eggs. "I hate that, too."

"You'd hate it more if I were bad at it."

Leo looks at me. After a moment, he turns back to the fridge. "French toast?"

"Why do you think I'm here?"

"I'm your only friend in the entire world?"

"No one better," I say. "Why waste time with anyone else?"

"I guess I can't argue with that."

Leo gathers the rest of the ingredients he needs. After setting a pan on the stove, he gets out a bowl and starts cracking eggs into it. He adds milk and cinnamon before mixing everything together with a whisk.

"How'd you get to be so handy in a kitchen?" I say.

"Necessity," he replies. "Your culinary skills peak at microwaving popcorn or opening a can of soup and eating it cold."

He's not wrong. I laugh as he cuts thick slices from a loaf of brioche bread that came from a bakery down the street. It makes amazing French toast, but I still say, "You don't have any Wonder Bread?"

"It's too early in the morning for you to be such a pain in my ass," Leo says. "Say something nice, or I will eat all the French toast right in front of you."

I smile. "You are the bestest, most handsome, smartest bar owner in all of Boston and probably New England, if not the entire East Coast."

"Probably?"

"I've never been outside of Boston, so…" I shrug.

"Fair enough," Leo says. "Now make yourself useful and start the coffee."

"Yes, sir." I slide off the stool and move into the kitchen. "You know, you never told me why you're awake so early."

"You mean aside from the pain in my ass sitting in my kitchen, demanding to be fed?"

I get the coffee out of the cupboard. Italian roast. "That's hurtful. I didn't demand. You offered."

"So I did," Leo says. "I am awake at this ungodly hour because I have a meeting later."

"What kind of meeting?" I ask, adding water to the coffee maker.

"Just adult stuff you would have no interest in."

"Everything all right?"

"Everything's fine."

"Promise?"

"Promise."

His tone is weird. I look at his back. "You'd tell me if something was wrong, right?"

He looks at me over his shoulder. "Nothing's wrong. I promise."

That tone wasn't any less weird than the first. Nothing may be wrong, but there's something he's not telling me. We don't lie to each other, though. I'm not sure what to think about that.

I nod and turn back to the coffee maker. "Uh-huh. If you say so."

While I wait for the coffee to finish, I get the syrup out of the fridge and set it on the counter. I get a couple of mugs next and fill them both with coffee before bringing them over to the counter.

"What's with the distrust?" Leo asks.

"What's with the vague answers?"

"It's early, I'm tired, and you're on your weird planning-a-job high."

"I don't have a planning-a-job high."

"Yeah, you do." Leo laughs. "You get off on it."

"I do not."

"You do."

"Okay, fine. It doesn't suck, but—"

"It does for me."

"You worry about me too much."

"I worry about you the exact right amount." Leo puts two slices of French toast on a plate and sets it in front of me. "Now shut up and eat your breakfast."

I pour some syrup onto my plate. "You should serve French toast at the bar."

"It's not bar food."

"Any food served at a bar is, by definition, bar food," I say. "You could serve French toast sticks with a little cup of syrup. That would be amazing. I would definitely order those."

"Yes, but would you pay for them?"

"Probably not. But other people would," I say. "Drunk people love breakfast foods. It's a proven fact."

"Oh yeah? Read that in a medical journal somewhere?"

"On the Internet."

"Nothing untrue to be found there." Leo sets down his fork. "All right. Tell me about the job."

"I shall be liberating something from some guy's safe in an office building."

"Did Jay tell you the right safe this time?"

"I'll find out when I get there."

Leo's lips thin into a line. He takes a deep breath. "Say something not terrifying, or the next time you come searching for breakfast, you'll find nothing but tofu."

"Why would you say something so horrible?"

"Skye. I am not kidding."

"This job is easy and extremely well-paying," I say. "And after my inevitable triumph, I will eat whatever vegetable you wish to serve me."

"Whatever vegetable?" Leo asks, and I nod. "It's a deal."

"Good."

"You're gonna be sorry you said that."

"I already am." I stand. "I'm gonna go so you can get ready for the mysterious adult stuff you don't want to tell me about, but thanks for breakfast."

"You coming to the bar later, or can I actually seat paying customers at your table?"

"Jeez. What is your obsession with paying customers?"

"Are you coming tonight?"

"Eventually. After the job."

"The office job? Already? You just got it."

I shrug. "It's a one-night-only deal."

"You hate those."

"Yeah, well, the money's really good."

"If you need money—"

"I don't need money. I just like it."

"Skye."

"What?"

We both know what. What I don't know is how hard Leo will choose to push me on it.

He shakes his head. "Some people date on Friday nights."

No pushback at all. Interesting. I smile. "How pedestrian."

"When was the last time you went on a date?"

"Hey, a guy asked me out for drinks just yesterday."

Leo nods. "And was this guy a mark or a beard?"

He knows me entirely too well. "A beard," I admit. "But it still counts."

"No, it doesn't." Leo sighs. "Be careful."

"I always am."

"Skye," he says as I head for the door. "I mean it."

"Me, too," I say. "I'll see you tonight."

6

I DRESS MUCH DIFFERENTLY FOR my next visit to the Skyreach Building. No more business junior executive. More cat burglar chic. Not only is black slimming, it's helpful when one wants to hide in the shadows, so I opt for black leggings, black fleece, and a black knit cap. For tonight, at least, Tessa Martin is super into fitness.

I walk like a woman on a mission through the front doors and into the lobby. It's quiet except for the sounds of the Celtics game. The security guard at the desk looks up as I approach.

"Can I help you?" he says. No trace of suspicion.

I smile. "I can't find my phone. I just want to see if I left it in my office." I pull my bag in front of me. "Do you want to see my ID?"

He shakes his head and waves me off before turning back to his TV. That was easy. I should send the Celtics a thank you note. Tessa's badge gets me past the turnstiles and to the elevator bank. When the doors open, I step inside, making sure to stay as close to the panel as possible, and select the ninth floor.

As the elevator makes its ascent, my heartbeat quickens. I like planning jobs, but I *love* this part. It's exciting, thrilling—the moments before the curtain rises and the show begins. I have a plan; I know my lines. I am ready. In and out, with a big fat paycheck waiting for me at the end of it. This is what I live for. This is what keeps me alive. *Has* kept me alive.

The elevator stops. The doors open. I take a deep breath and step out.

Showtime.

The majority of the overhead lights are off, but there's plenty of light available to make my way to Tessa Martin's office and use her badge to open the door. Sliding the badge into my pocket, I step inside and close the door behind me.

Tessa Martin has a nice office. My office is a booth in a bar. A nice bar that doesn't serve fries, but the drinks are strong and usually free, so that's not nothing. Tessa's space is clean and neat and looks professionally decorated with subtle feminine touches. No pictures on the wall. No pictures on the desk, either. Not that I'm here to investigate the woman who will very likely be questioned about her supposed presence in the building tonight. I should probably feel bad about that, but I'm more interested in the air vent behind her desk.

After removing a headlamp and a multi tool from my bag, I set it on the floor and drag Tessa's desk chair against the wall. I climb up on it, balancing on the armrests to reach the vent. It's not as large as I had hoped, but I'll fit. My bag won't, unless I want to drag it behind me. Which I don't. It can stay here. I don't need tools for the safe, and a flash drive can fit in my pocket. I return to the bag long enough to fetch my knife and slide it into the cell phone pocket of my leggings. Better safe than sorry.

The vent cover comes off easily, and I set it on the chair before boosting myself into the metal shaft. Turning on the headlamp, I crawl on my belly toward my goal.

Once I reach the other office, I peek through the slats. Dark and quiet. No one's working late. Always helpful. I carefully dislodge the cover and lower it onto the leather sofa directly beneath the vent. No one's in the cubical farm, so I climb out.

I go behind the desk and remove the picture from the wall to reveal the safe. The same make and model as described in my paperwork. Hallelujah.

Let's get this done.

The safe is not a difficult model to crack, which is a little surprising, given all of the security standing in between the entrance to the building and the safe itself. But maybe that's the reason. Maybe they figured they didn't need a more difficult safe because the obstacle course leading up to it would be deterrent enough for most people.

Most people. Not me.

As soon as I hear the final drop, I pull back and open the safe door, but before I can look inside, fluorescent lights come on behind me. Shit. I drop to the floor behind the desk and switch off the headlamp. My office remains dark, but who knows who's here and where they're going. If anyone comes in here, I'm dead. I glance at the exposed and open safe. If anyone even *looks* in here, I could be equally dead.

Voices. Two, maybe three. Male. One terrified. The others threatening. Easing the knife from my pocket, I peek over the top of the desk. Four men. Three closing in on the fourth. The fourth has his hands out, trying to keep the others at bay. He rounds a desk and continues to back up. Right toward me. Are they coming in here?

I lower my head as much as I can without losing my viewpoint. They're still heading right for me. I'll never make it to the vent without being seen. If they come any closer, I'll have to hide under the desk. There's nowhere else to go.

The man in trouble bumps up against the glass door. His hands are still in the air, palms facing out. I should be ducking under the desk or working on my ability to turn myself invisible at will, but instead I'm a goddamn deer in headlights, staring at the three aggressors. At least two of them have guns, but it's the third man who scares me.

I have seen a lot of scary things in my life, but he just may be the scariest. At a glance, he's old and frail, like some kind of ancient, corporeal ghost, but the way he's looking at the man pinned against the door tells a different story. His eyes are cruel. This man is capable of hurt. His voice, if I heard it, would be raspy, maybe barely above a whisper, but powered by the promise of pain. I've known people with eyes like his. I stay away from people with eyes like his. It didn't take long to learn that lesson, and I have never forgotten it. I never will.

But I don't move. If I move, they'll see me. If they see me…I don't want to think about what might happen then. I have to stay still and hope like hell they're not coming inside.

The man in trouble is now blubbering so fast I'm not even sure he's saying any actual words.

The gray ghost shakes his head. He flicks his wrist.

A gun goes off.

A splatter of blood and bone and brain matter hit the glass where the man's head used to be. The rest of him hits the floor.

I gasp.

Three sets of eyes look at me.

Well, shit.

7

RUN. I HAVE TO RUN.

But where am I going to go? My only ways out are the vent through which I entered and the windows behind me, and unless there's suddenly rock climbing equipment to take advantage of, or a giant safety net to jump into, the vent is the only viable option. That only puts so much distance between me and them.

But any distance is better than standing still.

The two gunmen fire their guns at the door, and I dash toward my exit. As the glass splinters and shatters, I haul myself into the vent and crawl back to Tessa's office. I fall out the other side, hitting my head on the corner of the desk. I stagger to my feet and run for the door.

They're behind me. Shouting, arguing, deciding. Pursuing. Are all three of them coming after me? I don't look. It doesn't matter how many are coming. They have guns. I have a headlamp and a multi tool. And a knife. Except…where did it go? I pat all my pockets but come up empty.

Great. Not only did I bring a knife to a gun fight, I lost the damn knife.

Shit.

I punch a button on each of the elevator panels. Up, down, up, down, all the way along the line. When the first set of doors open, I rush inside and pound the button to close the doors and a button for a lower floor. Someone slams into the doors as the elevator starts its journey.

My knees give way, and I collapse on the elevator floor. I rest my head against the wall for a moment, then glance at the control panel. I'm headed for the fourth floor. Which means I need to get off before then.

I stand and locate the access panel in the ceiling. The handrails give me the boost I need to climb out of the car and onto the top of the elevator. I put the panel back in place. It's not like it matters. When the elevator opens and the guys see that it's empty, they're gonna know where I went. But again, I have to try something.

As soon as the elevator stops, I climb the framing and pry open the doors on the fifth floor and shimmy out. It's lit only by a few overhead lights. Low light, no sounds, no people. Perfect. Keeping my head down, I stay close to the wall and make my way toward the stairwell.

The stairwell is equally dark and silent. The goons must have concentrated their efforts on the elevators and the exits. Are they on the fourth floor now? Did they go down to the lobby? Are they covering both?

The lobby is probably my best bet. Fastest to the street and closest to a crowd of people into which I can disappear. I open the stairwell door just enough to ease through. It's quiet here, too. The only noise is coming from the guard's television. I creep to the end of the corridor and peek around the corner at the rest of the lobby.

No sign of anything or anyone except the guard at his desk. I don't like it. It's too easy. Did the bad guys decide not to pursue me? Are they focusing instead on the dead guy? No, they can't do that. They can't let me go. I saw what they did. I saw their faces, and they know it. They'll come after me.

I have to go now. I have to chance it.

I hurry across the lobby. There's a lingering scent in the air. Gunshot residue. Nitroglycerin or whatever it is. Cordite? Whatever it's called, a gun was fired here. I don't even have to go all the way to the desk to see that they killed the guard, too. One shot, middle of his forehead. I stop. There's nothing to be gained by stopping, only things to lose. Life and limb at stake, but I stop anyway.

"There she is!" a man shouts.

My head snaps toward the elevator bank to see the two gunmen coming toward me. I run for the doors. Once on the street, I look for a crowd without finding one. This goddamn city is wall-to-wall people except for the one goddamn time I actually *need* it to be.

I break left and run, stripping off my gloves as I do so. One lands in the street, the other in a trash can. My hat ends up in an alley.

I look over my shoulder. They're still behind me. They're gaining ground. Shit, shit, *shit*—what am I going to do? How am I—

I stumble and hit the ground hard. My palms skid against the concrete, but I push back up and keep moving. I can't stop moving. If I stop, they'll catch me. I really don't want them to catch me.

Glancing over my shoulder again, I see one man still in pursuit. Where did the other one go?

The man raises his gun and fires. It hits the wall on my left, sending a spray of brick and mortar into the air. I shy to the right and go down again as my feet run out of sidewalk. A second shot rings out. I curl up in the street. Did it hit me? Doesn't feel like it, but even if it did, what am I going to do? Stay here and let him shoot me again? I stand and bolt across the street. I'm barely on the sidewalk when I run into another obstacle.

A person. A man.

He raises a gun and yanks me out of the way and fires at the guy chasing me. As my pursuer dives for cover, my protector shoves me into the back of a van and climbs in after me.

He slams the door shut and yells for someone to drive. The van pulls away from the curb as though it's a Lamborghini and not a utility van. I fall on the floor. The man swears and helps me sit up.

As he hovers over me, I see what's dangling around his neck.

A badge. An FBI badge.

Fuck.

8

THE FBI. THE FUCKING FBI. *Shit.* Out of the pan and into the fire. Fryer? However that expression goes, that's my life at this very moment. I can't believe I ran from murderers only to end up in the back of a windowless van with a goddamn FBI agent. Two agents. Someone's driving this thing.

"Name," the agent says. "What's your name?"

I can't tell him my name. I might still have the stolen ID on me. Maybe that will be good enough to pass until I can get the hell out of this.

"Tess. Tess…" Shit. What was the last name? "Martin. Tess Martin."

"Okay, good." He switches on a dome light. "Tess, I'm Ryan—Agent Daniel Ryan. I'm with the FBI." He snags the badge dangling around his neck and steadies it to show me. "Are you hurt? Did they hurt you?"

I have no idea. I don't think so, but there's entirely too much adrenaline coursing through my system to be sure. I shake my head.

"How many were there, Tess? How many did you see?"

"Three. I don't…I don't know where the other two went."

"Okay, that's okay."

"They killed the guard," I say. At least I think they killed the guard. It's possible there is more than one murder squad running around the building, but it does seem unlikely.

"What guard?"

"In the building. The night security guard. I-I don't know his name, but they shot him in the head."

"It's okay. You don't have to worry about them. We're gonna keep you safe."

I'd like to laugh, but that's probably not a good idea. Agent Daniel Ryan doesn't look completely incapable of protecting someone, but he didn't see the gray ghost. He doesn't know what that man's capable of doing.

They just shot that man. Men. They shot both of them in the head like it was nothing.

I drop my head in my hands, then immediately hiss at the resulting sting. I straighten. Why did that hurt?

Agent Ryan grabs my hand. I curb the impulse to put him on the floor and step on his neck. Assaulting an FBI agent will not improve my night any.

I pull my hand free. "What the hell do you think you're doing?"

"I'm sorry. I didn't mean to scare you." Agent Ryan holds up his hands but points to my head. "Your hands are bleeding, and so is your head. I just...I'd like to take a look at them, if that's all right with you."

No, it's not all right with me. I really don't want him to touch me, but what would Tess do? What would a normal, non-criminal person do in this case? Faint? Throw up? Let the federal agent look at their bleeding extremities while fainting *and* throwing up?

"Okay?" Agent Ryan asks, hands still in the air.

No, it's not okay, but Tess would probably say yes. I breathe deep and nod. My hands form fists while he shifts closer to examine my head.

I'm bleeding. How long have I been bleeding? Did I leave behind a blood trail? My bag's still in Tessa's office, but I wore gloves. There shouldn't be any prints for anyone to find, but if I left a blood trail…Shit. I hit my head on the desk. Is that when it started? Did I bleed all the way out of that building? If that's the case, all I can do is hope the FBI is more distracted by the two dead men than by anything I may have left behind.

Agent Ryan moves away to fetch a first aid kit. He sets it in his lap and opens it. After putting on a pair of latex gloves, he turns my hands over to look at my palms. The left one is bleeding. The right doesn't seem to be. He runs an alcohol swab over my skin and I wince.

"All right?" he asks.

I nod. He applies a bandage to my palm before turning his attention back to my head. Another alcohol wipe. More wincing. After another look at my head, he sorts through the kit for an appropriate bandage.

"Is it that bad?" I ask as he sets the bandage over my right temple.

"You'll be fine." He sits back and removes the gloves. "Are you hurt anywhere else?"

How the hell would I know? I didn't even know my own damn head was bleeding until I touched it.

"I don't think so," I answer.

He restores order to the first aid kit, then puts it back where he found it. He then moves to the front of the van to speak to the driver. What are the odds I can slip out the back while they're talking about…whatever they're talking about. Of course, there's a chance that me jumping out of a moving FBI vehicle might inspire the FBI to come after me. It'll be better, maybe, to sit tight for now. An opportunity to escape will present itself soon enough.

I hope.

9

WE DRIVE FOR WHAT FEELS like hours, but I have no idea how much time is passing. Maybe time isn't passing. Maybe the windowless van is some kind of place that goes unaffected by time. Maybe it just feels that way because I am a thief more or less in FBI custody and, as soon as the FBI figures that out, I will be the textbook definition of 'screwed'. Maybe it's better if time doesn't move at all. My very own stay of imprisonment.

But regardless of the time issue and the possibly-being-arrested issue, I continue to sit in the back of the windowless van with an FBI agent and a shit ton of surveillance equipment. They were watching someone. Who? Why? The pursuit and gunshots spilling out into the street must have interrupted their assignment. What's happening with that case now that the FBI is dealing with me? Are some other bad guys getting away with murder—perhaps literally—because Agent Ryan intervened to save my life?

He's still sitting near the driver, whispering from time to time, but watching me from the corner of his eye. Is he worried about me? Suspicious of me? It would make sense. My lie will only work so long. It may have already expired, for all I know.

They could be discussing what to do with the thief in the back of their van.

When the van finally slows to a stop, Agent Ryan opens the door and climbs out. He looks around, then beckons to me to join him. Getting out of the van won't be any worse than staying in it, so I oblige him. The second he closes the door, the van takes off, leaving Agent Ryan and me standing alone beneath a street light on a corner. I don't recognize the cross streets.

"This way," he says.

He leads me to a brick apartment building. We go inside and take the stairs to the fourth floor. Stopping at a door marked 4F, he reaches into his jacket pocket for a set of keys. He unlocks the door and opens it. He walks inside and flips on a light switch.

"Come on in," he says, moving on.

I walk in cautiously. Has Agent Ryan brought me to his own home? That can't be procedure. Something is very wrong here. *More* wrong, maybe. It's not like anything about this situation is right.

"Uh...Agent Ryan?" I say.

He comes back to close and lock the door. "You can call me Ryan. You don't have to worry about the 'agent' part."

Oh, I really do. "Okay, Ryan...where are we?"

"My apartment."

Why are we at his apartment? Shouldn't we be at some FBI field office or something like that? What isn't he telling me? I'm sure there's a lot he's not telling me, but this...Something is seriously off here.

"The bathroom's back through the bedroom, if you want to get cleaned up," he says then. "I can find you some other clothes to wear."

Why would I need other clothes? I look down. My leggings are torn at the knees. My fleece is ripped and looks wet. Why would it be wet? I run my fingers over the spot and pull them away to see them stained with blood. Shit. Is that all from me? Well, if nothing else, I need to undress to check for injuries.

I wipe my hand on my leg. "Can I use your shower?"

"Yeah."

He leads me through the living room and kitchen down a hallway to his bedroom. He's definitely not one for decoration. Everything is utilitarian. Functional, not fancy. He lives like Jay. Like me.

Ryan turns on the light in a small and unfortunately windowless bathroom. There's a vent in the ceiling, but there's no way I could fit in there. He points out the towels folded in a basket on the floor before removing a first aid kit from the cabinet hanging above the toilet.

"In case you need it," he says, setting it on the sink. He gestures to the tub. "Shampoo and all that stuff is in there. Use whatever you want. I'll leave some clothes on the bed for you."

As soon as he walks out, I close the bathroom door and lock it. While Ryan moves around the bedroom, opening and closing drawers, I open the cabinet above the toilet. Spare toilet paper and cleaning supplies. I open the mirrored cabinet over the sink. Aspirin, toothpaste, toothbrush, shaving supplies. Nothing interesting. Nothing useful. Outside the bathroom, another door closes and then I hear nothing at all. Does that mean Agent Ryan has left the room? I close the medicine cabinet and unlock the bathroom door. I crack open the door and peek out.

Alone at last.

I creep over to the bedroom window and look out, catching a glimpse of the tell-tale Citgo sign. Fenway, then. All right. That's helpful. I at least know where in Boston I am. What is less helpful is the fact that there's no fire escape. No ledge. No obvious handholds. I seriously cannot catch a break tonight.

I trudge back to the bathroom and lock the door. If you can't escape 'em, you might as well take advantage of their hot water.

When I get out of the shower, I wrap myself in a towel and use the first aid kit to take care of my injuries. I skip wrapping my palms. They're skinned, but treating them would be a waste of gauze. The worst is the gash on my left knee, but even that isn't too bad. No stitches required. I'll live. God knows I've had worse. A lot worse.

I open the bathroom door just wide enough to ensure that I'm still alone. Unless Ryan's hiding under the bed or in the closet, I am. I venture out and look at the clothing on the bed. Sweatpants, a T-shirt, and a hoodie. At least I'll be cozy.

Ryan knocks on the bedroom door. "Everything okay in there?"

"Yeah," I say. "I'll be out in a minute."

Once he walks away again, I get dressed. The clothing is predictably too large, but if my arrest is imminent, it's much better than the towel.

After running Ryan's comb through my hair, I walk out of the bedroom. My host is in the kitchen, removing mugs from a cupboard. A gun is on the counter in front of him. He clearly doesn't view me as a threat of any kind. But there is a threat. Multiple threats, even. I need a weapon. My knife was lost somewhere in the Skyreach, and I can't imagine Agent Ryan will give me one, so I'll have to procure one. The knife block next to the stove is my best bet. Grab a knife when his back is turned and keep it in the hoodie's front pouch.

"Coffee?" he asks, putting three mugs next to the gun. "Tea?"

Three mugs. He's expecting company. Another FBI agent, maybe? That's the kind of night I'm having.

"Tess?" Ryan says. "Would you like some tea?"

The only tea I want right now is the Long Island variety. I shake my head, but he makes me some anyway. Chamomile, from the smell of it.

He sets the mug on the table and gestures to a chair. "Do you take anything in your tea?"

Whiskey. Lots of whiskey. I sit down. "No, thank you."

Ryan sits across from me with his own tea. "How's your head?"

"Still attached."

"How's the rest of you? Anything you need a doctor for?"

Hell, no. Of course, that guy could have shot me in the gut and my answer would still be the same. I shake my head. "No, I'm fine. Just scraped up a bit."

"Okay," Ryan says. "We need to talk about some things."

I would think so. And he doesn't even know the half of it. At least I hope he doesn't.

"What things?" I ask.

"How long before you're missed?"

"What?"

"Is there anyone waiting for you at home? Significant other? Kids? Dog?"

Leo. Leo's waiting for me. He's probably standing at the bar, staring at my empty booth, trying not to lose his mind over the fact that I'm not sitting in it, giving him shit over the menu. But I can't tell the FBI that.

"Tess?" Ryan prompts.

I shake my head. "No. I, uh, I live alone."

"Okay. And what about work? Your co-workers, your boss? If you don't show up for work tomorrow, what happens?"

"Nothing," I say. "I'm...I'm on vacation. No one will notice I'm gone at all. Not for a while."

Oh yeah. It's a great idea to tell an FBI agent who clearly has something shady going on that I'm a single woman whom no one would miss if she were to disappear. I'm going to end up in some hole in the basement. But what else can I tell him? If I claim Tess Martin has a family, they'll look for said family. If I tell him about Leo...No. I can't tell them about Leo.

"Okay," Ryan says again. "Now, I—"

Someone knocks on the door. Ryan immediately reaches for the gun and heads toward the living room. As soon as he's out of sight, I leave my chair and pull the paring knife from the block and stick it in the front pouch of my sweatshirt. I return to my seat, keeping one hand on the handle.

Ryan returns a moment later, another man behind him. Older, out of shape. He's wearing jeans, a crewneck sweater, and a gun on his hip. Standard issue. Yep. Another FBI agent. Yay.

"This is my partner, Jonas," Ryan says. "Jonas, this is..."

His eyes focus on something behind me, lingering briefly before settling on me. He knows I have the knife. What will he do about it?

"Tess," Ryan says. "This is Tess Martin."

Jonas sits across from me. "You got any coffee?"

Ryan pours him a cup and then joins us at the table.

"You wanna tell me why you got me out of bed in the middle of the night?" Jonas asks.

Ryan starts talking, explaining how their surveillance was interrupted by gunshots and a certain someone running away from the bullets and the man firing them. Jonas nods from time to time while stealing glances at me. I contribute nothing.

"You okay?" Jonas asks when Ryan finishes. "Both of you?"

"Yeah," Ryan says. "We're okay."

Jonas looks at me. "Why were you there?"

"I work there," I lie.

"Little late to be working, wasn't it?"

"I couldn't find my phone. I thought I might have left it in the office, so I went to check."

"Did you find it?"

I shake my head. Jonas seems satisfied, at least for the moment, and turns to Ryan.

"Now what?" he asks.

"We need a plan," Ryan says.

"You need to tell me why we're having this conversation here and not in the office."

Ryan shakes his head. He doesn't want to talk about it in front of me. Why? What were they doing at the Skyreach? Who were they watching?

"So we're doing this?" Jonas says.

Ryan nods. "Yeah."

"If that's the case, you know who we need."

I don't, but Ryan tilts his head back. He stares at the ceiling for a while, then sighs and looks at Jonas.

"She's gonna kill us."

Jonas laughs. "She's gonna kill *you*. I'm not going anywhere near her."

Who? I look between the two men, but neither of them offer any additional details. Who the hell could they be talking about? A terrifying crime boss? A cranky criminal informant?

"You should drive." Jonas reaches into his back pocket for his wallet. He pulls out a wad of cash and leaves it on the table. "I'll cover for you and keep an ear out for anything coming over the wire. If there were murders—"

"There were," I murmur.

Both men look at me now. I look into my mug as though I've never seen chamomile tea as fascinating as this particular brew.

"She saw the guard," Ryan says.

Jonas nods, then jerks his head toward me. "What are you doing with her?"

"She's staying with me," Ryan says.

I am? I lift my head and narrow my eyes at him, but he doesn't notice. Don't I get a say in any of this?

"Okay." Jonas pushes away from the table and stands. "Do I need to remind you to be careful?"

Ryan shakes his head. "I'll walk you out."

Together, they leave the kitchen, talking quietly as they go. I stay right where I am and sigh. I should have just gone out the bedroom window, lack of handholds be damned. A four-story free fall never hurt anyone. Much.

When Ryan returns, he leans against the wall and folds his arms across his chest. "Paring knife?"

"Fits in my pocket," I say.

He nods. "I scared you when I took the gun to the door."

"No, it scared me when those assholes tried to kill me."

"Keep it, then, if it makes you feel better," Ryan says. "But I'm not going to let those guys anywhere near you."

Sounds likely. "So," I say, "where are we going, and who's going to kill you when we get there?"

Ryan smiles. "You'll see."

10

WE TAKE HIS CAR—A Crown Vic, of course. Ryan drives, speeding just slightly. I sit in the passenger's seat, my hand on the knife in my pocket, and keep an eye on the side mirror. One of the advantages of driving this late is the lack of normal Boston traffic. A tail would stick out more, but no one appears to be following us. While that's lucky, it seems suspicious. They have to be looking for me. For us, really. The gray ghost is not going to be the type to just shrug it off. Has Ryan thought of that? Is that why we're now heading out of town?

My chest tightens a little as we leave the Boston city limits. I've never done that before. Left the city. Feels weird, especially under these circumstances. What other firsts are in my immediate future?

According to the compass on the dashboard, we're driving west. Eventually, we turn south and cross into Connecticut—hey, my first time out of state—not stopping until the sun is up and rush hour is in full swing. Ryan pulls into a gas station and parks next to an open pump. He takes out his wallet and counts the cash inside.

"I'll grab some food for us," he says. They're the first words either of us have spoken since we got in the car. "There are probably cameras inside, so if you come in, leave the knife here and put your hood up."

The hood I can live with. I'm less thrilled about leaving my only protection behind, but he's watching and I do need to pee. I stash the knife in the glove compartment and raise my hood. We get out of the car together and go inside. While Ryan walks toward the beverage coolers in the back, I head straight for the ladies' room and lock myself inside.

There's no window, no possible source of escape, so I empty my bladder. While washing my hands, I look at my reflection in the mirror above the sink, focusing on the bandage covering my temple.

Carefully, I peel the bandage back. The swelling has gone down and the bleeding has stopped. That's something, at least.

Someone tries the handle, then knocks on the door.

"Just a minute," I say, pressing the bandage back in place.

"Jenny?" Ryan says.

I look at the door. Jenny? Is that supposed to be me?

Ryan knocks again. "Jenny? Are you all right, hon?"

Hon? I flush the toilet a second time and run the water for a moment before turning on the hand dryer. I unlock and open the door. He's standing there, looking like he's trying not to look concerned, a pair of plastic bags in one hand.

"You okay?" he asks.

Oh yeah. I'm great. I nod and pull my hood back up. Ryan gives me one of the shopping bags and then takes my free hand and leads me out of the store. Apparently, we're a couple now. He lets me go when we reach the car, and I walk around to get in on the passenger's side. He opens the driver's side door to place his bag on the seat before going to fill the gas tank. While he's distracted, I get the knife out of the glove box and return it to my sweatshirt pocket.

When the tank is full, Ryan gets back in the car and rummages through the plastic bag he left on the seat. He pulls out a disposable cell phone package and rips it open. He pops the battery in place and plugs the phone in to charge. The packaging and anything else in it gets dumped in the backseat. Next, he takes a bottle of water out of the bag and sets it in one of the cup holders.

"Water?" he says.

I shrug, and he puts a bottle in the other holder. The rest of the bag ends up in the backseat.

He motions to the bag in my lap. "Could you hand me a protein bar?"

I pass him the entire bag. He searches through it. It looks like pretty standard road trip fare. Not that I've ever been on a road trip before.

"Do you want something to eat?" he asks. "I don't know what you like, so I got some different options."

I shake my head. I'm not sure my stomach is up for food of any kind.

"Tess, I don't want to nag you, but you should eat something," Ryan says. "If you don't like any of this, I will get you something else, but you need to eat. Protein bar? Granola bar? Little thing of cereal? Mini donuts?"

I look at him. He has a single-serving container of Cheerios in one hand and a sleeve of mini powered donuts in the other. Cheerios are bad enough when there is milk. I sure as hell don't want them dry. I don't want the donuts, either, but I take them anyway.

"Thank you," he says.

He eats a protein bar before adding the rest of the food to the backseat stash. He starts the car, tells me to put on my seat belt, and pulls away from the pump.

"Jenny?" I say when we're back on the road.

He shrugs. "I didn't want to shout your real name."

He doesn't even know my real name, but I don't correct him. It's better he not know. For so many reasons.

"You know you actually have to ingest those donuts, right?" he says. "It doesn't count as eating otherwise."

I look at the donuts in my lap.

"Tess? Are you all right?" he asks.

"I'm fine."

"I need more than that. You need to tell me if something's wrong."

Of course something's wrong. I'm a thief lying to the FBI about who I am because angry criminals want to murder me for witnessing another murder. And in case that wasn't enough, I'm also in a car with an FBI agent, heading God knows where to do God knows what with someone who may or may not kill Ryan when she sees him.

"Are you hurt?" Ryan asks. "Sick?"

Yes. No. "I'm fine."

"Tess—"

"I'm fine, okay? I'm fine. I'm just…" In *so* much trouble. I sigh. "I'm still wrapping my head around the fact that…" Nope. That won't work, either. I shake my head. "It's just been a lot in the last day—not even a day because it hasn't even been twenty-four hours—but I'm just trying to keep my head above the metaphorical water here. That's using up a lot of energy. That's all."

"Then you definitely need to eat something."

Jesus Christ. As my other option is to listen to him hassle me further, I open the plastic sleeve and eat a damn donut. Powdered sugar drops on my shirt, my lap, the seat. I remove a second donut, tapping it a little to sprinkle more sugar on the upholstery. Petty, maybe, but it makes me feel better.

Ryan watches the sugar fall without comment, then turns his attention back to the road.

I have never been on a road trip before, and as the day passes, I wonder why some people seem to enjoy them so much. There's nothing to see, nothing to do, and nothing but disgusting, crowded restrooms at every stop. But that is how we spend the entire day, stopping only when Ryan deems it absolutely necessary. I stay silent, a passenger in this, in every sense of the word, until the sun starts to set and Ryan starts to look as though he's about to doze off.

"If you fall asleep, we're going to be in trouble," I say. "I'd offer to take over, but I don't know where we're going, and I also don't know how to drive."

Ryan glances at me. "You don't know how to drive? You must have grown up in the city."

"Yeah," I say. This is the truth. "Between the busses and the T, I never needed to learn."

I also never had the opportunity to learn. Kids who grow up on the streets often have bigger concerns than taking a driver's ed class. But Ryan doesn't need to know that.

He nods. "We'll find a place to stop for the night."

We're in Pennsylvania when he gets off the highway and pulls into the parking lot of a rundown motel whose sign claims to have a vacancy. He parks, and we go inside the lobby. While Ryan secures us a room, I hang back and count security cameras. There are a lot more than I would have expected at a place that looks like this. Are the owners paranoid, or does a lot of crime go down here?

We're assigned a room on the second floor. Ryan unlocks the door and makes a sweeping gesture with his arm.

"After you," he says.

I go inside and stop short when I see the single queen bed. "I am *not* sleeping with you."

"I'm not asking you to." Ryan nudges me forward so he can close and lock the door. "I'll sleep on the floor."

As he draws the curtains closed, I switch on the bedside lamp and glance at the floor. It doesn't look particularly clean, but I'll be damned before I offer to share the bed. There aren't enough pillow walls in the entire *universe* to make that happen.

"Do I need to worry about you disappearing in the middle of the night?" he asks.

I sit in a chair. Does he? No doubt I could do it. He's so tired, he'll be out in no time. I could easily go out the window or even the damn door, and he wouldn't know until he woke up the next morning.

Maybe that's what I should do. I'm off the grid about as much as any one person can get. If I make a break for it, I could just keep going and start over somewhere new. Change my name, change my appearance, change everything. But doing that would mean leaving Leo behind as well.

That might be better for him, though. I'm a liability. I was even before the gray ghost knew I existed. I'm even more so now. It would be best if I just disappeared, and Leo never heard from me again.

He would hate that, though. Really hate that. And me for doing it to him.

"Tess?" Ryan says.

"No," I say. "You don't have to worry."

Ryan goes over to the bathroom and flips on the light. He looks inside, possibly checking for assassins or escape routes. Next, he turns to the closet and removes a spare pillow and blanket. He spreads the blanket on the floor, pulls the comforter off the bed and throws it on top of the blanket.

He looks at me. "Are you hungry? Thirsty? Anything?"

God, no. Between breakfast and lunch, I've already had more to eat than I usually have all day long. All *week* long. If I eat anything else, I will literally explode.

Ryan sits on the bed to remove his shoes. "How's your head? Any pain?"

"No."

"Will you let me check it?" He gestures to his own temple, as though I might not understand what he means.

I slide back in the chair. "It's fine. You don't need to worry about it."

He looks at me for a moment, then nods. "I'm sorry about all of this. I know I'm coming across like some paranoid asshole, but I can help you."

Yeah. He can help me. Right into a jail cell. I look at my lap. "You say that like I have a choice."

"All right, there are some non-negotiable things in this scenario, but not everything is out of your control."

Like what? Ever since he threw me into his damn van, my existence has been alarmingly control-free. I'm pretty sure the only choice I've had thus far concerned breakfast foods.

"Okay," I reply. It seems like the safest option.

Ryan takes out his burner phone and sends a text before setting it aside. "You should try to get some sleep. We should leave early."

Picking up the phone, he goes into the bathroom and closes the door. I move over to the bed and take the knife out of my pocket. I turn it over in my hands, studying the blade from different angles. Stainless steel. Good quality. The kind that would be owned by someone who actually knows how to cook.

"Do I need to worry about that?" Ryan asks.

I lift my head. He's leaning against the bathroom door jamb, hands in his pockets. Does he ever do anything other than lean? Does his skeleton not support his body properly?

"Tess?" he says. "Do I need to worry?"

About me? No. In general? Probably. I shake my head and put the knife beneath the pillow.

"No," I say. "You don't have to worry."

11

IT'S STILL DARK WHEN RYAN and I get back on the road. Neither of us got any meaningful rest, but Ryan is apparently going to make up for that by guzzling coffee. I put my seat back and settle in for another day of excruciating boredom.

Three hours later, however, we arrive in Washington D.C., and Ryan parks in front of a line of two-story, brick row houses. This is where the terrifying crime boss lives? Seems a little…normal.

"Is this it?" I ask.

Ryan cuts the engine and removes the keys from the ignition. "Yeah. Leave the knife in the glove box, and…" He sighs. "Let's get this over with."

That's reassuring. I stow my knife before getting out of the car and following him to the end unit. Inside, I can hear the sounds of ABBA's *Dancing Queen.*

Ryan laughs. "Well, at least she's in a good mood."

He rings the bell. As soon as he does, dogs start barking. A lot of dogs. *Big* dogs, from the sound of it. Shit. I drop down a step.

"Don't worry," Ryan says without looking back. "The dogs are harmless."

But their owner isn't. Message received. The music cuts out, and the deadbolt is unlocked. I grip the handrail. If the dogs come out, I'm gone. I'd rather deal with the gray ghost and the armed assholes. And all their friends.

The door opens and a pretty brunette appears, the polite smile on her face disappearing when she sees Ryan.

"No," she says and starts to close the door.

Ryan puts his arm and foot in the door's path. "I just need to talk to him."

"Then find a phone," the woman says. "I'm sure you have a very nice one in your office. In Boston."

"Doesn't the fact that I'm here tell you anything?" Ryan asks. "Please, Nia. Let us in."

The woman—Nia?—seems to notice me for the first time. She looks me up and down before pushing open the door. "Fine."

Ryan motions for me to go first. I enter the house but stop when I see two large German shepherds blocking the hallway. Oh *hell* no.

"They only bite jackass feds, which I'm assuming you're not," Nia says to me. She looks at Ryan. "You, on the other hand, can wait here. I'll see if he wants to talk to you."

Ryan shakes his head. "I go where she goes."

Nia shrugs. "Not anymore."

She shuts the door and locks it.

"I don't think he's gonna like that," I say.

"Why I did it," Nia says, walking away. "Come on in."

As my other option is to stay in the foyer with the dogs, I ease my way around them and follow her into a small but sunny kitchen. A man in a suit is sitting at a table, eating cereal and reading over some papers in a manila folder.

"Who was it?" he asks, lifting his head. He looks at me. "Who's this?"

"Don't know," Nia says. "Ryan brought her."

The man puts down his spoon. "Where is Ryan now?"

"Front step." Nia glances out the window over the sink. "Unless he was dumb enough to try to come through to the back."

I look through a sliding glass door to see at least two more German shepherds roaming around. How many damn dogs live in this house? Are they why Jonas didn't want to come here?

The man smiles and stands. He closes his file. "I guess I'll let him in, then."

"If you must," Nia replies as he walks out of the kitchen. She looks at me. "Coffee? Something to eat? I pour a fantastic bowl of cereal."

"Just coffee," I say. "Please."

She turns, revealing her round belly. A pregnancy belly. The kind that's only noticeable in profile. Who is this woman? Is Jonas seriously afraid of her?

From down the hall comes two male voices. Ryan has made it inside the house. Nia makes a face as she carries a mug over to me. She really doesn't like him, does she?

"Have a seat," she says, putting the mug on the table.

She glances down the hallway, her expression not getting any cheerier, then picks up the cereal bowl and carries it to the sink. She drops it in, cereal and all.

"I'm not sure he was done with that," I say.

"He's done now." She points at the table. "I told you to sit."

I'm not sure I would call her terrifying, but she's certainly intense. I sit.

"What's your name?" Nia asks, sitting across from me.

"Tess," I say. Or is it Jenny? Ryan didn't specify when we got out of the car. But if I was supposed to be someone else, he would have mentioned that, right?

"Uh-huh. That's not your real name, is it?"

Is she some kind of clairvoyant? Maybe that's why Jonas is afraid of her. "What makes you think that?" I ask.

She smiles. "Does Ryan know?"

The voices are getting closer. I shake my head and Nia nods. Does that mean she'll keep my secret? Will her dislike of him work in my favor?

"How'd you meet Ryan?" she asks then.

"Near death experience."

Nia nods again. "That's how he gets all his girls. Isn't that right, Ryan?"

"I didn't hear what you said," Ryan admits as he and the other man enter the kitchen, "but I'm confident the answer is no."

"You always were smarter than you look," Nia says. "Of course, in your case, it would be hard not to be."

Ryan sighs, a half-smile crossing his face. "I always enjoy these little talks of ours, Nia."

"Then I am doing it wrong," Nia says.

"Nia," the suit guy says. "Maybe you could give him a break just this once."

Nia looks at him. "My break-giving abilities are entirely contingent on his reasons for being here and your involvement in it."

Suit guy hesitates. "Ryan needs help," he says. Nia snorts, and he points at her. "You can let some of them go by, sweets."

Nia folds her arms across her chest, then sits back in her chair and glares at Ryan. Much to my surprise, Ryan doesn't immediately drop dead.

He clears his throat. "Tess, this is Llewellyn Morgan. He's also an FBI agent, and he's going to help us."

Nia makes a disapproving noise. Llewellyn moves to her side, puts his hand on her back, and kisses the top of her head. She pushes him away, then stands and goes over to the sliding door and opens it. Two German shepherds race inside. They stop to sniff me and Ryan. Ryan scratches them between the ears. I resist the urge to climb on top of the refrigerator.

"I'm going to work," Nia announces. "Have fun putting yourselves in danger."

Now Ryan snorts. "Yeah. This coming from the woman who confronted—"

"Well, if I had waited for you to do it, I'd still be waiting," she says.

"I need you to take a sick day," Llewellyn says.

His tone is calm, as though Nia biting heads off federal agents is an everyday occurrence. Ryan did say she was going to kill him. Guess he wasn't wrong.

Nia looks at Llewellyn. "Why? What's happening?"

"Tess is in danger. I'm going to help Ryan get her out of it."

Now Nia looks at me. I'm not scared of her, but Tess would probably be intimidated as hell, so I shrink into my sweatshirt and pull the coffee mug a little closer. One of the dogs lays his head in my lap. Okay. *Now* I'm scared. God, I hope Nia was telling the truth about them only biting feds. I gingerly pet him between the ears.

Nia sighs. "What do you need me to do?"

"We left Boston in a hurry," Ryan says. "Tess doesn't have anything but the clothes on her back, and those are mine."

"What does that have to do with me?"

"Could you please go to the store and pick her up a few things?" Llewellyn asks.

Nia looks at me again. I concentrate on petting the dog. He hasn't bitten me yet, so I must be doing something right.

"Fine," she says. "You can crash in the guest room while I'm gone, if you want. You look like you could use the rest." She looks at Ryan. "You can have the couch, if the dogs are willing to share. Otherwise, there's the backyard. Or your car."

"Thanks for thinking of me," Ryan says.

Nia picks up her purse from the counter. She crosses the room, stops in front of Llewellyn, and puts her hand on his cheek. "Try not to die before I get back?"

He takes her hand and kisses her palm. "I always do."

Except for the kissing, the exchange feels very much like what Leo and I do before I go on a job. Nia doesn't like Llewellyn's work any more than Leo likes mine.

She frees her hand and walks out of the kitchen. The dogs follow her, but only one returns after the front door closes. I have no idea if it's the same one who put his head in my lap.

"Would you like to lie down?" Llewellyn asks me. "Nap, or...just get away from the dogs for a bit?"

"I'm not afraid of them," I say.

"Okay," he says. "The room?"

I really am tired, but I could use the privacy even more. I glance at Ryan. As he has no idea why I'm actually looking at him, he nods reassuringly. "Um...sure."

"Come on, then," Llewellyn says. "Let's go upstairs."

Llewellyn leads the way out of the kitchen, the dog pushing past me to stay even with him.

"*Gehen*," Llewellyn says as he walks and gestures toward the living room.

The dog stops and sits, his tail thumping, as he watches his master continue on without him. I move over as far as I can, glancing into the living room as I pass. The other dogs are sprawled out on the couch. Ryan will have to sleep on the floor. Or in the car. Maybe he'll let me sleep in the car, too.

We go upstairs, and Llewellyn points out the bathroom before pushing open a door at the other end of the hall.

"The guest room," he says. "Sorry about the mess."

I step inside. There's a full-sized bed across from the door and a variety of boxes and bags stacked up against the wall. Against another wall sits a white crib. This clearly will not be the guest room much longer.

We really shouldn't have come here. We shouldn't have brought other people into this. Especially not these people. What was Ryan thinking?

"I'm sorry," I say. "I'm sorry you were dragged into this, and that Nia's mad, and—"

"Nia will be fine. She has a...complicated history with the Bureau, but she'll be fine. You don't have to worry about her."

"Your wife has a complicated history with the Bureau," I say.

"Yeah."

"The Bureau of which you're a part?"

"Yeah."

"Must keep things interesting."

"You have no idea," Llewellyn says. "I'll leave you to it. Ryan and I will be in the kitchen if you need anything."

What I need is a phone and a way out of this mess, but I thank him and he walks out of the room. I close the door behind him.

Now what?

There are two windows to my left, overlooking the backyard. If there wasn't the possibility of even more damn dogs roaming the backyard—not to mention two federal agents sitting in the kitchen overlooking the backyard—it would be so easy to get out of the house. I could probably still do it. Presumably, Llewellyn and Nia's bedroom has a view of the street. No one's watching the street right now. I could escape. Just like I could have escaped from the motel in Pennsylvania. And likely even the gas station in Connecticut. So, what am I still doing here? What am I waiting for?

A better way out. If there is one. I don't want to disappear into thin air. I don't want to become someone else. I want to get back to Boston, back to Leo. I don't know if sticking around can help me do that, but disappearing sure as hell won't.

So I don't disappear. Yet.

I stay put. For now.

Sighing, I lay on the bed and look at the ceiling. Guess I'll take a nap after all.

12

I OPEN MY EYES AND look at the plain white ceiling above me. That's not my ceiling. I sit up and see a crib across the room. That's sure as hell not mine. Where the hell am I? How did I…Oh right. I remember now. How could I possibly forget?

I am in Washington, D.C. because I witnessed a murder, then lied to an FBI agent about who I am to keep my ass from getting arrested. Then I lied to two more federal agents because why not?

Shit. It would have been great if that had all been just a dream.

There's a plastic shopping bag sitting on the end of the bed that wasn't there when I closed my eyes. I really must have been out for someone to make it in and out of the room without waking me. I definitely don't like that. This whole experience has me on my heels, like I'm actually becoming the woman I am pretending to be.

I pull the bag closer to see what Nia picked out for me. Some short-sleeved crewneck T-shirts, a couple of pairs of jeans, a zip-up sweatshirt, some socks, a package of underwear, and a pair of basic cotton bras. She has a good eye for sizes. Too good, truth be told. I should be bothered by that, but really, in the grand scheme of shit that's gone wrong lately, having a stranger choose accurate clothing sizes for me doesn't register.

I change out of Ryan's clothes and into my new ones before venturing to the bedroom door. The house seems quiet. Too quiet. They wouldn't have left me alone with the dogs, would they? The TV's on downstairs, but that doesn't tell me anything. A lot of people leave the television on when they're not home. To keep their pets company. To deter thieves.

Not that it works.

I open the door and peek outside. No one's standing in the hall. No dogs come charging toward me. So far, so good. I head downstairs.

"Jesus Christ, Betty White!" Nia exclaims. "The goddamn answer is *snowflake*!"

Nope. I'm not alone. Nia's on the couch in the living room, a German shepherd on either side of her. The other two are lying at her feet. All four dogs look at me the moment I reach the bottom step. I freeze.

Nia glances over. "Oh, hey, Not-Tess. Did you sleep well?"

Not-Tess. Great. I walk closer. The dogs continue to watch my every movement. I've read that dogs can sense fear. What happens if they do?

"You okay?" Nia asks.

I nod and look at the television. She's watching an old game show. One of the people on screen does seem to be a younger Betty White.

Nia mutes the television's volume. "Are you hungry? Would you like something to eat?"

Would I? I don't feel hungry, but it's been a while since I ate last. I should probably have something.

"Hey, earth to Not-Tess. Can you hear me, Not-Tess?"

I look at Nia. "Could you stop calling me that?"

"Why? The guys aren't here, and the dogs don't care."

"They're not here? Where are they?"

Nia shrugs. "Off doing mysterious FBI stuff, I suppose."

"You suppose?"

"They didn't tell me, but one can assume," she says. "So? Late breakfast? Early lunch? Brunch, maybe?"

"Are you having any?"

"Please. I'm pregnant. I've had breakfast, like, six times already."

"So what's one more?"

"Exactly."

When she stands, all four dogs get up. She says something in what might be German, and they rush toward me. I flatten myself against the wall until the stampede passes, heading for the kitchen.

Nia chuckles as she walks by. "Not a fan of dogs, huh?"

"You have to admit four large German shepherds can be intimidating."

"They're babies, but don't tell them I said so. They think they're tough."

Nia opens the sliding door in the kitchen and sends the dogs outside. They roughhouse on the deck before chasing one another around the backyard. I'm guessing they're more than tough. Especially if they think Nia's safety is in question.

I sit at the table. "My lips are sealed."

"So, you want something to eat?"

"Sure," I say. "If it's not too much trouble."

Nia laughs. Loudly and without any humor whatsoever. It matches the complete lack of expression on her face.

"Compared to my life being put on hold and my husband being dragged into whatever you and Ryan have gotten yourselves into, breakfast isn't too much trouble," she says, a definite edge to her tone. "Especially because it's a choice between cereal and toast. If you want something more, you'll have to wait for the guys to come back. They cook. I don't."

"I'm sorry," I say. "I didn't know we were coming here. Ryan didn't tell me anything other than..."

Maybe it would be better not to tell her what Ryan said. She already doesn't like him. I don't need to make it worse.

"That I'd be pissed?" Nia asks.

"That's not an exact quote, but...yeah," I say. "What's the deal with you two? Why don't you like him?"

Nia raises an eyebrow. "Why doesn't he know your real name?"

I smile. "Call it a draw?"

Nia doesn't smile. Removing a box of donuts from a cupboard, she brings it over to the table and sits down. She helps herself to a donut. It's half gone before she turns the box toward me.

"I ruin your life and I still get donuts?" I ask.

"*A* donut," she replies. "And you haven't ruined my life. Yet, anyway."

"Just inconvenienced it."

"I don't like it when FBI business shows up unannounced at my front door."

"Your husband's an FBI agent."

Nia shrugs. "Nobody's perfect."

I take a donut from the box. "So, the guys just left us here? Did they also leave behind some armed guards?"

"Should they have? Does anyone know you're here?"

"Just the people currently staying in this house. And probably that Jonas guy."

Nia rolls her eyes. "That asshole."

"Does anyone like him?" I ask.

"Not in my experience."

One of the dogs scratches at the door, and Nia gets up to let them in. They tumble into the kitchen in a tangle of fur, teeth, and growls. Oh yeah. Total babies. Terrifying babies with enormous teeth.

"Is there anyone who should know you're here?" she asks, returning to her seat. "Family, maybe?"

No way I'm bringing Leo into this. I break off a piece of donut. "I don't have any family."

She looks toward the fridge. Its surface is clean and empty except for a sonogram print-out and a group photo with entirely too many people in it. Her family, maybe?

A family. A baby on the way. There are killers looking for me. I shouldn't be here.

I set the rest of my donut on a napkin. "I need to use the bathroom."

"Sure," Nia says.

I get up and maneuver around the dogs and walk out of the kitchen, quickening my pace once I'm in the hallway. I'll just go right out the front door. She may hear it—the dogs definitely will—but I can lose her easily enough.

"You know the house is under surveillance, right?" Nia says as I'm reaching for the doorknob.

I stop and glance at her over my shoulder. She's standing in the hallway, surrounded by German shepherds.

I turn around. "You said—"

"Did you really think they would leave their only witness to whatever the hell you witnessed here with nothing but me and four German shepherds for protection?"

"You think I need protection?"

"Ryan does."

Well, damn. I put my hands on my hips. Now what am I going to do?

"What's your deal, Not-Tess?" Nia asks. "Why don't you want to be here?"

"Why wouldn't I want to be here?" I say. "You've been so warm and welcoming."

"I told you—"

"You don't like it when FBI business shows up at your door. I know. I'm just trying to take that business elsewhere."

"Without the FBI."

"Can you blame me?"

Nia smiles. "No, but...Look, I know the kind of cases Ryan works in Boston, and I know that if he brought you here to my house to ask Lew for help in my presence, it's gotta be pretty bad up there."

I don't know the kind of cases he works. I don't know how bad it has to be for him to come here. I know he didn't want to involve the Bureau, and I know he didn't want to say why in front of me. I know Jonas didn't want to come anywhere near Nia. But I don't know what any of that means in relation to anything else.

Nia sighs. "Okay. Let me try this: If you leave, they will look for you, because your life is at risk. And because your life is at risk, they will take risks to find you, because that is what they do. But if you make them look for you and if you make them take those risks, therefore putting *them* at risk, I'm gonna be pissed," she says. "No doubt these criminals you're on the run from are formidable, but please believe me when I tell you that you won't like me when *I'm* pissed. Ask anyone. They'll tell you. Hell, they probably already have."

I'm not so sure I wouldn't like her when she's pissed. A smile is fighting to get out, but I keep it suppressed. Something tells me she would not find it an amusing or appropriate reaction.

"I'm just trying not to put *you* at risk," I say. "And...that." I gesture to her belly.

"You don't have to worry about us. We can take care of ourselves."

"Your unborn child can take care of itself?"

"They're very advanced," she says. "So, what's it gonna be? Are you staying, or am I putting you at the top of my mortal enemies list?"

It's harder not to smile now. "Do you actually have a mortal enemies list?"

"Walk through that door and find out."

The urge to do just that is strong, but I sigh instead. "Fine. I'll stay."

"Great."

"What do we do now?" I ask.

Nia shrugs. “How do you feel about the Game Show Network?”

13

I HAVE TO BE HONEST—I did not even know there was a Game Show Network. I did not realize anyone would be so interested in watching endless hours of old game shows, and that there would be enough people interested in watching endless hours of old game shows to structure an entire network around it.

But there is. And Nia, as it turns out, is more than interested. She's obsessed with the Game Show Network to the point where I suspect her unborn child will come out of the womb screaming about the retail price of toasters. She sits on the couch, once again surrounded by German shepherds, and yells out answers and contestant criticism with the passion of a normal person watching a beloved sports team. I sit in a chair to her left and ponder the merits of taking my chances with the well-armed bad guys.

As soon as the front door opens, the dogs charge into the foyer, barking fiercely. Llewellyn comes inside, and the dogs immediately go from being determined protectors to big, furry babies who should be ashamed by how goofy they're acting. Ryan slides in behind him and closes the door. He stands in the corner while the dogs swarm Llewellyn.

"*Gehen*," Llewellyn says, shooing them back into the living room.

They settle and escort him over to Nia where he bends down to greet her with a kiss. As he pulls back, he glances at the television and smiles.

"I see you had a productive morning," he says.

"More productive than you think," Nia replies.

I look at her. What the hell is that supposed to mean? The way Llewellyn tilts his head suggests he has the same question.

"You okay?" he asks.

"Be better if I had pizza," she says. "And breadsticks. With a side of pickles."

"Meat or no meat?"

"Yes."

"I'm on it." Llewellyn looks at me. "Any pizza topping preferences?"

I shake my head. "I'm not picky."

Or hungry, but there's no need to mention that. Llewellyn walks out of the room, calling the dogs to follow him. Ryan stays behind, pulling up an ottoman and sitting in front of me. We are in for a serious talk. Is this the part where he calls me out on my absolute rat nest of lies?

He looks at Nia. "Could you give us a minute?"

"I could," she says but doesn't move.

"Nia," he says.

"Hey, if you didn't want me involved, you should have thought about that before you knocked on my damn door."

What is Nia's deal? Is she just trying to be a pain in Ryan's ass, or is there something else going on? Is she only interested in this situation because of her husband's involvement?

"She can stay, if she wants," I say. "I don't mind."

Ryan looks between the two of us, perhaps calculating how much of a fight he would be in for if he were to argue and whether it would be worth the hassle. I can't decide for him, but I don't see the point in excluding her. Something tells me she would find out anyway.

He sighs and focuses on me. "The men who were after you. We think they believe you witnessed…a crime. Their crime."

Probably because I did. "What crime?" I ask. Sounds like something someone who hadn't actually witnessed the crime would say.

"There was a murder."

For a moment, I can see it again. Hear it again. Smell it again. Yes, there was most certainly a murder.

"Tess?" Ryan asks. "Are you—?"

"I, uh…" I shake my head. "I heard a…a noise."

"A gunshot."

Yes, it was. "I didn't know that. I didn't know what it was. I just went out to the hall to see if everything was all right, and they…" I swallow. "There they were. I saw the guns, and I…panicked." That's true enough. "I ran."

Llewellyn slips back into the room. Ryan is watching me closely. Nia looks bored. Are we keeping her from *Hollywood Squares*?

"You did the right thing," Ryan says. "But you weren't the only witness. There was someone else in the building that night."

Nope. "You mean the security guard? Because they killed him."

"No, someone who we believe actually witnessed the murder itself."

That part's true. "Who are they? Where are they?"

"We don't know, but we suspect they have good reason to avoid law enforcement agencies."

That is also true. "What reason is that?" I ask.

"We think they're a thief," Ryan says.

"Who just happened to be in the same place at the same time?" Nia asks. "Coincidence."

"Maybe," Ryan says. "We're looking into it."

Oh good. They're looking into it. I nod. "What does all that mean for me?"

"We're going to keep you safe," Ryan says, "but we need your help to do it."

Nia snorts. Llewellyn mutters, "Sweets."

"What kind of help?" I ask.

"How do you feel about looking at some pictures?" Ryan says. "See if you can identify the men you saw?"

At least I shouldn't be in any of the pictures. I hope.

I nod. "Okay."

14

AFTER LUNCH, LLEWELLYN LEAVES AGAIN. He doesn't say where he's going, only that he won't be gone long and he won't die while he's there. Does he say that every time he leaves the house? I get it, though. I pretty much have the same conversation with Leo every time I go on a job.

The problem is, though, we never know which time will prove to be the lie. Leo knows it, even if he won't say it, and I'm sure Nia does as well.

Ryan and I sit at the kitchen table, a laptop in front of me. I scroll through one mug shot after another, seeing faces I recognize, but not the faces I'm looking for. I'm unconvinced that will change. The gray ghost would be too smart, too careful, to have a mug shot in the first place. He'd also be smart enough to have lackeys with no record. This endeavor is like looking for a needle in a whole damn hayfield.

"Take your time, Tess," Ryan murmurs after a while. "No pressure."

"No pressure?" I look at him. "The longer it takes to find them, the more time they have to do whatever they're doing. Killing more people, probably."

"Which is why we're looking for them," Ryan says. "We won't stop until we find them."

"What if you can't find them?"

"We'll find them. Every picture that isn't them eliminates suspects and narrows the search. I know it seems slow and—"

"*Seems* slow?"

Ryan smiles. It's a fake smile. Probably the one he gives witnesses to placate them and lull them into cooperating with whatever useless busy work passes for investigating at the FBI.

"We'll find them," he says.

"Will you? They may not even be in this database," I say. "Not every criminal has a mug shot."

"I'm aware. This is just one avenue. You saw these men, so it's an avenue worth pursuing. We have others, and we are pursuing them as well."

Other avenues. What might those be? Will any of those roads lead to me? It's a goddamn miracle that none of them already have. I left things behind. I left *blood* behind. This lie should have fallen apart by now, so why hasn't it? Is the FBI really that incompetent?

"Tess?" Ryan asks. "Are you okay?"

Is he serious? I laugh. "Yeah. I'm fantastic."

"Is there anything you'd like to talk about?"

Plenty. And also nothing. How the hell am I supposed to know what's safe to say? I sigh. "When are you going to tell me what's going on here?"

"Ha!" Nia exclaims as she comes into the kitchen, all four dogs following her. "Don't hold your breath, Tess. The FBI doesn't share information unless they have something to gain from it."

Ryan smiles at the table, probably summoning his inner calm or whatever he uses to get through a conversation with Nia. She opens a cupboard and removes a box of dog biscuits. The dogs sit in front of her.

"Isn't that right, Ryan?" she says, giving each dog a cookie.

He doesn't look up. "The FBI isn't always at liberty to discuss details of a case with civilians."

"Tess isn't just someone in off the street, Ryan. She's your only witness."

"Not the only witness."

"The only one you have." Nia puts the box away. "Information should be a two-way street. You should try remembering that."

The Ryan versus Nia show is so much more entertaining than the Game Show Network. I put my chin in my hand. What'll happen next?

Ryan looks at her. "The last time I remembered that, I recall a civilian needlessly putting herself in a dangerous situation that ultimately ended with her in the hospital for…How many weeks was it?"

"Maybe that civilian wouldn't have had to do that if someone had been better at his job."

The conversation ends. Ryan and Nia glare at one another. If I had to guess, I would say Nia's trying to kill him with her mind and Ryan's daring her to do it. If only I had some popcorn.

The staring contest ends when one of the dogs whines and nudges Nia's hand with its nose. She looks at it and then at the clock on the wall.

"I'm taking the dogs for a walk," she says. "Don't burn down the place while I'm gone."

"We'll be sure to wait until you get home," Ryan says.

Nia rolls her eyes and smacks the back of his head as she walks by. She goes to the front door, the dogs swarming around her and yipping in anticipation. She clips leashes on their collars and somehow herds the pack out the door. The house settles into a welcomed, dog-free silence.

Ryan takes a deep, cleansing breath and looks at me. "Sorry about that. What were we talking about?"

As much as I want to ask about this whole Nia situation, I say, "You were about to tell me what the deal is."

"What deal?"

"The reason why you're an FBI agent looking to avoid involving his agency in…whatever the hell this is."

"What makes you think that?"

He's a shit liar. He's obviously not an undercover agent. He wouldn't last ten minutes. Ten *seconds*.

"I don't know. I guess maybe everything that's happened since I met you?" I say. "After you threw me in your windowless van, you took me to your apartment, you called your partner to meet you there, and when he showed up and immediately asked why we weren't in the office, you didn't want to talk about it. Instead, we took a road trip to recruit another agent in another city halfway down the eastern seaboard when a phone call could have taken care of that for you. I'm not an expert in FBI procedure, but we do seem to be operating a little outside the lines here. I want to know why."

Ryan studies me for a moment, then nods. Is he going to say anything? Do anything? Is a nod all I'm going to get? It better not be because a goddamn nod is nowhere near good enough.

"Corruption?" I ask. "Are your bosses corrupt?"

"They're not corrupt."

"Are you corrupt? You, Jonas, Llewellyn—all three of you?"

"We're not corrupt."

"Pretty sure that's what a corrupt agent would say."

"We're not corrupt," Ryan repeats. "Corruption is not the problem here."

"Then what is the problem?"

"This case." He sighs. "The three of us have been working it for a long time. More recently, it got…personal."

"Personal how?"

He shakes his head. "Just personal. Personal enough that the higher-ups removed us from the case."

Now we're getting somewhere. "But you never stopped working the case," I say. "Because it's personal."

"Yeah."

"So, when you were sitting in a surveillance van the other night, you were supposed to be..."

"Not doing that."

I nod. Interesting. "Why did we drive all the way here? You couldn't have just called Llewellyn and said something like, 'the crow flies at midnight' and hung up real fast?"

"The crow flies at midnight?"

"The game is on?"

"You like detective stories?"

"I like understanding my situation," I say. "Maybe you didn't want to call him on your phone, but you bought a burner on the way here. Also, they do sell burner phones in Boston."

"We decided no phones. To be safe."

"Paranoid, you mean."

"Maybe," Ryan says. "There was also you to think of."

"Me?"

"There's a pretty serious criminal contingent searching for you. Getting you out of Boston didn't seem like the worst idea in the world," he says. "Any other questions?"

"Does the FBI know about the murders?" I ask. "And by 'FBI', I mean someone in the Bureau other than you and the other two stooges."

Ryan smiles. "Yes, they know about the murders."

"Are they investigating the murders?"

"Yes. They're running their investigation. We're running ours."

"And what about me?" I ask. "Do they know about me?"

"Not so far as I know. They're looking for the thief. Not you."

I don't correct him. "Do you intend to tell them about me?"

"Only if it becomes necessary."

"Will it?"

"Don't know. I can't see the future."

Maybe that's my way out. Stick around long enough to help them identify the murderers, then scamper before anyone realizes I am their only witness. It could work, if I'm quick enough. And I'm pretty damn quick. It's just another timed job. Get in and out before security comes around.

"What happens if I do identify your suspects?" I ask. "What will you do with that information? What can you do?"

"I have friends who are supposed to be working this case. I will get the information to them, and they will take it from there."

"Without involving me?"

"No one knows you were there," Ryan says. "If I can keep it that way, I will. I promise."

More promises. I wish he'd stop making them. All I have to offer are lies.

"Either way," he continues, "you will be okay."

I have spent years learning how to read people. I know when someone's lying. I know when they're telling the truth—when they *think* they're telling the truth. Ryan believes he's telling the truth. He sincerely believes he can protect me. I don't, however, know if he's right.

But it's not his job to protect me. *I* protect me.

"If you want, I will take you to the field office and introduce you to the agent in charge of the investigation," Ryan says. "We'll tell them everything and they will take over. They will protect you. It will all be very above board."

The last thing I want is to walk right into an FBI office and become an official part of an official investigation. If there's a chance—however small—that I can get out of this without having to do that, then I need to embrace the hell out of it.

"What happens to you if we do that?" I ask.

"I will be in trouble with my bosses."

"What does that mean? Will you get fired?"

"Maybe. Fired, reassigned to an office in the middle of nowhere, permanently chained to a desk—lots of possibilities," Ryan says. "But what they choose to do is not your problem."

No, it isn't. But it isn't a solution, either. Sticking with Ryan may be my best bet. Not that I can tell him why I think so. What would Tess do in this situation?

"I don't want to go to the FBI," I say. "I'd rather stay with you."

"Are you sure about that?"

Nope. "Yes," I say. "You saved my life. Seems like the least I can do is try to save your career."

Ryan smiles. "I appreciate that."

Not as much as I appreciate the opportunity to *not* go to jail. I maintain eye contact a moment longer, then look back at the mug shots.

"Interrogation over?" he asks.

I gesture to the laptop. "I have bad guys to identify. Unlike you, who apparently has nothing to do but sit here and watch me do your job for you."

Ryan nods and stands. "I'll leave you to it, then."

15

While I continue to look through the mug shots, Ryan paces. He walks from the living room to the front door, toward the kitchen, then away from it again. He may not be sitting at the table staring directly at me, but he's still monitoring me closely. Because he really doesn't have anything to do but wait for me to identify his suspects or for Llewellyn to turn up something on one of those alternative avenues.

And I sincerely hope Llewellyn is having better luck because these pictures are leading absolutely nowhere.

If I were in Boston, I could be doing more. I would have alternative avenues of my own to explore. Rumors and whispers to chase down. Contacts who would know a hell of a lot more than the FBI. What are the odds Ryan would be willing to take me back there? Not to mention exploring those avenues without asking any follow-up questions or putting me in jail? There must be something I can do to make that happen.

"No luck?" Llewellyn says.

I jump and look at him. Shit, he's quiet. Most people can't sneak up on me. "Jesus, Llewellyn. How long were you standing there?"

"Sorry," he says. "You can call me Lew, you know."

Great. The only thing I like more than being on a first-name basis with an FBI agent is being on a goddamn nickname basis with one. I give him a thumbs-up.

He gestures to the laptop. "No luck?"

"Is that surprising?"

"No. These guys aren't amateurs." He sets a folder on the table. "Look through these and see if you have any better luck."

I open the folder to find a stack of photos. Not mug shots, but rather surveillance shots—security camera stills and maybe even some pictures taken with an actual camera with an excellent telephoto lens. I know these places. These photos are all from Boston. I sit back in my chair and scour each image.

While I do so, Ryan and Lew step out onto the deck. They close the sliding door to muffle their conversation. Ryan stands with his back to the yard so he can continue to monitor my lack of progress. Oh yeah, I'm definitely not feeling any pressure.

They're still out there when Nia returns home and ushers her canine cyclone into the kitchen. As they slurp water, she picks up one of the photos I have set aside. Her head soon tilts and her eyes narrow, and she glances toward the guys. When she notices me watching, she puts the photo back on the table.

"I was never here," she says and walks out of the kitchen.

As soon as she disappears into the living room, I pick up the photo. It's the inside of a shitty bar on Tremont Street—The Rebel Fly. The place is a Petri dish of illegal activity, so it's hardly a surprise to see it in a stack of surveillance photos. Jay practically lives there, but why does Nia know it? What did she see?

My second viewing doesn't tell me anymore than my first, but there's clearly something more I should know about The Rebel Fly. Another reason to go back to Boston. If I were there, I could just walk in and talk to the bartender. Angie knows everything that happens in those walls. But I'm not there. I'm here, and this stupid picture doesn't tell me a damn thing. I set the photo aside once more and return to the rest of the stack.

When the guys come back inside, Lew heads down to the living room. Ryan stays in the kitchen. He leans against the counter and watches me. I let him for a minute or two before I look up.

"If you're going to stare at me anyway, you might as well sit down and do it."

"Sorry," he says. "It's just that..." He smiles. "I have nothing to do but watch you do my job for me."

"Sounds exhausting." I gesture to the three open chairs. "Maybe you should take a load off before you overexert yourself."

"I am sorry about all of this," he says, sitting down. "I'm sorry you were caught up in it."

That makes two of us. I shrug. "It's not your fault."

"Doesn't make me less sorry."

That also sounds exhausting. How does he do it? How does he legitimately give a damn about someone he just met? Is that something people do? Is he the outlier, or am I?

"Everything okay?" he asks.

Not by a long shot, but I nod and go back to the photos.

By the time I finish going through the stack, everyone's in the kitchen, including all four German shepherds. Ryan and Nia sit at the table with me while Lew leans against the counter, arms folded across his chest. Apparently, no one has anything better to do than watch me do the FBI's job for them.

"Are there more photos?" I ask. "They're not in any of these."

"You're sure?" Ryan asks.

I'm not likely to forget those faces any time soon. Especially the gray ghost. "Yeah."

Ryan looks at Lew. "New players?"

"Possible," Lew says.

Possible, but not likely. They're just better players than the rest. I don't offer up my opinion, though. Tess probably doesn't have much insight into things like that.

Ryan rubs the spot between his eyes. "Okay, so the security cameras were down—"

"They were?" I ask.

"Yeah. Either the thief or the murderers disabled them before going in. We didn't even see you enter."

Well, the thief didn't do it, but that's something else Tess wouldn't know, so I reply, "Oh."

"So, we don't have any stills from the cameras to work with, and we don't have easy access to a sketch artist, either." Ryan looks at Nia. "Unless Colin could—"

Nia snorts. "Not unless you want some Picasso-looking shit. He probably knows someone, though. Not here, but in Boston, sure."

Ryan nods. "I think we gotta go back to Boston anyway. We're not going to be able to solve this thing from here. So, I'll go back, and Tess can—"

"Tess is going with you," I say.

Now Ryan looks at me. "What?"

"Tess can stay here. Right? That's what you were about to say? Tess can stay here while you go back to Boston and do whatever it is you do?" I ask. "Well, Tess isn't doing that. She's going back to Boston with you. I mean, I am. I am going to Boston with you."

"Where the murderers are looking for you?" Ryan asks.

I shrug, like it's no big deal. "You need my help."

"I do, which is why I need you to stay alive."

"Well, I don't plan on dying," I say. "I'm going with you."

"It's a bad idea, Tess."

"I've had worse."

"Tess, I can't let you—"

"We can make it work, Ryan," Lew says.

Both Ryan and I look at Lew, still leaning against the counter.

"El, come on," Ryan says. "It's not safe for her to—"

"Then we protect her."

"How? Where? We can't involve the Bureau, she can't go home, we can't go to my apartment because—"

"There's always the loft of squalor," Nia says.

Everyone looks at Nia, but only I seem to lack the necessary background. The loft of squalor sure sounds nice, though. Can't wait.

"He kept it?" Ryan asks.

Nia nods. "Uses it as a studio now. He won't mind if you crash there."

"You don't want to ask him first?"

"True. He may be hesitant when I tell him the favor would be for you," Nia says.

Lew smiles. "Call him, sweets?"

She reaches for her phone. "Sure. But only because you asked so nicely."

As she steps outside to make her call, I look at the guys. "Loft of squalor?"

"Her brother has a loft in South Boston," Lew explains. "You'll be safe there."

"She'll be safe *here*," Ryan says.

"You'll be safe there," Lew says to me. "We can keep you hidden and secure, and no one but us ever has to know you're in the city at all."

I nod. I'm not crazy about the part where I'll be trapped in something called the loft of squalor, but agreeing at least gets me back to Boston. I can figure out the next step once I get there. It'll probably involve an open window and a fire escape, though.

"Sounds good," I say. "Let's do it."

Ryan drops his head in his hands. "El—"

"It'll be fine," Lew says. "You'll be there with her, and we can get help securing the perimeter. We can do this."

Nia comes back inside. "You're good to go. He'll head over in the morning and set it up for you."

"Key?" Lew asks.

"Mine's still good," Nia says. "They won't have to interact with anyone."

Ryan lifts his head. "How much did you tell him?"

"Every last thing there is to know," Nia answers. "Because I know how much you love that."

"How much did you tell him?" Ryan repeats.

"As little as possible," Nia says. "This isn't my first time doing this. You don't have anything to worry about. From us, anyway."

"When you're involved," Ryan says, "I always have something to worry about."

Nia smiles. "Look at that. I guess we have something in common after all."

16

RYAN AND I LEAVE D.C. the next morning, well before the sun has actually risen, and head north. Because we're still avoiding toll roads, it takes even longer to cover the distance, but we arrive in Boston just after dark. I wonder if that was by design. Smuggle me in and out of places under the cover of darkness under the pretense that it's somehow safer.

Ryan parks on a side street in South Boston and we go around to the back entrance of an old brick building. It must have been a warehouse or factory in another life, but someone at some point made some half-assed effort to turn it into living space.

There's no elevator, so we take the stairs to the fifth floor and to a door marked 5C. Ryan fishes a key out of his pocket and unlocks the door. He steps inside and flips on the lights. I follow, bracing myself for my first look at the loft of squalor.

To the right is a wall of windows and a padded bench running along underneath them. Ryan goes over and pulls curtains across them. I don't see a door leading to the fire escape, but there must be an access point there. A window, probably. Which is fine by me. It wouldn't be the first window I crawled through.

Next to the windows is the living area—loveseat, coffee table, and a flat-screen television sitting on top of a bookcase whose shelves are bowing beneath the weight of books, sketchpads, and whatever else Nia's brother has stashed there.

To my left is a heavy bag and a set of free weights lined up against the wall. I like that. If there's hand wrap, I could maybe get a workout in. Unless Tess wouldn't be the sort to punch things. If she isn't, it's her loss because punching things can be therapeutic. And fun.

The kitchen is more of a kitchenette with a skinny and short fridge, a narrow stove, and an island that must double as a dining table, given the two stools set in front of it and the lack of any other table-like object.

A full-sized bed is set in an alcove in the back with a plastic milk crate on either side acting as nightstands. I look from that to the loveseat. Here's hoping it pulls out.

"The loveseat pulls out," Ryan says. "You don't have to worry."

I look at him, still standing by the windows. Is he a mind reader or just super attuned to my emotions? Not that I'm a fan of either one. I'm not. I much prefer to be an enigma to anyone I come across.

"You can have the bed," he says. "I'll take the couch."

"Are you sure?"

"Would you like the couch?"

"I would not."

"Then I'm sure."

That settled, I move on in my self-guided tour, passing a dresser and an armoire on my way to the one room in the loft. Must be the bathroom. I open the door, locate the light switch, and step inside.

The loft of squalor has a surprisingly nice bathroom. It's the only space that actually looks like it wasn't built during the industrial age. This room has been recently renovated. I suppose with a name like 'loft of squalor', I was expecting a bucket or a hole in the floor. I am both pleased and relieved to be mistaken.

I open the cabinet over the toilet. Aspirin and Band-aids. Nothing unusual or interesting. Under the sink are cleaning supplies, extra toilet paper—always nice to have on hand—a box of tampons—those could be useful, depending on how long this experience lasts—and a box of condoms. A big box. Jesus. Is this an art studio or a fuckpad? I really hope someone changed the bed sheets.

When I come out of the bathroom, Ryan is holding a black duffle bag.

"Where did that come from?" I ask.

"Jonas. He was supposed to bring some things by for me." Ryan gestures in the direction of the bed. "Nia said her sister-in-law would leave some clothes for you. They're probably in the dresser or the armoire over there."

I open the armoire first. It's mostly outerwear and sweatshirts in a variety of pastels. No black. In the drawers is a surprisingly large selection of T-shirts, leggings, pajamas, jeans, and socks. There are even unopened packages of underwear and sports bras in a couple of different sizes. Holy shit. Nia's sister-in-law has done a lot more than leave some clothing for me. She's provided me with an entire wardrobe. A pastel-based wardrobe, but still.

I close the drawers. "So, this whole thing is, like, a family affair now?"

"It's what they do."

It's what they do. He says that so casually, like there are people who do that. Which, I guess, there are, as here I am, surrounded by the evidence of it. A woman I don't even know put together all this for a total stranger because...why? Because Nia asked her to do it? Where the hell were these people when Leo and I needed it most?

"It's a lot," I say, sitting on the bed.

Ryan shrugs. "You know how family can be."

I don't, actually. Abandoned babies generally don't come with families.

"Is your family like that?" I ask.

Ryan perches on the back of the loveseat. "Pretty much. A little less intense, though."

Any family without Nia in it would be. "Fewer people who openly hate you?"

He smiles. "That's mostly theater. Nia doesn't hate me."

"Are you sure about that? Because I'm pretty sure the number one slot on her mortal enemies list belongs to you."

"The mortal enemies list? What did you do for her to bring that up?"

I'd rather not discuss that. I need to lull Ryan into complacency. Not ramp up the flight risk vibes. "I asked her about you."

Ryan laughs. "That would do it," he says. "Why did you ask her about me?"

"Curious."

"About what?"

"About why she hates you, about whether that's justified. About whether I can trust you."

Ryan stands, his relaxed demeanor disappearing with the action. "You don't trust me?"

Hell, no. "I don't know you."

He nods. "What can I do to change that? What would help?"

A time travel device of some kind to transport me back to a time and place when I wasn't in FBI custody or being hunted by killers. But I doubt he has access to one of those.

"Tess?" he prompts.

"I don't know."

"Okay," he says. "My name is Daniel Scott Ryan. I was born and raised in upstate New York. My family's still there—mom, dad, and two younger sisters."

"What are you doing?"

"Telling you about me. So you can know me better."

Huh. He really doesn't like that I can't trust him. I'm not sure I've ever met anyone who cared about that. At least not anyone who cared enough to do something about it.

"It might not work," I warn.

There's no 'might' about it. It won't work. Convincing me to trust a law enforcement official of any kind is a pretty tall order. The tallest. Like, that really tall building in Dubai kind of tall.

"Maybe not," Ryan says. "Still worth trying, though."

I can't decide if it's sweet or pathetic that he's trying so damn hard. I shrug. "All right, then. Knock yourself out."

He starts talking, telling me about a childhood that sounds sickeningly idyllic, like it was ripped out of some wholesome, family-friendly television show. A modern-day Waltons or something, with his neighbors, the Bradys, the Cunninghams, and the Cleavers. My childhood wouldn't fall into that category. If my childhood were made into a television series, it would only air on a premium channel because no basic cable network would be able to broadcast such a horror show without hefty fines from whatever government agency monitors such things.

"Do you miss them?" I ask.

"Sure." Ryan shrugs. "But Jonas, El, Nia…they're family, too."

"Nia's your family? Does she know that?"

"That really is mostly theater." He pushes off the couch and walks toward the kitchen. "Are you hungry?"

I'm not, but I follow Ryan and take a seat at the island.

He opens the fridge and smiles. "Looks like Nia's mom stocked the kitchen."

Of course she did. Ryan removes a casserole dish and sets it on the island.

"Want some lasagna?" he asks.

"No, thank you," I say.

"Are you sure? You have not lived until you've had Mrs. Kelly's lasagna."

That would suggest he's had it before. That maybe Nia really is family. That it really is mostly theater. I can't see her inviting anyone other than family over for dinner.

"I'm sure," I say. "How did you meet Nia and Lew?"

"I've known Lew since Quantico. We ended up working together when a case brought him to Boston. We both met Nia around the same time."

"Both vying for her affection?"

Ryan laughs. "No. Those two were always meant for each other."

"Pretty sappy, don't you think?"

"Doesn't matter. It's still true." He glances at me as he cuts out a serving of lasagna. "You okay?"

"You don't have to keep asking me that," I say. "I'm okay."

One thing my shitty childhood did prepare me for was shitty circumstances. I mean, there are definitely elements to this situation with which I'm far from okay, but things could be worse. A lot worse. I could be dead. I could be trapped in a true loft of squalor with the men from whom I'm trying to hide. This is what it is, and I can deal because I know what it isn't.

But Ryan doesn't know any of that, and I intend to keep it that way.

"It's okay if you're not," he says.

"Noted," I say.

Ryan looks at me for a moment, then nods. "Do you have any questions for me? About who I am? About the case? About…anything at all?"

I have a lot of questions about a lot of things, but that doesn't mean I should ask them. Unless I can find a way to do so that would sound less like Skye the thief looking for an escape and more like Tess the protected witness looking for reassurance.

Tess would probably be worried. Scared. People tried to kill her, which is likely not something with which she has had a lot of experience. It's not an everyday occurrence for most people. So, worried and scared would make sense. I can do worried and scared.

I glance over my shoulder at the now-hidden wall of windows. "Nia said the house in D.C. was under surveillance. Is that true?"

"Yes."

I look back at Ryan. "Does that mean there are people sitting outside of this building, too?"

"Yes."

"Who? Jonas?"

Ryan puts his plate in the microwave and starts it up. "Off-duty friends. A mixture of FBI and local police."

"Local police?"

"Nia's father is on the force."

Of course he is. Bad luck. It's all bad luck. If I had been a little quicker, a little better, a little...something, this wouldn't be happening. I wouldn't be here, surrounded by law enforcement whose friends are even more law enforcement.

While the lasagna reheats, Ryan gets a beer from the fridge and uses the island to remove the cap. "Want one?"

I want something a lot stronger than that. I shake my head. "Is it okay for you to drink while on the job?"

"It's okay. I won't get drunk. I promise."

"Are the promises of an FBI agent worth anything?"

"Someone's been hanging out with Nia too much."

Oh hell, Nia had *nothing* to do with that particular belief. But it's safer if he doesn't know that. "I can also tell you how much a nicely equipped Ford Escort would cost in California in the '80s."

Ryan grins. "She does love the Game Show Network."

The microwave beeps, and he turns to get his plate. He brings it back to the island and uses his fork to break the lasagna into smaller squares.

"I don't know what Nia might have told you," he says then, "but you can trust me, Tess. I will repeat that as often as you need to hear it because it's true. You can trust me. Lew and

Jonas, too. We will keep you safe while we find these guys. And we will find them. I promise you that, too. We'll find them as quickly as possible."

"That doesn't mean a damn thing," I say. "I know how slow an investigation goes."

"Oh yeah? How do you know that?"

Shit. I forgot I was supposed to be Tess. Tess likely would have been more accepting of his claim. I shrug. "Everyone knows that. Unless you're the right kind of person, justice is a slow train to arrive. If it ever does."

That piques his interest. He takes a drink from his bottle, then lowers it. "Are you speaking from experience?"

Yes. I shake my head. "No. I just pay attention."

"I'm sorry you feel that way."

"I'm sure you do. It's probably easier to do your job when you're not saddled with a disbeliever."

"A disbeliever? Is that what you are?"

Yes. "Maybe."

Ryan nods. "Then part of my job is changing your mind."

"What if you can't?"

"I will."

He won't, but I smile anyway. "I hope so."

17

THE FIRST THING I SEE when I open my eyes is a clock reading 8:18.

It's not my clock. I don't own a clock. Guess this means this goddamn nightmare is still very much *not* a dream.

Yipee.

God, I hate being awake this early. Not to mention waking up in yet another strange new place. It happens so infrequently that it always throws me. There's always the question of where I am and how I ended up there. And now, there's the need to remind myself of who I'm supposed to be. What's today's rundown?

The loft of squalor.

Still lying to the feds.

Still Tess, who is definitely not a thief nor affiliated with thieves in any way, shape, or form.

I really need to stop being Tess.

I sigh and roll onto my back to look at the ceiling. No escape options to be found there, so I sit up slowly. I don't want to wake my babysitter. He doesn't strike me as the type to sleep past eight in the morning, but I don't see him anywhere. I hear breathing, though. Strangely rhythmic breathing. What is

Ryan doing? Is he still asleep? Is he awake and lying on his back, staring at the ceiling, while waiting for a sign of life from me?

I slip out of bed to find out which.

Turns out, the answer is neither. Ryan's lying, shirtless, on his back on the floor, doing sit-ups. Or crunches. I don't know the difference between the two. I do know that Ryan looks good without a shirt. Really good. The man does not lack for muscle tone. I sit on the window seat and count reps. Who the hell knows how long I'll be stuck here. I should indulge in whatever pleasures I can find.

I'm up to forty when he notices me and freezes, mid-action. All hail the observation powers of the FBI.

"How long have you been sitting there?" he asks.

"Forty crunches," I say.

He completes the rep and lies back on the floor before propping himself up on his elbows and looking at me. "You're quiet."

"I have my moments," I say. "How many do you do?"

"One hundred."

"How many more do you need to do?"

"Ten."

"Well, carry on."

After a moment's hesitation, he resumes his workout. It would be weird—weirder, maybe—to keep watching, so I move on. I select some clothing from my new wardrobe and head to the bathroom to find out what kind of water pressure the loft of squalor has.

When I come back out, the loft smells like coffee, eggs, and bacon. Ryan is standing at the stove. Sadly, he is wearing a shirt. I leave my pajamas on the bed and go into the kitchen to get myself some coffee. I take it over to the couch to watch Ryan cook.

He glances at me. "Breakfast? I can make you some eggs."

I hate eggs. And eating breakfast. I shake my head. "I'm not big on breakfast."

He turns back to the stove. "You're not big on eating."

Jesus. When did Leo get here? "I eat fine," I say. "And even if I didn't, I don't see how my eating habits are any of your business."

"Touchy subject?"

"No," I say. "What's on the agenda today?"

Ryan removes the pan from the stove and sets it on the island. He doesn't look like he intends to move on just yet, but the burner phone on the counter dings before he can speak. He picks up the phone and reads the screen.

"Jonas is on his way here with the sketch artist," he says, typing a reply.

Never thought I'd be grateful to hear a sentence like that, but it does offer a way out of this conversation.

"You should really get cleaned up before they get here," I say.

"Yeah." Ryan looks around and sighs. "You should eat something. It's going to be a long day, and you should have something in your system to help you get through it."

"I'm not—"

"And I don't want to hear that it's not my business, Tess, because my business is making sure you're taken care of, and that includes protecting you from people trying to kill you *and* your shitty eating habits. Maybe you're not used to having someone look out for you, having someone care, but you have someone now, so do us both a favor and just eat something." He grabs his phone and stalks toward the bathroom. When he stops to pick up his duffle bag, he points toward the apartment door. "And don't you dare open that for anyone other than Jonas."

He goes into the bathroom and shuts the door. Apparently, Agent Daniel Ryan has a breaking point and I just pushed him past it. It makes me like him more. Leo might like him, too, except for that whole being-a-fed thing.

When the shower starts, I peruse the kitchen for breakfast options and find a box of strawberry frosted Pop Tarts in a cupboard. Good enough. I sit at the island to eat, making no attempt to do so neatly, and leave both a smattering of crumbs as well as the crumpled foil packet on the counter top. He'll either think I ate or suspect I just made it look that way. I'm curious to find out which.

I'm also curious if there's anything *useful* in this loft and start my search in the kitchen. In the liquor cabinet next to the fridge are half-empty bottles of Smirnoff and Jack Daniel's, an unopened bottle of red wine, and some gin. If the bad guys come knocking, I could always make Molotov cocktails.

There's a selection of knives in the silverware drawer, but Nia's brother is definitely not a chef. I run my finger along one of the blades. He's not big on knife maintenance, either. I don't know how these things could cut anything. Maybe they don't. Maybe that's why they're here. I put the knives back in the drawer and close it. Maybe he takes better care of his art supplies.

Tucked among the sketchbooks and writing and drawing materials, I discover a box of tools I suspect are used to sculpt clay or some clay-like substance. A lot of them look like things you might see at a dentist's office, but among them is a black folding knife. Three-inch blade. Actually sharp. Oh yes. This is much better.

The shower stops running. Time's up. Closing the knife, I slip it into the pocket of my jeans. I make sure the art supplies show no sign of having been disturbed and am back on the couch when Ryan exits the bathroom.

He doesn't acknowledge me as he drops his duffle next to the couch and goes into the kitchen. He looks at the mess on the island and then at me.

"Did you eat, or did you just make it look like you ate?" he asks.

His suspicion makes me smile. "I ate."

He nods. Still annoyed but trying not to show it. "Thank you."

The phone dings again. Ryan pulls it from his back pocket and glances at it. "They're here. You ready?"

Not in the least. "As I'll ever be," I say.

18

A COUPLE OF MINUTES LATER, Ryan lets Jonas and a fresh-faced young woman into the apartment. Jonas is carrying coffee and a box of Dunkin' donuts. The woman has a tote bag hanging from one shoulder and a sketch pad tucked under her other arm.

Jonas motions to her. "Sketch artist," he says as though this is how humans greet one another. That, or he thinks either Ryan and I are incredibly stupid. Maybe both.

The sketch artist offers her hand to Ryan. "I'm Carrie."

He shakes her hand. "Ryan. Thanks for helping us out."

"No problem."

He leads her over to me. "This is Tess. She saw the men we need you to sketch."

"Hi, Tess," Carrie says. "It's nice to meet you."

Weird circumstances, though. Hell, she's not even meeting *me*. I nod. "Hi."

Ryan brings her a chair, and Carrie sits down. She puts her sketch pad on the floor and digs through her tote bag. Ryan goes back to the kitchen where Jonas is halfway through a Boston cream donut. Ryan stands at the island and eats his now-cold breakfast. In between bites, he talks quietly with Jonas, but he's watching Carrie and me.

"Okay," Carrie says. "I think I'm ready."

She thinks she's ready? I look at her. The tote bag is now on the floor. The sketch pad lays unopened on her lap.

"Have you done this before?" I ask.

"Not professionally, but I understand the theory."

"There's theory behind this?"

Carrie nods. "There is. I'll show you." She opens the sketch pad. "Tell me how you spent that day—the whole day, not just when you encountered the men."

Let's see...I cased an office building, ate French toast with Leo, napped, and then broke into multiple offices, cracked a safe, witnessed a murder, ran from the murderers, and also lied to the FBI. A lot. I absolutely cannot tell her how I spent the day. Especially in the presence of two law enforcement officials.

"Why?" I ask. "What will that do?"

"You'll see. What time did you get up that morning?"

I sigh. What would Tess have done? "Well, I...I have to be at the office at nine, so I got up around seven. Did the usual—breakfast, shower, that kind of thing. Got to work on time, and—"

"How'd you get to work?" Carrie asks.

"The T. Wanna know what line?" I say. I hope not, as I have no idea where Tess lives.

"How crowded was the train?"

"Morning commute in Boston. What do you think?" I say. "Yeah, it was crowded. I got bumped into and felt up all the way to my destination."

"What happened when you got to the office?"

Holy shit. This is going to take *forever*. "The usual boredom and water cooler small talk. It was maybe a little worse that day because it was the last day before my vacation. Five o'clock took even longer to come around, you know? But as soon as it did, I left. The commute was the same going home as it was going in because commutes are like that."

"What made you go back to the office?"

Crime. "My phone. I couldn't find it and thought maybe I left it on my desk. So I went back," I say. "I talked to…" I swallow, remembering the sight of the bullet hole in his head. "I talked to the guard on duty, then went up to my office."

The chatter in the kitchen has stopped. The urge to look at Ryan is strong, but I keep my focus on Carrie. She still hasn't drawn a damn thing.

"What happened then?" she asks.

Gunshot. Red mist. Running for my life.

"I heard a noise—I didn't know it was a gun—and I went out to the hallway to see what it was. That's when I saw them. Three of them."

"Which one stood out the most? And why?"

The gray ghost. His eyes.

"The one without a gun," I say. "The other two had guns, but the other guy…He may have had a gun I didn't see, but…His eyes."

"Tell me about his eyes."

"They were…predatory, if that makes sense. Maybe it doesn't," I say. "The rest of him wasn't anything. He was older, white-haired. Colorless, almost. Not exactly gaunt, but slight. Flat, maybe. Like he'd blow over in a gentle breeze. If you passed him on the street or sat next to him on the T, you wouldn't think he was capable of anything, really, besides maybe breaking a hip. But his eyes were different. You run away from a man with eyes like that."

I catch movement out of the corner of my eye and glance at Ryan. He's not leaning anymore. What interests him more? The man I'm describing or the way I'm describing him?

Carrie starts sketching. She asks about the eyes' shape and size and color, every last detail down to the bags beneath them. When she runs out of questions, she continues to work for a few more minutes before putting down her pencil.

"Like this?" she says and turns the pad toward me.

My body instinctively withdraws when I see what she has created. If this is the theory, then it more than works.

"Yeah," I say. "Just like that."

By the time Carrie leaves, there are three sketches sitting on the kitchen island. The gray ghost and his two lackeys. Ryan and Jonas stand on opposite sides of the island, discussing their suspects. I stay on the sofa. I don't need to look at the sketches anymore. I don't want to.

I want to find the men themselves. Preferably from afar and well out of range of any weapons they have in their possession, but I want to find them. I don't want to sit here, listening to Ryan and Jonas speculate on their case. They may believe they know how criminals think, but I can do better. I can do *more.*

But I can't tell them that. Not without exposing myself. Which is selfish—so goddamn selfish. Two people are dead, and here I am, worried about being arrested.

Jonas gathers the sketches and walks out of the apartment without acknowledging me at all. Ryan locks the door behind him.

"Tess?" he says. "Are you okay? Do you need anything?"

I shake my head. "Where is Jonas going?"

"To talk to some contacts and see if we can put some names to those faces."

What kind of contacts? FBI? Local police? Criminal informants? Shit, will it even matter? Law enforcement won't know anything about the gray ghost. A CI might, but a CI who does know that man will also be smart enough to keep their damn mouth shut about it.

"Thank you for doing this," Ryan says. "I know it can't have been easy to relive that."

Easy. It was supposed to be an easy job. Easy in, easy out, easy money. Instead, I watched a guy whose name I don't even know get his damn head blown off.

"What was his name?" I ask. "The guy they killed. Not the security guard, but the guy in the office."

Ryan sits in Carrie's chair. "Edward Roberson."

Edward Roberson. So now I know his name. It doesn't change anything. I'm not sure why I thought it would. "Oh."

"Did you know him well?"

"I didn't know him at all," I say. Except that he and Tessa Martin worked together. She at least would have known his name. "I mean, we worked for the same company but in different departments. I know he liked…baseball. That's about it."

"So you don't know why a thief would have broken into his office?"

Probably something hidden in the safe behind the picture of Fenway Park. I shake my head again. "No reason I can think of. Was anything taken from his office? I think he had a safe. Maybe they took something from there?"

"Not that anyone can tell, or has been willing to tell us, but if Edward Roberson was mixed up with this case…" Ryan sighs. "He may have been the only person who knew what was worth taking."

Not the only person. Someone hired me, after all. Jay would know. Jay could give me a name. That person might know the gray ghost. If they were both trying to break into the same safe on the same night—presumably looking for the same thing—then that person might be the only one willing and able to identify the gray ghost.

"Tess?" Ryan says. "Are you—?"

"What if I can do more?"

He shakes his head a little. "Do more?"

"To find those men."

"Like what?" he asks. No judgment, just curious. "Do you know something about Edward? Did you see something else that night? Something you were too scared to tell me about at the time? If you know something, you should tell me. You can, you know. You can trust me."

I can't trust him. I wish I could, though, which is weird because Leo's the only person on the entire damn earth I do trust.

Ryan leans forward and places his hand on my knee. "Tell me what you meant."

I look at his hand. "I didn't mean anything. I don't know anything. I can't do anything. I just…I'm just sitting here, not doing anything, and…" I shrug. "I wish I wasn't."

Ryan nods. He pulls back and glances over his shoulder. When he looks back at me, he's smiling.

He stands and offers me his hand. "Come on."

I don't move. "Where?"

"We're gonna take out our frustration on the heavy bag over there."

I look at the bag and then back at him. "*Our* frustration?"

"You're not the only one who wants to be doing more," he says. "What do you think?"

I think it still doesn't make him trustworthy, but it'll feel good to beat the crap out of something.

"Yeah, okay." I put my hand in his. "Let's do it."

19

FEELING A BIT LIKE A diva with a wardrobe addiction, I change into clothing more suited for punching a heavy bag. I come out of the bathroom to find Ryan sitting on the coffee table. He's wearing the shorts and T-shirt from this morning.

He looks at me. "Hey, come sit. I need to wrap your hands to protect them."

Oh. He thinks Tess doesn't know anything about boxing or punching or fighting. Maybe she doesn't—I have no idea—but I do. Should I tell him that? Pretending otherwise will be exhausting. Telling the truth could be worse. But that's currently the story of my entire damn life, isn't it?

I sit on the couch. Ryan slides closer and takes my right hand. Picking up a roll of hand wrap sitting at his side, he gets to work. First the right, then the left. When he finishes, he sets the remaining wrap aside and carefully checks his work. Is he nervous or just overly protective?

He looks at me. "How does that feel? Okay?"

"Yeah. It's fine."

Ryan stands. "Ready?"

I nod and stand without thinking and collide with his body. He grabs my elbows and keeps me upright. Keeps me close.

"Okay?" he asks.

I seriously doubt it, but I say, "Yeah, I'm good. Thanks."

"Good." Ryan lets me go and walks away. "Let's warm up."

Oh, I do not have the patience to pretend. I ease past Ryan and walk over to the heavy bag, swinging and stretching my arms along the way. It's not much of a proper warm-up, but who the hell cares about that? Stopping in front of the bag, I check the distance, right my stance, and begin.

Ryan joins me, bracing the bag. "You've done this before."

I concentrate on my punches. "Once or twice."

"You take kickboxing classes or something?"

"You know," I say, "sometimes, it just feels good to hit something."

"You're not lying."

I pull my next punch and step back. "What?"

"You're not lying," Ryan repeats. "It does occasionally feel really good to punch something."

Oh. I resume my workout, now imagining the bag is wearing the gray ghost's face. "Or someone."

"That would be assault, you know."

I knee the bag. Once. Twice. "Only if you get caught."

Ryan laughs. "I'm not sure that's true."

It is where I come from. Tess likely has a different philosophy, though. I step back again and run my arm across my forehead. "Your turn."

He studies me for a moment, then nods. He starts slow, hitting the bag as though he's either disinterested or just really bad at boxing. Steadily, he loses himself in the rhythm and his jabs become sharper. He knows what he's doing.

That could be fun.

I move up and brace the bag. "Wanna spar?"

"With you?"

"You see anyone else here?"

"No, but—"

"Afraid?"

He glances at me. "Of you?"

"Is that so crazy?"

It is. It is really crazy. This isn't Tess. This is me. I should back off, but this is a much, much better feeling. Dangerous, but better. I want to be me again. Just for a little while. Damn the consequences.

"We don't have mats," he says, "or—"

"I promise I won't hurt you."

Ryan stops and drops his arms. He smiles, but it's different now. Whether or not he realizes it, he's not seeing Tess anymore. He's not seeing that damsel in distress he rescued from the bad guys. For the moment, anyway, he's seeing me.

A moment is all I need. Just one moment of normalcy—or as close to it as I can get.

He comes around the heavy bag to face me properly. "Let's see what you've got."

A rush goes through me. I haven't felt like this since I stepped off the elevator at the Skyreach. God, I've missed this feeling. Being capable. Being in control. Being powerful. Being *alive*.

It's trouble, the whole damn thing, but I raise my hands into a defensive position. Let's see what *he's* got.

He won't start anything, so I take a half-hearted swing at him, just to get things rolling, and he dodges it. His hands come up—not as high as they should be—but he doesn't attack. Looks like I'll be making the second move, too.

I lash out. His forearm comes up and absorbs the blow. I try again, harder this time. He blocks that as well. The movement is crisper. He's still holding back, but he's getting there.

Maybe the third attempt will be the charm. I stick with the same arm. After he blocks it, he swings at me with his other arm. I duck and sidestep out of the way. He shifts to keep me in front of him, hands creeping into position.

I land a kick to his ribs. He grunts and pitches forward, so I move in and attempt a punch. He blocks it with his arm, then turns sideways to check me with his shoulder. I feint to the left, and he takes the bait. I hit his chest. Ryan staggers back. Dropping down, I kick his legs out from under him. He ends up on his back on the floor and doesn't move.

Shit. Did I just break an FBI agent? There's probably a law or two against that.

After a moment, he laughs. "That is one hell of a kickboxing class."

He has no idea. I stand and hold out my hand. He takes it and I help him up, but he doesn't let go. Once again, he keeps me close. The look in his eyes is intense, and I am feeling...things that would be really dumb to act on. For a lot of reasons. I should push him away. I should put as much distance between us as possible.

But my fight or flight impulse is strangely dormant. Apparently, it's just as dumb as the rest of me.

"Were you holding back?" he asks.

I shrug. "Seemed only fair. You were holding back."

"How do you know that?"

"I know," I say. "Wanna go again? Maybe neither of us holds back this time, and we see who ends up on top."

The look in Ryan's eyes changes. Still intense—*really* intense—but maybe now he's imagining who would end up on top. What *is* going through his brain right now? That is, if his brain is doing the thinking at this moment. It may not be. Mine sure as hell isn't.

I lean forward. Bad idea. Such a bad idea.

Ryan's phone rings, and we both jump. He drops my hand and goes to the island. Turning his back to me, he taps the screen and brings the phone to his ear.

"Jonas," he says.

Jonas. Great. Another reason to dislike that man.

"Yeah," Ryan says then. A pause. "Yeah. Okay."

He ends the call and looks at his phone.

"Everything all right?" I ask.

Ryan turns around. "Yeah. Everything's fine. Well, nothing new is wrong, anyway, which is…" He grimaces and puts the phone back on the island. "It's good."

Okay, that's weird. Because of me or something Jonas said? I nod. "Are you all right? Did I hurt you?"

He smiles. "No, you didn't. I'm good. I'm…" He shakes his head and points toward the bathroom. "I need to shower."

Ryan walks away. The bathroom door closes and the shower starts up.

I unwrap my hands. I should let this go. I shouldn't pursue it anymore. It's stupid and dangerous and I need to be smart and careful.

I drop the wrap on the floor and head toward the bathroom. I hope he didn't lock the door. Tess doesn't know how to pick locks.

He didn't. I walk in. Ryan doesn't notice. He's standing under the spray, one arm braced against the wall in front of him. I admire his backside as I strip off my clothes. He doesn't notice that, either.

I open the shower door and step inside.

Ryan turns. His jaw drops but no sound comes out. I close the door.

"What…What are you doing?" he asks, his voice hoarse.

What does he think I'm doing? "Conserving water."

"Conserving water?"

"For the environment." I put my hands on his chest and back him against the wall.

"Jesus, Tess."

"If you want me to go, just say so."

"We…" He swallows. "We shouldn't."

"That's true," I say. It is possibly the worst idea in the history of ideas. "Does that mean you want me to go?"

"No. But…" His hands find my hips. "Are you sure you want—?"

I kiss him. He definitely kisses me back.

"I'm sure," I say.
He nods. "Okay, then."

20

THOUGH WE SPEND THE NIGHT together in bed, I wake up alone the next morning. I sit up and look around the loft. Where did he go? Why didn't I hear him leave?

On the crate to my right is the box of Pop Tarts with a Post-it note attached to the front. I don't recognize the handwriting, but it has to be Ryan's. I pull the note off the box.

Need to take care of some things. Be back soon. Stay here and don't open the door for anyone other than Lew or Jonas.

I put down the note. He's not here. He has left me alone. I don't know where he is, what these mysterious things are that he's gone to take care of, or why Lew would be knocking on a door that's a good five hundred miles away from where he is, but none of that really matters at this moment because I am alone.

I get out of bed and walk to the windows. Opening the curtains, I examine the street below. If I were surveillance teams set up to keep an eye on the building, where would I be? How many of them are there? There's at least one on this side and one watching the back. I don't have a view of that street from here. I'll have to go up to the roof.

The roof's a possibility. Depending what's on either side of this building, I could use it to get onto the roof of a neighboring building and walk out of that one instead. Or maybe just walk right out of this one. Even if the surveillance teams see me, and even if they follow me, I could lose them. Go where cars can't follow or ditch them in a crowd if they follow me on foot. I could—

Someone knocks on the door. I look at it over my shoulder. Who might that be? Ryan has a key; he wouldn't need to knock. His note mentioned both Lew and Jonas, but would either of them really be here without Ryan? They might, if something happened to Ryan.

Shit. Did something happen to Ryan? What the hell did he do?

The person knocks again. I go over to the door and peek through the peephole to see Nia standing on the other side. With tote bags. Why does she have bags? Is she moving in?

"I know he told you not to open the door," she says, "but open the damn door already. I really need to pee."

I open the door and let her in. "What are you doing here?"

Nia holds out the tote bags. "Bringing you supplies. And using the bathroom. I wasn't kidding about needing to pee."

As soon as I take the bags, she hurries away. I put the bags on the island and start to unload them. A carton of milk and some orange juice. A couple of boxes of healthy cereal. More Pop Tarts. Word certainly travels fast.

"Don't you think D.C. to Boston was a little far to travel just to deliver Pop Tarts?" I ask when Nia emerges from the bathroom.

"Don't flatter yourself," she says. "We're in Boston to visit family."

"Which means you're really in Boston so Lew can work with Ryan and Jonas on the case none of them are supposed to be working on."

Nia shrugs. "Don't know what you're talking about. We're here to visit family."

"Well, then, shouldn't you be visiting your family? Is it even safe for you to be here?"

"It's my brother's loft. It wouldn't be the first time I've been seen in this neighborhood."

"Yeah, but your brother doesn't live here anymore."

"No, he lives in the suburbs, like a proper boring, married person."

"He doesn't seem to be the suburbs type."

Nia sits at the island and opens the Pop Tart box. "Funny what children, or the prospect of them, does to people."

I glance at her belly. "When are you due?"

"Both far too soon and not nearly soon enough."

Does that mean I don't have the right to ask a personal question, or is Nia just contrary by default? Of course, it's entirely possible for both options to be true.

I nod. "Well…good luck with that, I guess."

"Thank you," Nia says. "How's it going here? You and Ryan getting along?"

Her tone puts me on edge. What does she mean by that? Does she know what Ryan and I did yesterday and last night and technically this morning? Did Ryan say something to Lew? To Nia?

"It's fine," I say quickly. Too quickly. If she didn't know before, she will now. "We're fine."

Nia smiles. She looks at the unmade bed, then back at me. I don't know why, but I am completely horrified.

"Well," she says. "Good luck with *that*."

"Give me a break," I say. "Ryan is not that bad."

"At sex?"

"He's not bad at sex. He's…" Holy *shit*. I did not know a person could be this mortified and not immediately drop dead from embarrassment. I shake my head. "You know what? I am not talking about this with you."

Nia laughs. "Colin usually has condoms in the bathroom. You know, if you need them."

"I don't…We didn't…" I sigh. "We found them."

Nia laughs again. "Let me know if you need more."

"I really won't."

"Because he's bad at sex?"

"No, I meant…Shut up."

Nia laughs even harder. "Oh, shit. I am so happy I came over here today. This is—"

Her phone rings then, and she chuckles as she digs it out of her coat pocket. She glances at the screen and makes a face. Her amusement fades.

She accepts the call and brings the phone to her ear. "Mom."

She slides off the stool and wanders away while listening to whatever her mother has to say. She doesn't contribute much to the conversation, just nods a lot and says, "Uh-huh" from time to time. I get a glass and pour myself some orange juice.

"Yeah, okay, Mom. Listen, I gotta go," Nia says. "My beer's getting flat, and the sushi's getting warm, so I'll talk to you later. Okay, bye!"

She ends the call and walks back toward me.

"Sorry about that," she says. "Even though we are currently staying at her house, and I literally just saw her before I came over here, my mother still felt the need to call to make sure her grandchild is all right. Not her daughter, mind you. Just the baby."

I doubt that. The woman who filled a fridge with food for a complete stranger probably cares a hell of a lot more about her daughter, grandchild or not. But what do I know? I've never had a mother call and check in on me for any reason.

I fold the empty tote bags and set them in front of her. "Thanks for the supplies. Thank your mother, too. It's nice that she cares."

Nia raises an eyebrow. "Are you kicking me out?"

"Is there a reason to stay?"

"You mean besides me not wanting to go back to my parents' house?"

"Yeah, besides that."

"Well, if I leave now, I won't be able to tell you what I know about the case the guys are definitely not working on."

"How do you know anything about this case?"

"I don't suck at eavesdropping," she says. "Interested?"

Yes. I shrug. "Maybe."

"Oh please. You don't like being kept out of the loop any more than I do."

I really don't. "What's your plan?"

"My plan is I tell you what I know, then we go check it out."

"We?"

"I really don't want to go back to my parents' house."

"You shouldn't go. It could be dangerous."

"Let's hope."

What is wrong with her? "Nia," I say. "The baby?"

"It's fine. I'm not giving birth today."

"Not the point I was making."

"I know," Nia says. "But here's the thing...I feel the need to exert some goddamn independence, and I'm thinking that you do, too. Unless you're over it now that you and Ryan are orgasm buddies."

There is something seriously wrong with this woman. "We are not orgasm buddies."

"Then he *is* bad at sex."

"He's not..." I squeeze my eyes shut. My head hurts. "What do I have to do to make you stop talking?"

"Change into some walking-around clothes, and let's take a walk."

I open my eyes. "We can't just walk out of here. The entire building is being watched."

"Fortunately, I know where the surveillance teams are camped out," Nia says.

Okay, so that might be helpful. Even if absolutely nothing else comes out of this field trip, just learning where the surveillance teams are situated will be worthwhile. Once I find them,

I'll find the vulnerabilities. Once I find the vulnerabilities, I can do just about anything.

"Well?" Nia says.

"Ryan's gonna be pissed," I say. He didn't even want me to open the goddamn door, and now here I am, planning to follow Nia right through it.

"All the more reason then," Nia says.

Maybe. "If you do this," I warn, "you will be actively working against the FBI's investigation."

"The doctor did say I should stay active."

"You will be actively working *against* your husband."

"Wouldn't be the first time." Nia glances at her phone. "Clock's ticking, Not-Tess. Are we doing this or not?"

This is a terrible, terrible idea.

I nod. "We're doing this."

21

I LEAVE THE LOFT OF squalor looking like someone hosed me down with Pepto-Bismol. Pink joggers, pink warm-up jacket, and a pink knit cap to cover my hair. As much as I hate looking like a goddamn highlighter, it will be a disguise in itself. No one who knows me will ever recognize me like this.

Nia and I walk down to the lobby. I keep my hand in the jacket pocket, fingers gripping my new knife, and gravitate toward the wall to maintain the illusion that Nia is on her own. She walks up to the doors and stops to take out her phone. She pokes the screen, then brings the phone to her ear.

"Okay," she says, looking at me, "across the street is a green rustbucket that I think used to be a Toyota in another life. I'm going to mosey on over there—"

"Mosey?" I say. "You're going to mosey?"

"Yes, I am going to *mosey* on over there and tell the two gentlemen sitting inside that you're being a model cooperating witness," she says. "While they're busy looking at me and not the entrance to this building, you sneak out to the left and wait for me on the corner the next block over. Think you can handle that?"

God, I hope so. "Yes, I can handle that."

"Good. Also, if you decide to ditch me, I will be forced to reach out to my husband and your boy toy."

Jesus Christ. I roll my eyes. "I won't ditch you."

"You better not."

Nia lowers the phone and sticks it back in her pocket. She walks outside and heads across the street to a green sedan. The driver's side window goes down and she leans on the car door. I inch up to the doors to check the situation on the sidewalk, my hand clutching the knife tighter. I don't have a lot of time to waste, but I would feel better with at least a little cover. As soon as I see a pair of women walking in the right direction, I ease open the door and time my exit so I'm walking just a half step behind them. I peel off when I reach Nia's pre-selected meeting spot and lean against the wall.

I hate having to wait for her. I hate having to involve her in any of this. Ryan—the FBI, I mean—will be pissed enough that I snuck out. I can only imagine how much more displeased they—or, at the very least, Lew—will be when they find out Nia came along with me.

But I want to know what they know. I need to know if it's something. As soon as I find out, I can ditch Nia. I don't care how bored she is, she shouldn't be involved with this. And not just because if I spend much more time with her, I just may kill her myself.

"Oh good," she says when she finally shows up, "you can follow direction."

I push off the wall. "Where are we going?"

"I'll tell you when we get there."

She leads the way to the nearest T station and we take the red line to Downtown Crossing, then switch to the orange line and head towards Charlestown. I'm sure it doesn't mean anything that we're going that way. Lots of people live there. Lots of things happen there. The fact that I also happen to call it home is just some funny coincidence.

We get off the train at Sullivan Square and walk toward Bunker Hill Street. Okay, so the coincidence is feeling a little less funny now. My heart feels like it's now beating in my damn ears. I'm surprised Nia can't hear it. But it's okay. This still doesn't mean we're heading to my apartment. How would the FBI have found it? It wasn't as though I left behind a calling card at the scene of the crime. Except for my blood. I wasn't bleeding a lot that night, but I was bleeding. There could be blood and skin tissue on Tess's desk. I rested my head against the elevator panel, so there could have been some left there as well. But if I did leave blood behind and if the FBI did find it, that shouldn't have led them to my home. I've worked very hard over the years to stay out of the system. Hell, the apartment isn't even rented in my name. So, even if they did, somehow, link that apartment to the crime scene, it doesn't necessarily lead to me.

Yet.

I hold my breath as we near the turn toward my apartment. If she goes left, I'm going to need a contingency plan. Ditch her? Let her call Lew and Ryan and whoever else to hunt me down?

But instead of turning left, Nia keeps walking. Okay. I should feel relief, but I don't. If not my apartment, where *are* we going? What else is around here that could possibly be connected to the Skyreach? Who even knew…Oh.

Jay.

We're going to Jay's apartment.

Which makes even less sense. How did the FBI get Jay's address? What possible connection could there be between Edward Roberson and Jay? Jay met with clients, not the people whose safes I would be breaking into.

"You okay?" Nia asks.

"Yeah," I say. "Just…nervous, I guess. Has the FBI been here yet?"

"Waiting on a warrant or something," she says. "I think it's around this next corner."

It is. At least it's late enough in the day that Jay shouldn't be home. He should already be at The Rebel Fly by now. I have to hope so because I'm pretty sure Nia's planning to walk right up to the front door and knock.

"Do they have the place under surveillance?" I ask. I don't see any city utility vans or Crown Vics or dark-colored SUVs with tinted windows anywhere, but that doesn't mean they aren't set up somewhere else. Across the street, maybe.

Nia turns the corner. "The whole point of this was to avoid the feds. Do you really think I'd bring you to an address the FBI was actively watching?"

"I don't know. You might."

"Well, I didn't. They're not watching the place." Nia gestures to a building. "This is it."

Yes, this is it. Great. I would have hated to be wrong about that.

Jay lives in the basement unit, which comes with its own entrance. Nia walks down the three steps to the door and knocks. No answer. She tries the doorknob. Locked. She steps back and studies the building, then glances side to side.

"Cover me," she says.

Cover her? What is she planning to do? Blast her way in?

She opens her bag and rummages through it. If she pulls out some C-4, I'm gone. She finds what she's looking for, then awkwardly sinks to her knees.

"What are you doing?" I ask.

"I'll tell you what I'm not doing," she says. "I'm definitely not picking this lock in order to gain unlawful entry to this residence, that's for sure."

I look over her shoulder. Are those bobby pins? "You're picking a lock using bobby pins?"

"Do you have a better idea?"

I do, actually, but I'm not me. Tess isn't supposed to know anything about lock picking. Or this apartment.

I sigh. "No."

"Then be a good lookout and turn around."

Am I really going to let a pregnant woman sit on her knees and commit a crime with bobby pins? It's hardly the most ethical thing in the world, but then again…I am a thief. What do I know about ethics? Besides, I have to admit I want to know if she can do it.

I turn to watch the street. "Your husband is an FBI agent."

"That is the rumor."

"And your father, I believe, is a cop."

"Chief of police, but yes."

"Yet, here you are, using hair accessories to break into someone's house."

"I specifically said I definitely wasn't doing that," she says. "What's your point?"

I shift to check her progress. The technique is clumsy but not bad. If she devoted more time to it, she'd be better than me. Well, maybe not *that* good, but still, far better than a civilian has any right to be. Especially a civilian with that many ties to law enforcement.

"An act of rebellion, or do you live a secret life of crime?" I ask.

"A girl can't do both?"

A girl most certainly can. "You don't really seem the type."

"All the better for people to underestimate you. I'm guessing you know all about that."

What makes her think that? I mean, she's not wrong, but still. Nia seems a little too good at reading people for my comfort.

I look back at the street. If the FBI has this address, why aren't they sitting on it? If it's important enough to require a warrant, why aren't they watching it in the meantime? Maybe they are, and Nia just doesn't know it. If that's the case, they've hidden themselves well. I don't see any signs of surveillance anywhere.

Nia cackles. "And that's how we do it, people."

I look at her. She grins at me as she pushes the door open.

"See?" she says. "Easy peasy."

Oh yeah. Super easy, and not at all slow. I go down the stairs to help her up. "Impressive."

She gestures to the apartment. "After you."

I glance inside. It looks neat. Entirely too neat for Jay. The man's a goddamn slob. Unless he had a personality transplant and hired a housekeeper since I saw him last, we won't find anything good.

I still need to look, though. I need to know. Nia, however, doesn't.

"You should stay out here," I say.

"Why would I do that?"

"Because we don't know what we'll find in there."

"Which is why I'm going in."

"Nia, please," I say. "Just...stay out here."

"Why?"

"I'm trying to protect you, you maniac," I say. "Not to mention your unborn child, who most definitely needs protection because its mother is crazy. Stay out here."

"No."

I sigh. "Fine. Come inside. Just don't touch anything."

She scoffs. "This is not my first break-in."

Seriously. How did this woman end up married to an FBI agent? I shake my head and step into the apartment. Not only is it clean, it smells like someone attempted to clean but missed a pretty big spot. Probably the couch. Jay salvaged it from the sidewalk on trash day. He likes doing that—picking up whatever other people have discarded and using it to his advantage. Furniture. Food. Electronics.

Me.

I walk in farther, sidestepping to the left to avoid the spot on the floor that squeaks. Professional habit. No one's around to hear any tell-tale signs of company, wanted or otherwise. Which wouldn't be odd—Jay's usually gone by this time anyway—except something's off. Someone has been here. Someone who wasn't Jay.

I turn into the kitchen and stop. Well, that explains the smell.

A body.

Not just any body.
Jay.

22

THEY CUT HIS THROAT.

He's on his back, eyes open and gaping at the ceiling. Blood pools around his head and shoulders. This is not the first corpse I've seen—it's not even the first one I've seen this *week*—but it's not getting any easier.

Did Jay know the people who did this? He may have. Nothing looks disturbed. There was no forced entry. It wasn't a robbery. It wasn't random. They came here for him. They came here to cut his throat and walk away without leaving a mark.

Except for the dead body on the kitchen floor.

I look up. On the counter next to the refrigerator, aimed right at the entrance to the kitchen is a webcam. That's not Jay's. I guess the murderers left more behind than just the body. Is the gray ghost on the other end? Is he watching me right now?

"What are you—?" Nia gasps. "Oh my God."

She fumbles through her bag, and I turn around just as she's pulling out her phone. Shit.

"What are you doing?" I ask, moving to block her from the camera's view.

"Ordering pizza," she says. "There's a dead body on the floor. What do you think I'm doing?"

I take the phone from her hand. "You can't call the police."

"I'm not calling the police."

"You can't call the FBI, either. We're not supposed to be here."

"I think murder would take precedence over breaking and entering."

"You don't understand," I say. "We can't be here. We need to leave right now."

Nia looks at the body. "I need to call someone. We can't just...leave it here."

I should leave her here. That's what I should do, but instead I continue to shield her.

"Look at me," I say. She does. "Now look just slightly to your right. There's a camera on the counter, recording everything we do."

Her eyes dart in that direction.

"Now look back at me," I say. She does. "Obviously, I don't know for sure, but if I had to guess, I would say that the people who did this are sitting on this place to see who comes looking for the guy who used to live here. And that's us. They're probably on their way here as we speak, so we need to go. *Now.*"

Nia nods. She actually looks a little uncertain, maybe even scared. I give her phone back, then grip her arms above the elbow, and back her out of the kitchen. As soon as we're both clear, I turn her around and point her toward the door.

"Did you touch anything?" I ask.

"Just the door when we came in."

"Go," I say. "Wait outside, but don't go up to the sidewalk yet."

For what I suspect is the first time in her life, Nia doesn't argue. She walks straight outside and stands there while I wipe the doorknob with my jacket.

"You could be destroying evidence," Nia says. "If whoever did this—"

"They would have done the same thing." I step outside and close the door behind me. "They wouldn't have left any evidence behind."

"How do you know that?"

Because it's how I would do it. Well, except for the murder part. I don't kill people.

"I watch a lot of television," I say. "Now, *please,* stay here a minute."

I walk up the steps to check out the street. Nothing appears different or suspicious. This is probably as good as it's going to get.

"All right. Let's go." I look at Nia. Her phone is to her ear. "What the hell are you doing?"

"We have to call someone."

"We have to go far, far away from here. We can't stick around and wait for the goddamn cops."

"I get that. It'll be fine."

"Why? Who did you call?"

"Not Lew. Not the FBI. A friend, okay? It'll be…" She holds up her hand, then says, "Noah? It's Nia."

She's quiet for a moment, listening with a seriousness I didn't realize she possessed.

"Yeah, I know," she says. "Noah, listen, I'm sorry about this, but I need a favor." She's quiet again. "The kind where I give you an address and you check it out without asking any follow-up questions." More silence. "I don't know. Come up with something."

She glances at me, eyebrow raised. What does she want from me? Am I supposed to come up with something? Because I did, and she's currently ignoring it.

"There's a dead guy on a kitchen floor," she says. "I thought someone should know about it."

She gives him the address and ends the call.

"Now can we get out of here?" I ask.

"Not yet."

I am going to leave her here. I am just going to walk away and let her stand around to see who shows up first—this Noah guy or whoever was on the other end of that camera feed.

Except I can't do that. As much as I would love to do it, I can't. Mortal enemies or not, she's Ryan's family.

I look around. There has to be a better place to wait than right in the damn doorway. Across the street is an alley between two buildings. It's not as good as fleeing for our lives, but it should still give Nia a decent view of this building while providing us with some semblance of shelter.

"Well, can we at least go somewhere a little less exposed?" I point out the alley. "Like, over there?"

Nia looks. "Yeah. Okay."

I take her hand and pull her across the street and into the alley. She stays near the sidewalk and leans against the wall of one building. While she keeps an eye on Jay's apartment, I watch the street. Nothing else will be coming out of that apartment. The danger will be coming from somewhere else.

"Who's Noah?" I ask while we wait. "How do you know him?"

"Family friend," Nia replies.

"So, he's a cop," I say. Nia glances at me. "You don't seem to have any friends who aren't tied to law enforcement."

"They are few and far between," she agrees. "There's a dead man in that apartment over there. Don't you think a detective might be useful?"

"Probably depends on the detective."

Nia turns back to the street. "Noah's a good guy. You don't have to worry."

Oh, I do. I really do. But it's been a while since I first spotted the webcam. If whoever was watching the feed was sending armed people after me, I would know it by now. They would be here by now. They would have been close and ready to strike the moment their target was acquired. If they're not here yet, they may not be coming. Here and now, anyway.

It takes about fifteen minutes for the first car to arrive. It's unmarked, but too economy-class to belong to anyone working for the gray ghost. This must be Noah. A woman gets out on the driver's side, dressed in a black pantsuit with a sky-blue blouse under a black blazer that doesn't hide the gun on her hip. A similarly dressed, dark-haired man gets out on the passenger's side, aviator sunglasses in place. He rests his arm on top of the sedan while he surveys the area. If he notices Nia, he doesn't react. He and the woman talk to each other across the car, then he closes the car door and walks around to join her.

"Is that Noah?" I ask.

Nia nods. She leans forward, as though she intends to step out of the alley, and I put my hand on her elbow to keep her back.

"Who's the woman?" I ask as they walk toward Jay's apartment.

"His partner. Patricia."

The moment they head down the stairs and disappear from view, I tug on Nia's arm. "Come on. We need to go."

"Where?" Nia asks.

To make sure these assholes haven't eliminated the only other person in my life.

I smile. "I'll tell you when we get there."

The Thieves' Den is crowded, especially for the time of day. A lot of people day drinking on a weekday. More power to them. If I wasn't toting around a pregnant pain in the ass, I would join them. I keep my hand clamped around Nia's wrist as I make my way to Robbie behind the bar.

"Where you been, Maggie?" Robbie says.

So not the time. "Is he here?"

"Office." Robbie nods at Nia. "She with you?"

Leo's okay. He's really okay. I exhale a shuddering sigh of relief. "Yeah. Bring her something non-alcoholic?"

Robbie nods, and I pull Nia toward my booth.

"Maggie?" she asks.

"Not the time." I stop at my booth and point to it. "Sit. Stay."

She sits, and I go through the kitchen to Leo's office. He's sitting at his desk, reading over some paperwork, but glances up as I enter. He's unshaven. I can't remember the last time I saw him unshaven. The bags under his eyes make it look like he hasn't slept since we last saw each other. Probably because he hasn't.

"Where the hell have you been?" he exclaims, pushing out of his chair. He freezes and looks at something behind me, then retakes his seat. "Who's this?"

"What?" I look over my shoulder to see Nia standing there. "What are you doing? I told you to sit and stay."

"Yeah," she says. "Turns out, I'm not a dog."

I sigh and gesture to a chair in the corner. "Sit. Stay. Be quiet."

She salutes me. "Yes, Commandant Tess."

As she moves to the chair, I turn to Leo. He mouths, *Tess?*

I shake my head and close the office door. "Jay's dead."

Leo temporarily forgets about how pissed he is. "Dead?"

I nod and mime cutting a throat. "When did you see him last?"

"I keep tabs on you. Not him." Leo points at Nia. "Who is that?"

"My bodyguard," I answer. Nia laughs.

Leo doesn't. "Who is she?"

"You really don't want to know."

I sit in a chair in front of the desk and mouth, *FBI.* Leo's eyes widen so much I'm afraid they'll fall out of his head. He opens his mouth but closes it again.

"Can you ballpark it?" I ask.

"The night you disappeared," Leo says. "He came in, I asked him where you were, he said he didn't know. I told him to get the fuck out until he did know. Now, will you please tell me where the hell you've been and what the hell is going on?"

Not with the FBI's wife and the police chief's daughter sitting behind me. "The job went sideways."

"Sideways?" Leo echoes. "Jay's dead, you've been missing for *days*, and now you're here with whatever"—he waves toward Nia—"*that* is. Sideways doesn't quite cut it."

I lean in. "Jay sent me on a job, and now he's dead, and there are scary men with guns—and I'm guessing at least one knife—trying to find me. Probably to kill me."

"Been there, done that," Nia mutters.

Leo looks at me as he gestures to her in exasperation.

"I know," I say. "Believe me, I know, but she stays with me."

Leo takes an exceptionally deep breath. He holds it for a few seconds before exhaling through his nose. "You think whoever's looking for you found Jay instead?"

"It's possible," I say. "Could you ask around? See what you find out?"

He nods. "How do I get in touch with you?"

"You don't. I'll contact you."

He sighs. "Are you okay?"

I don't even know anymore. "Yeah."

Leo reaches across the desk. His fingertips graze mine. "Make sure it stays that way?"

"I can take care of myself, you know," I say.

He smiles and squeezes my hand. "Don't remind me."

23

I ESCORT NIA OUT OF The Thieves' Den. As soon as we're on the sidewalk, my legs stop. Which is not ideal. I can't stop now. My life may be a raging, out-of-control trash fire, but I still have a major pain in my ass with which to deal.

"All right," I say. "I don't care what you think about it. I am taking you back to your parents' house right the hell now. Where do they live? How do we get there?"

Nia rolls her eyes like she's some goddamn petulant teenager. "We should take the T."

We get on the orange line and head toward downtown, switching to the green line and heading out of the city. Of course her family lives in the suburbs. I look out the window at the houses and backyards. Why would anyone choose to live here? What's even out here besides white picket fences and boredom?

"So," Nia says, "you knew that guy."

I look at her. "You mean Leo?"

"No. The dead guy. What did you call him? Jay?"

"Yeah," I say. It's not like I can deny it now. At least not successfully. "I knew him."

"How'd you know him?"

"Family friend."

"You told me you didn't have any family."

"Jay wasn't family."

"Maybe not, but Leo is."

"We're not related."

"Like that matters," Nia says. "You've clearly known each other forever, and he clearly cares about you."

"That makes him family?"

"Or a boyfriend, maybe. Well, ex-boyfriend, I would hope, given your recent activities with a certain FBI agent."

I laugh. "Leo is not my boyfriend. He is not now, nor has he ever been, my boyfriend. I'm not his type."

"He likes redheads?"

"Men."

"Oh."

"You have a problem with that?"

"Why would I have a problem with that?"

"People are assholes."

Nia nods. "That is true, and I'm no exception, but I don't give a shit about that."

"Good for you."

"It doesn't make him any less your family, you know."

What the hell is it with Nia and family? I look at her in exasperation. "I'm not you. I don't have group photos on my refrigerator or walls. I don't have a mother calling to check in on me every damn day. Or any day, for that matter. I've *never* had that."

"You have Leo," Nia says. "You can call it what you want, but he's your fucking family, you dumbass. He jumped down your throat the moment he saw you, was totally pissed that you hadn't been by or checked in, and he kicked out your family friend, Jay, for not being worried enough about you. Family are the people who care enough to get pissed at you when you do stupid shit."

"Speaking from experience?" I ask, and Nia shrugs. "Leo's a friend. Not family."

"Liar."

"Why does it matter to you what I consider Leo?"

"There are very few people I give a shit about, and admittedly, most of those people are German shepherds, but I love my family," Nia says. "Even if they're jerks and I want to kill them, I still love them. Everyone should have that."

"Not everyone gets that."

"That's when we make our own. Like you did with Leo. So why deny it?"

"None of your damn business."

"That's rude," Nia says. "After everything we've been through?"

"I hardly know you."

"We have found dead bodies together."

"One body."

"Well, how many have you found with Leo?"

"No comment."

"No comment. Jesus, you're fun." She laughs and looks up. "Come on. This is our stop."

We exit the station and start walking along a street. I haven't been to this part of town before, but it doesn't seem to lack for anything other than residential buildings. It does not appear that Nia is taking us to her parents' house at all. I really should have figured. I am not only off my game, but my game has, in fact, packed up and left Boston altogether.

"In here," Nia says, pointing out a building on a corner. The sign above the door reads *The Howling Sailor.*

"Your parents' house is a bar?" I ask.

"Hey, I don't judge your life." Nia opens the door. "Let's see if they're home."

I follow her inside. The Howling Sailor is a far cry from The Thieves' Den. This is the dive bar other dive bars aspire to be. This is a place that would serve fries, if the rats hadn't already eaten them all. What's more, it's a goddamn cop bar. The haircuts alone make it obvious. Of course Nia brought me to a goddamn cop bar.

We walk around tables and patrons to the bar at the back. Two stools are open right in the center. My favorite place to be. She takes one and gestures to the other. I sit at an angle to watch as much of the room as possible. No way in hell will I be turning my back to a room full of cops.

Nia leans forward. "Hey, Frank!"

The man behind the bar looks over and shakes his head. He wipes his hands on a towel and heads over to us.

"I am not serving you," the man says as he leans over to kiss Nia's cheek.

"Not even club soda? Or water?" she asks. "You're going to deny a pregnant woman water?"

"You want club soda or water?"

"God, no. I want whiskey," she says. "But I'll settle for water."

The bartender glances at me as he fulfills her request. "Who's this?"

"A fun, new friend," she says. "Frank, Tess. Tess, Frank."

Frank sets a glass of water on the bar. "You want something?" he asks me.

"Vodka. Top shelf," I say. "Put it on her tab."

Frank puts a shot glass in front of me and pours some Grey Goose in it. That's a surprisingly quality choice. I just assumed that in a place like this the top shelf option would be lighter fluid. He sets the bottle next to the glass.

"You don't need to leave the bottle," I say.

"If you've been hanging with this one"—he nods to Nia—"you probably need it."

"Nice," Nia says, but she's smiling.

"They don't pay me to be nice."

"Good thing."

Frank rolls his eyes. "Where does your husband think you are?"

"This isn't the 1950s, Frank. He doesn't need to know where I am."

"Uh-huh." He looks at me again. "Enjoy."

He walks away. I pick up my glass and do a shot.

"Come here often?" I ask.

"I'm married, you know," Nia says.

"And hilarious." I gesture to the room. "This is a cop bar."

"That a problem?"

Yes. "No. Just an observation."

"Oh. I thought it might be a problem because you're a thief."

Look at that. Things just got worse. I pour more vodka into my glass. "Could you say that a little louder? I don't think the cops in the back heard you."

"Are you, by any chance, the thief my husband and my mortal enemy are currently looking for?"

Well, I knew the truth would come out eventually. I sigh. "It's possible."

Nia nods. "Yeah. You're gonna have to tell them that. Like, today. And if you don't, I will."

I'm surprised she hasn't already told them. She really didn't want to stay at her parents' house, did she?

"When did you know?" I ask.

"I knew something was up when you first walked into my house using an assumed name. I didn't confirm anything until today, though."

"You didn't tell Lew?"

"Lew and I don't keep secrets. He knows I have doubts. He'll know the rest soon enough, unless you tell him first. And you really should tell him first. It'll go better for you, if you do."

"Better than what?"

"Dunno. Jail?"

I do the second shot. "I could run away before they get here. You'll never be able to catch me with that belly."

Nia snorts. "Joke's on you. I couldn't even catch you without the belly. I don't exactly run," she says. "But…we do happen to be sitting in a cop bar at which I am a well-established and—dare I say—beloved regular. If you want to avoid a scene, you might want to stay right where you are."

"Ladies," Lew says, moving up behind his wife.

"Besides," Nia continues, "I already told him we were going to be here."

Of course she did. I look at Lew.

"Let's talk," he says.

24

WHILE NIA STAYS AT THE bar, Lew and I move to a corner booth. Out of habit, I sit with my back against the wall. Lew sits across from me. His expression is the epitome of seriousness. If I tried to call him by his first name, he'd probably respond that his first name is Agent. I can't see this going well for me. At all.

"Where's Ryan?" I ask.

Lew holds up a finger. A moment later, Frank stops at our table with two mugs of what I think is supposed to be coffee.

"You good?" he asks Lew.

"Yeah. Thanks, Frank."

"I'll keep an eye on Nia."

Lew smiles. "Don't tell her that."

"I know better."

Lew glances at the bar and sighs. "You know what? Call Patrick. Have him come and take her home."

Frank laughs. "Oh, she won't like that."

Lew shrugs. "Today's not a day where I worry about that."

"I'll take care of it," Frank says.

He walks away. Lew turns his attention to me.

"Ryan is at the loft," he says. "I told him I would track you two down."

"But you've known where we were the entire time."

"Yes."

I nod. "What does Ryan know? What did you tell him?"

"That your story didn't sit right with me. That I thought you were likely hiding something."

"Because Nia told you so?"

"Nia thinks the FBI is the federal equivalent of the Keystone Cops, but we can occasionally work things out on our own."

I have no idea what the Keystone Cops are, but that probably doesn't matter much at this time. "Did he agree with you?"

"Again, we're not dumb."

"Then why—?"

"You're still in trouble. There are still people trying to kill you."

I look at the table. "Yeah."

"So, start at the beginning and tell me what happened."

I pull the mug closer. "Is there any version of this story that doesn't end with me in jail?"

"Won't know until I hear it."

I really don't want to do this, but I do seem to be running short on options. Perhaps the fact that he's willing to hear me out at all is an encouraging sign.

"My name isn't Tess," I say.

Lew's expression doesn't change. "What is your name?"

"Skye."

"Last name?"

"Walker."

"Your name is Skye Walker?"

"My parents loved *Star Wars*."

"What's your real last name, Skye?"

"I don't have one."

"Are you like Cher?"

"Or a kid who fell through the cracks of the system a long time ago."

"You would have had a surname when you entered the system."

"Probably did."

"But you don't know it."

"Like I said, it was a long time ago."

"Was your name Skye when you went into the system?"

"No."

"How long have you been Skye?"

"Long enough."

Lew nods. He picks up his mug and sips the coffee. "Why were you at the Skyreach that night?"

"I was working a job."

"What kind of job?"

"Safecracking."

"What was the target?"

"Wall safe."

Lew sighs. He looks as though he could use a bit of Irish in his coffee. "What was *inside* the safe, Skye?"

I shrug. "Don't know. I had only gotten the door open when I was interrupted."

"What were you supposed to take from the safe?"

"Flash drive. And no, I don't know what was on it."

Lew nods again. "How did you get this job?"

"Through my agent."

"Agent?"

"I don't have a better word for it," I say. "Potential clients contacted him. He contacted me when he had a good fit. He thought this would be one of those jobs."

"You don't know who hired you?"

"I never meet the clients. They never meet me. It's better that way."

"What's this agent's name?"

"I imagine the morgue has him listed as a John Doe."

"The murder victim?" Lew asks. "The one who had his throat cut?"

I nod.

"What's his name?"

"I called him Jay. Other people called him Jimmy. I don't know if those were first names, last names, or even real names."

"How long had you been working with him?"

"Fifteen years, maybe."

Lew sits back, studying me. Probably doing math in his head. Calculating how long I've been a thief.

"Was he the Fagin to your Oliver?" he asks.

He's sad now. Sad for *me*. The goddamn gall.

I frown. "Don't do that. Don't feel sorry for me. Don't try to explain away my misdeeds, okay? I *survived*. I survived when I had no business doing any such thing, and I built a life out of *nothing*."

"A life outside the law."

"I think you just described half of D.C.'s population."

"Maybe more," Lew says. "Did Jay make you a thief?"

"No."

"He just helped you parlay it into a career." Lew nods. "Okay. Tell me about this job."

"I received an envelope with the safe specs and day and time. I showed up to crack a safe and witnessed a murder instead."

"You didn't pick the night?"

"The client claimed it was a one-night-only kind of thing."

"So the murderers could have been there for the same reason."

I shrug. "It's possible. Probable, even. Hell of a coincidence otherwise."

"Yeah," Lew agrees. "You say you never meet your clients, but do you have a way to find out who they are?"

"Anonymity is the point. I don't want to know who they are. I don't want them to know me," I say. "Jay was the only one who knew both."

"Did he keep records of any kind?"

I laugh. "I mean, it's possible, I guess."

"Can you do better than 'it's possible'?"

"No, you know what? I can't. I can't do better than 'it's possible' because I don't know. I don't have any answers for you. I wish I did because I would love to get my life back. Or *a* life, anyway, but right now I don't have any more to offer you. Because all I know is that I watched Edward Roberson get shot in the head. Now the three men who were in that office, either doing or ordering the shooting, are trying to find me so they can shoot *me* in the head. I'd really like to avoid that, if at all possible."

"So work with me."

"I *am*," I say. "I don't know if Jay kept records. If he did, he never showed them to me."

Lew looks me over, tapping his index finger on the table. The jury is now deliberating my guilt. My future. I raise a brow and look back. Let him do his worst. I can take it.

"What other work do you do? What else have you done?" he asks. "Is it always safecracking and larceny, or do you hire out for other types of jobs as well?"

Yeah, right. I sit back and fold my arms across my chest. "That was my very first job ever."

"Skye, if we find evidence—"

"You won't. There's nothing to find."

"Because that was your very first job ever."

"Yes."

"In fifteen years."

I don't flinch. "Yes."

Lew looks unconvinced. Can't imagine why.

"There's nothing to find," I repeat. "I am good at what I do."

He relaxes a little. "How would you know? That was your very first job ever."

"I don't kill people," I offer. "Which I think puts me ahead of the other three people who walked out of that building that night." I shrug and pick up my mug. "For what it's worth."

The coffee's cold now, but I take a sip anyway. It tastes like the rats had a hand—or something else, perhaps—in making it. I put the mug down and gently push it aside.

Lew sighs. "I will see about getting you a deal."

"A deal? Like, my cooperation with your investigation in exchange for not throwing me in jail?"

"Yes."

"Okay. How will you make that happen, given that this entire investigation is unsanctioned by your bosses because your involvement in this case was deemed inappropriate?"

"I have friends in the Bureau. I can make inquiries."

"Will that work? Will they go for it?"

"Probably. You wouldn't be a big enough collar for the Bureau to care about letting you go."

"Thanks for the ego boost," I say, and Lew shrugs. "Will Ryan go for the deal?"

"I'm not sure they'll ask his opinion."

"I'm asking."

"No one knows what Ryan will do except for Ryan. And whatever suspicions we had..." Lew shakes his head. "You two have something going on. I don't know any details—and I'd prefer to keep it that way—but it'll make it worse. He'll take it hard."

I nod. Makes sense. What makes less sense is that I care at all about what Ryan will think.

"If I can get you a deal," Lew says then, "it will be under the condition that you don't lie to Ryan, you don't lie to me, and you definitely don't lie to my wife."

"I won't promise the last."

"Skye—"

"I won't promise it," I say. "If something comes down to me telling Nia a lie, or me letting her get hurt, I'm gonna choose the lie. Don't even try to tell me you'd want me to do differently."

"I'd prefer she not be in a situation that could lead to her getting hurt."

I laugh. "Pretty ballsy of you to lecture me on the importance of your wife's safety when you're the one who used her in some secret undercover sting operation to get the truth out of a suspicious witness."

"We had it under control."

"Oh yeah? So then you knew there was a dead guy in that apartment?"

"Mostly under control," Lew concedes. "We thought it might have been your apartment."

"Well, it wasn't." I sigh. Now that we're talking about Nia's safety, I suppose there's something I should tell him. It'll piss him off, but he should know. "Did you go there?"

"Yes."

"Did you see the camera in the kitchen?"

"Yes. The feed had been cut, but we saw it."

I nod. "It was on when we were there."

Lew's face changes. I thought he was serious before, but now it seems as though I need to redefine my understanding of that word. Or steal a dictionary or a thesaurus the next time I'm in a bookstore.

"Did they see her?" he asks.

"I don't know. I tried to shield her, and I got her out as quickly as I could, but…maybe."

Lew points at me. "Don't fucking move."

He slides out of the booth and stalks away. He pulls out his phone and angrily jabs at the screen. I lean to the side to peek at the rest of the room. So many cops. All of them staring right at me. Jonas is the only one I recognize. He's sitting at a table near the exit. I'd say he looks pissed, but I've never seen him look any other way. Maybe that's his happy face.

I move back to the middle of the bench seat. Lew's on the other side of the room, still talking on his phone. There's a vein in his neck that looks about ready to pop. Wherever Nia is now, it'll soon be surrounded by armed guards. Inside and out. She's going to love that. And me, for causing it.

When Lew returns to the table, he's still mad.

"I didn't have to tell you about the camera," I say.

"You think that helps your case?"

"I think it helps you protect her."

"You didn't have to take her there in the first place."

"Again, she took me there. At your direction. She's also the one who broke out the bobby pins so she could definitely not use them to gain unlawful entry to Jay's apartment *and* refused to stay outside when I told her she should," I say. "So maybe you could take it down just a notch there, Agent Tough Guy."

Lew looks at me. He nods and takes a deep breath. Then another one. His phone dings. He glances at the screen, visibly relaxes, then sets the phone aside. Nia must be accounted for now.

"Tell me about The Thieves' Den," Lew says. "Why did you go there?"

"It's where I would meet Jay. I wanted to ask the bartender when he had seen him last."

"If that's true, why did you ask the guy in the back office? Leo?"

I sigh. "You and Nia really don't keep secrets, do you?"

"No."

"Kills the mystery, doesn't it?"

"We seem to be doing just fine in the mystery department," Lew says. "Who's Leo?"

"Leo is my family. He's my brother. Not biologically, but...He's my brother."

"He was with you in the system?"

"Yeah," I say. "Until we weren't."

Lew nods. "What did he have to say about Jay?"

"The last time he saw Jay was the night of the job. Jay wasn't worried that I hadn't showed up, which Leo didn't like. Leo kicked him out, and that was the last time he saw him alive. From the looks of things, it was pretty close to the last time anyone saw Jay alive. But I'm not a medical examiner, or a coroner, so that's just a guess."

"What is Leo looking for now?"

I don't like this. I don't want him on the FBI's radar. "Okay, before I say anything else, you have to understand that Leo isn't like me. He's legit."

"Then I'm sure our investigation will show that."

I grip the table's edge. "No. No, Lew. You cannot investigate him."

"I think we can."

"Jesus Christ, are you listening to me? You can't do it. If people find out he's being investigated—"

"You could give us more credit, you know."

I shake my head. "No. No, I can't."

"Skye—"

"Make the deal for him. I don't care what happens to me. Do whatever you want to me. Throw me in prison. Give me to the murderous gunmen. Whatever. I don't care," I say. "But Leo needs to be protected. He's clean; he's legit. He can't be a part of this."

"You already made him a part of this."

"Well, you can't make him a bigger part," I say. "Come on, Lew. You fucking G-men look the other way all the goddamn time when the upper class is fleecing the entire damn country. You sure as hell can leave Leo alone."

Lew looks at me like I'm not railing against him or having a meltdown on the other side of the table. This is payback, isn't it? Nia was in danger, so now they're going after Leo. These goddamn people.

"What is Leo doing for you?" Lew asks. "What is he looking for?"

"Lew," I plead. "Don't do this."

He appears unmoved. "Just answer the question."

I don't care who they are. I don't care what they could do to me. If they go near Leo, I will fucking *murder* them.

"He is asking around to see if anyone knows anything about Jay. That is it. That is all. There is nothing illegal about that."

"Who is he asking?"

"A network to which you wouldn't have access, being the pig-headed, asshole federal agent that you are."

"Pig-headed?"

I shrug. "If the head fits."

Lew smiles. "You can relax, Skye. I have no intention of going after Leo if I don't have to."

"If you don't have to?" I say. "Why would you..."

My chest tightens. I struggle to breathe. Goddammit.

"You're going to use him," I force out. "You're going to use him as collateral."

"Incentive."

"You're going to use him to keep me in line."

"Only if you make me. If you hold up your end of the deal—"

"I will."

"Then he's going to be okay. I promise."

I hate this man so very much. *Hate.* Except 'hate' doesn't even begin to cover it. I shake my head. "I can't trust your promises."

"I know. But he's going to be okay anyway."

"He better be," I say. "Because if he isn't, I'm gonna..."

Lew waits.

I sigh. "I'm gonna let you use your imagination."

"All right, then." Lew slides out of the booth. "Come on."

"Where are we going?"

"To talk to Ryan."

25

LEW DRIVES. I SIT IN the passenger's seat and contemplate throwing myself out of the car. Sadly, we're not going anywhere near fast enough for it to kill me. Stupid Boston traffic.

And stupid Lew with his stupid extortion plan. Except it isn't stupid at all. It's smart. Brilliant, even. I will have no other option than to cooperate with whatever bullshit he comes up with because I can't risk them going after Leo for any reason.

I should have ditched Nia when I had the chance.

I should have done a lot of things.

Like not slept with an FBI agent, for one. Because now I have to tell that FBI agent that I lied to him. A lot. About a lot of things. According to Lew, Ryan will take it hard. He's big on trust and wanted me to trust him and thought he could trust me.

He was very wrong about that.

So he'll take it hard. What does that mean exactly? What will he do? Will he take it out on Leo? Will Lew do anything to stop him if he tries?

We pass the loft of squalor and park on a side street. Lew turns off the engine. I stare out the windshield.

"Skye," he says, "are you—?"

"Can I talk to him alone?" I ask.

"If you like."

There is nothing about this situation I like. Why do I care about this? How did I get attached? Except for Leo, I am not someone who gets attached to anyone. Anything. Attachments make life harder. How did I forget that?

"Can I go up alone?" I ask.

"No."

"Will you wait in the hallway?"

"Yes."

Good enough. Or as good as it's going to get, I suppose. We get out of the car and go up to the loft of squalor. Lew unlocks the door and steps aside.

I walk into the apartment and close the door behind me. Ryan's sitting at the island, eating lasagna. What is it with that goddamn lasagna?

He looks at me. "Did you and Nia enjoy your day out?"

"I'm sure she's had better days."

He sets down the fork and turns on the stool to face me directly. "Did something happen? Is she all right? Are you?"

If I don't do this, Lew will. Or Nia. I'm not sure which would be worse—though Nia would likely take too much pleasure in telling him.

"Tess?" Ryan says.

I take a deep breath. "My name isn't Tess."

"What?"

"My name isn't Tess," I repeat. "Tess is someone who kind of looks like me and works for Pearson Pharmaceuticals on the ninth floor of the Skyreach Building."

"What are you…" He stops as he works out the truth. Like Lew said, they're not dumb. "You're the one we've been looking for. You're the thief."

He's at least the third person today to say that to me, but this is definitely the worst. "I wish you wouldn't call it that."

"No? What would you call it? Acquisitions specialist?"

"No, I'd call it 'thief'. I just wish someone with the ability to arrest me would call it something different."

"Why?"

"I don't want to be arrested?"

"No, Tess. *Why*? What was your plan?"

"I didn't have one. I was just trying to keep my head above water."

"By lying."

"By any means necessary," I say. "I don't always have the luxury of being picky about how that happens."

He stands. "That's bullshit, Tess."

"That's still not my name, Ryan."

"What is your name?"

"Depends who you ask."

"I'm asking you."

"Skye. My name is Skye."

"Do you have a last name?"

"Not usually."

"What's on your driver's license?"

"I don't have one of those. I don't know how to drive, remember?"

"Birth certificate, then."

"I've never seen one, but if it does exist, it probably says 'Jane Doe' or whatever name they give to abandoned babies."

Ryan pulls back a little. His brain is maybe registering that information, but his heart is still entirely focused on the me-being-a-liar part. He shakes his head. "I thought you were just scared."

"I was."

"I thought you were scared to tell me what you saw because you were scared for your life."

"I was," I say, though I'm reasonably sure he's not listening to me at all at this point.

"But no," he says. "It turns out you're a thief."

"Yeah."

"Jesus Christ, Tess."

"Skye."

"You're the thief. You're the goddamn thief."

"Yep."

He jabs an angry finger in my direction. "*You're* the goddamn thief."

"Still true."

"You're the goddamn *thief.*"

"Yeah, this conversation will take a lot longer if you insist on repeating everything twenty times."

"Tess, don't—"

"Skye."

"Skye," he echoes.

He stares at me. Not moving, not speaking. Just staring with a complete lack of emotion I would find impressive under different circumstances. My chest aches, but I'm not sure why.

That's a lie. I know why. I don't understand it, but I know why.

Ryan nods. I hold my breath.

"You're under arrest," he says.

I exhale. "Ryan—"

"Turn around."

"Ryan—"

"Turn. Around."

I turn around. He cuffs my hands together behind my back while reciting my rights. I've never done this before. I've seen it on TV and have seen it happen to other people, but I have never been arrested. It feels weird, a little like it's not actually real, or that I'm somehow standing outside of my body watching someone else be taken in. Because of Ryan, maybe? Because he's hurt and angry? Because he's hurt and angry because of me?

I knew I was going to be in trouble. And here I am.

"I'm sorry," I say when he stops talking.

Ryan nudges me toward the door, keeping his hand on my arm as he opens it. Lew's in the hallway, leaning against the opposite wall, but he straightens when he sees us.

"No," he says and blocks the way.

"Move, El," Ryan says.

"No." Lew backs us into the apartment. "You're not doing this."

"She's a thief," Ryan says.

"I know."

"She's the thief we've spent days looking for."

"I know."

"She knew we were looking for her and she didn't say anything."

"I know."

"She..." Ryan hesitates. "She lied."

"I know," Lew says. "But you can't do this. If you take her in, this is all over."

"That's the plan."

"If you take her in, we're exposed."

"So?"

"If you take her in, *she's* exposed."

Why is Lew trying that tactic? What difference will that make to Ryan now? He wants to expose me. Arrest me. Lock me up and throw away the key.

And apparently, I'm just going to stand here and let him do it. Why? Why am I just standing here? I can slip cuffs. I can get away from men. I can get out of this. Slip the cuffs, hit the guys where it counts, run out the still-open door or onto the fire escape, and get as far away as fast as my little legs can carry me.

But instead, I'm just standing here. Like I don't know how to slip cuffs or incapacitate men, or...anything else. I'm standing here like I'm actually Tess whatever-her-last-name-is, shocked—simply *shocked*—that this thing is happening to her.

"Fine." Ryan releases me. "She's your problem. Do whatever the fuck you want."

He pushes past Lew and storms out of the apartment, slamming the door behind him.

Lew looks at me. "You okay?"

Most definitely not. I shrug and start working my way out of the cuffs. "Depends on what the fuck you decide to do with me."

"I'm going to keep working this case with your help," he says. "Unless you prefer I do something different?"

I shake my head.

"Okay, then." Lew glances around. "Give me a minute to find a key for the cuffs."

"Don't bother." I slip the cuffs and hold them out. "Here you go."

Lew smiles before taking them. "Thanks."

26

LEW IS SHOWING NO SIGNS of leaving.

While I watch from the couch, he sits at the island, typing furiously on his phone. Who is he texting? Ryan? Nia? Jonas? All three? What a conversation that would be. Ryan's pissed that I'm a liar and a criminal. Nia's pissed that she was sent back to her parents' house. Jonas may not be pissed, but he's probably making one hell of a case for why Lew should have let Ryan bring me in.

He should have done that, too. He should have stepped aside and let Ryan arrest me, but instead he stood in the way and said no. Why? Who am I to him except a thief who exposed his pregnant wife to indiscriminate murderers?

"You don't have to babysit me," I say. "I'm sure you have nine million agents watching this place now."

Lew doesn't look up. "The nine million agents are watching Nia. You're stuck with me."

"Nia will be pissed."

"Nia's already pissed. This is nothing." Lew sets his phone aside. "When did you eat last?"

"I'm fine."

"Not what I asked."

Lew stands and goes over to the fridge. He opens it and removes the casserole dish on top. The lasagna. He smiles and puts the dish on the island.

"Want some?" he asks.

"You don't have to take care of me," I say.

Lew gets two plates out and sets them next to the lasagna. "I'm not trying to take care of you. I'm trying to avoid eating alone."

"Too bad for you that I don't eat with blackmailers," I say. "You know, as a general rule."

"I'm not blackmailing you," Lew says, loading up the first plate.

"Feels like it," I say as he prepares a second serving. "I told you I wasn't hungry."

"Actually, you told me you don't eat with blackmailers. Not that you're not hungry."

"Well, I'm not hungry."

"Well, that is your loss because my mother-in-law is an excellent cook."

"That's what I've heard. Still not hungry, though."

Lew puts the first plate in the microwave and starts it up. "You really should eat something."

"Hey, funny story," I say. "I've never had a mother, and I sure as hell don't need one now."

"What about a friend?"

"Is that what you are?"

"I'm not your enemy, Skye."

"The hell you aren't." Suddenly, the loft of squalor is feeling a whole lot smaller, and the couch is feeling mighty close to the law enforcement official. I move to the window seat. "You're a goddamn fed, you've been lying to me all goddamn day—"

"To be fair, you spent longer than that lying to us."

I scoff. "What does a fed know about being fair?"

"I could have let Ryan take you in," Lew says. "You broke the law. Multiple laws, in fact. Arresting you would have been fair."

"Then arrest me. Or tell Ryan you changed your mind and he's free to arrest me. I'm sure he'll rush right over then."

"Is that what you want me to do?"

"I want you to stop talking to me like you're concerned with anything other than your damn investigation. You don't give a shit about me. You're only here because I can identify your murderers."

"And also because your escape artist abilities are above average."

"You think your presence makes a damn bit of difference?"

Lew shrugs. "You're still here, aren't you?"

"Don't flatter yourself. That has nothing to do with you."

"Oh yeah? What does it have to do with, then? Leo? Ryan, maybe?"

My stomach lurches. I draw my legs up to my chest and sit sideways on the bench. "None of your business."

The microwave beeps, and Lew swaps out the plates before starting it up again.

"Has Nia told you how we met?" he asks.

I roll my eyes. "Yeah, because she's so open about her personal life. Especially with new people whom she finds suspicious."

"That changes once you get to know her."

"How many people get that far?"

"Fewer than you think."

I doubt that. "You did. Obviously."

"It wasn't easy."

"I'm guessing Nia doesn't make *anything* easy."

Lew smiles. "I was undercover, here in Boston."

I get that. Lew would be a good undercover agent. He knows how to lie. "As what?"

"Her father's partner."

Wait. Does that mean… "You were an undercover cop going undercover as a cop?"

"Yeah. I know how it sounds."

"Nia can't have liked that."

Lew chuckles. "She did not. She was pretty mad when she found out."

"Nia? Mad? I can't imagine what that might be like."

Lew nods. "A lot of people have that same problem."

His deadpan delivery makes me smile. God damn this guy. I stand and walk over to the island. When I sit down, Lew pushes the second lasagna plate in front of me.

I don't touch the food. "Why were you undercover as her father's partner?"

"An investigation suggested there was possible corruption in a local police force. I was sent to find out where it was and how deep it went. Because I was new, and because that's how they did things, I was partnered with Nia's father."

"Please tell me he wasn't one of your corrupt cops."

Lew shakes his head. "Patrick Kelly is the furthest thing there is from a corrupt cop."

Patrick Kelly. That name sounds familiar. Why, though? Because he's a cop? That doesn't make sense. It's not like I keep track of every officer in the city. Why would I…Oh.

"I remember that," I say. "Some major cop corruption scandal. It was all over the news. That was you?"

He nods.

"You were shot, weren't you?"

"More than once."

"And Nia's dad, too, right?"

"Yeah."

I nod. "That's why it's personal."

"What?"

"Ryan said the case was personal to you—to the both of you. Is that because you were shot?"

"Should I not take that personally?"

"Most people would, I'm sure. But you?" I say. "I'm not sure you would."

"You don't know me that well."

"No, but…" I shake my head. "I think there's something else."

"Have you ever been shot?" Lew asks.

I shake my head again. Stabbed and beaten, yes. Shot? No.

"It changes things for you," Lew says. "Things you never thought would feel personal feel remarkably personal."

"I'm sure it does and they do. But if this case is personal enough that you and Ryan are willing to go to these lengths to keep investigating, there must be something else. Is it because they shot Nia's dad?"

"You tell me."

I lean in, resting my elbows on the island. "Probably not. I mean, I'm sure you like the guy and didn't like that someone shot him, but you're an undercover fed and he's a cop. You both got into that line of work knowing bullets could be part of the deal. So, it's something else. Someone else."

But who? Who would both Lew and Ryan care about that much? Who else was involved? What did the news report say? Two police officers were shot. A whole mess of corrupt cops were arrested. One died during the course of the investigation. I don't remember anyone else being mentioned, though. If someone else was involved, the media didn't seem to know about it.

"Did they kill a fellow agent?" I ask.

"No."

"Did they injure or maim a fellow agent?"

"No."

"Was it Nia?"

Lew's face loses all its humor. He quickly gets himself back under control, puts that mask back in place, but the damage is done. The secret is out. Nia, then. It's funny that Ryan took that so personally.

"What happened?" I ask.

Lew shakes his head. The game is over.

"But you're okay now," I say then. "All of you?"

Lew nods.

"And you obviously got the girl."

"It took a while, but yes, I eventually got the girl."

"Why did it take a while?"

"Secrets and lies, and some stupidity on my part." Lew shrugs. "Nia likes the truth, too."

Ah. At last, we have arrived at the point. Too bad for Lew it doesn't change a damn thing.

"Your situation with Nia and my situation with Ryan is not the same," I say.

"I lied to her. You lied to him. There may be a couple of similarities."

"The circumstances behind the lying make it very different," I say. "Besides, it's not like Ryan and I are in love or anything. We were just…killing time."

"Were you?"

I pull back a little. What is that supposed to mean? "Did Ryan say something to you?"

"He didn't tell me anything."

"Then how do you know anything happened?"

"I am a trained investigator. We occasionally notice things."

"Right. I keep forgetting the FBI isn't dumb."

Lew smiles. "I have known Ryan for a long time, Skye. He may not have said anything to me directly, but he doesn't think you were just killing time."

"Well, then, he's really dumb. If he thought last night was anything other than me alleviating some boredom, then he's probably too stupid to even be in your stupid agency."

"That would be quite the achievement."

Lew is an unflappable enigma. Perhaps this is why he could go undercover successfully. He can lie and very little seems to faze him. The only time I've seen him express any sort of negative emotion was back at the bar when he thought Nia might be in danger. Does he even have a breaking point otherwise?

Lew gestures to my untouched plate. "Are you going to eat that?"

"No."

"Then hand it over. We do not waste my mother-in-law's lasagna."

I glance at his midsection as I push the plate toward him. He doesn't look like he eats carbs very often. Or ever, really. Lew puts the plate back in the microwave.

"What happens now?" I ask. "With the case."

"Tomorrow, you and I will start our investigation."

I sigh. "Sounds like a plan."

27

LEW SNORES.

It's loud. Obnoxiously so. So much so that I'm shocked the entire damn building isn't shaking. That earthquake warnings aren't going off all over the city and the rest of Massachusetts. That people in California aren't asking one another if they feel that tremor. That there isn't some monster tsunami working its way across the ocean right now.

Ryan didn't snore. He was a quiet sleeper. An annoyingly early riser, maybe, but a quiet sleeper. I miss that now. I miss him. And not just because he didn't sound like a running chainsaw being fed into a wood chipper.

I shouldn't miss him, though. For any reason. As a general rule, one should not miss law enforcement officials who can and actively want to arrest oneself. One shouldn't sleep with them, either, but I can't quite bring myself to regret that. Not yet, anyway. There's plenty of other regret to deal with first.

I just can't do it here. Not with the world's loudest sawmill working overtime.

I get out of bed and walk over to the wall of windows. I carefully open the window on the end. No alarms go off. Lew doesn't wake up, so I climb out onto the fire escape and go up to the roof.

The city view sucks—there's nothing to see but taller buildings on all sides—but there's plenty to see on the street. The on-duty protection detail sticks out more at this time of night. Two SUVs. One sedan that seems to have people sitting inside it. One person standing on the sidewalk, smoking a cigarette next to a station wagon. This operation is being paid for with favors and good will.

I'd like to think that says a lot about the men with whom I am working. That when someone sends out the bat signal, an entire village responds, even without the promise of overtime or payment of any kind. Except maybe in beer. Or donuts.

My village is much, much smaller. And even smaller still now.

Because Jay is dead.

Jay is dead. It's been true for a while now, but it feels foreign. Or maybe unimportant. Which makes sense. He's not Leo. He was never my family. What did Lew call him? The Fagin to my Oliver? Maybe that's true. Without Jay, who knows what would have happened to me and Leo. We might have been okay. I might have figured things out for myself.

But for all of Jay's faults—and there were a lot of those—he did help keep us alive.

And now he's gone. Lying in a drawer in a morgue. Listed as a John Doe, unless they run his prints or some kind of DNA test whose results come back with a different name. An actual name.

It's strange to think that for as long as I knew him, I might not have known *him*. Does he have another name? Another life? Does he have…anyone? What happens to his body if he doesn't? What happens if no one claims him? Do they bury him in some kind of pauper's grave? Cremate him and dump his ashes in a communal hole in the ground along with the rest of the unknown and unclaimed? Flush him out to sea, like a goldfish? Here one day, gone the next, with no one noticing at all.

I'll be the same one day. Sooner rather than later, if the gray ghost has his way. Leo would claim me, though.

If he could find me.

The guy smoking his cigarette is wandering now. He's not even looking at the building he's supposed to be watching. This would be the perfect time to shimmy down the fire escape and disappear. Hell, I wouldn't even have to work that hard. Quick, quiet, and gone. My specialties. The FBI wouldn't be able to find me.

But they could find Leo. They know exactly where to find him. It's my fault. It's all my fault. I didn't think it through. Why didn't I think it through? Everything I've ever done to protect him, and I go and fuck it all up in a single afternoon.

I have to limit the damage now. I just have to. Staunch the bleeding anyway I can. I'll stay here and play the FBI's stupid games and make damn well sure they have no reason to go anywhere near Leo. It doesn't mean they won't do it anyway, but I have to try.

Which means I'm going nowhere but back to bed.

I climb down the fire escape and return to the loft of squalor. As I'm closing the window, a light comes on behind me.

"You came back," Lew says.

I flip the lock on the window. "Turns out, I have nowhere to go."

"Skye—"

"Just...don't." I turn around to see him sitting in a chair next to the pullout. "Okay? Let me brood in peace?"

Lew nods. "Okay."

I get back in bed and pull the covers over my head. A moment later, the lights go out.

Maybe tomorrow will be better.

Maybe.

28

I WAKE TO THE SMELL of freshly brewed coffee. Lifting my head, I see Lew standing at the island, his phone to his ear. Judging by his face, he's talking to Nia. Or listening to her, I suppose, as whatever's happening on the other end of that call doesn't actually seem to involve him saying anything.

I get out of bed and go use the bathroom. When I come out, I walk over to the kitchen and sit on a stool. Lew's still on the phone. Has he even gotten a word in at all, or has Nia just been yelling at him the entire time? He glances at me and gets a mug out of a cupboard. He pours some coffee into it and sets it in front of me. It's almost another full minute before he puts the phone down.

"Nia hang up on you?" I ask.

"Yeah."

"So, she's mad, then."

"She's been happier."

"What about Ryan?" I ask.

Lew gets out a frying pan and sets it on the stove. "He's definitely been happier."

No shit. I roll my eyes. "Have you heard from him?"

"No. But he's okay," Lew says. "Ryan will come around eventually. You don't have to worry."

Oh no, I still have plenty of things about which to worry. The possibility of a future relationship with an FBI agent just isn't one of them.

Not that I thought there was a future there.

Because I didn't.

Don't.

Lew opens the fridge and removes the milk and a carton of eggs. What is the FBI's obsession with eggs? Are agents required to eat them for breakfast?

"How'd you sleep?" he asks as he pulls out a mixing bowl.

"You snore. Loudly. And a lot."

"Sorry about that," he says, expertly cracking an egg into the bowl. "I'm making an omelet. Would you like one?"

"No."

"You didn't eat dinner last night. You should eat something this morning. If you don't want eggs, there's cereal or Pop Tarts. I could even make you some toast."

"I'm not hungry."

"Something solid, Skye," he says. "We have murders to solve and a case to crack. Can't do any of that on an empty stomach."

He has no idea how much I've been able to do on an empty stomach. "What will you do if I refuse to eat?" I ask. "Arrest me?"

"I will look at you with disapproval."

"Wow. Scary."

"You know, not everything needs to be a fight."

"Not in my experience."

Lew sighs. "Just humor me and eat some damn toast, Skye. Please? We have a lot to do today."

I finish my coffee and eat some damn toast. After I shower and dress, we leave the loft and get back in Lew's car. He drives to Charlestown and parks across the street from Jay's apartment.

I look at the building. "What are we doing here?"

"Investigating," Lew says, unbuckling his seat belt.

He wants to go *inside*? I look at him. "Investigating what? Haven't the cops and FBI already been over the place?"

"Now I want you to look. You knew the vic. They didn't. You may see something they missed."

I don't want to go in there. Not now. Or ever again. "I didn't come here very often," I lie.

"You've been here, though, right? Before yesterday, I mean."

"Yes."

"Then let's go."

I get out of the car and follow Lew across the street. A police officer is standing watch at the front door of Jay's apartment. I drop back, but Lew goes right up to him. After they shake hands and exchange pleasantries about what a nice day it is to walk through a murder scene, or whatever they're discussing, the officer holds out a box of latex gloves.

Lew pulls some out and looks at me. "You, too."

I inch closer and take the gloves Lew hands me. Next, we're given coverings for our shoes. Once we're properly outfitted, the officer opens the door and Lew and I go inside. The door closes behind us, leaving us alone. There's still the faint scent of decomposition, but now it's mixing with chemicals.

"What are we looking for?" I ask.

"Anything. Anything that could tell us who did this, anything about the job, anything," Lew says. "We're not picky. We'll take any information we can get."

"The job?"

"Fagin's the only one who knew both sides, right? It's possible he kept records, right?"

"Jay," I say. "His name was Jay."

"Maybe Jay kept records."

"If he did, I never saw them."

"Where might he keep them?"

I look around. I don't know how to do this. This is not what I do. How does it work? Where do I begin?

"Skye," Lew says, and I look at him. "Tell me about yesterday. Did anything stick out to you?"

"You mean besides the dead guy in the kitchen?"

"Yes. Anything besides that?"

I shrug. "It was clean. Neat. Jay, as a general rule, was neither of those things. I knew someone had been here, that it probably wouldn't mean anything good…I asked Nia to stay outside, but she, uh, refused."

"Sounds like her," Lew says. "Anything else?"

"Not really. We weren't here very long," I say. "So, you want me to go through the place?"

"Yes."

I nod and walk through the apartment to the bedroom in the back. I've never had a reason to be in his bedroom before, but it's as neat as the rest of the place. It's sparsely furnished—just a full-sized bed and a chest of drawers. There aren't even any pictures on the walls. Not a lot of options for hiding spots. The dresser seems too formal for Jay, so I start there.

I sit on the floor and open the bottom drawer. After removing the clothing, I check for a false bottom. None. I take the drawer out completely and turn it over to look at the underside. Nothing. I set the empty drawer to the side and move on to the next.

Lew watches from the doorway. He doesn't tell me that they've already done what I'm doing now. Maybe he doesn't know. Maybe he doesn't care.

There's nothing unusual in any of the drawers, so I pull the dresser away from the wall to look behind it. Neither the dresser nor the wall have any hidden secrets to offer. I didn't think they would, but it's better to check. Who knows what the Bureau is actually capable of.

I slide the dresser back against the wall and return the drawers and the clothing to their proper place before turning to look at the rest of the room. Guess the bed is next.

There's no headboard or footboard, so I strip the sheets—thank God for gloves—to look at the mattress. It shows no signs of having been altered in any way, but I run my hands over the surface and along the sides to make sure.

I look at Lew. "Help me move it?"

He steps into the room and we lift the mattress off the box spring and prop it up against the wall. The underside of the mattress hasn't been touched, either. The box spring is more of the same. This is a goddamn waste of time.

"Has it occurred to you that the murderers already took anything worth taking?" I ask as we reassemble the bed.

"Of course it did. And I'm sure they did."

"Then what the hell am I doing?"

"Finding me the empty spot that proves there was something worth taking."

What if I don't find that? What happens to me? Does my entire deal depend upon my finding something? I really have to hope not, as I search both the closet and the floor without turning up one damn thing of interest.

I go from the bedroom to the bathroom. Lew once again waits in the doorway.

"Tell me about Jay," he says as I work.

"He was a guy who exploited homeless kids. What's there to know?"

"Homeless?"

"You have your past. I have mine."

Lew's quiet for a moment. Then he asks, "If he targeted kids, why were you still working for him?"

"I wasn't working for him. I was working with him," I say. "And that was my very first job ever, remember?"

"You're not supposed to lie to me, remember? We have an agreement, Skye."

"Until we have a written and signed agreement, we don't have anything but me helping you out because you threatened Leo. And also because men with guns are actively hunting for me."

"I'm working on it," Lew says. "I don't know what might have happened to you in the past—"

"Goddamn right you don't."

"—or who you might have dealt with, but they weren't me. If I tell you I'm going to do something, I'm going to do it."

"No, you're going to *try* to do it. That's what I remember you telling me," I say. "And that is pretty damn far from a guarantee."

"I'll prove it to you, if you give me the chance."

Ryan said that, too. Look what happened there.

I stop working and turn to Lew. "Say I give you this chance. Say I take a big, damn chance on a near total stranger who works for a government agency I trust about as far as I could throw you. Which, to be clear, is not far at all. It would be the exact opposite of far."

"Okay. Let's say that."

"What happens to me when you fail?"

"I won't fail."

"What happens to me when you fail?"

Lew looks at me. I stare back. If he wants me—expects me—to trust him, then he needs to goddamn earn it.

Lew shakes his head. "I suppose you either go to jail or go into hiding."

Well. Those would be the options, wouldn't they? Points to Lew for telling the truth, I guess. Here's hoping I get my deal before he drops dead from exertion.

"I could go into hiding, you know," I say. "I could disappear, and you would never find me."

"Maybe."

"Not maybe. I would. You guys would find Jimmy Hoffa before you'd find me."

Lew nods. "Maybe that's true, but you won't do it. Because Leo has a life here. One from which he can't just walk away."

Lew's wrong about that. Yes, Leo does have a life here, but he would walk away in a heartbeat if I asked him to. He would have the getaway car packed and running before I even finished the sentence. Neither of us could drive it, but I'm sure he'd have a plan for that, too.

"Skye," Lew says, "I will get you a deal. I will make that happen."

"Yeah. Sure."

"You don't believe me."

"You work in law enforcement, Llewellyn. As a professional liar, I might add," I say. "Of course I don't believe you."

"I don't do that anymore."

"What? Lie?"

"Work undercover."

"But you still lie."

"Something we have in common, I think."

Yeah. Maybe. Either way, it's a good place to end this conversation. Before I say anything I'll regret. Anything *else,* maybe. Way too much has been said already.

I go back to work. The bathroom doesn't offer up any hidden secrets or places to hide them, so I return to the front of the apartment. I stop short of entering the kitchen and look at the floor. The body isn't there anymore, but I can still see it. There was just so much blood. A surprising amount of blood, really. I thought Jay had nothing in his veins but nicotine and cheap whiskey.

There's nothing in them now, I suppose.

"Skye?"

"What happens to his body?" I ask. "What happens if no one claims him?"

"I don't know, but I can find out."

"Yeah. Okay."

"Do you want to claim his body? If no one else does?"

Do I? What would I do with him? Have him cremated and scatter his ashes at The Rebel Fly?

"Why would I?" I say. "It's not like he was anything to me."

"It's all right if he was."

"Well, he wasn't," I say. Shit. I *hate* this conversation. What made me even ask the question? "You know, I could do this job a lot faster if you would just shut up and let me do it."

"My apologies." Lew gestures to the remainder of the apartment. "Have at it. I won't interrupt again."

He doesn't, either. He remains absolutely silent while I comb through the kitchen and the living room, looking for something that doesn't seem to exist. Either the murderers already took it, or Jay didn't keep it here to begin with. For all anyone knows, it could be taped under the table in his booth or behind his favorite urinal at The Rebel Fly.

Or maybe there was never anything at all to find.

When I have exhausted all possible options, I look at Lew. He's standing in the middle of the living area, hands on his hips, and nodding slowly, as though trying to figure out what comes next.

"All right. Well, I appreciate you looking," he says finally. "Let's go."

He heads toward the door. I take a last look around. Will this be the last time I'm ever here? Do I even care? What the hell is wrong with me?

"Are you coming?" Lew asks.

I look at him, still walking away. My gaze drops to his feet. What's wrong with this picture?

"Wait," I say.

Lew stops. "What?"

"Walk back toward me."

Lew does as I ask. The floor doesn't make a sound.

When he reaches me, he holds up his hands. "Well?"

I brush him aside and walk over the floor myself. Still no sound. I step on and around the spot. Nothing. I bounce a little. Was it like this the other day, too? Did I just not notice?

"What are you doing?" Lew asks.

"The floor is supposed to squeak here."

"You know where the floor is supposed to squeak?"

"Always good to avoid squeaky floors in my line of work."

"This is a basement apartment."

"So what? They can't have squeaky floors? Only mold and mildew?"

"They have concrete floors, Skye. Concrete floors generally don't squeak."

"Well, this concrete floor does. Or did."

I move to where the carpet meets the kitchen's linoleum floor. Extracting the knife from my pocket, I use it to separate the carpet from the subfloor. There's no resistance whatsoever. Someone has done this before.

"How long have you had that knife?" Lew asks.

"Found it in the loft of squalor," I say. "Do you want me to keep going, or do you just want to scold me for carrying a three-inch blade that I haven't used on anyone or anything other than this carpet?"

Lew doesn't answer.

"Look, this is what you asked me to find," I say. "This is something unusual. It's weird and doesn't make any sense and sticks out. Maybe it's nothing, but maybe it's something. Let's find out which."

Lew nods and helps me pull up the carpet. There's no pad underneath, but there is a lone plank of wooden flooring.

I look at Lew. "Wood floors squeak."

"Yes, they do."

I don't need the knife to remove the plank. Beneath, in a space apparently chiseled out of the foundation, is a thick, black book. I ease it out of the hole and open it. The pages are filled with gibberish that I can't read, but I've seen enough of Jay's penmanship to know he wrote it.

"Not-so-little black book," I say.

Lew holds out his hand. "Client list?"

"Makes sense. A job ledger, maybe," I say, giving him the book. "I doubt I was his only…independent contractor."

Lew flips through a few pages. "Okay. We'll take this with us. You can take a closer look at it later."

"Me?"

"You speak Fagin. At least better than anyone else we know of," Lew says. "Now, let's get this covered up and go see Leo."

29

THERE IS NO AVAILABLE STREET parking in front of The Thieves' Den. Lew finds a space a few blocks over and pulls into it. As soon as he cuts the engine, he holds out his hand, palm up.

"Knife," he says.

"What?"

"Give me your knife, please," he says. "As well as any other weapons you may have on your person."

"Are you serious?"

"Yes."

"The only thing I've stabbed with that knife was an older-than-dirt carpet."

"And it will remain the only thing you stab with that knife."

"Come on. I found you a pretty big clue."

"Possible clue." Lew flexes his fingers in a 'gimme' motion. "Knife. Now."

I sigh and hand over the knife. He puts it in his jacket pocket. Sure. Because that'll prevent me from stealing it back. Dumbass. I roll my eyes and get out of the car.

Lew secures the ledger in the trunk and we head to the bar.

"The Thieves' Den," he says as we approach. "A little on the nose, isn't it?"

I shrug. "Leo likes it."

Lew opens the door for me. I take advantage of the opportunity to retrieve my knife and return it to my own pocket.

It's still early in the day, so there aren't many customers inside. A couple sits at a table by the front window and a lone man is staring into a half-empty pint glass at the far end of the bar. Robbie's prepping garnishes while Dolly leans over the bar, giving him a view of her ample cleavage.

I walk up to them. "Is Leo here?"

"He's always here," Dolly says. She straightens as she studies Lew like he's an option on the appetizer menu. "You're new."

I take Lew's left hand and lift it, pointing to the wedding band on his finger. "He's married," I say. "Tell Leo I'm here, would you?"

Robbie nods, looking at Lew. He knows something's up. "Dolly."

Dolly sighs, as though going out back to talk to Leo is a major inconvenience. As she turns and walks away, I drop Lew's hand and push him toward my booth.

"Dolly," he says. "Is that her real name?"

"I'm not sure anyone knows," I say. "Sit down. Shut up."

He grins as he obliges me. A minute later, Robbie comes over with my usual order. He sets it down and looks at Lew. "You want something?"

"Whatever's on tap," Lew replies, and Robbie walks away. Lew looks at my drink. "Come here often?"

"You and your wife need some new material," I say. "Are you planning to tell Leo who you are?"

"By which I assume you mean my unfortunate association with a certain law enforcement agency?"

"Yeah."

"Yes," Lew says. "I have no reason to keep it from him. Do I?"

"Well, he doesn't like the FBI anymore than I do, but no," I say. "If you trust me at all, you can trust him."

Leo arrives then with a plate of food, along with silverware wrapped in a napkin. He sets them on the table while looking at Lew with suspicion. "Every time you come in here lately, it's with a new friend. What's this one's name?"

I look at the plate. Some kind of meatballs, maybe, with a red sauce for dipping. "Would it kill you to put fries on the menu?"

"Mags," Leo says.

"Mags?" Lew echoes. "How many aliases do you have?"

"Who can keep track?" I look at Leo. "Do you have time to sit?"

"I sit, you eat."

I point to the plate. "That?"

"You want junk, you go to Applebee's. If you want me to sit and talk to whoever the hell this is, you eat what I give you."

I sigh and slide over to make room for Leo. "Sit. I'll eat."

Leo sits and looks at Lew. "You have a name?"

"I'm Lew."

"Who the hell are you, Lew?"

"Just someone trying to help out our girl here."

Our girl? I raise an eyebrow at Lew. He nods toward the plate. Jesus Christ. Now there are two of them. I unroll the napkin and pick up the fork. It would be wrong to stab him with it, right? Instead, I stab a meatball. I could always throw it at him.

"You throw that, and you're cut off," Leo says, still staring down Lew. "Not just for today, but for the rest of eternity."

There are times when I hate how well he knows me. I eat the damn meatball, then gesture between the two men with my fork. "So, you two gonna talk, or are you just gonna whip 'em out on the table while I go get a tape measure?"

"We'll wait for you to finish eating first," Lew says.

"Are you FBI, too?" Leo asks him. "The last one was FBI."

"The last one wasn't FBI," Lew says.

I stab another meatball. "No, she just sleeps with them."

"She sleeps with one of them," Lew corrects. "Nia has—"

"Issues?" I interject. "I'm just guessing."

Lew gives me a look that could freeze over hell. I can take all the shots at him and the FBI that I want, but Nia is off limits. He and Leo may have more in common than I initially thought. I put down the fork and hold up my hands in apology.

"Nia would have laughed," I say. It's possible that I'm right.

"Nia's not here, and I'm not her," Lew replies. He looks at Leo. "Skye tells me you're asking around about Jay. About who may have killed him."

Leo looks at me. "He knows your name. How does an FBI agent know your name?"

"Well, I'm guessing multiple agents know it by now," I say, and Lew shrugs. "It wasn't my idea. It was the cost of doing business."

"What business is that?" Leo asks.

"Figuring out who killed Jay, who's trying to kill me, and maybe stop them from doing that," I say. The FBI doesn't care about Jay's death or my life as much as they do other things, but that's what Leo will care about most. "I'm a protected witness or something like that."

"Which brings us back to my questions," Lew says to Leo. "You're asking around about Jay?"

"Yeah, but Skye only asked me yesterday," Leo says. "There hasn't been time to turn up anything yet."

"If you do find something, how were you going to tell her?"

"We hadn't worked out that part yet," I say.

"Okay. Let me help with that." Lew takes out his wallet and removes a card from it. He slides it across the table. "If you hear anything that Skye should know, call this number, leave a day and time, and I'll be here."

Leo doesn't touch the card. "If Skye isn't with you, you get nothing."

Lew rests his elbows on the table. "We're trying to keep her safe. It's harder to do when we're parading her all around the city."

"You're trying to keep her safe? You're using her to identify your suspects."

"Which will go a long way to keeping her safe."

"Sure. But you want me to believe that you or your bosses wouldn't dangle her on a string to catch a bigger fish?"

"You're right. They would," Lew says. "But this particular operation isn't exactly sanctioned by my bosses."

"Why?" Leo asks.

Lew shakes his head. "That's a long story."

"I've got nowhere to be," Leo says.

I sigh. I don't have anywhere to be, either, but this is exhausting. "They're running an off-the-books investigation because the case is personal to them, which is something their bosses don't like and wouldn't approve of, but if we play along, there's a possibility I might get out of this mess without dying or going to jail."

"A possibility?" Leo asks.

"Lew's going to try to get me a deal."

"Try?"

"Well, he's not supposed to be working this case, so the process may be a little more challenging than it would normally be."

"Jesus Christ." Leo looks at Lew. "Do your bosses know about her?"

"Not currently," Lew answers.

"Great. Really, that's even better," Leo says. "Now you're telling me you have to protect her from both the murderers *and* your own agency."

"I'm telling you I *will* protect her," Lew says.

Leo laughs. "Do people really believe you when you say shit like that?"

"It's not a lie."

"Oh, look! You did it again," Leo says. "Hold on. Lemme go put out a sign. Live comedy at The Thieves' Den. Don't miss it!"

Lew turns to me, not appearing particularly frustrated but more unimpressed with Leo's feelings on this subject. If he's looking for me to offer up some support or reassurance, then he's shit out of luck.

I shrug. "He has a point."

"Yeah, I do," Leo says. "You can claim whatever you want, but I know the truth. You care about your case. I care about *her*."

Beneath the table, I put my hand on Leo's leg and squeeze slightly. His hand covers mine and returns the gesture.

"I care about her, too," Lew says.

Leo shakes his head. "Not as much as I do."

"Of course not," Lew says. "But the fact remains that Skye is in trouble, and we have the ability to help her get out of that trouble. She, in turn, has the ability to help us stop these people from doing more harm. So yes, I am going to use her. But she's going to use me, too."

"I think you'll find that Skye can take care of herself."

Lew nods. "A lot of people in my line of work think that. I still end up investigating a lot of murders, though."

Leo grips my hand.

"I don't doubt that Skye is very good at taking care of herself, but here's the thing," Lew continues. "The people looking for her are very good at taking care of people who are very good at taking care of themselves. Whatever you think of me or my agency, it's probably fair. I don't care about that. I just don't want Skye's to be the next body I come across."

"Skye would like to avoid that as well," I say. My voice sounds strange. Like it doesn't belong in this conversation, even though I am its subject. "If that matters to anyone."

Lew looks at me. "It matters."

"It's her life," Leo says. "If she's not with you, you get nothing from me."

Lew nods. "Then she'll be with me," he says. "Now, let's talk about what we need."

30

AS SOON AS WE RETURN to the loft of squalor, Lew sets the ledger on the kitchen island and pulls out his phone. He walks away as he places a call and puts the phone up to his ear. A moment later, he lowers the phone, shaking his head with irritation. Must have called Ryan, and Ryan let it go to voicemail because he's pissed at me. And at Lew for protecting me.

Lew sighs and calls someone else.

"Hey, Jonas," he says. "Yeah."

He glances at me and goes out to talk on the fire escape, positioning himself to be able to see inside the loft. Bathing in the warm glow of Lew's trust, I sit on one of the stools and open the book. Let's see what Jay was hiding.

Jay's writing is worse than chicken scratch, but it's definitely code. If I could figure out the key, I could read everything. Clients, jobs, the thieves who pulled them, maybe. It can't be too difficult to break. Jay wrote it, for crying out loud. How complex could it be?

All right. Each page has eight columns. Five columns are numbers. Dates and profits—total, his cut, and the thief's, probably. How much did he cheat all of us?

The first and last columns are consistently six numbers long. Those must be dates. Day, month, and year. Job received and job completed, maybe? I flip through the pages to find the last entry. Assuming the last entry was the job he gave me, it would be incomplete because I never came back.

Until it was too late.

Sure enough, the last entry in the book only fills five of the eight columns. The first column is probably the date he accepted the job. I'll come back to that. Columns two, three, and four are all six letters that don't spell any actual words. One of them is my name. Or Magpie, anyway. Columns two and three have repeated letters, which 'magpie' does not, so column four must be me.

I go over to the art supply shelves to find a sketch book and something resembling a pencil. I take them back to the island, open the sketch book to a blank page, and write down the alphabet. Using 'magpie' as the key, I decrypt the other two columns.

Column two: EDROBE

Column three: LEDGER

Column four: MAGPIE

Three and four are self-explanatory. I was supposed to steal a ledger. EDROBE, though…Like Edward Roberson? The murder victim? Was he also the client?

I hear a key slide into a lock and look at the door. Someone's here. Unless Nia gave a key to the murderers because she was pissed at me, I know exactly who that someone is. Closing the sketch book, I stand and move to the end of the island to face the door.

It opens, and Ryan steps inside. I don't relax. Too bad it wasn't the murderers.

Ryan looks at me as he closes the door and then glances around the rest of the loft.

Assuming he's searching for Lew, I point to the fire escape. "He's talking to Jonas. Probably because you didn't answer when he called you."

Ryan walks toward me, maintaining solemn and angry eye contact until he notices the open book on the island. He frowns as he studies it.

"What's that?" he asks.

"I'm pretty sure you trained investigator types call it a clue," I answer.

"Where did it come from?"

"Jay's apartment."

"Jay?"

"Fagin."

"Who found it?"

"I did."

Ryan looks at me. "Lew took you there? Why?"

"Your guys didn't find anything when they processed the scene. Lew thought I might."

Ryan gestures to the book. "And you found that."

"Yes."

"What is it?"

"Working theory is a job ledger."

"Theory?"

"It's written in code," I say. "Lew wanted me to try to crack it."

"You're going to crack it."

"I'm going to try," I say. No need to mention that I've already done it. Not to him. "Unless, of course, you'd rather I not."

"It's evidence. You shouldn't be handling evidence."

"Oh. Well, I can get a baggie to put it in, and you can run it down to headquarters. See what they make of it."

Ryan looks at the floor.

"But you can't do that, can you?" I say. "Because your investigation is still under the table or off the books or in the shadows or wherever, which means I'm the best hope you've got."

Ryan lifts his head and stares at me. Out of the corner of my eye, I see Lew coming back inside, but I don't look away from Ryan.

"Hey, Skye," Lew says, "I…" He stops when he sees Ryan. "You're here."

Ryan turns to Lew. "You took her to a crime scene."

"And she found us a lead. How about that." Lew joins us at the kitchen island. He looks at the open book, then at me. "Figure it out?"

"Maybe," I say. "But I have a question."

Lew nods. Ryan does nothing.

"How did the FBI find out about Jay?" I ask. "Or, the address, at least. How did they find that address?"

"I don't know," Lew says.

"Well, it had to be through Edward Roberson, right? Either his office or his home?" I ask. "That's where they would have started looking for clues, right?"

"I obviously can't say for certain, but that is a reasonable assumption," Lew says.

"Okay, so that means something in one of those two places led to Jay," I say. "Which means Jay and Edward Roberson had a connection."

"The man did send you to break into Roberson's safe," Ryan says, his voice as flat as his expression.

I look at him. "Yeah, but Jay met with clients. Not targets." I turn to Lew. "Do you have a picture of Edward Roberson? Preferably, you know, one with his head intact?"

"I can get one," he says. "Why?"

"I want to find out who knew him and what name they knew him by. A picture would help with that."

Lew nods. "Where are you planning to do this?"

I shrug. "It's ladies' night at The Rebel Fly."

"How do you know The Rebel Fly?" Ryan asks.

"I'm a thief, Ryan. How do you think I know?" I respond. "The Rebel Fly was like Jay's office. He probably met Dead Ed there, which means someone there will know about it."

"Dead Ed?" Lew says. I shrug again.

"Jonas and I will go to The Rebel Fly," Ryan says.

"And do what?" I ask. "Be ignored?"

"You don't know—"

"I do know," I say. "If you and Jonas go in there, you won't get anything but saliva in your drink."

"I wasn't planning to flash my badge."

"You won't have to. They'll make you the second you walk through the door, if not sooner," I say. "They won't talk to you."

"But they'll talk to you," Lew says.

"Yeah," I say. "They will."

Lew glances at Ryan. Ryan shakes his head.

"I'll go with her," Lew says.

I examine Lew. If I have to have a chaperone, he is the best choice of the three. They'll have a harder time making him. He might even make it all the way to the bar first.

"Can you at least pretend you don't know me?" I ask. "I have a reputation to protect."

Lew smiles. "Yeah. I can do that." He looks at Ryan. "Call Jonas. Let's make a plan."

31

JONAS COMES OVER WITH A pair of pizzas, and the guys gather around the island to discuss their plans over a slice. Ryan stands with his back to me. I sit on the couch and look at the back of his head because I'm apparently someone who does things like that now.

Fortunately, Ryan doesn't notice. Lew, however, does. He puts a slice of pizza on a plate and brings it over to me. I take it because I suspect he won't leave me alone until I do.

"It'll be okay," he says quietly.

I hate how he keeps presuming what I'm thinking and feeling. I absolutely despise that he may not be completely wrong.

I huff. "Liars gonna lie."

"Takes one to know one."

"Are you twelve?"

Lew nods at the plate. "Eat your dinner."

He returns to Ryan and Jonas. I look at the pizza. Pepperoni. I peel off one pepperoni slice and eat it, then put the pizza on the couch and go back to watching the FBI make this whole thing more complicated than it needs to be. All I need to do is walk through the door and ask the bartender what they know.

The most planning that takes is figuring out whether to walk or take the train.

Maybe I should just go without them. Slip out the window, down the fire escape, and be on my way. Assuming the surveillance teams are in the same places they were earlier, there's a possibility I could get to The Rebel Fly and back before anyone even notices I'm gone.

It would be better than just sitting here, watching the back of Ryan's head while he refuses to acknowledge my existence in any way.

But if I do that, will it blow back on Leo?

I glance at the guys. All right, so maybe I won't leave the building, but I can't sit in this room any longer.

I get up and walk over to the windows. None of the guys notice. I climb out the window onto the fire escape and then up to the roof. Looking over the side, I pick out tonight's surveillance teams. A minivan and another SUV. Will they be invited to go along on the field trip? Because if this excursion needs anything, it's more damn cops.

I move away from the edge and sit on the ground with my back up against an air conditioning unit. Taking the knife out of my pocket, I open and close the blade while watching the sky slowly darken. Good thing I can't draw any parallels between that and my current situation. Otherwise, I might have to sit here, thinking deep thoughts about where and how everything went so very wrong.

Taking a last-minute job.

Joining Ryan in the shower.

For example.

"Didn't I take that away from you already?" Lew asks.

I look up to see him climbing onto the roof.

"Not successfully," I say.

I close the blade as he walks toward me. When he stops in front of me, I hold it out.

He shakes his head. "Keep it, for now. Take it with you tonight. Just in case."

I put the knife in my pocket. "Does that mean you and the boys are done coming up with your overly elaborate plan to infiltrate the criminal establishment?"

"Overly elaborate?"

"It's The Rebel Fly, not the Legion of Doom."

"We don't like to take chances with protected witnesses," Lew says.

I shake my head. "You're gonna make it worse."

"If our plans concerned you so much, maybe you should have stuck around and helped us make them."

"Yeah. Because two-thirds of your circle has so much interest in anything I have to say."

Lew shrugs. "You're going. They're not."

"Are they really not going?"

"They'll be in unmarked cars. One watching the front entrance, one watching the back."

"And you?"

"I am going in with you, but I will pretend not to know you for as long as I can."

"What does that mean?"

"That means I will be there to watch your back," Lew says. "And if anything happens—"

"Oh my God. Nothing's going to happen."

"Skye," Lew says sharply. "There are trained killers hunting for you. They killed Edward Roberson, they killed Jay, and now they are looking for *you*. It could be that they made the same connection to The Rebel Fly that you made, and it could be that they are there now, waiting for you to show yourself."

I hadn't actually thought of that. "And you're still going to let me walk in there? Your...protected witness?"

"Yeah," Lew says. "But I am going to have your back. And if anything happens—if anything even seems like it's going to happen—then I am going to be there to protect you and get you the hell out alive."

What did Nia tell me back in D.C.? They will take risks for me because my life is at risk. I sure as hell don't deserve that.

"Nia will be pissed if I let you do that for me," I say.

"How happy is Leo right now?" Lew asks. I shrug. "You're not letting me do anything, and Nia is not your concern. Infiltrating the Legion of Doom is."

I roll my eyes. "It's not the Legion of Doom."

"It is tonight," Lew says. "Act like it."

I nod and stand. "In that case, I'm gonna need a few things."

"What things?"

"Two words," I say. "Black. Leather."

32

THOUGH I DON'T SEE WHO acquires or delivers them, my wardrobe requests are fulfilled, and I leave for The Rebel Fly looking and feeling more like myself. Denim and leather and boots—with a three-inch blade secreted away in my pocket. No offense to Nia's sister-in-law, but this is more my style.

Lew and I take the T to the Park Street station, riding in separate cars. From there, we walk down Tremont Street, Lew trailing behind me. I'm not supposed to look at him, unless there's trouble of some kind, and I don't need to. I can feel his eyes on the back of my head, like his gaze is one of those child harnesses parents put on their toddlers.

As we get closer to The Rebel Fly, I start checking out the cars parked on the street. Ryan and Jonas left the loft before we did, in order to get in position, but I don't know what vehicles they were using, or who's supposed to be watching which entrance. It doesn't much matter, though. It's not like I really want to interact with either of them.

I walk inside the bar. The difference between this place and The Thieves' Den is staggering. The Rebel Fly embraces its roots and clientele and works hard to create an environment in which they'll feel comfortable. It's dark and seedy, and every liquor bottle behind the bar contains a fair amount of water. Only the regulars know the secrets to getting the good stuff.

I make my way through the room, nodding to the patrons who nod to me. Angie's tending bar tonight. That's a lucky break. If Edward Roberson came here, she would know it.

There are no open seats at the bar, so I wedge myself in between two occupied stools. On my left is an old man nursing a beer while eating peanuts from the communal bowl. On my right is a young guy wearing an Emerson sweatshirt, with a pint in his hand and what looks suspiciously like his wallet sticking out of the top of his jeans. An over-served frat boy. My favorite kind.

He leans toward me and slurs, "S'up, sexy? Buy you a drink?"

"No, thanks," I say, waving Angie over. "But you can piss off and give me your seat."

He pats his lap. "We can share it."

Yep. Definitely over-served. Or maybe just plain stupid. I grab his hand and bend his middle finger back past the point of comfort. "I can also break your hand. What do you think about that?"

He grins. "I like a girl who likes it rough."

I yank his finger out of joint. His head rears back as he howls in pain, and I take the opportunity to relieve him of his wallet.

"Bitch," he spits out.

"Tell your friends," I say. "Now get out of that seat and this bar before I break your other hand."

He swears at me again as he slides off the stool and stumbles toward the exit. I sit down and move his abandoned pint to the side. Flat domestic beer has never interested me.

"What did I tell you about assaulting my customers?" Angie says, stopping in front of me.

I sigh. "Make sure they've paid their tabs first."

"Yeah. And did you do that?"

I open the wallet and thumb through the surprising amount of cash inside. What a dumbass. I take out a hundred dollar bill and offer it to Angie. "He asked me to give you this. Said you should keep the change."

"Goddamn right he did." Angie takes the money and tucks it beneath her bra strap. "The fuck you doing here? Thought you were too good for this place."

"I am."

"Well, if you're looking for Jimmy, he ain't here."

No, he really isn't. I shake my head and remove Edward's picture from the inside pocket of my jacket. "I'm looking for this guy, actually. You seen him around?"

Angie leans over the photo. She smiles. "Oh yeah. That asshole. Yeah, I've seen him."

"Got time to talk?" I ask.

She glances over her shoulder. "Yeah, gimme a minute." She reaches down and gets me a bottle of Sam Adams. Removing the cap, she sets it in front of me. "On the house."

I pull a fifty from the wallet. "On my new bestie."

"Even better."

Angie takes the bill and tucks it next to the hundred. She heads back down the bar, checking in with her customers. At the other end is Lew, chatting up a townie whose low-cut dress is at least two sizes too small. What would Nia think of that? If I had a phone, I'd take a picture and send it to her. I do, occasionally, enjoy chaos.

Lew leans in to talk to Angie, who gets him his own bottle of Sam Adams. The townie nearly spills out of her dress when placing her order. Angie makes a rum and Coke, which, at The Rebel Fly, is more a watered-down Coke with a splash of watered-down rum. It's a complete waste of money, but the townie doesn't seem to notice as she concentrates on flirting with Lew.

Angie waits on another guy—whiskey on the rocks—before returning to me. She jerks her head to the left. "Let's go."

I return Edward's photo to my pocket and follow her through the storeroom and out the back door. She leans against the wall, takes out a pack of cigarettes, and shakes one out. She offers me the pack. I decline with a wave of my hand and glance at the cars parked on the street. I don't see either Ryan or Jonas.

Angie lights her cigarette and takes a long drag. Her eyes close for a moment before she exhales and looks at me. "So, a few days back, this asshole comes in, looking like…well, not like he did in your picture, that's for fucking sure. He don't belong here, you know, but he ordered a beer and paid in cash, so what the fuck do I care?"

"Is that why you remember him?" I ask. "He didn't belong?"

Angie laughs and takes another drag. "Nah. So, after a while of looking around like some fucking kid at Disney World, this dumbass says to me that he's looking for a thief, like we have them on the fucking menu or something. I'm thinking this asshole's the worst fucking cop I've ever seen, and I tell him to piss off."

"Did he?"

"Probably would've." Angie taps the ash off the end of her cigarette. "But Jimmy overheard him and came by. Took him to his booth."

So they did know each other.

Angie blows a smoke ring at me. "That why you looking for him? He owe you money?"

"Something like that," I say. "Did you get a name?"

"Yeah, we exchanged business cards," Angie says. "No, I didn't get a fucking name."

"Had to ask," I say. "How many days back was this? Do you remember?"

"Oh fuck." Angie scratches her cheek with her thumb. Cigarette ash falls with the motion. "What was it? A week, maybe?"

That's why Jay was late. He was supposed to meet me at The Thieves' Den but stayed to talk to Edward. To get the time-sensitive job he then offered me.

"Haven't seen him since," Angie says. "The dumbass, I mean, but Jimmy ain't been in, either. Where's he been? You know?"

The morgue. I look at the cars again. There's a Jeep Cherokee with a D.C. plate, but I can't see if anyone's behind the wheel.

"Vacation," I say.

Angie snorts and drops the cigarette butt on the ground. "Jimmy on a fucking vacation. Sunbathing and sightseeing and shit. I like that. You're funny, Maggie."

"Always have been." I turn my back to the street and look at Angie. "You have your knife on you?"

"Yeah."

"Can I borrow it?"

"Yeah." Angie shifts to pull a switchblade from its concealed spot at the small of her back. She hands it over. "That ain't street legal, you know."

I tuck the knife inside my jacket. "Neither am I."

"Hey," Angie says. "You in trouble?"

Yes. "No more than usual."

"Well, that's good to hear." She straightens. "I gotta go back. You coming?"

I open the frat boy's wallet and pull out the remaining cash. I hold it out. "I was never here."

"You never are." She takes the bills and tucks them into her back pocket. "What about Hollywood at the bar?"

"What?"

"Hollywood. The guy who followed you in."

That must be Lew. Did he manage to reach the bar before she made him? "It's okay. He's harmless. He thinks he's protecting me."

Angie snorts again. "Don't he know you can take care of yourself?"

"I said he was harmless, not smart," I say. "Appreciate you asking, though."

"Gotta take care of my regulars."

"Yeah," I say. "No one's come in asking about me, though, right?"

"Not that I heard."

That's something, at least. "If that changes, tell Leo?"

"Yeah."

"Not over the phone."

Angie hesitates, then nods. "Yeah," she says. "What are you into, Mags?"

"You really don't want to know."

"You in over your head?"

Most definitely. "Not yet." I glance back at the street. The Jeep Cherokee is still there. "I gotta go."

"Want me to tell Hollywood you left?"

I smile. How much would I love to see Lew's reaction to that? "He's not that dumb." I toss the frat boy's wallet into the Dumpster. "See you."

I walk away, shrugging into my jacket a little. I'm on the next block over, heading back to Tremont Street, when the Jeep Cherokee pulls up alongside me. Ryan's behind the wheel, but I get in anyway.

"Well?" he says.

He doesn't look at me. I don't look at him, either. Two can play at that game.

"Edward Roberson hired someone to break into his own safe," I say. "Why would he do that?"

Ryan pulls back onto the road. "Let's find out."

33

RYAN AND I ARE THE first to return to the loft of squalor. He immediately goes over to the windows to close the curtains before leaning against the wall to text people. Probably Lew and Jonas, but he doesn't say anything to me. He hasn't said anything at all since we pulled into traffic.

Which is fine. It doesn't bother me at all. I don't have anything to say to him, either.

I remove Edward Roberson's picture from my jacket and leave it on the island next to a gold wedding band. Must belong to Lew. I didn't notice that it was missing. Good detail, smart to do so, but does Nia know he does that? She can't like that very much.

Slipping out of the jacket, I take it over to the armoire to hang it up, keeping Angie's knife in the inner pocket. Lew's bound to confiscate the other knife when he gets back. I need to make sure Angie's stays a secret. Next, I get some yoga pants and a T-shirt out of the dresser and head toward the bathroom to change. Ryan looks at me, his thumbs frozen over his phone.

"You can relax," I say. "Not even I can escape from this bathroom."

Ryan blinks, then looks back at his phone. I go inside the bathroom, close the door, and lean against it. Hard to believe this could suck anymore, but I'm sure it'll find a way soon enough.

After I change, I leave the bathroom. Still no sign of Lew or Jonas. Ryan's moved from the windows over to the heavy bag. He stands there, his back to me, and pushes the bag a little with his bare fist. I'm sure there's no significance to that, so I go sit on the couch to wait.

I glance at the clock on the kitchen wall. What is taking Lew so long? Did I give him too much credit and he simply hasn't realized I left? Did he stay behind to see how far he could get with his townie? Maybe he and Jonas went somewhere else instead of coming straight back here. If Ryan told them what I told him, they could have taken that information and done…something with it. Where would they go? What could they do? Who could they ask?

Why do we need to ask anyone? The man hired someone to break into his own safe. Surely I can figure out why. Why would Edward Roberson hire someone to break into his own safe? Why would anyone? Insurance? It wouldn't be the first time someone attempted some form of insurance fraud. But it doesn't feel right here. He was hurried; it was a time-sensitive job. The man was desperate for a thief. One night only. Could he have been trying to protect the thing in his safe?

Not that I really know what the thing was. A flash drive of some kind. Whatever it was, the gray ghost must have it now. I even made it easier for him to get it. I did everything but empty the damn safe. While his goons were chasing me, he probably walked right over Edward's body to get what he wanted. And while I was being whisked away in an FBI surveillance van, he was…

An FBI surveillance van. The FBI was watching someone. *Ryan* was watching someone.

"Why were you there that night?" I ask.

Ryan turns to look at me. "What?"

"At the Skyreach. The night we…met," I say. "You were there for a reason. Who were you watching? Dead Ed? The gray ghost?"

He hesitates. Why? He doesn't trust me enough to tell me?

"The building," he answers.

"You were watching the building?" I say. "What was the building suspected of doing?"

"It wasn't…" Ryan sighs. "We've been working this case for a long time—I told you that—and our last lead, before he disappeared into WITSEC, worked in that building. We've been hoping that watching the building might get us another lead."

"And instead you got me."

"I thought you were in trouble."

"I was."

Ryan folds his arms across his chest and looks at the floor. "We didn't know about the ghost. You led us to him."

"Does it matter if we can't find him?"

Someone knocks on the door. Ryan walks over to it. "We'll find him."

He puts his eye to the peephole, then opens the door. Jonas strolls inside. Well, that's not going to help anything. Where is Lew?

Jonas goes over to the island and pulls out one of the stools. He sits, leaning his elbow on the island while looking at me. I look back. On the list of things that intimidate me, Jonas is nowhere to be found.

"So," he says, "you're the thief."

"Did you just figure that out?" I ask. "Your buddies didn't tell you earlier?"

"You lied to us," Jonas says, "and now you want a deal."

I look at Ryan. Or his back, anyway, as he's now staring at the wall as though it's something featured in the Louvre and not the exposed brick of the loft of squalor. "Seriously? Didn't you tell him anything?"

Ryan doesn't acknowledge that either Jonas or I exist.

"You think you deserve a deal?" Jonas says.

"I think I'm not a big enough collar for the Bureau to give a shit about me," I say. Lew wasn't wrong about that. "You're much more interested in the gray ghost and what effect taking him down can have on your case. So, if giving me a deal can help you do that, who cares what I may or may not deserve? Who cares what happens to me?"

Jonas glances at Ryan. I decline to do the same. Ryan doesn't care. Not anymore.

"Don't much like letting thieves walk," Jonas says.

"Unless they're rich or politicians, you mean. Doesn't seem to be much of a problem then." I shake my head. "You're just pissed because your partner got his feelings hurt."

Ryan's looking at me now, but I stay focused on Jonas.

"Or because you're a criminal," Jonas says.

I nod. "Right. I'm sure that's all it is."

There's another knock at the door then. Lew has arrived at last. Ryan lets him in.

"How's it going here?" Lew asks. "Everyone okay?"

Despite my absolutely shitty mood, I grin at Lew. "Hey, Don Juan. Where's your new girlfriend? Did you take her home and introduce her to your wife?"

Lew picks up his wedding ring and slides it back into place. "You, of all people, must recognize a beard when you see one."

I laugh. "Does Nia know you do that?"

"How do you think we met?" Lew says. "Need I remind you that flirting is actually legal whereas assault—"

"Assault?" Ryan says.

"Oh please," I say. "I did every woman in that place a huge favor. Including your girlfriend."

"Still illegal," Lew says.

"What assault?" Ryan asks.

"Only if he reports it, which he won't," I say. "And if he did, somehow, decide to report it—which, again, he won't—

no one there saw one goddamn thing because I was never there."

"Someone needs to tell me about this assault," Ryan says. "*Now*."

Lew points at me. "You *were* there."

"Not according to the bartender. Or the patrons."

Lew shakes his head and walks toward me. "You don't know—"

"I do know," I say. "Nothing will come from the drunken frat boy. He was so drunk, he may not even remember what happened. He'll be fine, and so will your investigation."

"What assault?" Ryan says.

Lew stops in front of me and holds out his hand. "Knife."

"You know, there are still murderers looking for me," I say.

"Which is why Ryan, Jonas, and I carry guns." Lew flexes his fingers. "Knife."

I roll my eyes and pass over the knife. "This is dumb."

"I agree. I shouldn't have to keep doing this."

"Well, do a better job of hiding it this time."

Lew walks away and gives the knife to Jonas, who looks at it and then at me before putting it in his jacket pocket. Yeah. Okay. That'll work. I have no intention of getting close enough to Jonas to do any goddamn thing.

"What. Assault," Ryan says.

Lew looks at Ryan as though he didn't realize anyone else was in the room. "Don't worry about it."

"Don't worry about it?" Ryan gapes at Lew. "You just told me she *assaulted* someone."

I shrug. "Only a little."

Lew sighs. "That's not helping, Skye."

"Oh," I say, "I wasn't trying to help."

Jonas shakes his head in disgust. "You're not trying to help. You have a *deal*."

"No, what I have is Lew's word that he's going to *try* to get me a deal," I say. "Which is very different from an actual deal."

"Skye," Lew says.

"No." I stand and look him in the eye. "You know what? No. Just...no. I'm done. I'm done taking shit from this asshole"—I jerk my thumb toward Jonas—"and I'm done in general. Get me a damn deal, or don't, but if you don't send him home right now, I'll be gone by morning. And I'm confident enough that I'm warning you now instead of just doing it."

"Skye—"

"You will *never* find me," I say. When Lew opens his mouth, I add, "Him, too."

Lew sighs again. He doesn't look mad, though. Just...sad.

He doesn't break eye contact with me as he says, "Jonas, why don't you go home? We'll talk to you in the morning."

Jonas stands. "Goddammit, Llewellyn. You can't—"

"Clock's ticking," I say and walk away.

As it's a stupid studio apartment with nowhere else to hide, I return to the bathroom and lock the door behind me. The boys are fighting. About me. Loudly. I turn on the shower to help drown out the sound. It doesn't help much. I sit on the floor, my back against the door, and listen.

"For fuck's sake, Llewellyn," Jonas says, "you're losing sight—"

"If I'm losing it, then you've lost it," Lew says. "Whatever else she is, Skye is a *person*. You keep forgetting that. And *you*...You knew what you were doing. Grow the fuck up."

"I didn't know who I was doing it with," Ryan says.

"Grow up anyway," Lew replies. "We need her."

Jonas laughs. "We don't—"

"We do," Lew says firmly. No argument allowed. "Neither of you want this done as badly as I do. Neither of you want these guys as much as I do. They almost killed me. They almost killed Patrick, and they—"

"We know," Jonas says. "That's why we've been doing this. That's why we've been working this goddamn case since our bosses and yours ordered us off it. We sat in that hospital room every night and—"

"And Nia never left," Lew says. "I am going to take these assholes down, and I need Skye's help to do that. If that's something you can't accept, I understand, but get the hell out. Even if it is something you can accept, get the hell out. Either way, Jonas, go home. I'll call you when I know what happens next."

The only sound then is the shower. What are they doing now? Is the fight over? Are they in a Mexican standoff? Are Ryan and Jonas's heads exploding because Lew sided with the common criminal over the brotherhood?

I jump when a door slams shut. Who left? Who stayed?

A moment later, someone bangs his fist against the bathroom door.

"Turn off the damn water and get out here," Lew shouts.

Lew has a breaking point, too. Another time, another place, and I would find it funny. After he walks away, I get up, turn off the shower, and open the bathroom door. I stick my head out and glance from side to side. Jonas is gone. Ryan's sitting at the island, an open bottle of Jack Daniel's in front of him. I don't see Lew, though. What happened to him?

"Where's Lew?" I ask.

Ryan starts to look at me but stops and looks at his whiskey instead. "Fire escape. He got a call."

I step out of the bathroom. "Who?"

"Didn't say." He picks up his glass and has a drink. "Tell me about the assault."

"You don't have to worry about it."

"Tell me anyway."

I walk toward Ryan and stand on the other side of the island. "There was a drunk frat boy who offered to let me sit in his lap. I offered to break his hand. He said he liked a girl who liked it rough, and I called his bluff."

"How?"

"I dislocated the middle finger on his left hand. He called me a bitch, and then he left."

Ryan lifts his glass. "You can't do that."

"Yeah. It's good you're looking out for rich, white, young men," I say. "They have so little protection in this world."

Ryan has another sip of whiskey. "You do that a lot."

"Tell the truth?"

"Oh yeah. You're known for telling the truth, aren't you?"

"Probably not," I say. "But that was true."

"That was sarcasm."

"What was? What you said or what I said?"

Ryan shakes his head. "I don't even know."

I watch him have more whiskey. "Well, by all means, have another drink. That'll definitely help."

"Can't hurt."

I don't know about that. I look away when Lew climbs back into the loft. He closes the window behind him and walks toward us.

"That was Leo," he says. "He wants to meet tomorrow at noon."

"Did he say what he had?" I ask.

"No. If you're not with me, I get nothing, remember?" Lew looks at Ryan. "I have somewhere else I need to be. You'll have to go."

I don't want to go anywhere with Ryan. "That wasn't what you promised Leo. You told him you would be there."

"You being there will be more important," Lew says. "The fed will be interchangeable to him."

Ryan shakes his head. "She's not going."

"Part of the deal," Lew says. "Leo won't talk to us unless Skye's there, too."

"We're just going to let them run this thing?"

Them. He spat the word out of his mouth as though it had a foul taste to it. I shouldn't be surprised, but I am. I shouldn't be hurt, but I am. I walk away and sit on the couch.

"They got us a lead. In fact, every lead we have has come from Skye or Leo. So yes, for now, they get to call the shots," Lew says. "I thought we settled this, Ryan."

"You settled it," Ryan mutters.

I look at him. Drunk, angry, and conflicted. Such a terrific combination.

"Damn right I did," Lew says. "Are you going to be able to do this?"

Ryan looks at me. As soon as our eyes meet, I turn away.

"Ryan," Lew says. "Can you do this, or should I ask Jonas to—?"

"No," Ryan says. "I'll do it."

He finishes his drink and walks across the room to go out on the fire escape. He stands there, his back to the loft. To me.

I look at Lew. "Still think it's gonna be okay?"

Lew doesn't answer.

34

RYAN AND I SPEND THE night in estranged silence.

I would say it would be time better spent working on the case, talking through the things we know, and developing theories about the things we don't, or maybe building one of those collages on the wall you see on all the detective shows, but Ryan won't talk to me about any of that. I'm just the bloodhound now. I find the clues. I don't get to know what happens next.

The silence stretches into the next day. We get ready, side by side, like some married couple who long ago lost interest in interacting with one another, and walk into The Thieves' Den at exactly noon.

Robbie's tending to a couple at the end of the bar. I go directly to my booth and sit with my back to the wall. Ryan sits across from me.

"What is this place?" he asks.

"A bar."

"I know it's a bar. I was asking…" He shakes his head. "Never mind. Where's this Leo guy?"

"He'll be out in a minute."

"How do you know?"

I point to the nearest security camera in the ceiling. "I walk in, he comes out."

"You two know each other well then."

"Better than anyone."

Robbie comes over to the table and looks at me. "You drinking?"

Someone's picked up on the tension. All we did was walk in and sit down, and Robbie can still tell something's up.

I shake my head. "Too early in the day."

"We're here to see Leo," Ryan says.

"He knows," I say. "Thanks, Rob."

Robbie steps back toward the bar. He maintains eye contact with me and nods toward Ryan. I shake my head.

Ryan glances over his shoulder and watches Robbie walk away. "What was that about?"

"Robbie's concerned I'm in distress," I say. "But don't worry. I assured him I was not."

Ryan looks back at me. "Why would he think you're in distress?"

"Dunno. He must think you're coming across like a real asshole right now."

Ryan blinks. "I didn't say or do anything."

"You didn't have to."

Ryan sits back. He glances again at Robbie. Robbie's back behind the bar, prepping garnishes while keeping an eye on me.

Ryan looks at me, his expression conflicted. "Skye, we—"

He stops when Leo approaches the booth, plate in hand.

Leo looks him over. "Another new friend?"

"I'm not sure 'friend' is the right word," I say, "but this is Ryan. He works with Lew."

Leo puts the plate down and sits next to me. "Ah. More feds. Fun."

"Nice place you have here," Ryan says.

"Pays the bills," Leo replies. He nudges the plate toward me. Diced tomatoes and God knows what else piled on thin slices of toasted bread. "What happened to the other one?"

"Prior commitment," I say. "We're stuck with Ryan."

"You're stuck with me?" Ryan says.

"Sorry. He's stuck with me." I look at Leo. "He's mad because I lied to him."

"Because no one ever lies to feds?" Leo says.

"Guess not." I gesture to the plate. "What even is this?"

"Bruschetta," Leo says. "It's like a fancier mini pizza. Eat it."

"It looks like what you throw up after you eat pizza," I say. "Pass."

"Can we please just talk about what we came here to discuss?" Ryan says. "You summoned us here. Why?"

Leo angles himself to look at me. "Got an address for you. Not sure if they're the guys you're looking for, but the chatter is promising."

"What address? What chatter?" Ryan asks.

"Is he always like this?" Leo asks me.

"I told you he's mad at me," I say. Then, because Leo won't tell Ryan anything directly, I ask, "What chatter?"

"Lots of talk about tracking down a stray and tying up loose ends. They're putting out feelers for information. Anyone with anything useful can go to this address." Leo gives me a folded piece of paper. "Word is they'll pay for a tip that pays out."

"You think I'm the stray?" I ask.

"If I had to guess."

Ryan holds out his hand. I drop the paper onto his palm.

He slides out of the booth. "Don't go anywhere."

I salute him. He walks to the other side of the bar, his phone already to his ear.

Leo drapes his arm across the back of the booth. "So, you fucked him."

I should have known he would be able to tell. I sigh. "Yeah."

"What the hell were you thinking, fucking a fed?"

Thinking. Yeah. I was totally doing that. I shrug. "I don't know. I was bored and he looks really good shirtless."

"Jesus, Skye."

"I know. But you would have fucked him, too."

"I highly doubt that."

"Oh yeah? See him without a shirt on and say that."

"No abs are that good." Leo shakes his head and sighs. "Tell me you only fucked the one time because you were bored and you will never, ever do it again."

"He's mad at me. He won't want to sleep with me ever again."

"That is not what I wanted to hear. Tell me you're done with him."

Hard to believe we could be anything else. "Yeah, we're done," I say. "Why would you think otherwise?"

"Because he's mad at you, and you're upset about it."

"I'm not upset," I say. "Worried, maybe, that this whole thing will end with me in prison—"

"You're only *maybe* worried about that?"

"Shut up," I say. "What's at that address? Do you know?"

"Restaurant in the North End."

"Real or a front?"

"Both, maybe? I'm not sure. For all I know, it's some mom-and-pop place that's currently being occupied by whatever fucking mob you've gotten yourself involved in." Leo nudges my leg with his knuckles. "Here. Take this before your babysitter comes back."

I take the object from his hand. A lock pick set. I slide it into my jacket pocket, next to Angie's knife.

"What else do you need?" he asks.

"A lot, but this is a start," I say as Ryan ends his call. "He's coming back."

Ryan returns to the booth but doesn't sit down. "Let's go," he says to me. He looks at Leo. "Thank you for the intel. If you learn anything else—"

"I'll be sure to contact your much more pleasant counterpart." Leo stands and looks at me. "Don't die?"

I nod. "I'll do my best."

35

WE DRIVE BACK TO THE loft of squalor in silence. Upon our arrival, Ryan locks the door but doesn't put the chain in place. Expecting company, then.

Is there going to be another meeting of the minds? Will it be both Lew and Jonas, or has Jonas not been let back into the club yet? Did someone look into why Edward Roberson might have hired someone to break into his own safe, or did last night's argument squash that lead? Maybe nobody cares anymore about Dead Ed or why anyone was hired to break into a safe because Ryan was dumb enough to sleep with a lying, conniving thief. If that's true, does that mean none of them care anymore about whether that thief meets the same fate as the other three victims in this case?

Lew might. He has at least attempted to acknowledge I am a human being. But I can't rely on that. I can only rely on myself. I have a knife and a lock pick set the FBI doesn't know about. It's not much, but it's a start. And if that's all I get to work with...Well, I've done more with less.

But as I'll only be able to keep the tools I have as long as they continue to not know about them, I go straight to the armoire to hang up my jacket.

"How do you know Leo?" Ryan asks.

I close the armoire and turn around. Ryan's sitting at the island, leaning with his elbow on the countertop, and his eyes fixed on anything other than me. Wants to ask personal questions. Still won't look at me. Sounds about right.

"We grew up together," I say.

"In the same foster home?" he asks. When I don't answer, he makes eye contact. "El told me you grew up in the system."

Great. What else did El tell him? "Oh."

"It's nice you two had one another."

What is Ryan doing? Why is he doing it now? "Yeah. Nice." I swallow a laugh. "That's what our childhood was. A regular fairy tale."

"What does that mean?"

"That means El didn't tell you everything."

"Like what?"

I shake my head. "It's not relevant to the case."

"I'm not asking because of the case."

"Then why are you asking? I thought I had no value to you outside of this case. I'm just an asset. Well, not even that, really. I mean, you don't want *them* involved at all, so what does that make me? A necessary, temporary evil?"

Ryan looks away again. "I know I've been—"

"An asshole?"

"You did lie to me."

"I lie to a lot of people. You're not special."

Ryan nods. "You want me to apologize for being mad?"

"I don't want anything from you," I say. "Lew and I made an arrangement. I'm gonna do what I can to hold up my end. You can do whatever you want."

"Except talk to you."

"If you want to talk about the case, we can talk about the case," I say. "But I don't know why we would ever need to talk about anything else."

"I'm just trying to understand."

"Understand what?"

"You."

"Why?"

Ryan shakes his head. "I don't know. Maybe…" He takes a deep breath. "Maybe you're right, and we should only talk about the case, but…"

But. There's always a but. What is his?

"But what?" I ask.

"I don't know."

I nod. "Compelling argument."

I walk over to the couch and sit down. I pick up the remote and turn on the television. Three women are standing in a kitchen set making some kind of food. I don't care about cooking or food or whatever small talk they're making while they cook their food, but it's better than conversing with Ryan about our doomed fling.

Ryan stands in front of the television. "This is how I figure it out."

"Figure what out?"

"I don't know. You? Us?"

Trying to figure me out? I don't like that, but that's a game I've played before. I win every time. Most every time. Trying to figure *us* out, though? Nope. I don't like that at all. That is a game in which I have no interest.

Besides, there's nothing to figure out. There is no us. There can't be.

"So," I say, "the idea here is I tell you my life story, and you decide…something."

"I don't know. I guess."

He guesses. Well, then. I set the remote aside. Time to bring out the heavy guns.

"Leo and I did grow up in the system. That's true. At least until we were about eight and we ran away. After that, we lived wherever."

"What does that mean? On the streets?"

"Well, we were eight and neither of us had a trust fund, so yeah. We lived on the streets, in shelters, abandoned buildings, and anywhere else we could find."

"That's why you started to steal."

"Seemed like a better choice than dying," I say. "I'm sure you disagree, though."

"Skye—"

"Met Jay—sorry, *Fagin*—when I was ten. I was in Quincy Market because it's crowded and full of distracted tourists who carry cash. It was pretty easy pickings. Jay—I mean, Fagin—was there, probably for the same reason. Or maybe he was trolling for kids he could recruit to steal for him. I don't know. It never came up. It didn't really matter to me, you know? He fed us, so we stuck around."

"So, Leo's a thief, too?"

I shake my head. "Leo doesn't steal. I wouldn't let him."

"You wouldn't let him?"

"He didn't have the talent."

"Talent?"

"Yeah. Talent," I say. "It takes talent, and he didn't have it. It wasn't worth the risk, so I didn't let him steal. He's not a goddamn thief."

"Talent," Ryan repeats. "Jesus Christ."

I see we won't be moving past this point any time soon. I sigh. "Look, I know you think I'm the Bill Sikes in all of this, but—"

"The who?"

"Bill Sikes. From *Oliver Twist*?" I say. Does he not get the reference? "You've been calling Jay 'Fagin' since the body was found. Do you really not know why?"

"No, I know why. I'm just...surprised, I guess."

"That I get the reference? Why?"

"You just seem..." He shrugs. "You're pretty well-read."

"For an uneducated, homeless street urchin, you mean?"

"No. Of course not. I didn't mean—"

"Why not? It's accurate," I say. "But that's the nice thing about libraries. They don't require their patrons to have or spend money. They have heat in the winter and air conditioning in the summer, bathrooms, water fountains, and a lot of their programs come with free refreshments. And if you're not too dirty and not too noisy, they'll let you stay and read as many books as you want."

"Why did you…What happened?"

"What do you mean?"

"You were in the system, right?" he asks. "Foster care?"

"Which is, of course, universally known as a system without flaws or cracks through which kids can fall."

"Which was it for you?"

"Both. We were better off on our own."

"Why? What happened?"

He doesn't get to know that. I shake my head. "We couldn't stay there."

"Why?" he asks. I say nothing. After a moment, he nods. "You were…"

Not me. But he doesn't get to know that, either.

"Did you tell anyone?" he asks then.

"Tell who? The adults doing the abusing or the adults who put us there in the first place?"

"What about—?"

"There wasn't anyone, Ryan. No one we could trust but each other."

"That's still true, isn't it?"

"Never had a reason to think otherwise."

That's a direct hit. As pissed as he is, he still hates thinking I don't trust him. Poor, well-intentioned idiot. How has he survived in this world for so long?

"What about The Thieves' Den?" Ryan asks.

We're dangerously close to venturing into interrogation land here, but I say, "The business is clean. It's legit. All the proper whatever is in place and up to code. I don't know the terminology. I don't run a bar."

"Did you finance it?"

"It's Leo's business," I say. "And if you're curious how an uneducated, homeless street urchin came to own and operate a bar—"

"I am."

"He got a job as a kid at a restaurant doing whatever they needed done. He was too young to work there legally, so they paid him in cash under the table. They didn't pay him much, but he couldn't exactly complain, and besides, there were other benefits."

"Like what?"

"First dibs on Dumpster diving," I say. "He always knew when there was something worth going in for."

Ryan's face contorts. He's horrified, disgusted. Maybe even guilt-ridden.

"Plus," I continue as though he isn't fighting a losing battle against revulsion, "Leo learned a lot about the restaurant business. That job led to other jobs, which led to other opportunities, which eventually led to The Thieves' Den."

Ryan's expression hasn't changed. "Skye, I—"

"Stop. Don't do that," I say. "I don't want to hear it. The look in your eyes is more than enough. You feel sorry for us. You pity us, and I don't want you to do that. I don't give a damn what you think of what I had to do to survive. I don't care that you're now feeling guilty about your suburban childhood with your happily married parents and the roof over your head and the food that magically appeared on the table every night without having been dug out of the trash or scammed from the library. There is literally nothing you could say right now that I would want to hear, so just don't say anything."

Ryan walks over to the window. He looks at the city through the gauzy curtains. He probably looks at a lot of life like that. Through a hazy filter that makes it appear so much better than it really is.

"I'm sorry," he says. "I'm sorry that happened to you. To you both."

I fold my arms across my chest. "Does that mean you understand me now? You've decided whatever you needed to decide?"

Ryan returns and sits on the coffee table. He leans forward and rests his elbows on his knees. "Look, what happened between us..."

How will he end that sentence? What happened between us was fucking amazing? What happened between us was a mistake? What happened between us was a fucking amazing mistake? So many possibilities.

"...shouldn't have happened," he finishes.

He can say that again. It shouldn't have happened. I should have known better.

Ryan clears his throat. "You are a—"

"Thief?" I offer.

His head ticks, agreeing while trying not to agree. "A witness. My witness," he says. "I should have...I should have known better. It was my job—it *is* my job—to look out for you, to protect you, and I'm sorry I didn't. I'm sorry."

"*We* should have known better," I say.

"Maybe, but you're not a fed."

"And I thank God every day that's true."

Ryan straightens. "You don't have much faith in law enforcement, do you?"

"I don't have *any* faith in law enforcement."

"Because you're a thief?"

"Well, that certainly doesn't help."

"Then why?"

Maybe we can go back to discussing our doomed fling. I shake my head. "It doesn't matter."

"I think it does."

"You also thought sleeping with me was a good idea, so what do you know?" I say. "It doesn't matter, Ryan. Not to the case. Not to anything. Let it go."

Ryan looks sad now. I think we have achieved acceptance.

Someone knocks on the door, and I glance at it. Lew must be here.

Ryan walks away. I grab the remote and turn up the volume. The three women are now sitting in armchairs discussing anti-aging beauty tips. From the corner of my eye, I watch Lew enter the apartment.

"Everything okay here?" he asks.

"It's fine," Ryan says.

I smile. It's kind of nice that he's such a shitty liar. I never have to wonder if he's telling the truth.

Lew nods. "Skye?"

I look at him. "It's all good."

There's a moment where the only sound is daytime talk show chatter.

"Uh-huh," Lew says. "Well? What did Leo have for us?"

"Got an address," Ryan says. "Apparently, the chatter is promising."

"All right, then," Lew says. "So…who's up for some surveillance?"

36

EXCEPT FOR THE PART WHERE I have to sit with two other people in a windowless van with no fresh air and a weird smell, running surveillance is a lot like planning a job. Only way more restrictive and incredibly boring.

Ryan and Lew sit with their backs to me, studying a pair of monitors intensely, like they're watching a riveting movie with endless action instead of what I'm pretty sure is the most boring street in all of Boston.

This set-up will only get us so far. Recording the people entering and exiting the building will only tell us so much. It's a goddamn restaurant, for crying out loud, chosen for the exact purpose of people walking in and out. And there's been plenty of that. People going in and leaving shortly thereafter with takeout. None of them, however, have been the three men for which we're actually looking. We need to go inside. Everything's happening inside those damn walls.

The guys probably can't go inside. They would need a warrant or probable cause. I, on the other hand, don't need either of those things. I just need an unwatched entrance. A building this size must have at least one.

Ryan and Lew won't go for that, though. They'll just trot out the line about not putting me at risk and maybe utter some bullshit about how the plan is completely illegal.

So maybe I don't ask them. Maybe I just go. They're so engrossed in the world's worst reality show, they may not notice I'm gone until it's too late.

Worth a try.

I stand. They don't notice. I inch toward the door. They don't notice. I ease the handle down. Ryan points to something on one of the monitors and Lew leans in to take a closer look. I open the door and slip out, then close it as softly as I can. Apparently, they don't notice because neither of them comes after me.

One thing I did learn from my time in the van is where the cameras' boundaries are. I stay well out of their range as I cross the street and approach the building from the rear, stopping on a corner to look over the scene. No one's standing guard on the loading dock. There seems to be a lack of obvious security cameras, too, but that doesn't seem right. Even if it is just a mom-and-pop place, they must have a camera somewhere. It's just hidden better than most.

But regardless of where a camera may or may not be, I have to make a decision. The longer I stand here, the greater the chance that Ryan and Lew will notice my absence. If I'm going inside, I need to do it now.

I move toward the back door, keeping my head ducked as much as possible. If there are cameras, they hopefully won't get a good look at me. When I reach the door, I try the handle, but it doesn't budge. That would have been too easy. I get out my brand-new lock pick set and work the lock.

As soon as it gives way, I step inside and close the door behind me. I walk down a short corridor into an industrial kitchen. A surprisingly empty kitchen, given how many take-out bags have left this establishment. A front, then. At least today.

The double doors which lead to the dining room have little round windows in them, and I walk up to take a look. A few people sit at tables, obviously bored, but none of them are the three men from the Skyreach. Maybe they're not here. Or maybe they're somewhere else in this place.

I back away from the doors and turn around. Where's the manager's office? I find another hallway, which leads past an employee locker room and bathroom, then through a storage room filled with nonperishables and sundries a restaurant would need if it wasn't always a front, or at least wanted to look that way.

And a staircase. I take it up to the second floor. There's a landing at the top and a door with a frosted glass window. I try the doorknob, but it doesn't open. I get out the lock picks again.

I open the door to see an office. No people. Desk, loveseat, filing cabinet. Framed pictures of Fenway, Gillette, and the Garden on the wall, not arranged in any discernible pattern. I ease inside and quietly close the door behind me. There's bound to be something here. I just need to find it.

I start with the desk, looking over the papers scattered across its surface. Beneath the food order forms and employee schedules is a calendar with notes scribbled on it. None of it means anything to me until I see *Skyreach* written almost illegibly in one of the boxes. The date is the same as when I was sent there. One night only.

Maybe this is the place after all.

After a fruitless search of the desk drawers, I move on to the filing cabinet. Three drawers filled with manila folders containing what looks like personnel files and tax records. Everything looks, to the best of my knowledge, legit.

That leaves the pictures. If I were a hidden wall safe, where would I be?

There's nothing behind either Fenway or the Garden, so that leaves Gillette. I remove the frame and find a wall safe with a combination dial behind it. Not even a fancy safe. Just a boring, run-of-the-mill variety. I smile. This is normal. This is something I can do. In my sleep, even.

I press my ear to the safe and get to work. It's not much more of a challenge than picking the locks. That's a surprise. And a little embarrassing. These guys are supposed to be master criminals. I could have pulled this job when I was ten. Hell, *Leo* could have pulled this job when he was ten.

Which doesn't make sense. The gray ghost is better than this, better than cheap locks, no cameras, the name of the goddamn *building* written on a desktop calendar, and a safe a two-year-old could crack. So what did he do? Outsource to some locals? But why these locals? It was a last-minute, one-night-only job. Maybe he was as pressed for time as Dead Ed. Any thief in a storm, or whatever. Or maybe using them was his way of insulating himself and his organization. After all, the FBI is currently sitting outside of this building, not wherever he's hiding.

I open the safe and search the contents inside. Two physical ledgers. One with the real numbers, one cooked, I would wager. If I had a camera, I would take pictures of the pages for the guys to analyze later. I could just take the books with me, but they're bulky and their absence would be noticed the moment someone opened the safe. Best to leave them here, maybe.

I glance back in the safe. Blending in with the dark interior is a flash drive. What are the odds it's the same drive I was hired to steal before? Given my string of especially shitty luck, they're probably not great, but if this drive was secured in a safe, there must be *something* worth protecting on it. I take it out and slide it into my bra.

The sound of creaking floorboards catches my attention. Someone's coming.

Shit.

I shove the books back inside the safe, close the door without locking it, and put the picture back in place. Now me.

Where can I hide? Under the desk? Behind the office door? Just throw myself out a window and hope for the best?

Behind the door is closest, so I scramble into place and put my hand on the switchblade in my pocket. I hold my breath as the door opens and someone steps inside.

"Skye?" Ryan whispers.

I release the knife and peek around the door. "What are you doing here?"

"What are *you* doing here?" he hisses. "You're supposed to be in the van."

I step out. "Well, so are you. Are you even allowed to be in here? Don't you need a warrant or something?"

"I'm here looking for my protected witness who can't seem to stay out of trouble," he says. "Now let's get out of here before the wrong people find us."

Someone whistles, and Ryan steps back to look into the hallway. He moves toward me then, using his arm to herd me back. Lew rushes into the office and closes the door.

"They're coming," he says. "We need another way out."

That leaves the windows. I go to the closest and look out. "There's a lip. We can make it around the corner and climb down from there."

Lew nods. "Good. Let's go."

Someone hits the door. Lew throws his shoulder against it and grabs the knob to keep it closed. Whoever's on the other side isn't deterred. Maybe I should have stayed in the van.

Lew looks at me. "Is there a safe in here?"

"Maybe."

"Is it already open?"

"Possibly."

"Skye," Ryan says. "Do it."

As I remove the picture and reopen the safe, Ryan opens the window.

"Do you want me to take anything out of it?" I ask Lew.

"No. Just leave it open." He tosses a black billfold to Ryan. "Get her out of here. I'll buy you as much time as I can."

What? No. He's not serious, is he?

Ryan tugs on my arm, but I don't move.

"Go," Lew says. "Skye, go. Now."

Ryan drags me to the window. "Dammit, Skye. We gotta go."

"But Lew—"

"He'll be fine. Now go."

I climb through the window and cling to the brick as I inch my way right to make room for Ryan. He follows me and promptly swears as he fumbles to keep his grip and footing and balance.

"This is not a ledge," he says.

"I said 'lip', not 'ledge'. Now concentrate, or you're going to fall."

I coach him through where to put his hands and feet, and we work our way along the wall and around the corner. The fire escape is all the way at the other end of the building, and we're coming up on another set of windows. We can't very well go past those. Not without knowing who or what may be inside. I glance down. It won't tickle, but we shouldn't break anything or die.

I stop.

"What?" Ryan asks.

"You're going to hate this part," I say.

"Why? What do you want me to do now?"

"Let go," I reply, then do so.

37

I HIT THE GROUND, TREMORS running up my legs. My hand presses against the pavement to keep myself upright. I look up. Ryan's still on the lip, looking at me. Inside the restaurant, alarms are being raised. People are yelling. They will find us. Especially the dumbass still clinging to the outside of a damn building.

"Let go!" I say.

Ryan shakes his head but does it. When he lands, he starts to fall back, but I step behind him and prop him up.

He looks at me over his shoulder. "Okay?"

I nod. "You?"

Doors open. Ryan spins around and pushes me in the opposite direction. "Go, go, go."

I am no stranger to running away from people chasing me. I have a finely tuned fight-or-flight reflex, but this time, it's wrong. It's the right thing to do—I think—but it's still wrong. Lew stayed behind. We can't just leave him there, but here we are, running away. We don't even go back to the van. We just run, looking for some distance between us and our pursuers, and maybe a nice crowd in which to get lost.

Once we're on Washington Street, we stop running. Then Ryan stops moving altogether. That's no good. Walking's okay, but we need to keep moving. I grab his hand and pull him along.

"Skye, wait," Ryan says. "Stop. We gotta stop."

Stopping is a terrible idea. We should really keep moving, but Ryan needs to get his shit together first. I can't keep dragging his distracted ass through the city. Looking around, I steer us down Causeway Street and toward North Station.

On our way in, an older man is walking out, putting what looks like a flip phone into his coat pocket. An easy mark with an ancient phone. That could be useful. I don't have one, and who knows if Ryan has his, and we may need to make a call at some point. As we pass one another, I use my free hand to lift the phone and tuck it away in my own pocket.

Once inside, I keep moving until I see an alcove and shove Ryan into it. At the other end is a door marked 'Authorized Personnel Only' with a keypad lock. Not impossible to hack but it would take a while. Okay, so this won't be a way out. Just a temporary resting space. Here's hoping the bad guys don't find us first.

If they even are still chasing us. It's possible we lost them. It's also possible they declined to pursue us because they have Lew. A bird in the hand is worth two in the wind or however that expression goes. We are in the wind, and they have one in their hands.

They have Lew. Goddammit.

"Fuck," Ryan says. "Just…fuck."

I have nothing to add. That is the perfect sentiment for this situation. This is why I like working alone because—Jesus Christ—what am I supposed to do with knowing that Lew's probably having the shit beat out of him right now because I didn't stay in the goddamn van?

Ryan punches the wall. "Fuck! They're gonna kill him."

I move to the other end of the alcove to keep an eye on the crowd. "No, they won't."

"How do you know that?"

I don't know that. But the alternative is believing they will kill him or maybe already have. I can't think that. I can't live with that guilt.

"Because they don't want him," I say. "They'll use him for leverage to get what they do want."

"They want *you*, Skye."

"I know. You should give me to them. We should go back right now and make the trade."

"They'll definitely kill you."

I don't see the problem with that. I don't know how Ryan does. All his problems would be solved then, wouldn't they?

"No, I'm not doing that," he says. He drags his hand through his hair and looks at the ceiling. He closes his eyes and breathes deep. Exhaling slowly, he opens his eyes. "Okay. We need…Shit. I don't have my phone."

I take out the phone I acquired earlier and offer it to him.

"You have a phone?" he asks.

I shrug. "I do now."

He stares at me for a moment, then his face performs an impressive array of gymnastics as he realizes what I said and what it means.

"Are you serious?" he says then.

"Never hurts to be prepared," I say. "Do you want to make a call or not?"

Ryan sighs and takes the phone. He types in a number and walks a few steps away to converse with someone. Jonas, I would guess. Who else is left?

"Yeah," he says, walking back toward me, "we'll meet you there."

He ends the call and starts to hand me the phone but freezes. Probably remembering it's not actually *my* phone so much as stolen property. I take the phone, remove the number Ryan called from the log, and wipe it down before tossing it in the nearest trash receptacle.

"Where are we going?" I ask.

38

WE GO BACK TO THE loft. Jonas is standing outside the door when we arrive. It's a mark of how shitty the situation is when I actually feel some relief to see him.

"What's going on?" he asks.

Ryan shakes his head. "Not out here. Come inside."

Ryan unlocks the door and the three of us enter. I remove the flash drive from my bra and set it on the island. That goddamn thing better be worth it.

"Wait...where's Morgan?" Jonas asks. "Wasn't he with you?"

Ryan sighs. "They got him."

"Jesus Christ." Jonas points to me. "What did she do?"

"I didn't do anything," I say.

I walk to the bathroom and close myself inside. Shedding my jacket and casting it aside, I sit on the floor with the door against my back. No one follows me. They have other things to do—other, more pressing concerns with which to deal. I can't hear what they're saying, but it's obvious what they're talking about. What went wrong. What to do now. How to get their man back. What to do with the thief who let it happen.

I didn't do anything. It's true. I watched a man get shot in the head without doing anything to stop it. I watched Lew get taken down without doing anything to stop it. I watched him sacrifice himself to protect me without doing one goddamn thing to prevent it. I didn't even say *no, stop, don't do that*. I didn't tell him I wasn't worth it. I didn't do anything, and now they have Lew.

And the FBI has me.

I need a phone. I need to contact Leo. He found them once; he can find them again. If we can make contact, I can arrange for a trade. Me, for Lew. It'll work. They don't want him. They want me. If I play it right, Ryan and the FBI won't need to know. There's time. They'll have to tell Nia what happened, and then they'll have to deal with the ensuing volcano of rage. That won't be quick. I can do this. As soon as they leave, I'll go. It doesn't matter if agents or cops or the damn National Guard are watching the building. Even if they see me leave, I can lose them. I can—

Someone knocks on the bathroom door.

"Skye?" Ryan says, knocking again.

I stand and open the door. "What?"

"Are you..." He reaches for me but stops short, his hand staying in midair. "Are you all right?"

Why is he asking that? I shake my head. "I'm fine."

"You're crying."

Am not. Am I? I turn to look in the mirror. Well, shit. I am crying. When did that start?

Ryan comes into the bathroom and closes the door. "Skye—"

"I'm fine." I wipe my hands across my cheeks.

He looks unconvinced. Probably the tears. His hand rises, falls, then rises again. Torn between comforting me and hating me. I don't mind the hate. That's familiar. That's comfortable. Deserved, even.

"I'm sorry about Lew," I say. "I'm sorry I didn't..."

"It's not your fault," Ryan says, but it's lacking any true commitment. It's just something he's said a million times before to persons of interest or witnesses or whatever I am. It's muscle memory, his lips, teeth, and tongue forming the words without any thought or meaning behind it.

It's okay, though. He shouldn't offer me comfort. He shouldn't. I don't deserve it.

I don't deserve it, but I want it anyway. Need it. Crave it. Maybe I could just take it. I'm a thief; that's what we do.

I step toward him, take his face in my hands, and kiss him. His arms wrap around me as he returns the kiss, deepens it. We're kissing as though our lives depend upon it, but it's not enough.

I need more.

My hands drop to fumble with the button and zipper on my jeans.

Ryan pulls back slightly to give me room but keeps his forehead against mine. "What are you doing?"

"Taking off my clothes," I say, easing my jeans over my hips. "Join me, won't you?"

He hesitates, then steps back and reaches for his belt. I remove my shoes and jeans before stripping off my panties and shirt. Ryan picks me up, turns to press me against the door, and finds his way inside me.

He stills and lowers his head to my shoulder.

I run my fingers over his hair and cup the back of his neck. "Ryan. *Please.*"

Lifting his head, he looks at me. Through me. He takes my hand from his neck and pins it against the door near my head.

"Please," I whisper.

He starts to move. I nod. Yes. Yes, this is what I want. What I *need.* I wrap my legs around him and put my free arm around his neck. He looks away, keeping his head close to mine as his lips graze my mouth and neck.

Faster now. Harder. This won't last long. Ryan lets go of my hand, but I keep it against the door to brace myself. The wave is building. Close. So damn close. Just a little more. I tilt my head back and close my eyes as the wave reaches its crest.

Soon after, Ryan achieves his own release. But even after we're both spent, neither of us move. I'm not sure either of us can move. Hell, I can barely *breathe.* I open my eyes, not looking at anything at all, as I wait to see if my breathing will return to normal. Ryan's head drops to my shoulder, and he buries his face in the crook of my neck. His breath on my skin suggests I'm not the only one struggling for oxygen.

"Skye?" Ryan gasps. "Are you…"

I am. I feel *better,* which makes me feel worse. Fuck.

"Put me down," I say.

I unhook my legs and he carefully lowers me to the floor. I keep both hands on the door and lean back, unsure my legs can hold me up.

Ryan runs his hand over his face. "We shouldn't have done that."

No, we shouldn't have. I feel like shit again. Ryan looks like he feels the same way. He stands motionless for a moment, then nods and starts to right himself.

He looks at me as he zips his jeans. "Get dressed. We need to go talk to Nia."

I shake my head. "She won't want to see me. I'll stay here."

"If I leave you here, you'll be gone when I come back."

Yes. Yes, I will. "What's wrong with that?"

"I can't just let you…" He sighs. "Dammit, Skye. You know damn well why I can't do that."

"Because I'm your witness. Because protecting me is your job."

"Yes."

"And for no other reason."

I don't know why I say it. I know what this is and what it isn't, and it will never be anything more than this: an angry, frustrated coupling against a goddamn door.

Ryan picks up his shirt and pulls it on. "No," he says, not looking away. "No other reason."

Jesus Christ. A bullet to the chest would hurt less.

I nod. "I'll be right out."

39

INSTEAD OF GOING TO NIA, we end up at a high rise in the heart of the city. Jonas takes the lead, and Ryan follows close behind me. Entirely too close, considering our particular circumstances. I'm not sure why he's being so clingy until I see the FBI sign on the wall near the elevators. I stop short, but Ryan puts his hand on my back and gently pushes me onward.

This is an FBI field office. Lew's capture has officially ended the unsanctioned investigation.

The office is a beehive of activity, little worker agents in dark-colored suits all doing whatever it is they do when one of their own has been taken. Ryan ushers me into a conference room and directs me to wait. I walk around the oval table in the center and stand with my back to the windows overlooking the city. I've seen the skyline. I don't need to see it now. It's more important to watch the door.

After a while, both Ryan and Jonas join me. Ryan paces at the opposite end of the room. Jonas sits at the table, drumming his fingers on the mahogany surface. What are they doing? Why are they just...waiting? Shouldn't they be doing something? Like I'm one to talk. Each second that passes puts us farther away from Lew, but thank God Ryan and I took the time to fuck against a bathroom door.

Nia barges into the room. "Where the fuck is he? What did you fucking do?"

Maybe that's why they were waiting. Jonas stands. Ryan stops pacing and looks at her.

"Nia," he says, "I am sorry—"

"I don't want to hear that you're fucking sorry, Ryan," she says. "I want to know where my goddamn husband is."

"He was captured," Ryan says. "They moved him. We don't know where he is now."

Nia doesn't move. She doesn't yell. Her hands grip the back of one of the chairs. For support? In preparation of picking it up and throwing it at someone? I can't tell. This is the moment before Vesuvius explodes and Pompeii is buried by lava and ash.

"I am pregnant, Ryan," she says, her voice low and calm.

"We will get him back. I promise," Ryan says. "You won't have to raise this child alone."

Nia's eyes widen. "Fuck that. I am not talking about that," she says. She's not as calm now. "I'm saying that if you make me take my pregnant ass out there to get Lew back on my own that I will kill you. And if you thought I was going to kill you the last time, it will be *nothing* compared to how hard I will kill you this time.

"Because this time, I'm hormonal. This time, my ankles are swollen. At least I think they're swollen. I don't know because I can't remember the last time I *saw* my ankles. I have to pee every ten minutes, and I have barely slept in months, so I swear to God that if you make me do your goddamn job, I will fucking *murder* you, and no jury will ever convict me because no one likes FBI agents that much!"

"You need to calm down," Jonas says.

Shit. Even I know that's the wrong thing to say. Nia lunges at him, but Ryan intercepts her before she makes contact. He holds her close and murmurs something in her ear. She continues to fight against him and he continues to talk to her until she slumps against his chest. The reprieve only lasts seconds before she shoves him away.

"Agent Jonas? Agent Ryan?" a new voice says.

Standing at the door is a young female agent holding out a phone. Jonas walks out first. Ryan keeps his hands in a defensive position, as though he expects Nia to go off the handle again. She doesn't. As soon as Jonas is clear, Ryan makes eye contact with me. He jerks his head toward Nia and drops his hands before walking out of the room. The door closes behind him, leaving Nia and me alone. She walks to the windows and looks out over the city.

What the hell does Ryan expect me to do here? I'm just as responsible for Lew's capture. More responsible, even. Does he really think Nia will be interested in talking to me? In listening to me?

"So," I say, "do you assault a lot of federal agents?"

"Only the ones who deserve it."

I nod. "Maybe you should sit down. The stress—"

"I'm fine."

"Nia, you can't—"

Her head whips in my direction. "Don't fucking tell me what I can't do."

I straighten. The FBI may be afraid of her, but I'm not the FBI. "You can't go after Lew. Not like this."

"I'm not helpless."

"No, but you're...very pregnant." I glance down. I can't see her ankles, either, but I add, "Swollen ankles and all."

She shakes her head. "I can't leave it to them. I won't."

She goes back to staring out the window. I believe her. She won't leave it to them. I can practically hear her brain formulating a rescue plan and how many goddamn bobby pins she'll need to pull it off. Lew put his life on the line for me. Because of me. I sure as hell can't repay that by letting Nia do the same.

I glance at the door to make sure it's still closed. "You don't have to. I'll do it. I'll get him back."

Nia turns around. "How?"
"I'll give them what they want."
"What's that?"
I swallow. "Me."

40

NIA REFUSES TO LEAVE. I'M not given the option. I stand in the corner while she sits at the head of the conference table. Together, we watch the small team of agents at the other end of the room try to figure out what the hell they're going to do next.

I also need to figure out what *I'm* going to do next. If I'm going to get Lew back, I need to ditch the FBI. Their methods will waste time, time Lew may not have. So I guess that means my first task is to get out of here unnoticed. It shouldn't be too difficult. They're so distracted by the Lew situation, I could get away with a lot of things. Getting out of this room and this building will be child's play. They'll notice my absence eventually, but with a little luck, it'll be too late by then.

Nia looks at me. "Will you be doing anything at any fucking point?"

"I told you I would."

"Yes, but so far, all I've seen you do is a fantastic fucking impression of a potted plant."

"Anyone ever tell you you swear too much?"

"Every goddamn day," she says. "So?"

Ryan walks out of the room. Jonas is deep in conversation with a couple of other agents.

I step out of the corner. "I'm working on it."

"Work harder," she mutters as I pass.

The other agents don't notice me slip from the room. Ryan is walking away, head angled toward the floor as he rubs the back of his neck. I catch up with him in an empty hallway.

"I want to help," I say.

He turns around. "You've done enough already. Go back inside and stay there."

"I can help," I say. "I know I'm not an agent—"

Ryan scoffs. "You're right about that."

"—but I'm also not Nia."

"I'm not so sure about that."

Strangling him would be counterproductive, so I roll my eyes and sigh. "Has she ever lied to you?"

Ryan shakes his head.

"Then I guess I'm not her," I say. "I can help you, Ryan. I have certain...skills that could be useful in these circumstances. Let me help."

"No."

"Just so we're clear—you saying 'no' won't keep me from getting involved."

"A jail cell might."

Yes, that might do it. I've never attempted to escape from jail, but if he were to arrest me, I'd have to work it out damn quick.

"Then again, it might not," I say.

He studies me. Thinking. Brooding. Hating me, maybe. Because of me, his family's in danger. Why wouldn't he hate that?

"You know I can help you," I say. "Do you really want to risk your family because you're mad at me?"

"Mad at you?"

"You can't possibly claim that you're *not* mad at me."

"No, I'm saying *mad* doesn't even cover it," Ryan says. "They have him because of you."

"I know."

"If you had just stayed in the goddamn van—"

"I know. Okay? I know!" I say. "I know this is my fault, and now I want to fix it."

"You can't."

"Jesus Christ, Ryan. Stop this. I am a weapon in your arsenal. Use me."

Ryan puts his hands on his hips. "How would you have done it?"

"Done what?"

"If I had left you in the loft, what would you have done next?" he asks. "I know you were planning something. Tell me what."

"Track down the gray ghost and arrange a trade."

"How?"

"I was going to ask Leo for help. He found the address before. Whoever gave it to him could maybe help me find the ghost himself."

"Leo could do that?" Ryan asks. "He could track them down and arrange a meet?"

"Trade, Ryan. *Trade,*" I say. "They don't want to meet. They're not interested in talking terms. They just want me."

"Well, I can't give you to them."

"Yes, you can," I say. "And what's more, you should. Use the trade to find them. Use it to get Lew out of there. Then use it to take them down. Or out. Or…I don't know. Just use it. Use me."

"And when they kill you?"

"Then they kill me," I say. "How is that a problem?"

Ryan shakes his head. "I am not talking about this with you again. Goddammit, Skye, you're wasting time."

"*You're* wasting time! I told you what to do back at the train station, but instead you just keep moving us farther and farther away. I'm trying to get us back there."

"You're going to stay out of it," Ryan says. "And this is the last time I will say that. If I have to say it again, you're going to be in handcuffs."

"I can get out of handcuffs."

"Then I will put you in jail."

"I can get out of jail."

"Then I will put you in the deepest, darkest hole I can find on the face of the earth in order to keep you out of the god-damn way," Ryan says. "Don't push me anymore on this, Skye. Don't do it."

Okay. This is getting us nowhere. Time for something more drastic. I hold up my hands in surrender.

"Go back to the conference room and stay there," he says.

He turns around and walks away. I let him get a few steps ahead before silently moving up behind him and kicking the back of his right knee. He goes down, putting his hands out to break his fall, but looks back at me.

"What the—?"

I kick him in the face, and he slumps to the floor, unconscious.

"Sorry," I say and then walk away.

41

I DON'T HAVE A LOT of time. I didn't have a lot of time even before I assaulted an FBI agent, but now it's even worse. As soon as Ryan wakes up, or the FBI realizes I'm gone—whichever happens first—they're going to come after me. And they're going to know where to start looking. It's not as though I have a lot of options at this point.

I use the back entrance to The Thieves' Den. The kitchen staff nods at me before returning to their work. Leo's office is empty, the light off. I start toward the bar but step out of the way when one of the bar-backs comes into the kitchen with a tub of dishes.

"Upstairs," he says to me.

I thank him and go back outside and use the fire escape to access Leo's apartment. The living room is dark, but there's a light on in the bedroom. I use Angie's knife to carefully jimmy open the window and slip inside.

Two glasses and a bottle of wine sit on the counter. A trail of clothing leads from the kitchen to the bedroom. Leo's going to be more than pissed, but there's no time to wait for them to finish.

I knock on the bedroom door before pushing it open. "Hey, sorry to interrupt, but I really need to interrupt."

There's a tangle of flesh and bedding and indignant groans and swearing. A polite person would look away, but I look right at the bed. Leo looks back at me, murder in his eyes. His playmate is shocked, but cute.

"What the fuck, Maggie?" Leo says.

"I need to talk to you. Put some clothes on." I point behind me. "I'll be out here."

I close the bedroom door and go to the kitchen to fetch the bottle of Ketel One he keeps in the cabinet above the fridge. I get a glass and pour a decent amount of vodka in it. Just enough to take the edge off but not enough that I'll be too drunk to get Lew back once I track him down. If I can track him down.

I hear the shower start, but Leo comes out from the bedroom, wearing boxer briefs and the same pissed-off expression as before. He moves through the apartment, gathering the discarded clothing.

"He's cute," I say, sitting at the table. "What's his name?"

Leo glares at me. "Jesus Christ, Skye."

"His parents set him up with that one."

"I'm going to kill you," Leo says.

"Well, you're going to have to get in line," I reply. "Because there's at least one criminal organization and one law enforcement agency ahead of you."

"Oh no, no, no—I've known you the longest, so I get to jump the line."

"Normally, I would agree that that is your right, but I'm going to need you to relinquish that claim for the next twenty-four to forty-eight hours. Maybe longer."

"How much longer?"

"Possibly forever."

"Why? What the hell happened?"

I swallow a mouthful of vodka. "I'm really sorry about this, but you have to send Jesus home. I need your help."

Leo sighs. "Fuck, Skye."

I nod. "If that's what you have to say now, just wait until I tell you what happened."

"What happened?" Leo asks.

"Lew's being held captive by murder-happy mobsters, and also the FBI is probably on their way here. Or will be soon."

"Why?"

"In addition to getting one agent kidnapped, I may have assaulted another."

"Define 'assaulted'."

"Knocked unconscious."

"Intentionally?"

"Yes."

"Every breath you take somehow makes my life just that much harder," Leo says.

"Cheer up. That might not be an issue much longer."

After glowering at me once again, Leo walks out of the room. I finish my vodka and am pouring myself more when he and Jesus emerge from the bedroom fully clothed. Jesus does not look impressed. I can't blame him for that.

"Sorry about this, Jesus," I say. "It's nothing personal. I think you're cute together."

Leo rolls his eyes and walks Jesus to the door. He apologizes, then kisses him fiercely before they part ways. Leo closes and locks the door behind him.

"I suppose you used the window," he says.

"I didn't have time for the chain." I gesture toward the bedroom. "I didn't know you'd have company."

"We're not all loners like you." Leo sits across from me and takes the vodka. "Tell me what happened."

"We went to run surveillance on that address you gave us. Only the FBI's version of surveillance involves sitting in a van and not actually doing anything, and—"

"And you got bored."

"I decided to be proactive."

"Because you were bored."

"Fine. I was bored," I say. "But sitting in the stupid van didn't tell us who was actually in the restaurant, so I snuck out of the van and went inside to find out. Ryan and Lew came after me and it turns out that, yeah, it was the right place. Lew stayed behind to give Ryan and me time to get away."

Leo nods. "And the assault?"

"I want to track down the guys again and arrange a trade. Ryan doesn't want that to happen. I had to get around him somehow."

"So you knocked him unconscious."

"Yes."

Leo drinks straight from the bottle. "Arrange a trade," he says after he swallows. "You mean you for Lew?"

"What else would I mean?"

"They'll kill you."

"Everyone keeps saying that, like I don't already know." I put my glass on the table. "I am aware of the consequences, Leo. Help me track down these guys. Agree to whatever they want, but only after you get proof of life."

"Do these guys know they kidnapped an FBI agent?"

"I don't know, but just in case they don't, maybe don't tell them that."

"You really want me to do this?" Leo asks.

"I *need* you to do this."

"Skye, come on," he says. "Forget the FBI. You're here now. You're free now. We could just go."

"Go where?"

"Wherever we want. Somewhere there aren't people trying to hunt you down and kill you."

"You have a life here, Leo. You have the bar, Jesus—"

"His name isn't Jesus. And it was just a first date."

Liar. I nod toward the door. "That wasn't a first date kiss, Leo. I know what you're trying to do, and I appreciate that you would do it for me, but I need you to stop wasting time and start making calls."

He sighs and reaches for his phone. "You should eat something. If you're going to give yourself over to mobsters who want to kill you, you shouldn't do it on an empty stomach."

Sounds like a fair trade. I nod and go back to the kitchen. While he starts making calls and pacing around the apartment, I make a peanut butter sandwich. Leo wanders into the kitchen, phone to his ear, and takes some carrot sticks out of the fridge. He puts them in front of me, points at them, then at me, before walking back out. I return the carrots to the fridge. I'll be more damned than I already am if carrots are going to be my last meal.

When I finish my sandwich, I swap out my jacket for a hoodie from Leo's closet and put it on, transferring both Angie's knife and my lock picks to the kangaroo pocket. I look out the bedroom window. No sign of the FBI on the street. I go to the living room and look out that window as well. Still no angry people in cheap dark suits and sunglasses. Does that mean they haven't yet noticed unconscious Ryan in the hallway? Maybe they're not interested in looking for me yet because they have one missing agent and another unconscious.

They'll come eventually, though. Regardless of reason, I did assault Ryan. The Bureau won't let that slide. *Jonas* won't let it slide.

"I have the girl you're looking for. I want to make a trade," Leo says.

I turn to look at him. This is it.

"Yeah," he says. "Her for him."

I roll my eyes. Why is the concept of a trade so difficult for everyone to grasp?

"No, I want proof of life," Leo continues. "You don't get her without it."

I hold my breath. Please, let there be proof. Please, let Lew be alive.

Leo lowers the phone. "One question."

"Name of the safe house," I say, and Leo relays the request.

"Loft of squalor," he says a moment later.

I close my eyes and nod. He's alive. Lew is alive. For now.

"Okay," Leo says, sitting at the table. He catches my eye and mimes writing on something. "Name the time and place."

I grab a pad of paper and a pen from the kitchen counter and give them to him. He scribbles something down.

"She'll be there. Make sure he is," Leo says. "You let him go and she's all yours. If he's not there—and not in one piece—the deal's off, and you'll never find her."

Leo ends the call. He rips off the top sheet and hands it to me. Faneuil Hall Marketplace. Tomorrow. Right smack in the middle of the day. It'll be crawling with people by then.

"At least it's somewhere familiar," Leo says.

"What do you think?" I say. "Shooter on a rooftop?"

"They only want you dead. They don't care how it happens," Leo says. "They get you to walk out in the open, take the shot, and walk away."

And then they kill Lew because they have a thing against leaving witnesses behind.

"Think Lew will be there?" I ask.

"I do. They'll need him to draw you out, and it'll need to be him, too. They couldn't use a hooded decoy or anything like that. It'll stick out too much," Leo says. "But once they see you?"

All bets will be off. I get a bullet in the brain, Lew gets knifed in the kidney, and we both die in the middle of Faneuil Hall. The tourism board will be so excited.

I sigh. "How do I get him back alive?"

"Maybe you don't. Maybe you can't."

"I still have to try. He's Ryan's family and Nia's everything, and—"

"And that means you have to kill yourself?"

"And Lew gave himself up to protect *me*," I say. "I'm not leaving that debt unpaid. I'm going to get him back."

"And with what plan are you going to do that?"

"I don't know yet."

I glance at the clock on the wall. Eighteen hours until the exchange. If they're planning to shoot me on sight—and why wouldn't they?—then I need to find Lew before the exchange. I pick up the paper. I know where they're going to be. Or at least I know where one guy with one decent rifle will be. How can I use that? Start at the end point and work my way back? It's not a great plan, or even much of a plan, but it is a plan.

Kind of.

"What about Ryan? Or the rest of the FBI?" Leo says. "Can they help?"

"Ryan's unconscious, and the rest of the FBI's gonna be mad at me about that," I say. "I'm doing this alone."

"You are capable of doing a lot of things on your own, but this is not one of them," Leo says. "If you try to do this alone, you'll get yourself killed. You need some kind of backup."

"No. They'll be expecting me to have backup. So I'm not going to do that."

Leo laughs. "That is the dumbest thing I have ever heard, and I have known you for years."

"Well, trying to be smart about things isn't getting me anywhere except in more trouble," I say. "Maybe it's time for a change."

"Yes, you being dead will be quite the change."

I stand. "Be sure to remember me fondly."

"I'll remember my hoodie fondly since I'm never going to see that again."

"You might. When the FBI finds my body, maybe they'll ask you to confirm identity."

Leo stills. He shakes his head. "Suddenly, this game isn't so funny anymore."

"When was it ever funny?" I say. "Take care of yourself, Leo."

I force myself to move toward the window and open it. Taking a deep breath, I start to climb through.

"Skye," Leo says when I'm halfway onto the fire escape. "His name is Linus."

I look at him and smile. "Leo and Linus. Sounds like kismet to me."

"I'd really like to introduce you properly sometime. Make sure I can do that, okay?"

"I can't promise that."

"Then lie to me."

I shake my head. "We don't lie, Leo. Not to each other."

"Lie to me. Just this once. Please, just..." Leo sighs. His eyes are bright and shiny with tears he's trying not to let out. "Tell me you can take care of yourself. Tell me you'll be okay."

I don't want to do it. I don't want to lie to him. The chances that this will be anything other than a one-way mission are so small. Me telling him anything other than that will be false hope. We don't do false hope.

"Skye," he says, his voice close to breaking.

I swallow down some tears of my own. "You're really worried about your hoodie, aren't you?"

"Yeah. I am."

I nod. "Family dinner, Saturday night. You bring Linus. I'll bring the wine."

Leo smiles. "You don't like wine."

"You and Linus do."

"Okay, then," Leo says. "Saturday night. It's a date."

I slip out the window and down the fire escape. I pull the hood over my head and start walking toward my apartment but stop short at the sight of Jonas leaning against his black Crown Vic.

Smarter than the average bear after all.

"Well?" he says. "You arrange a trade?"

"It's done."

"Good." He pushes off the car and opens the driver's side door. He jerks his head toward the passenger's side. "Get in."

42

I DON'T MOVE. "I DON'T have time to be arrested right now. Not if you want Lew back."

"I'm not planning to arrest you. Not yet, anyway," Jonas says. "Get in the car."

"My mother taught me to never get in cars with strangers."

"You don't have a mother."

"I have a mother," I say. "I just don't know who or where she is."

"Heartbreaking," Jonas says. "Now get in the damn car."

"Where are we going?"

Jonas shrugs. "You tell me."

I sure as hell am not going to tell him where I live, but he's clearly not going to go away until I give him something. His car's already pointed north, so I gesture to the street. "Head that way."

I walk around to the passenger's side and get in the car. As soon as I have buckled my seat belt, Jonas pulls into traffic.

"I'm surprised you let me ride up front," I say.

"So am I. You should be in cuffs right now."

Yes, I should. But the fact that Jonas didn't put me in cuffs or in the back of the car, and referred to my plans as a 'trade' and not a 'meet' is encouraging. Or as encouraging as I suspect Jonas ever gets.

"Has he woken up yet?" I ask.

"He has."

"Is he okay?"

"Has a hell of a headache, but he'll survive."

I knew that already. "How mad is he?" I clarify.

Jonas glances at me, then looks back at the road. "Tell me about the trade."

Was I really expecting anything else? I sigh. "I got proof of life, so I told them they could have me if they let Lew go. They agreed. End of story."

"Morgan's okay?"

"He's alive."

Jonas nods. "Where and when is this trade taking place?"

"I can't tell you that."

"Yes, you can."

"No, I can't. I won't. If I tell you where and when this is happening, you'll stake out the place because the FBI *loves* to stake out places. And if you stake out the place, the bad guys will know it, and you'll never get Lew back."

"So I'm just supposed to let you go in there on your own?"

"Yes."

"I'm just supposed to trust that you'll do what you say?"

"Yes."

"I'm supposed to trust a *thief* to—"

"Yes, Jonas. Jesus Christ!" I roll my eyes. "Yes, I am a thief, and yes, I am asking you to trust that I'm going to get Lew back."

Jonas shakes his head. "Ryan won't go for that."

"Which is why I left him unconscious in a hallway."

"Yeah. He didn't like that, either. Neither did I, by the way."

"Which is why I didn't ask either of you before I did it," I say. "I had to do it this way, okay? Ryan wasn't going to arrange the trade, so I did it for him."

"There's nothing to stop them from killing you."

"Do you care about that?"

"I care about getting my agent back. If you walk into their trap, they can kill you, then Morgan."

"I have that covered," I say.

"Do you?"

I don't, but I'm not about to admit that to him. "Don't worry about it. Lew's getting out of this."

"What about you? Are you getting out of this?"

No. No, that's not going to happen. I turn away and discreetly wipe my eyes with the hoodie's sleeve. "How 'bout them Bruins?"

Jonas sighs as he stops for a red light. "Ryan won't like that, either."

Why? He wants to be the one to kill me himself? I glance at Jonas. "What about you?"

"I think Ryan's life—*my* life—would be vastly improved if he had never met you," Jonas says. "But…I don't like what losing you will do to him. He can't admit it at the moment, but it's true. Things would be a lot simpler if you did die."

"So maybe you don't tell him you found me," I say. "Maybe you tell him I wasn't at Leo's."

Jonas looks at me. I concentrate on the road. The light changes, but Jonas doesn't stop staring.

"The light's green," I say.

We don't move. Cars behind us honk. Jonas continues to stare. The honking becomes laying on the horns. Jonas still doesn't move. Cars start pulling around us, the drivers screaming obscenities and flipping us off.

When the light turns back to red, Jonas faces front. He flips on the turn signal and takes a right, pulling into the first available space against the curb and puts the car into park.

He doesn't look at me. "You make this happen, or I will hunt you down and you will *wish* those assholes had killed you."

I already do. "I'll make it happen."

"Here." Jonas reaches into his jacket and pulls out the knife he confiscated from the loft of squalor. He hands it to me. "Now get out of my car."

I add the knife to my stash in the kangaroo pocket and reach for the door handle. "Yes, sir."

Jonas drives away as soon as I close the car door. I pull the hood over my head, check the cross streets, and turn toward home.

43

I HAVEN'T BEEN TO MY apartment since the night I left for the Skyreach. There's no reason to think the gray ghost knows about it. Jay never had the address, and I don't know how else they would have found it. Still, I approach the building carefully, sticking to the shadows on the other side of the street. There's no obvious signs of danger, so I cross the road and head inside.

Skipping the elevator, I take the stairs to the floor and apartment directly above mine. The guy who lives here is at work this time of day, so I pick the door lock to gain entrance and use his living room window to access the fire escape and climb down to my apartment.

It's dark. No sign of life. That's not likely to change. I could keep sitting here, watching nothing happen, or I could get on with it. As Lew's life is still in the balance, getting on with it wins.

Using the knife Jonas returned, I jimmy open the window and slip inside the living room. No lights come on. No one shoots me.

Hooray.

I head to my bedroom, making sure the shades are drawn before turning on the lights.

First up—a wardrobe change. Black leggings, T-shirt, fleece, and sturdy shoes for climbing. What all the best-dressed thieves are wearing this season. And every season. After tying back my hair and concealing it beneath a black knit cap, I pull my tool box out from under my bed to look at the options. All my best tools are probably in some FBI evidence locker by now, but I have others. Not that I know what I'll need for this particular job. I'm new to rescue missions. Weapons would be traditional, but I lack anything other than short, easily concealable blades. Maybe I'll just take my lock picks and a knife or two. Stick with what I know. This is bound to be a one-way mission, regardless of what I bring, so why waste time worrying about it?

Stashing the lock picks in the inside pocket of my fleece, I then exchange Angie's and Colin's knives for a better blade and slide it into the right-side pocket on my leggings. I take a small push knife secured in a necklace sheath and slip it over my head, tucking the knife itself into my bra.

All right. What else?

A headlamp. I have no idea what the light situation will be. Better to have it and not need it than to be fumbling around in the dark.

I'm putting one in my jacket pocket when a door opens. *My* door.

Someone's in my apartment.

Shit.

I rush to the light switch and turn it off. A light comes on in the living room. I take the knife out of my pocket and open the blade. Because that'll be a lot of help against men with guns. I look over my shoulder at the bedroom window. I'll have to go out that way.

"Skye?" Ryan calls. "Are you here?"

What the hell is he doing here? How did he find this place? I walk out of the bedroom and go into the living room.

He's standing near the door. There's a bandage on his head, the skin around it already turning various shades of purple and yellow. He glares at me—if looks could kill, I would be very, very dead—for a moment before his gaze flicks down to the knife in my hand.

"You do like blades," he says.

"They have their uses." I close the blade and slide the knife back into its pocket. "What are you doing here?"

"You assaulted an FBI agent."

"Did I?"

"You did."

I lean against the wall. "Oh. Are you here to arrest me, then?"

"Any reason I shouldn't?"

"You need me to get Lew back," I say. "I know where the exchange is happening. You don't. And even if you did know—which, again, you don't—you would still need me. I'm the one they want."

"They can't have you."

"I already told them they could. Can't take it back now," I say. "This is the right thing to do here, Ryan. You know it is."

"What would you know about doing the right thing?"

"Only what I've read in books," I say. "If I don't show up, they will kill Lew. Nothing else matters here. If you want a chance—just a *chance*—to get Lew back, I have to be at that exchange."

Ryan sits on the couch and starts to lower his head into his hands. He stops before any contact can be made and tips his head back instead.

"You should go home," I say.

"You can't do this alone."

"I can't do this with you. Look at you! You should be resting at your own house or the loft of squalor. Even a hospital or a park bench somewhere. I don't care where you go, but you're not coming with me."

"You're not going without me."

"Big talk for a guy who's probably seeing two of me right now."

He lifts his head and looks at me. "You didn't hit me that hard."

"I didn't hit you at all."

"You kicked me in the face."

"That's a serious allegation. Do you have any proof to back up your claim?"

"You mean besides your fucking bootprint on my cheek?" Ryan says. "Cut the bullshit, Skye. I don't want to play games here."

"Neither do I. You're not going to arrest me, and I'm not going to tell you anything, so—"

"I don't need you to tell me anything."

"What does that mean?" I ask. "Did you wake up with psychic powers?"

Ryan leans to the side and reaches into his back pocket. He pulls out a folded piece of paper. Son of a bitch.

"You went to see Leo," I say. "And in addition to that piece of paper, he also gave you this address. And the key you used to get inside."

"You thieves are so smart."

"Some of us are," I say. "If the FBI stakes out that location, you'll get your agent killed."

"That's why I didn't tell the FBI."

Huh. Didn't expect that. I meet his eyes. "Not even Jonas?"

"True or false," Ryan says. "Jonas knows what you're planning to do and decided to let you do it anyway."

True. I shrug. "I haven't seen Jonas since I walked out of the conference room. How would I know what he knows?"

Ryan's jaw ticks as he stares at me. I don't flinch.

"No," he says finally. "Not even Jonas."

"So, it's just you and me."

"Against the world."

"I suppose there are worse odds."

Ryan drops the paper onto the wooden crate. "What's your plan?"

I push off from the wall and walk toward him. "I know where they're going to be in"—I check the clock on the wall—"sixteen hours. That gives me about fifteen hours to find Lew first."

"And how are you going to do that?"

"Start at the exchange point and work my way out."

"The exchange point?"

"Well, the only other lead is the restaurant, and I'm guessing you guys already looked into that. If you found something viable there, you'd be acting on it. You wouldn't be here asking me what I'm doing."

Ryan nods. "There was a van—some commercial laundry service that doesn't exist. It showed up shortly after you and I…We couldn't confirm it, but we think they put him in there."

Or it was a decoy. A little misdirect to buy themselves some time and space. I nod. "Where did you lose it?"

"Sumner Tunnel. We're looking for it, but even if we find it, there won't be anything left there to find."

No, there won't. They'll have wiped it down or burned it or done something to destroy any evidence. The van, regardless of whether Lew was actually ever in it, is a dead end. But if the FBI is looking for that, it'll keep them out of the goddamn way.

"Let me guess," I say. "You guys are now searching the airport."

"It's a possibility."

Not a good one. I shake my head. "They're still in Boston. If anything, they switched vehicles at Logan and drove right out again."

"Is that how you would have done it?"

"No, that's not how I would have done it. I don't kidnap people," I say. "Lew is somewhere in Boston. He has to be."

"Why? Why does he have to be?"

"Because if he isn't, we've already lost," I say. "I don't want to lose. I don't want to tell Nia we lost. Do you?"

Ryan shakes his head.

"Okay. So Lew is somewhere in Boston," I say. "They wouldn't have had time to move their entire operation, and what's more, they wouldn't have wanted to. Not because of me. Not because of some no-name, local thief. That gray asshole has built an empire in this city, and he is not going to give it up because of me. So they are here, and Lew is here, because they are going to use him to get to me, and they will not kill him—they will *not* kill him—until they're sure they have me. Which means we have time to find him first."

"By starting at the exchange point and working our way out," Ryan says.

"Unless you have a better idea?"

"No, but...it's a lot of ground to cover on our own. We need help," Ryan says. "What about Leo?"

I shake my head. "Leo's done everything he can. He stays clear of whatever happens next. What about that guy? The one Nia called. The detective."

"Noah Wiley?"

"I didn't get a last name, but the first name's right."

"He's a cop."

"But not a fed. He might have some useful resources."

"He doesn't know you, and he might have heard my name, but he doesn't know me."

"He knows Nia, which means he probably knows Lew, and even if he doesn't know Lew, he still knows Nia and her entire damn family," I say. "Maybe he would help us to help them."

Ryan nods and tosses me his phone. "Call Nia. Ask her to reach out to Noah."

"Why me?"

"We don't have time for me to go twelve rounds with her over how incompetent I am."

Fair enough. I find Nia's name in his contact list and call her.

"What?" she says when she answers.

"It's Skye. I need—"

"Did you get him back yet?"

"Still working on it, but I need your help. Can you talk to Noah? See if he'll help me with something?"

"Yes."

"And can you also not tell the FBI or anyone else that I asked you to do this?"

"With pleasure."

She ends the call. A couple of minutes later, the phone buzzes with a text. I glance at it. An address.

I show the message to Ryan. "Know where this is?"

Ryan nods. "Let's go."

44

THE ADDRESS LEADS TO A downtown police precinct. I hesitate on the sidewalk across the street from the building. Willingly walking into a police station for any reason is one of those things thieves are just not supposed to do. Ryan's in the middle of the crosswalk when he notices my absence. He stops and looks at me.

"Are you coming?" he asks.

I nod and force myself to take that next step. This is how we get Lew back. This is how I even out the scales.

It is only by repeating those two facts to myself over and over again that I make it to the doors. Through the doors. Up to the desk behind which sits a uniformed officer. The officer lifts his head and I drop back. Ryan can handle this.

Ryan flashes his badge. "We're looking for Noah Wiley. He's expecting us."

The officer points to his left. "Bang a right at the conference room. You'll see him."

Ryan thanks the officer and we go in search of Noah. The hall opens into a bullpen with desks clustered together in groups of two and four. It's not quite a cubical farm but pretty close.

The man I saw outside of Jay's apartment is sitting at a desk by himself. Gone are the aviator sunglasses, so when he looks up, I see the faint flicker of recognition in his brown eyes. Great. I love it when cops recognize me.

I lightly hit Ryan's arm. "Over there."

Ryan changes direction and we approach the man behind the desk.

"Noah Wiley?" Ryan says.

"Yeah." Noah leans back in his chair as he looks me over. "You're Nia's friend?"

Did Nia call me that? Surprising, given the circumstances.

"That depends on how this whole thing plays out," I say.

Noah gestures to Ryan. "Who's this? Nia didn't say there would be two of you."

"She didn't know he'd be here," I say, "but he's helping me help her."

Ryan shows his badge again. "I'm Daniel Ryan. I work with Nia's husband."

Noah nods and looks at me. "And you? Who are you?"

"The less you know about me, the better for all involved," I say. "But you can call me Tess."

Noah raises a brow. "Okay. What do you need?"

"Is there someplace private we can talk?" Ryan asks.

"Yeah," Noah says, standing. "Come on."

He leads us into a conference room and closes the door. Wanting some space between me and the cops, I move around the table to put my back against the opposite wall. Ryan stays near the entrance with Noah. None of us sit.

"All right," Noah says. "Tell me what you need."

"What did Nia tell you?" Ryan asks. "We're not trying to be difficult. It's just a sensitive situation."

Noah leans against the wall near the door. "Nia said her husband is in trouble and Tess here is trying to get him out of it. But since she didn't tell me who you were or what the trouble was, and she has ties to multiple law enforcement agencies, yet is sending two people to me, I assume you need to stay well under the radar and maybe just slightly outside the law."

Slightly. Sure. "Good assumption," I mutter.

Noah glances at me. "How far outside the law are we talking here?"

I shrug. "Depends on what we find."

Ryan doesn't disagree. His family's in danger. There are very few lines he wouldn't consider crossing right now. I'll have to cross them for him.

Noah looks at Ryan, probably waiting for some sort of assurance that we're not about to destroy the city. Ryan doesn't say anything.

"Okay," Noah says. "How can I help?"

"We need access to camera feeds—security, traffic, whatever we can get our hands on—starting in and around Faneuil Hall," Ryan says. "Both real-time and maybe some older footage, too."

"How old?" Noah asks.

"Two or three hours," I say.

"Are you expecting or hoping to find Llewellyn on any of these feeds?"

Ryan shakes his head. "That's not likely. We're hoping to find the people who took him, then follow their trail back to where they're holding him."

"And you think some of them will be in or around Faneuil Hall?" Noah asks.

"It's a theory," I say. Neither Ryan nor I mention that those people may be snipers waiting for their chance to shoot me in the head.

"All right," Noah says. "You can use my computer. Start with the real-time feeds, and I'll work on seeing what else I can get you."

"Don't tell your partner about this," I say. "Or anyone else."

Noah looks at me, then at Ryan.

"Please," Ryan says. "If you can."

Noah nods and walks out of the conference room. We follow him back to his desk. He sits down and logs in, then stands and motions to Ryan to take the chair. Ryan sits and starts typing. Noah walks away. I watch him approach the woman I saw with him at Jay's apartment. Patricia, I think Nia called her. They have a quick and quiet conversation by the coffee station. She glances over. As soon as we make eye contact, I break it and move to stand behind Ryan.

Real-time traffic feeds appear on the monitor. They're the right area, but they're not showing enough of the sidewalk. We need a better angle. Ryan seems to agree, as he scrolls through the options until he finds one he likes. I lightly scratch my arms. My skin is itchy. Being in this place is giving me hives.

"There," Ryan says.

I look at the monitor. He pauses the video and points at the screen, but I already see it. A man, carrying a long duffle bag. I've seen him before.

"That's him," I murmur. "That's one of them."

Shit. They're really doing it. They're setting people in place to shoot me the moment I set foot in their sights. My stomach tightens and my throat closes up. Apparently, there's a difference between thinking something's a one-way mission and seeing concrete evidence of it.

"Skye?" Ryan asks in a low voice.

"I'm fine." I gesture vaguely at the monitor. "We need to find out where he came from."

"We will. Just—"

"Just nothing. Focus on finding Lew, okay?" I say. "And my name is *Tess*."

"Hey." Ryan grabs my hand. "I won't let him get near you."

"Look at the bag, Ryan. He won't have to get near me." I free my hand from his grasp. "Stop screwing around, and do your damn job."

Ryan sighs and turns back to the monitor. I step away. I need some air. Or a toilet in which to vomit. I turn abruptly and smack into Noah.

"Everything okay?" he asks.

"Bathroom," I say.

He points to the right. "Down there."

I rush down the hallway until I find the women's restroom. I go inside and into the first stall, dropping to my knees just in time to avoid puking on the floor.

When I have nothing left inside me, I sit on the floor and put my back against the wall. What the hell is wrong with me? There is no time for this.

Standing, I flush the toilet and exit the stall. Noah's partner is leaning against one of the sinks.

"Okay?" she asks.

"Bad sushi," I say.

I step up to the sink next to her and turn on the faucet to rinse my mouth.

Patricia offers me a paper towel. "Your friend out there asked me to come in here and check on you."

I take the paper towel and wipe my mouth. "He's not my friend."

"Does he know that?"

"Apparently not." I toss the towel in the trash. "Tell him I'm fine. I'll be out in a minute."

Patricia straightens. "Tell him yourself. He's just outside the door."

She walks out of the bathroom. Ryan starts to say something but stops.

"Ask her yourself," Patricia says.

Ryan comes into the bathroom. I grip the sink as I look at his reflection in the mirror.

"You okay?" he asks.

"Bad sushi," I say.

"You know I know that's a lie, right?"

"You find him?" I ask.

"Skye—"

"Tess."

Ryan sighs. "Yeah. I'll show you."

We go back to Noah's desk. Ryan sits down, and I look over his shoulder at the frozen image on the monitor. Shit. That's the shooter, all right. The same goon from the Skyreach walking out of a building with his duffle bag, like he's off to the gym. Or the shooting range.

I look from him to the building. Standard brick box. Tall windows, lots of small panes. Not the kind I can fit through.

"What is it?" I ask.

"Old factory. Others surrounding it have been renovated and converted into condos. Some are in the process of being renovated. This one's listed as owned by a developer, but they don't seem to be making much progress on the project."

By design, I bet. It's a good cover. You could smuggle in all sorts of things right in bright daylight that way. Construction workers, contractors, even people in suits could go in and out all day long unnoticed by anyone around them.

"What do we do now?" I ask.

"How would you do it?" Ryan says.

I shake my head. "I don't do rescue missions. I don't know how to plan for that."

"Then plan a heist. You're a contract thief. Lew's the package," Ryan says. "How do you do it?"

"I can't…I need more information."

"There is no more information. This is all we have," Ryan says. "Come on, *Tess*. You were going to do this all on your own before I showed up. How would you have done it?"

I run my hands through my hair. How would I do it?

"Is there a satellite image?" I ask.

Ryan turns back to the computer and clicks the mouse a couple of times. An overhead view of the neighborhood appears on the screen.

Ryan points to a rooftop. "That's our building. How do you get in?"

I lean in to take a closer look. The building on its left is residential now, complete with a rooftop patio. The distance between them looks manageable.

"I would use the roof of that building to get on the roof of the other. That'll be the weak point. They'll cover the doors, but they may not think about the roof. A lot of people don't."

"Okay. You're on the roof. Now what?"

I tap a light-colored rectangle on the roof's image. "That's either a door or a vent. We can use that to get inside."

"A vent?"

"It's an older, industrial building. The vents will be bigger." I glance at him. "You should be able to fit just fine."

"Okay. Good. Then what?"

"Well, ideally I'd know where the package was and what kind of security stood between me and it. But we'll have to start at the top and work our way down."

"Okay. Good. What else?"

"Extraction," I say. "I can't just stick Lew in a backpack and walk out the front door."

"Can we go back the way we came in?"

"Possible, but...we don't know if he'll be able to do that. I got proof of life, so we know he's alive, but there's no telling how badly he's hurt. What if he can't run? Can't walk? Can't...anything?" I say. "We should have a couple of different exits in place, just in case."

"The T?" Ryan asks.

I shake my head. "It's too far away, especially if Lew is hurt. Besides, the trains are hard to time. It has to be something we control fully."

"Cars, then. Multiple cars."

"How many do you have access to?"

"Without telling anyone what we're doing? One," Ryan says. "What about—?"

"Don't say his name in here," I say. "Besides, he can't drive."

"You need more help," Noah says.

Both Ryan and I turn to look at him, standing on our left. How long has he been there? How much has he heard?

"We do," I admit. "But it can't be you."

"Why not?"

"Think about what you've overheard and make an intuitive leap," I say. "It can't be you."

"It can be," Noah says. "And it should be."

"Why is that?" I ask. "You know this isn't exactly sanctioned by people you would approve of. Why do you want to get involved?"

Noah smiles crookedly as he scratches his chin. "I don't know what kind of partnerships you've had in the past—"

"I don't have partnerships," I say.

"I could have guessed that," he says. "So, you don't do partnerships and, clearly, you don't do trust, but you should trust me when I tell you that you don't want to let Nia down. You don't want to live with what happens when you do."

I should have pressed harder to get their story. Sounds like it's a good one.

"Look, Patricia and I are going to grab some food," Noah says. "If there's a note with addresses and a time left behind while we're gone, then we'll cover it. If not..." He shrugs. "Then we won't."

"Fair enough." Ryan stands and extends his hand to Noah. "Thank you for your help."

Noah shakes Ryan's hand and walks away. Patricia joins him and they head out of the room.

As soon as they're gone, Ryan turns to me. "Well?"

I suppose there are worse ideas. I sigh. "Figure out where you want them."

Ryan looks at the map, his thumb tapping his lips as he considers the possibilities. Removing a couple of Post-It notes from a stack on the desk, he scribbles two addresses. He looks at his watch and writes down a time. After hiding the notes under the keyboard, he picks up a business card from the holder, takes out his phone, and creates a contact for Noah Wiley.

"We should go," Ryan says. "We have a big night ahead of us."

45

OUR NEXT STOP IS RYAN'S apartment. Has he been here at all since the night we met? Is this where he went after he found out who I am? He doesn't say anything about it as he parks the car in the lot behind the building and we walk up the four floors to his front door. By the time we get there, he's looking exceptionally pale and tired.

"Are you okay?" I ask as he unlocks the door.

"I'm fine."

"Are you, though? You don't look fine."

Ryan opens the door and walks inside. "That's because a crazy woman kicked me in the face."

"You probably had it coming," I say, following him in. He heads for the kitchen, leaving me to close the door. "Seriously, Ryan. If you're going to drop dead from the effort of walking up four flights of stairs, then maybe you should stay here."

"I'm fine."

"I can't rescue you both."

"You won't have to rescue me. I'm fine."

I nod. "There's a difference between being fine and being able to mount a covert rescue operation against a well-armed criminal organization."

His hand forms a fist. He raises it like he intends to hit something but only brings it down on the table with all the force of a gentle tap.

"Goddammit, Skye," he says. "What do you want from me?"

"I...don't know, but I don't want you to die."

"Maybe you should have thought about that before..." He shakes his head. "Never mind."

Sounds like a plan to me. There's no good way to end that sentence. Better to let it just hang there, awkward and unfinished. Finishing it offers nothing. Finishing it would imply there's some sort of anything between us with a shelf life that hasn't already expired.

Which there isn't.

There can't be.

Ryan gestures to the couch. "Just...stay here, would you?"

I sit. He walks toward the bedroom. A few minutes later, he comes back with a duffle bag of his own and puts it on the table.

"Do you know how to use a gun?" he asks, unpacking weapons and ammo.

I stand and walk over to the other side of the table. "I don't want a gun."

"That's where you draw the line, huh?"

"Get caught with a gun, and it's a lot worse. Get caught without one, and—"

"And you can tell a federal agent you're nothing more than an innocent bystander."

"I *am* an innocent bystander," I say. Ryan glances at me. I shrug. "Relatively speaking."

He grunts and looks away again. "You didn't answer the question."

"What quest—oh. Uh, yeah. I know how to use a gun."

Ryan nods and holds one out. Small. Black. Smith & Wesson.

It's nothing I can't handle, but I shake my head. "I don't want that."

"This isn't about what you want. Take it. Don't be afraid to use it."

I don't take it. "I'm a lot of things, Ryan, but I'm not a killer."

"They are."

Good point. I take the gun. "Do you have…I can't walk in there with a gun on my hip, and I'm not sticking it down my pants. Do you have a shoulder holster I can use?"

He looks at me again, then returns to his bedroom. I put the gun on the table. I much prefer knives. Ryan soon comes back with a black leather holster.

"Try this," he says. "I'll help you with the straps."

I take off my jacket and slide on the holster. I turn so Ryan can adjust the fit. As his fingers brush my skin, I close my eyes.

"How does that feel?" he asks.

I need a moment to realize he's talking about the holster and not other things.

I open my eyes. "Good. It's good."

His hands drop and he moves away. He puts a gun into a shoulder holster of his own and a backup revolver on his ankle.

He nods toward the gun I left on the table. "You're taking that with you. I mean it."

I pick up the gun, check the safety, and put it in the holster. I put my jacket back on and zip it.

"What else do you have on you?" he asks.

"Lock picks. Headlamp." I hesitate. "A couple of knives."

"Is that all you take on a job?" He walks over to a cupboard and removes a glass from it. "Lock picks and a knife?"

He fills the glass with water from the sink, then sets it on the counter. He puts his hands on the counter next and leans against it.

"Depends on the job," I say. "You need aspirin?"

"What?"

I go to his bathroom and get the aspirin out of the medicine cabinet. I bring it back to the kitchen and put the bottle in front of him.

"Take some damn aspirin," I say. "I'd tell you to take whatever damn meds the damn doctor prescribed because they'll be much more effective than this over-the-counter crap, but if you're still thinking that you should come with me, you shouldn't be high while doing it."

Ryan straightens and picks up the bottle. "How did you know where I keep the aspirin?"

"I looked when I was here before."

"You went through my medicine cabinet? Why?"

"Wanted to see if there was anything useful. Which there wasn't." I nod at the bottle. "You need me to open that for you? Maybe crush up some pills and mix them into some juice?"

Ryan smiles. "No."

"Then what are you waiting for?"

His smile fades. "Maybe you should stay here."

"Are you kidding?"

"No. You're..." He shakes his head. The movement makes him wince. "You shouldn't be there. You're a civilian."

"I may not be a super secret agent like some, but I'm not a civilian, either," I say. "And out of everyone in the apartment right now, I'm the only one without a head injury. You're the one who should stay behind."

"Well, I'm not doing that."

"Well, neither am I," I say. "How many more times do we have to have this conversation? Every minute you stand here, arguing with me, is another minute those assholes have Lew, and it's another minute we come closer to having to tell Nia we failed. So get your shit together before someone knocks you unconscious again and goes to take care of the problem on their own."

Ryan wastes another minute looking at me. Then he nods and opens the aspirin bottle. He shakes out a couple of tablets and swallows them dry.

"Someone, huh?" he says, putting the bottle back on the counter.

I shrug. "One mystery at a time."

"Yeah." Ryan picks up his keys and sticks them in his pocket. "If you die, I'm gonna be pissed."

I smile. "Me, too."

46

RYAN PARKS ON A SIDE street two blocks over from the factory. He gets a backpack out of the trunk and we walk toward our target. My heart is pounding a lot harder than it normally is on a job. I'm not feeling my usual rush, either. Now, I feel dread and worry. All the eggs are in a single basket, and I'm taking that basket straight into the center of the hornets' nest.

I walk up to the front doors of the condo building and hit every button for every unit until one buzzes us inside. We take the elevator to the top floor, then use the stairs to gain access to the roof.

We walk toward the factory. I don't see any security prowling the rooftop. When we reach the edge, I lean over to look toward the street. Cameras on the front and back corners that will be trained on the doors, maybe the surrounding street. There's a side door directly below us. I don't see a camera there. The distance between the two buildings isn't a problem. For me, at least. I can't say the same about Ryan. He doesn't do this sort of thing every day.

And he definitely doesn't do it with a head injury. I glance at him. He's looking worse. Pale. In pain.

"Can you do this?" I ask.

"I can do this." Ryan checks his watch. "They should be in place by now. I think this is as good as it's going to get."

I walk away from the wall. It's not a huge gap, but a running start is still required. Ryan follows me, putting his pack on his back.

"Don't use your hands to break your fall," I caution. "It'll be a lot harder to use your gun with busted wrists."

"I'm not planning to fall."

"Your body may have other ideas." I take a deep breath. "Last chance to back out."

"I'm with you until the end," Ryan says. "Even if that is in the next hour."

I smile. "Gotta love a positive attitude."

Ryan sighs and looks at me. "Skye, I just…If this is the end, I want—"

Oh hell no. I run and leap over the gap, easily landing on the factory roof. When I look back, Ryan is already in motion. He hits the roof and skids across the surface. His hands are tucked close to his chest, so I move to the access door. It's locked, but I'm prepared for that. It's a relief to have to deal with such a normal damn problem. I remove the picks from my pocket and set to work. By the time Ryan has joined me, I've finished.

I put the picks away and open the door. "After you."

"Get your gun out," Ryan says as he moves inside.

I leave the gun where it is and follow him. The roof access leads to a U-shaped floor, open to the space below. There's a set of stairs leading down at the other end. Five doors to the left, five more on our right. Offices, closets, and at least one bathroom, I would guess. It looks deserted, certainly not like they're keeping a hostage here, but we'll still have to look. We have to open every door and every door we find behind those doors. Until we find Lew.

Ryan puts a finger to his lips. Because, as a thief, I don't know that being quiet is the key to not being discovered.

I roll my eyes and whisper, "You go left, I go right. We meet at the stairs."

He shakes his head vigorously and motions that we should stay together.

"The longer we're here, the greater the chance that we'll be found," I say. "We need to clear this floor, and it'll go a lot quicker if you go left and I go right."

Ryan nods and pulls me close. "Take your gun out of the holster," he says in my ear. "And be careful."

I get the gun out and pretend to disengage the safety. He nods again and moves to the left. When his back is turned, I go right.

The first room I come to is completely empty with no other doors leading anywhere else, so I move on. The second room is also empty, but there's a door inside. Behind that door is nothing but some copy paper boxes. Since Lew couldn't fit inside them, I go back out to the hall.

It continues that way. Every door I open leads to an empty room. When Ryan and I meet at the stairs, it's obvious he's found more of the same.

Which is all right. I thought it would be that way. Lew's an important hostage. They weren't going to leave him alone and unguarded on a deserted floor in an abandoned factory.

Ryan and I both look over the side to the floors below. Nothing but wooden crates to be seen, but the bad guys will be there somewhere. And Lew. He'll be there, too.

Unless he's not here at all.

Shit. That's a bad thought to have. He has to be here. He will be.

"We stay together," Ryan says. "Watch each other's back."

I nod. Seems prudent, as we're about to literally walk down into another level of hell filled with an undetermined number of guns and bad guys.

Ryan leads the way down the stairs. My heart is pounding even harder and faster now. Ryan stops at the sound of voices. They're far enough away that I can't tell how many people are talking. Ryan moves again, slower than before. I push against his shoulder. I'm all for caution, but slow and steady will only get us so far. Ryan glares at me. I nudge him again.

He makes some hand gestures that mean nothing to me. Either he wants me to slow down and stay behind him or the FBI needs entirely too many gestures to tell someone to go fuck themselves. I nod to placate him. Ryan nods as well and moves on.

He stops again at the bottom of the stairs. Evaluating options, maybe, or possibly making sure to pose for any security cameras in the area. The voices are coming from the right, so I duck under the railing and head that way, using the plethora of wooden crates for cover. What are they smuggling in those crates? Guns? Drugs? Kidnapped FBI agents?

The voices are louder now. I'm getting close. I press myself against the wall. It sounds like they're just on the other side of this wall. If I go any farther, I could be exposed.

I still have to look, though.

I crouch down and slowly peek around the corner.

The gray ghost is sitting at a desk inside a temporary office with glass walls. The other goon from the Skyreach is there, too, standing on the ghost's left and pointing to something on the desk. Behind them is a wall of monitors. I'm too far away to see what's on them, but they're assuredly security camera feeds. More than what I saw outside. I glance at the ceiling. Are they watching the interior as well?

A hand lands on my shoulder. I shrug it off and turn, raising my gun, and end up pointing it in Ryan's face.

For fuck's sake. I lower the weapon. "What are you doing? I have a *gun*, jackass. Did you forget?"

"You left the damn safety on," Ryan says. "And what are *you* doing? We're supposed to stay together."

I point over my shoulder. "Gray ghost. In there."

Ryan's entire demeanor changes. He beckons me out of the way and takes my place. He crouches and cautiously looks around the corner. When he turns back, he rests his head against the wall for a moment before looking at me.

"Switch off the safety," he says, "and stay with me."

I give him a thumbs-up and leave the safety as is. Ryan goes back the way he came. I follow, watching both our backs and the ceiling.

Ryan stops behind another crate. I stop behind him, glancing upward, and finally see a camera. If there's one, there's more than one. Like rats or cockroaches. No alarms have been raised, but the gray ghost is not dumb. If he's watching, if he knows we're here, then he can deal with us quietly. He'll check the perimeter, figure out if we were stupid enough to come without backup of any kind—which, of course, we were—and then trap and kill us.

Like rats. Or cockroaches.

I look away from the camera to see a man appear on the other side of the room. He stands alone at the start of another hallway. He looks bored. Someone on guard duty, maybe? His hostage is all tied up with nowhere to go, and he's left with nothing to do but pace the hallway and wait for something to happen. It's the most promising lead we've had since we broke in. There's no way in hell we're not going to look.

I reach out and snag Ryan's sleeve. When he looks at me, I point out the guard. Ryan nods. He makes some more hand gestures I would probably recognize if I had gone to FBI school, but I don't need them to know how to make my way across a room unseen. I've been actively trying to be invisible my entire damn life. I give him another thumbs-up and creep away. Ryan growls before scrambling to catch up.

I stop behind a concrete pillar and wait for the guard to turn and walk in the opposite direction. As soon as he does, I move toward him and kick the back of his knee. He goes down the same way Ryan did, and when he turns to look at me, I hit him with the gun. He falls unconscious on the floor. I put my gun back in the holster and search the guard. Gun on his hip. I pull it from the holster and hold it out behind me while patting him down with my free hand. No other weapons. No keys. I don't need them, but they are a time saver.

Ryan takes the gun from my hand and leaves a pair of plastic restraints in its place. I secure the guard's wrists behind his back and then his ankles.

Ryan drags the man out of the way, leaving him on the floor against the wall. "That's what it looked like, huh?"

"I don't know what you're talking about." I look at the hallway. Clear of other people. Two doors. I gesture to the one closest to us. "Check the door."

Ryan tries the handle. "Locked."

That's my cue. I get the lock picks out and kneel in front of the door. The lock is old and simple. Even Nia and her bobby pins could have made quick work of this lock. I get to my feet.

"Behind me," Ryan says.

Ryan puts his back against the wall. When I'm in place, he shoves the door open. Nothing happens. No gunfire, no bad guys come pouring out. Ryan motions for me to hang back, then moves into the room.

"Skye," he says. "Get in here."

47

IT'S NOT A ROOM SO much as a closet. No way out other than the way we came in, and the only light source is a single, exposed lightbulb in the ceiling. Lew is cuffed to a chair in the center of the space. One on each ankle. His hands are secured together behind his back. His head is hanging down, but the gash on his cheek is proof that he's taken a serious beating.

Ryan points to the door. "Watch our exit."

Or I could pick the locks keeping Lew attached to the chair, but whatever. I put my back against the wall and keep an eye on both the hall and the guys. My gaze immediately goes to the ceiling. Camera. Right there. If someone is looking at those monitors, there's no way we haven't been seen. The clock has been ticking since the moment we entered this building, but it's counting down a lot quicker now. No point in mentioning it. We're either leaving with Lew or we're not leaving.

I really hope it's the first.

I check on the guys. Ryan crouches in front of Lew. He feels for a pulse and removes a gag from Lew's mouth. He pats Lew's unbloodied cheek.

"El? You in there? El, wake up." Ryan touches the cuff on Lew's ankle and looks around to the back of the chair. "Can you pick the cuffs?"

I honestly thought he would never ask. "I can, but if he's unconscious—"

"Just get the cuffs open," Ryan says. "I'll keep watch."

We swap places. I take the lock picks out again and start with the ankle cuffs. If I release his hands while he's out, he'll just fall flat on his face. Sadly, there is no time for such hilarity.

Lew starts to come to as I finish the second ankle cuff.

"Ryan," I say, moving behind the chair.

"Ry?" Lew's head droops again, then turns toward me. "What is…Skye?"

"Hi," I say. "Stay awake, okay?"

Ryan abandons his post to join us. His gun is still out. "El?"

"I'm okay."

"Can you walk?"

The cuffs give, and Lew slumps forward. I drop the picks to catch his arm and keep him upright.

"El?" Ryan says.

"I'm okay," Lew says. "Just…give me a minute."

Ryan looks at me and jerks his head toward the door. I recover my picks and put them back in my pocket. As I walk by, Ryan holds out his gun. Oh good. The only thing I like more than carrying one gun is carrying two, but I take it and move into position.

Lew stands. His knees buckle and Ryan catches him.

"Nia get a new dog yet?" Lew asks.

"Not yet," Ryan says. "I think we may have gotten you back just in time."

Lew closes his eyes. "Good. That's good."

Ryan drapes Lew's arm around his shoulders. "Come on, El. We gotta go." He looks at me. "We clear?"

I glance at the ceiling camera. Probably not, but what's the other choice? We barricade ourselves in this glorified closet and tunnel our way out with a set of lock picks? I look from side to side, and then nod.

"Is it just you two?" Lew asks.

"You don't think that's enough?" Ryan says.

"You already look like you lost a fight."

"Skye did that."

"Allegedly," I say, my attention more on what's coming our way. Footsteps. People not trying to be quiet. People who have no reason to try. I'm not sure how many of them there are, but they're heading right for us. I look at the door to the left. What are the odds it leads to a damn exit?

I turn toward Ryan and Lew. "Hey, Butch, Sundance? Do you think you can move things along? We're about to have company."

"Shit," Ryan says. "How did they know we're here?"

"Camera in the ceiling," I answer.

Ryan looks up. To his credit, he finds it quickly. "How long have you known that was there?"

"A while."

"You could have said something."

"We hadn't found what we came for yet," I say. "But now we have Lew and only one possible way out, so move your asses down the hall already."

Ryan and Lew start toward the door, Lew still leaning heavily on Ryan. I don't know what's behind that door, but we're going to need a goddamn miracle to get us all out of this alive.

I walk backwards, Ryan's gun up and ready. The second I see someone round the corner, I shoot, driving them back.

"Faster would be better," I say over my shoulder, then fire again as another goon appears.

As soon as the door opens, the goons make their move, coming out in force, guns firing. Bullets fly around me, striking various targets. A sharp pain tears through my right arm, near the shoulder. Mother*fucker*. I clench my teeth to keep from crying out. Hurts like hell, but I don't think it's a direct hit. Just a graze. I straighten and return fire.

"Skye," Ryan says. "Let's go."

He grabs my arm and pulls me back. As soon as we make it through the door, he pushes it shut and leans against it.

"See if you can find a way out of here," he says.

I hand him his gun and look around. A storage room. Floor-to-ceiling metal shelving units holding metal tins. I glance toward the ceiling. An industrial-sized vent. Would work for me, but Lew couldn't make it up there. I jog to the other end of the room to see what, if anything, is there.

A door. There's a door. Thank God there's a door. I run down and push against the handle. The door opens, and I get a glimpse of a street light. Even better.

"Skye!" Ryan calls. "Help! Now!"

I run back. He and Lew are losing the fight to keep the door closed. Grabbing a metal folding chair, I drag it over and pull Lew away.

"Door in the back," I order. "Start moving."

I wedge the chair beneath the door's handle. It won't hold them long. Bullets come through the door. Ryan and I shy to the left and sit side by side on the floor.

"There's a door in the back. I think it leads outside, or at least gets you closer to it. Probably that side exit we saw from the roof," I say, taking my gun out of the holster. "You and Lew need to get the hell out of here."

"*We* need to get the hell out of here, Skye. All of us."

I shake my head. "Lew's too slow. Someone has to stay behind to buy the other two time."

"Then it'll be me."

"I can't support Lew's weight. Not long enough to make it out, anyway." I jerk my head toward the bad guys. "I can, however, slow them down."

"How will you do that?"

"Fight like a thief."

A window above our heads shatters and glass rains down on us. I duck my head, but Ryan shields me with his body. As soon as the shower ends, I push him back.

"You have to go," I say. "Lew needs all the time he can get."

"Skye—"

I put down my gun and kiss him. Hard. One more for the road. "Shut up and go. Don't stop. Just get to a car and go. I will be faster on my own, and I will meet you at the loft."

Ryan nods. "You better."

He pushes up off the floor. Staying low, he goes after Lew. I pick up my gun, disengage the safety, and rest my head against the wall. Okay. How the hell am I going to do this?

First step, get some breathing room.

As soon as the gunfire stops, I pop up and shoot through the broken window. I get off three shots before I have to hit the floor.

Okay. How does a thief fight? We don't. We hide in the shadows and avoid being seen so we don't have to fight. If we're doing our damn jobs right, no one even knows we were there until we're long gone. But it's too late for that. They know I'm here. And I have to keep their focus here.

I glance up at the wonderful industrial-sized vent in the ceiling. If I were alone, I would be disappearing through that right now. But that won't give Ryan and Lew the time they need. I'll need something more.

I look at the tins on the shelves. Paint thinner.

Fire could work.

I scramble to the shelves, grab a tin, and twist off the cap. I throw it toward the door and reach for a second tin. Clear liquid spills out. It's not the most thorough job ever, but I don't need to burn down the entire factory. I just need to slow the bad guys down. Distract them. Give them something else on which to focus. There's a lot of money tied up in this place, in one form or another. They can't let it burn.

The door finally gives way, and the goons come rushing in. I pick up my gun and start shooting at the tins, firing until the sparks catch fire. The goons shout. One of them jumps back, his pants on fire.

That's as good as it's going to get, so I bolt for the back. My hand's on the door when someone grabs me and drags me back. I drive my elbow into their gut. They grunt and release me. Spinning around, I aim the gun at his midsection. I pull the trigger, but nothing happens. Out of ammo. Fuck.

The goon sneers and launches himself at me, taking me to the ground. The gun is jolted from my hand as my head bounces off the concrete, but I push up, aiming for his eyes with my thumbs. He pulls back, so I drag my nails down his cheeks.

He snarls and puts his fist in my face. My field of vision explodes with stars. Knife. I need my knife. I fumble to find the pocket and remove the blade. Flipping it open, I stab it into the goon's body. He howls and pulls away. I lose my hold on the knife, but I slide back and get on my feet. He reaches for me, and I jump back. It's not a jump so much as a I-now-have-a-head-injury backwards stumble, but points for effort, if not style.

He lunges again, hands outstretched, and falls short. When he looks up, I bring my fist down. He catches my wrist and twists. I scream as I stomp on his nose. He lets me go and I stagger back. The only knife I have left is the push blade in my bra. I reach for it, but my fingers can't even grasp the chain.

Shit. The knife doesn't matter, does it? I look over my shoulder. How far away is the door? I can't keep doing this. I'm not going to be on my feet much longer. I can't climb, either. Not now. I am…I am in trouble.

I laugh. This is it, isn't it? I hope Ryan and Lew got out. It would be a goddamn shame if—

Something—someone?—hits me from behind, landing a blow to my right side before I shove them off. I turn to look at the goon and see my knife on the floor. If I can get to it, maybe I can—

A gunshot has me ducking. It's loud and close. Did it hit me? Did I get shot? The goon falls to the floor and doesn't move, arms flopping out to the side. Oh. *He* was shot. How did that…

I look over my shoulder. Ryan. Lowering his gun.

"That was entirely too close!" I exclaim. "Were you aiming for him?"

"Not the time, Skye," Ryan says. "The factory is on fire."

My side is on fire. That asshole did more than punch me. He stabbed me, didn't he? With my own damn knife. Shit. I am *never* gonna live that down.

I slump against the nearest shelving unit. "Seemed like a good idea at the time."

"I'm sure it did. Let's go."

Wonder how far I'll get. I push off the shelves and take a couple of unsteady steps. Ryan rushes toward me. I don't discourage him. He moves to my right and grabs my arm. I cry out and he freezes.

"Jesus, Skye," he says.

I shake my head. "Just a graze. Keep going."

He moves to my other side and more carefully drapes my left arm around his shoulders. He puts his arm around my waist. It hurts more than my arm, but I bite my lip to avoid making a sound.

As we shuffle toward the exit, he pulls out his phone. He hits a button and brings the phone to his ear.

"We're coming out now," he says. "Be ready."

I breathe deep as we step out into a narrow alley. Ryan's forced to drop behind me but puts his hand on my back. I keep my hand on the factory wall for support.

"Who are we looking for?" I ask. It takes a surprising amount of concentration to form the words. That's not good. Here's hoping I make it to the car before I pass out.

"Noah," Ryan says. "He's coming to us. Just keep going."

I can do that. I laugh. I can't do that.

"How badly are you hurt?" Ryan asks.

Pretty badly. "Just bruised," I lie. "I'll be okay."

As soon as we clear the alley, Ryan moves back to my side. My legs are heavy, like they have weights attached to them. My knees give out, and Ryan catches me around the waist. He half carries, half drags me to a silver sedan sitting at the curb. He opens the back door and helps me inside, climbing in after me. The car takes off.

I tip my head back and rest it against the seat. Hope Noah doesn't mind blood on the upholstery.

"So," Ryan says, "fighting like a thief. How'd that go?"

"You got Lew out, didn't you?" I wince and press my hand to my side. "You did get Lew out, right?"

"Lew is free and clear and on his way to the hospital," Ryan says. "Where you need to be."

I pull my hand away to look at the blood covering my palm. "I don't…"

A wave of pain works its way through me. I close my eyes to ride it out. Ryan turns my hand and swears. His fingers probe my side.

"She's bleeding," he says. "Can you go any faster?"

The car accelerates. I crack one eye open to watch Ryan pull off his jacket. He presses it against my side.

"You're overreacting," I say. "It's just a scratch."

"You're either a liar or you don't know what 'scratch' means," Ryan says.

I laugh. "Maybe both."

"Where else, Skye? Where else are you hurt?"

I close my eyes. God, I'm so tired.

"No, no, no." Ryan pats my cheek. "Skye, stay awake. Talk to me."

I shake my head. "No talking. No point. We don't work out."

"Hey. Hey!" Ryan says.

Why is he shouting? He's sitting right next to me. Does he think I can't hear him?

"I told you, Skye. I told you I'd be pissed if you died. Don't you fucking die on me!"

What a damn drama queen. "Not dying. Just...sleepy."

He shouts some more, but I'm drifting away. It's quieter now, which is nice. I just need to sleep. Just for a little while. We can go back to fighting later.

I lean into the darkness and let go.

48

JESUS CHRIST. IT'S LOUD IN here. Wherever here is.

I open my eyes to see a drop ceiling that will definitely not support my weight. Wherever I am, I'll need a different way out.

That does beg a question, though. Where am I? On my back. On a bed. Somewhere loud. And clean. Too clean. Like someone washed everything down with antiseptic. Does that mean…Shit.

The hospital. Not ideal, but at least it's not a jail cell.

I lift my head to get the lay of the land. My left hand is cuffed to the bed. My right hand is in some kind of splint. Fuck. My clothes are gone, replaced by a hospital gown. Double fuck.

How long have I been out? The last thing I remember was being in Noah's car. Now I've been stripped and handcuffed to a bed in a hospital. It's clearly been a while.

All right. What else? The bed is shielded by a curtain. Lots of activity happening on the other side, so I'm probably in the emergency room. There are the unmoving shadows of two figures on the other side of the curtain. Guards? Guards and handcuffs. Apparently, Ryan thinks I'm more of a Houdini than I actually am.

The curtain moves, and a nurse, accompanied by a female police officer, comes inside. She pulls the curtain back in place before looking at me.

"You're awake," she says. "How are you feeling?"

Trapped, mostly. "I don't seem to be feeling much of anything," I say.

She nods. "We gave you something for the pain."

Terrific. That will definitely help me get out of here. I glance at the cuff I currently lack the ability to remove. Maybe the painkillers don't matter at all.

"Where's the guy who brought me here?" I ask. "Ryan. Uh…Agent Ryan. Daniel Ryan. Of the FBI."

"I'm not sure," the nurse says.

I look at the officer. "Do you know where he is?"

She shakes her head.

"What about Noah…something? Willard, maybe?" I say. "He's a detective. Is he around?"

"Don't know Detective Willard. Don't know where Agent Ryan is," the officer says. "I don't need to know, either. My orders are to make sure you stay wherever this nice woman wants you to stay."

I move my wrist to make the handcuff jingle. "Well, can you at least take this off? You can't really think I'm a flight risk."

"Sorry," the nurse says. "It stays for now."

Of course it does. "What about the rest of me?" I ask. "Give me the rundown."

"Your wrist needs a cast, your arm needs some stitches, and your side probably needs surgery."

I shake my head. "I don't want surgery."

"You may *need* surgery."

I *need* to get out of here. I don't need anesthesia and more unconsciousness. "I don't want it. Get me one of those forms to sign. All the forms. Whatever I need to sign to get out of here. You bring them, I'll sign them."

"And with what hand will you sign those forms?"

Mean. But fair. "I will use my teeth," I say. "Please?"

"No."

"I don't think it's legal for you to keep me here against my will."

"There are, occasionally, exceptions," she says. "But hang in there. We'll get you out of the ER as soon as we can, and you can be handcuffed to a bed in a private room."

Despite the situation, I laugh. "You are really mean, you know that?"

She shrugs. "Just call me Nurse Ratched."

"No offense, but I'll probably call you worse than that."

"You won't be the first." She pats my leg and walks away. "I'll be back."

I look at the officer. She doesn't appear to be going anywhere. Now that I'm awake, I warrant direct supervision.

"Do you know Lew?" I ask. "Uh, Llewellyn something. I don't remember his last name, but seriously, how many goddamn Llewellyns can there be? He's married to a hot mess whose dad's some kind of police chief around here. Ring any bells?"

The officer glances at me. "Yeah, I know him. Her, too."

"Is he here in this hospital?"

"Yeah."

"Is he...How is he?"

"Don't know anything about that."

"Do you really not know, or are you just not willing to tell me?"

The officer looks me over with a critical eye. Her name badge reads FARLEY. What does she know about me and this situation? Maybe she doesn't know anything other than I am handcuffed to this goddamn bed, and that doesn't exactly happen naturally.

"I really don't know," she says finally. "But if an officer had died or was close to it, it would be a lot different around here."

That's one thing to be glad for. I could be trapped in an ER filled with angry law enforcement officials instead of dealing with a single, seemingly indifferent one.

I nod. "Thank you."

Officer Farley goes back to ignoring me without actually ignoring me. I look again at my left wrist and turn it to judge the tightness of the cuff. The metal chain jangles just enough to catch her attention and she looks at me, her eyebrow arched.

"Just trying to get comfortable," I say.

"Uh-huh."

When she looks away, I lean forward as much as I can and crane my neck to check the ER for anyone familiar. Ryan, maybe, or Noah, or his partner whose name I can't remember. Or Jonas, even. I was unconscious for a while. Someone must have told him what happened by now. I don't see any of them. I don't even see any other police officers or anyone giving off federal agent vibes. Where is everyone?

Maybe they're with Lew. Makes sense. The point of this whole damn thing was to get him back. Of course Ryan would stick with him.

They could also be dealing with the aftermath of the rescue op. I did set fire to a factory filled with a fair amount of flammable materials and bad guys. That probably required some attention as well.

Shit. I caused so much damage. I hope to hell that Lew's deal works out. Otherwise, I may spend the rest of my life in cuffs or behind bars. Maybe both.

The effort of sitting up becomes too much, and I lie back against the pillow. I'm no expert, but I suspect the meds are wearing off. Which is good. I need to be clear-headed if I'm going to escape. Not that I have any idea how I can do that when I'm attached to the damn gurney. Maybe I could chew off my hand, like an animal caught in a trap. Officer Farley will never notice that.

I'm still cuffed to the damn bed when Nurse Ratched returns with two men wearing scrubs. Orderlies, maybe?

"How's your pain level?" Nurse Ratched asks.

Awful. "Terrific."

"Would you like something for the pain?"

Yes. "No."

Nurse Ratched looks at my right side. She doesn't believe me. "We're going to move you to a room now."

I sit up. Does that mean the cuff's coming off?

"Cuff stays on," Officer Farley says, not looking at me.

"Thanks, Officer Bubble Burster," I say, and she smiles.

The orderlies wheel my gurney out of the curtained area. Officer Farley walks on my left and Nurse Ratched stays on my right, like she's my emotional support nurse or something. We all get in an elevator. I don't see what floor is selected, but given the length of time we're in the little metal box, it's much too high to be an easy escape. I lie back against the pillow and look at the access panel in the ceiling while thinking about the good ole days when I wasn't handcuffed to a damn gurney.

We get off the elevator, and the orderlies move my parade float down a hallway into a small patient room with a single bed. The gurney is positioned next to the bed. Nurse Ratched pulls back the blanket covering me.

"Can you move over on your own?" she asks.

I shake my left hand. "Not with this goddamn thing on."

Officer Farley comes over and unlocks the cuff. "How about now? Can you manage it now?"

I glance at the orderlies standing by. I don't want them touching me, so I nod and slide over, my body hating every motion, no matter how minor. I am feeling every last bruise from that fight. Not to mention the stab wound and the broken bones. Too bad I am entirely too tough for painkillers.

As soon as I'm on the bed, Officer Farley puts the left guardrail in place and reattaches my cuff.

I look at it, then at her. "Gee. Thanks."

She nods and retreats to the hallway. The orderlies leave with the gurney. Nurse Ratched buzzes around the room, fiddling with all the things I've only ever seen on television.

"Aren't you afraid to be alone with me?" I ask.

She laughs. "I've seen a lot worse than you."

I jangle my cuff. "You sure about that?"

Nurse Ratched leans lightly on the guardrail. "One cop who's waiting outside the room? Yeah, I've seen worse than you."

"You really are mean."

"I know. You're a badass," she says. "Are you such a badass that you're going to continue to refuse pain meds you obviously need?"

I can't go anywhere. I might as well be high while I'm trapped. I sigh. "No."

"Good girl," she says. "I'll be right back."

She walks out of the room. Officer Farley steps back inside and stands by the door. She nods at me. I don't return the gesture, a move which I'm sure hurts her feelings immensely. A moment later, she looks to her right, then turns and holds out her hand. "Name?"

"I'm her damn brother," Leo says. "Let me in."

How the hell did Leo find me? Officer Farley looks at me. I nod, and she moves out of the way. Leo comes into the room, the expression on his face warring between being pissed and being relieved.

I'm in trouble.

"Hi," I say.

49

"SO," LEO SAYS, WALKING TOWARD me. "You survived."

"Such as it is." I look at Officer Farley. "Is there any way you might consider waiting in the hall so my brother can scold me in private?"

"She stays cuffed to that bed," Officer Farley says to Leo.

"No argument here," he replies.

Officer Farley walks out, pulling the door closed behind her.

Leo pulls up a chair and sits at my bedside. "What's the damage?"

I check that the door is closed before saying, "I set a factory on fire."

"I meant damage to *you,* but good to know you can now add arson to your list of talents."

I sigh. "Broken wrist. Stab wound. Bullet—"

"Someone shot you?"

"At me. It was just a graze."

"Just a graze," Leo echoes. "Is it over?"

"I don't know. Maybe. Maybe not," I say. "I don't know if they got what they needed. I don't know if they got *anyone.* No one's told me anything, but if they didn't—"

"If they didn't, we're leaving," Leo says.

"I made a deal."

"You didn't agree to kill yourself for them. If they can't take it from here, we're leaving. We're getting the hell out of Boston and starting over somewhere far away from here."

"What about the bar?"

"There are other bars."

"What about Jesus?"

"His name isn't Jesus."

"You gonna leave him behind?"

"If I have to."

"I don't want that for you."

"I don't want *this* for *you*." Leo leans forward. "Look at you!"

"I am…I will make a full recovery."

"How long will that last? How long before they put you in danger again?"

"To be fair, they didn't want to put me in danger this time," I say.

"But they did anyway."

The door opens again, and Nurse Ratched reappears empty-handed. She smiles at Leo. "You must be the brother."

"I am," Leo says.

"You seem to be lacking drugs," I say when she turns to me.

"Yeah. About that," Nurse Ratched says. "The doctor's coming to talk to you."

Shit. If that's happening, that means…I shake my head. "I don't want surgery."

Leo stands and moves to my side. "She needs surgery?"

"She does."

"I don't want it," I say.

"No one cares what you want," Leo says. "You're having surgery."

Nurse Ratched attempts to conceal a smile. "Your brother's wise. You should listen to him."

I laugh. "You say that like I've been given a choice here."

"I'll let you pick the color of your cast," she says. "How about that?"

"You let everyone do that."

"Not when they're handcuffed to the bed."

"Black," Leo interjects. "If you have it, she wants black."

"Like his heart," I say, and Leo scoffs.

Nurse Ratched's smile grows. "I'll let them know," she says. "The doctor will be in shortly, and we'll get you prepped for surgery."

Leo thanks her as she walks away. I don't. That'll show her.

Leo looks at me. "I can't believe you were stabbed and shot—"

"Grazed," I say.

"—and are about to have surgery," he continues, "and you didn't even call me. What the hell, Skye?"

I shake my handcuff. "Sorry. Apparently, we haven't gotten to the I-get-a-phone-call portion of my detainment," I say. "How did you know I was here?"

"Oh, your friend, Nia, called the bar and asked to speak to me. Can I just tell you how excited I am that all your FBI connections know right where to find me?"

"You're one to talk. You told Ryan where I lived."

"He knows where I live. It seemed only fair."

"I told you—"

"I know what you told me. I still didn't want you to go after Lew alone."

"So you told the feds where to find me."

"I told *Ryan* where to find you," Leo says. "The feds wouldn't have cared if you walked out of that building alive. I knew Ryan would."

"*I* didn't care if I walked out of that building."

"That is not making the argument you think it is. If you want to kill yourself, Skye, you'll have to find another way to do it."

"I don't want to kill myself."

"Are you sure about that?"

I sigh. "I was trying to do the right thing."

"So was I."

"Well, you shouldn't have told Ryan anything," I say. "Just because you think there's something between us that isn't there doesn't mean—"

"Oh please."

"We have rules, Leo. We need those rules to survive."

Leo nods. "We do. We do have rules. We have had them for a long time, and we needed them to survive. You're right. We needed them to survive, and because we had those rules, we did survive. You made sure we survived. I am here right now because you made sure *I* would survive."

"Do you have a point, or are you just trying to break some world record for the most uses of the word 'survive' in a single paragraph?"

"You never stopped trying to survive."

"Do you know how stupid that sounds?"

He glares at me. "It's time for the rules to change. We're not those kids anymore. We don't need to be so guarded about everything all the damn time."

"You don't decide that. *We* decide that," I say. "But you told an FBI agent where I lived."

"I told Ryan where you lived."

"Stop pushing that narrative, like there's some difference between him and all the law enforcement people we have known."

"There is a difference, even if you're too stupid to see it," Leo says. "But it doesn't matter because this isn't even about you and Ryan."

"Who else would it have been about? Who else is even left?"

"Me, you idiot. *Me*." Leo jabs his fingers against his chest. "Did it ever occur to you that maybe I did it for me? So that the goddamn FBI wouldn't walk into my bar or knock on my door to ask me to identify your body?"

"Leo—"

"You are my fucking family, Skye. You always have been my family—my *only* family—and you damn well know it," Leo says. "I wasn't going to let that go without a fight. Be pissed at me all you want—I can live with that—but I would do it again."

"I'm not pissed at you," I say. "I just…I wish Ryan didn't know where I lived, okay? Because I'm me, and he's—"

"I know you think Ryan's mad—"

"I woke up handcuffed to a bed." I shake my wrist, in case Leo somehow hadn't noticed. "I'm *still* handcuffed to a bed."

"Of course you're handcuffed to the bed! You're a flight risk, Skye! You are the little illustration next to the phrase 'flight risk' in the damn dictionary! And yeah, Ryan is probably mad at you, but it's because he cares about you."

"Ryan does not care about me. I mean, he cares about arresting me, but that's about it."

Leo shakes his head. "That's not it. You may not be able to see it or admit it, but he cares about *you*. A lot. And that's something we have in common. Hopefully, the only thing we have in common."

There's a knock on the door. Leo and I look over to see Ryan standing just inside the room. Oh fuck. How long has he been standing there? How much of that conversation did he hear?

Ryan looks at me for a long moment before turning to Leo.

"Leo," he says.

Leo stands. "Ryan."

"Could I…I need to talk to Skye," Ryan says. "Alone. Please."

Leo looks at me. "I'm going to talk to your doctor, and then I'll be out in the waiting room. If you attempt to ditch me, or do any other stupid thing, I'm gonna be pissed. *More* pissed."

"I'm not going anywhere," I say, glancing at Ryan.

Except maybe jail.

50

AFTER LEO LEAVES, RYAN CLOSES the door. He doesn't move any closer, just looks at a spot on the wall beyond my head. I'm uncomfortable, but I'm not sure how much of that can be attributed to my injuries and how much is because of the awkward silence. The silence is okay, though. As long as he isn't saying anything, he isn't reading me my rights and arresting me.

"How are you feeling?" he asks finally.

"I'll be fine," I say. "I've had worse."

Now Ryan looks at me. There's a lot about me he doesn't know. More than he actually does know. More than I ever want him to know.

"How's Lew?" I ask.

"He'll be okay. God knows he's had worse, too."

Good. That's good. This was all worth it, then. I nod. "Is Nia here yet?"

Ryan smiles. "You didn't feel the disturbance in the force?"

"No, but they did give me some painkillers." I nod toward the door. "What's with the guard? And the handcuffs?"

"I wanted to talk to you."

"You need a guard and cuffs for that?"

"Earlier, you jumped off a building to avoid talking to me."

"That is…mostly accurate," I admit. "But we were also on a rescue mission, not a leisurely walk through the park."

"And if I took you on a leisurely walk through the park?"

The idea of doing that makes me smile. "Didn't think you were the leisurely-walk-through-the-park type."

"I could be," he says. "You don't know me that well."

Lots of that going around. Ryan moves toward me and sits in the chair on my left.

"You came back for me," I say.

"I did."

"You weren't supposed to. You were supposed to get Lew out of there, and—"

"And I did that. I got him out of the building and into a car and to a hospital," Ryan says. "He will be fine. But you—"

"Are also fine," I say. "Or I will be. Eventually."

"Yeah. Because I"—Ryan jabs a finger against his chest—"came back for you." He shakes his head and looks at the floor. "You were losing that fight, Skye. Hell, you had lost that fight. If I hadn't come back for you—"

"Your life would be a lot simpler right now," I finish.

Ryan's head snaps up so fast, I worry he may have given himself whiplash. "Why would you say that? Why would you ever—?"

"It's true," I say. "You may not like it, but it's true. Things would be a lot easier for you—for everyone—if I had gone into that factory and never came out again."

Ryan tilts his head to the side. Guess he didn't give himself whiplash after all.

"Things would be easier if I let that guy kill you?" he says.

"Am I wrong?"

The anger drains from Ryan's face. Now he looks tired. Defeated. "Why is it every single person in your life values your life more than you do?"

I feel like I've been punched in the gut all over again. I shake my head. "That's not true."

"Really?" Ryan jerks his thumb toward the door. "Should I go get Leo and ask him what he thinks?"

"Leave him out of this."

"Because he'll agree with me? It sure sounds like we have that in common."

"How much did you overhear?" I ask.

"Enough."

"Enough? What does that even mean?"

"You said…In the car, you said there was no point in talking because we don't work out," Ryan says. "Was that the blood loss speaking, or do you really believe that?"

"Do you think there's a world where we do work out?" I ask. He can't, can he?

He's still for a moment, then shakes his head. "I'm going to let Lew and Jonas take over your case from here."

It's for the best. We can't keep doing this, going around in the same circles only to come back to the same conclusion. We don't work out.

We can't.

"You're going to let them do that, or are your bosses pissed?" I ask.

"Both."

The door opens again. This time, Nurse Ratched comes in. She stops short when she sees Ryan. "Oh. I'm sorry to interrupt, but we need to prep our patient here for surgery," she says. "Are you done?"

Ryan looks at me. "Yeah, we're done." He stands and walks toward the door. "Take care of yourself, Skye."

Hard not to sound more final than that, but before he can leave, I ask, "Are you in trouble?"

Ryan smiles. "Since the day I met you."

I say nothing as he walks out.

51

I CAN'T REMEMBER EVER BEING this tired in my entire life. Maybe nobody has ever been this tired in their entire life. Seems unlikely, though. Lots of people in the world. Surely one of them has been more tired than this.

Which really sucks for them because this…is the worst.

Getting free of it is like trying to swim to the surface from a deep, dark, underwater trench. Or what I imagine that would be like if I were someone who knew how to swim and could do something like that.

Which I am not.

I should learn to swim. It could expand my skill set. For underwater thievery. And not drowning.

When I finally make it to the surface, I breathe deep and open my eyes. It's pretty dim, but I can still see the ceiling that won't support my weight. Which might not matter. I don't think I could go anywhere anyway. My chest hurts. My side hurts. My…*everything* hurts. Why does…

Oh right. The hospital. Surgery. I'm still here. Made it to the other side. That's good, I suppose.

"Welcome back," Lew says.

I turn my head to the left to see Lew sitting in a chair. His face looks puffy and bruised. There's a bandage on his cheek. It's like he spent a fair amount of time getting punched in the face.

I squint at him. "Your face is…"

Lew raises a brow.

I lift my hand to wave him off. It no longer seems to be cuffed to the bed. Progress, maybe? "Relax, you big peacock. You're still preternaturally handsome. You just look…hurt."

"I've had worse," he says. "A lot worse."

"Who hasn't?" I lift my head to look around the room. That hurts, too. "Where's Leo?"

"He went to get you some things from home. He'll be back in a little bit."

I lay my head on the pillow. "I don't need anything from home. I'm not staying."

"I know you think so."

"I mean it."

"I know."

Always such a smug asshole. "What are you doing here?" I ask. "Why aren't you in a hospital bed?"

"They discharged me."

"Why you and not me?"

"I didn't get stabbed. You did."

"Only a little," I say. "You got the shit beat out of you."

"Only a little," Lew says. "How do you feel?"

Like not answering that question. "Where's Nia?" I say instead. "Filing for divorce?"

"She is at her parents' house," Lew says. "Probably not filing for divorce."

"Lucky you."

"She knows this is occasionally the job."

"Occasionally?"

"I don't go undercover like I used to."

"Because of Nia."

"Because my face was featured across a lot of media after my last case in Boston. Makes it harder to go undercover when people recognize you," Lew says. "It wouldn't be safe for me or for the people working with me."

"Is undercover work ever really safe?"

"Is thieving?"

"What's life without a little risk?"

"You call this a little risk?"

"I'm still alive."

"Pretty low bar there, isn't it?"

"It's high enough."

"For what?"

Survival. "What about my deal?" I ask. "Do I still have one of those?"

Even in the low light, I clock his disappointment with my question. Why? Because I don't have a deal?

"You do," he says finally.

"But?"

"But...you have a choice to make," Lew says. "You can keep going the way you've been going, keep doing what you've been doing, or..."

Always with the drama, this one. "Or?"

"Or you do something different."

"Something legal, you mean."

"That deal only covers what happened the night of the murders and your lying about it to the FBI."

"Lying? The deal covers lying?"

"Lying to a federal agent is against the law, Skye," Lew says patiently.

Oh. "Well. What fun is that?"

"It's not supposed to be fun," he says. "You don't have immunity for anything you may have done before—"

"I told you that was my very first job ever."

"Okay, but it wasn't," Lew says. "You don't have immunity for what you might have done in the past, and you don't have it for anything you may choose to do in the future."

"Hence the choice," I say.

He nods. "Yeah."

"Let me guess. You think I should give up my life of crime."

"No, I think you should continue to risk your life when you don't actually have to," Lew says drily. I roll my eyes and he adds, "Come on. Did you really think I would say anything else?"

"No, but you don't have to be a jerk about it."

"You say 'jerk', I say I don't want to have to arrest you someday. And I really don't want to have to investigate your disappearance or murder or—"

"Well, unless you're moving back to Boston, you won't have to do any of those things," I say. "And I don't know why you guys keep treating me like I'm some goddamn kitten stuck in a tree. I am not helpless. You don't even know half of what I've survived or half of what I've had to do to survive. The key word there, in case you missed it, is *survive*. Because I am a survivor, so stop acting like me being murdered is some foregone conclusion."

"You're right. I don't know what you had to survive, and I don't know what you had to do in order to survive, and I don't doubt that you are a survivor," Lew says. "The key word there, in case *you* missed it, is my use of the past tense."

"That's not a word."

"Shut up and listen," Lew says. "You survived. Past tense. You did what you had to do, and you made it out. Not only that, but you got Leo out, too."

I shake my head. "Leo got himself out."

"You got him out," Lew says. "You know how I know that? Leo told me. While we were sitting here, in this room, waiting for you to wake up, following the surgery you had for the major stab wound in your side."

"It's not that major."

"It required surgery."

"Minor surgery," I say. "And I only got this stab wound because I was saving your sorry ass. Did you and Leo talk about that?"

"No, we were talking about how my sorry ass only needed saving because I had to save your sorry ass first."

"Are you talking about the restaurant? About how you and Ryan followed me in?"

"You were supposed to be in the van."

"Well, so were you," I say. "I break into places for a damn living. Those guys never would have known I was there. You made it worse. Ryan made it worse. Neither of you should have been there."

"You shouldn't have been there."

He's so goddamn calm. Here I am, railing at him, and there he is, sitting in that chair like we're talking about the weather. And not even interesting weather, like a three-day blizzard or a major hurricane. How does he do it? Is he some kind of robot? Is that how he's managed to stay married to Nia?

"You didn't need to be there. You didn't need to take the risk," Lew says. "You did once, I know. But you don't now."

Jesus Christ. This has got to be the worst intervention ever. "What am I supposed to do then?" I ask. "Sit at home and learn to knit?"

"Stop. You're supposed to stop. Stop taking risks you don't need to take."

"It's not a—"

"Yes, it is. You are good at what you do, but it's still a risk. A pretty damn big one," Lew says. "If you won't do it for you, do it for Leo."

"Oh, fuck you," I say. "Don't you fucking use him."

"I'll use whatever tools I have at my disposal to help convince you."

"Leo wouldn't want to be considered a tool or used by the FBI."

"In these specific circumstances, I think he'd make an exception," Lew says. "We can ask him when he gets back, but it might be easier and quicker if you can find a way to accept the very real truth that there are people in this world who want you to remain in this world."

"Did he ask you to tell me this?" I say. "Is that why he's not here right now?"

"He didn't ask me anything. He didn't have to," Lew says. "I can see it. Even though I am…" He shakes his head. "Whatever unflattering thing you care to call me."

"You mean like 'FBI agent'?"

"Yeah. Like that," he says. "Leo really didn't say anything to me. He didn't ask me to do anything. I imagine he would view it as a betrayal of some kind."

"Funny. That didn't stop him from telling the FBI where I lived."

"He told Ryan where you live."

"Lived," I say. "And there's no difference between Ryan and the FBI."

"There's a big difference."

It doesn't feel like there's much of a difference at all. But maybe the fact that Ryan's not sitting here, that he passed the case off—passed *me* off—to Lew and Jonas means otherwise. If he didn't care, he would still be here.

The lies we tell ourselves. I smile because it seems like a better choice than crying.

"Is Ryan why you're here?" I ask. "Did he want you to help me see the error of my ways?"

"He didn't ask me to do anything except take over the case. But I don't think he would mind if you were to reconsider your career choices. He would also like you to remain in this world."

I sigh.

"Sucks, doesn't it?" Lew says. "Having people care about you."

"It's certainly inconvenient," I say. "Especially when they won't shut up right after you've woken up from surgery."

"Does that mean you'd like me to be quiet?"

"No, I think we should never stop talking. Ever."

Lew chuckles. "I can take a hint."

"Can you?"

"Yeah. I can," he says. "Just promise me you'll think about what I said."

"About giving up my livelihood?"

"There are others."

Easy for him to say. He gave up the undercover life to go work for the Smug Asshole department of the same government agency. What am I supposed to do? Being a thief is all I've ever done. It's all I've ever known. If I don't do that, what else is out there?

"You know," Lew says, "someone with skills like yours, the experience you have…" He shrugs. "We can use someone like you."

"You already did."

"That's not what I meant."

"Well, I know you're not suggesting I join the injustice department."

Lew laughs. "I am not. I know better than that."

"Then what are you suggesting?"

"We're not the only people you could help."

The door opens, and Jonas steps inside. He summons Lew with a jerk of his head.

Lew looks at me. "Just something to think about," he says. "Sit tight for a minute?"

Some people think they're so funny. I flip him off with my good hand. He smiles and limps over to Jonas.

52

LEW AND JONAS STAY IN the room, talking in hushed tones, each of them glancing at me at various times. What happened? Did my deal fall through? I should have known better than to trust Lew. I should have chewed my fucking hand off back in the ER.

I sit up. It hurts like hell, but I can manage. I *will* manage. I glance at the window to my right. Does it open? What floor are we on?

"Do not go out that window," Lew says without looking at me. "Don't even *think* about getting out of that bed."

The smug asshole strikes again. I sink back against the pillow. "Well, then, do you want to tell me what you're talking about over there? Because you're really freaking me out."

Lew turns and smiles. It does not ease my anxiety.

"We got them," he says. "We got them all."

"Them?" I ask. I don't want to assume. He has to say it.

"The gray ghost and the other two men from the Skyreach. We got them."

Yeah. I'm going to need more. "And by 'got them' you mean?"

"They're in custody. All three of them," Jonas says. "Plus a few more."

"You're sure it's them?" I ask.

Jonas comes forward and pulls the rolling table in front of me. He removes some photographs from his jacket and lays them on the table. "You tell me. See anyone familiar?"

Lew helps me sit up, putting extra pillows behind my back for additional support. Thoughtful jackass. I push him away and look at the photos. Booking photos. Eight of them. Three of the men I've never seen. One is the man I knocked out at the factory. Another is the guy who stabbed me. Two are the henchmen from the Skyreach. The last is the gray ghost.

Shit. Could this thing really be over?

I separate out two of the photos. "They were in the factory." Next, I slide the henchmen photos over to the side. "These two shot Edward Roberson. They tried to shoot me." My fingers hover over the picture of the ghost. I don't want to touch it. "This is the man who told them to do it."

"You're sure?" Jonas asks, sitting in the chair. Lew stands behind him and leans against the wall.

"I'm sure," I say. "You're sure they're in custody?"

"Yeah."

"How long will they stay there?"

Jonas shrugs. "Probably depends on how good their lawyers are. But our lawyers are pretty good, too."

"Do you have enough to hold them? Charge them?" I ask.

"I think we do." Jonas grimaces as though experiencing sudden and acute gastrointestinal distress. "Thanks to you."

My brow furrows. "Me? How did I do that?"

Jonas holds up a plastic bag containing a flash drive. "Look familiar?"

"Is that the drive I…acquired from the restaurant?" I ask. Jonas nods. "Then there must have been something on it. Something incriminating?"

"Yeah."

"They really put something incriminating on that?" I think I'm insulted.

"They didn't. We think Roberson did."

"Why would he do that? Was he new to crime?"

"Yeah," Jonas says. "He took the place of the last guy—"

"The WITSEC guy," I say. Jonas frowns. "Ryan mentioned him. I don't know anything else about him, though."

Jonas nods. "Right. Well, we thought the organization would attempt to recruit someone new, and it looks like they thought Roberson would be their guy. Maybe he knew what happened to his predecessor, maybe he didn't, but our best guess is he thought he needed insurance to protect himself."

"That's stupid. These guys don't care about insurance," I say.

"You know that. I know that," Jonas says. "Roberson didn't."

I shake my head. "It got him killed."

Jonas shrugs. "Don't know about that, but it didn't help."

No, it really didn't. I nod at the photos. "Did they happen to confess? Are they talking at all?"

"Four words," Jonas says. "And four words only."

"I want a lawyer."

"Got it in one."

That's not surprising. Those would be the only four words I would say, too. "Will they confess? Can you hold them if they don't?"

Jonas glances at Lew. Lew nods.

Jonas looks back at me. "Your ghost won't confess to anything. We both know that. He won't confess, and his lawyer will get him out. Afterward, he may keep a lower profile for a while. He may leave Boston altogether. I don't know."

Or he could stick around and send other people after me because I'm still a damn thorn in his side. Have they thought of that? Do they care?

"What about the shooters?" I ask.

"They had guns on them when we arrested them. Those guns might match the weapons used to kill Edward Roberson and the security guard. And if they don't…" Jonas shrugs. "You're not the only one who saw them. They won't get the lawyer the ghost gets. They'll talk. They'll deal."

They'll get a deal. They killed a security guard. They killed Edward Roberson. They probably killed Jay. They tried to kill me—more than once, even—and they'll get a deal. The justice system at work.

"Skye, look at me," Lew says. When I do, he continues. "They will go to prison. They will do time."

"Don't make promises your agency won't keep."

"They killed two men—"

"They killed more than two."

"Only two we can prove," Jonas says.

Will they even bother trying to prove the third? Do they care? Why spend time and resources figuring out who slit a man's throat when they have nothing to gain from it? Jay's death has no bearing on their case. He isn't anything to them. He isn't anything to anyone.

Almost anyone.

"I want his remains," I say.

Jonas looks confused.

Lew does, too, briefly. Then he nods. "Fagin, you mean." He immediately holds up his hand in apology. "Sorry. Jay."

"They're gonna cremate him," Jonas says.

"Then I want his ashes," I say. "If that's okay."

"That's okay," Lew says. "I'll make sure you get them."

I nod. I should thank him, but all I manage to say is, "Good."

"Skye," he says then. "You—"

"What does all this mean for me?" I ask.

"You got a deal, don't you?" Jonas says.

I glance at Lew. He nods.

"I do," I say.

"Well, there you go." Jonas stands and gathers the photos from the table. "You identified our suspects, helped us take them into custody, and found us a possible new avenue in our investigation. I'd say you held up your end."

"So…this is it?" I ask.

"This is it."

"Are you disappointed you won't be able to arrest me?"

Jonas laughs. "I'm sure I'll get another crack at it soon enough."

"I might surprise you," I say.

"Then again, you might not."

That does seem to be the more likely of the two. Got to appreciate the man keeping it real. "Then we're done?" I say. "Like, really done?"

"God, I hope so," Jonas says.

"Yes," Lew says. "I need to bring by some paperwork for you to sign, but other than that, we're done."

"I need to sign something? I wasn't supposed to exist, and now I need to sign something?"

"Trust me?" Lew asks.

I scoff. "You want me to trust a fed?"

"I want you to trust *me*," Lew says. "Can you do that?"

No. Hell, no. But this is probably one of those situations where it's too late for that. I sigh. "Better you than Jonas, I suppose."

Jonas rolls his eyes and heads for the exit.

Lew smiles. "I'll take it. Get some rest, okay?" he says, following Jonas. "I'll bring your agreement by later."

"Hey, Lew?" I say before he can go. He looks at me. "Thank you."

He nods and walks out.

53

THREE DAYS LATER, HOWEVER, I am still in the damn hospital, and Lew has yet to return with my deal. That's what I get for trusting him. Or *not* get, I suppose, as I have nothing to show for my efforts except a black wrist cast and a still-healing and itchy surgical scar on my side.

Not to mention a rather concerning tendency to spend my waking hours watching daytime television. It's not like I was a genius before, but every day I remain here, staring at that damn TV, I get just a little bit dumber. The worst thing is that Saturday morning television is somehow even worse than the weekdays. I may cave and start watching the Game Show Network soon.

Deal or no deal, I need to get out of here.

"I have good news," Nurse Ratched announces as she walks into the room.

I highly doubt that. Her idea of good news is that it's pancake day in the cafeteria. Still, I mute the television and look at her.

She smiles. "You can go home this afternoon."

Well, that *is* good news. I drop the remote and throw back the blankets, but Nurse Ratched blocks me before I can get even a single toe on the floor.

"This afternoon," she repeats. "*Late* afternoon. Your brother will be coming to get you, and when he gets here, you will be discharged. Not before."

"Why do I have to wait?" I ask. "I don't need a chaperone."

"You need to take it easy until your body is fully healed. Something tells me you'll be much more successful at that if you have some supervision."

That is probably not the most inaccurate statement ever. I sigh and settle back on the bed.

"Good choice," Nurse Ratched says.

"I don't recall being given a choice."

"We always have a choice."

I roll my eyes. "Don't take this personally, but I really hate you."

"I know," she replies. "But think of it like this: You've made it four days already. You can last a few more hours."

We'll see about that. I pick up the remote and unmute the volume. Looks like I'll be watching the Game Show Network after all.

I'm in the middle of a *Family Feud* marathon when there's a knock on the door. I look over to see Lew and Nia walk into the room. Well, Lew walks. Nia waddles.

"I hear you're going home today," Lew says.

I turn off the television. "That's the rumor. What are you doing here?"

Lew holds up a legal-sized envelope. "Got something for you."

"My Get Out of Jail Free card?" I ask.

"Something like that."

It's about damn time. I look at Nia as I climb out of bed. "And what are you doing here?"

"You did what you promised to do, so I wanted to thank you," she says. "And also use your bathroom. I really need to pee."

She goes into the bathroom and closes the door.

I look at Lew. "It seriously must take you guys forever to go anywhere."

Lew smiles. "What did you promise to do?"

"Save your sorry ass," I say. "Envelope, please."

Lew hands it over. I set it on the bed to open it, then hold it upside down to shake out the contents. Nothing comes out.

"Here," Lew says. "Let me help."

He takes the envelope back and removes a stack of paper. "One copy for you. One for me."

I take the stack. So this is an FBI deal. "It took you long enough to bring this. I was starting to think you had lied to me."

"*Starting* to think?" Lew asks, and I shrug. "I was concerned that if I brought it sooner you might be tempted to leave the hospital before you should have."

"*Might* be tempted?" I ask, reading the first page. I stop when I see the name printed on the paperwork and look at Lew. "Skye Walker?"

"Your parents must have been *Star Wars* fans," he says.

Or smug assholes with too much time on their hands. I roll my eyes and start looking over the rest of the deal. Nia comes out of the bathroom and Lew helps her sit in the chair. They wait quietly while I continue to read. There's quite a lot of lawyer speak, but I think I get the gist of it. Seems legit. Or as legit as the FBI ever really gets, maybe.

"This is it, then?" I say when I finish. "I'm free to go or whatever?"

"You'll never have to see any of us again," Lew says.

Something aches in my chest a little. Don't know why. "None of you, huh?"

"Unless, of course, you give us a reason to come looking for you," Lew says.

"Wouldn't want that." I can't want that. We don't work. We could never work.

"Skye?" Lew says. "Are you—?"

"Yeah, yeah, yeah." I drop the paperwork. "Crime doesn't pay. I get it."

"On that note..." Nia pulls a folded piece of paper from her bag and holds it out. "Here. In case you need it."

I take the paper and unfold it. *Jitters. Newbury Street. Lacey.* "What is this?"

"It's a coffee place on Newbury Street," Nia says. "My friend Lacey is the day manager there. She'll give you a job if you need one."

"A job?"

"A legal one."

That sounds like it'll pay well. "I don't know that I'm much of a barista."

Nia shrugs. "You could learn."

"That easy, huh?"

"Never claimed it would be easy," she says. "Perfect caramel lattes are difficult to master."

"It's possible I wasn't talking about the coffee."

"No shit." Nia looks at Lew. "I gotta pee."

He helps her up. As she returns to the bathroom, Lew pulls the tray table over. He puts both copies of the deal on top and offers me a pen.

"Two signatures, and we're gone."

I take the pen in my left hand and write *Skye Walker* in shaky letters in the appropriate spot on each page. Lew then folds one copy and tucks it into his jacket pocket. The other he puts back in the envelope and lays it on the bed.

"Have you considered what we talked about?" he asks.

"Not even a little."

"Well, then, would you like my advice?"

"No, but I'm guessing you'll offer it anyway."

He nods at the envelope. "Take that life and do something good with it."

"Your definition of good and mine are pretty different."

"Maybe not so different."

"Or maybe incredibly different."

Lew smiles again. "You can help us without helping us, you know."

Nia comes back out before I can ask what the hell he means by that.

"You done?" she asks Lew.

He nods. Nia walks right up to me with the intensity of a hungry, feral Rottweiler who probably has to pee. I brace myself.

"I don't think either of us are huggers," she says, "but…"

She throws her arms around me and hugs me tightly. I wince as an uncomfortable amount of pressure is applied to still-healing areas of my body.

When she releases me, she steps back and nods. "Thank you." She then looks at Lew. "Let's see if we can make it to the lobby before I have to pee again."

She turns and walks out of the room. Lew follows, lagging behind just long enough to give me a small salute. Then he's gone. They're all gone. For good.

I look at the envelope. What would be a good use of that life? Helping them without helping them? Even if I knew what that meant, is helping the FBI in any way something I'd want to do? I already helped them with their stupid case. What more could they want?

Well, it is a government agency. What else can I expect from them? All take. No give.

I look at the envelope again. Except for that, anyway.

There's another knock on the door. I look over, expecting to see Nia needing the bathroom, but Leo comes in instead.

"You good?" Leo says. "All packed and ready to go?"

No, I'm not good. Nor have I packed. But I am ready to get the hell out of here. I smile. "If you had taken any longer, I would have left without you."

"You wouldn't have dared." Leo comes over to the bed and gestures to the envelope. "What's that?"

I pick it up and hand it to him. "A new life."

54

AFTER PACKING MY BELONGINGS INTO a tote bag and collecting a couple of prescription bottles from Nurse Ratched, Leo and I leave the hospital and take a cab to his apartment. He gets out of the car first and helps me out—not that I need it—then walks behind me to the building as though I am a toddler taking my first steps or an elderly person in danger of falling and breaking a hip. When we near the door, he rushes ahead to open it for me. I may be hurt, but this is really overkill.

"You're being ridiculous, you know," I say.

"Shut up," he replies.

We go upstairs to his apartment. Leo unlocks the door and pushes it open. He lets me go in first.

"Okay," he says, closing the door behind us, "you're taking the bed, and—"

"What?" I turn to look at him. "I'm not taking your bed. The couch is fine."

"The couch is *not* fine. You just got out of the hospital, and you're still recovering from surgery."

"Minor surgery."

"You're not sleeping on the damn couch, Skye. End of argument."

"You keep this up, and I'll just walk home."

"Oh please. We both know you're never going back to that apartment."

No, I won't be going back there. I can't. It's too bad. It was a real shithole, but it was mine.

"I won't be here any longer than I have to be," I say.

Leo pulls me in for a tight hug. "Stay as long as you need. Stay forever, if you want. In fact, I would prefer it."

The sincerity in his voice makes me want to cry. As I am entirely too tough for that, I laugh instead. "Jesus would love that."

"Will you please stop calling him that?"

"Probably not anytime soon." I free myself from Leo's arms. "I appreciate the offer, but I can't stay here indefinitely. Jesus will only tolerate me being here for so long. I'm not looking to ruin your relationship."

"I wouldn't have *Linus* if you hadn't…I wouldn't have survived our childhood without you, and Linus knows that," Leo says. "And he knows you're not going anywhere. He gets to decide if that's something he can deal with."

"And if he decides he can't?"

Leo shrugs. "Then it's his damn loss. Because I am an *amazing* catch."

"Check out the ego on you."

"It's not ego if it's true." Leo hands me the tote bag. "Now, go put your crap away in the bedroom. Linus is coming over."

"He is? Why?"

Leo gives me a look that suggests I have forgotten something obvious. It's not his birthday or a holiday. What's left?

"It's Saturday," Leo says. "Family dinner night."

Family dinner night? Since when do we have family dinners? Where did he even get the idea? It's not like we…Oh. That's right. Me. He got the idea from me.

"You know I wasn't being serious about that, right?"

"Well, I *am* serious, and it *is* happening. In about an hour." Leo points to the bedroom. "Go get ready."

"Jesus and I are going to bond over how mean and bossy you are."

"Can't wait." Leo heads to the kitchen. "Go!"

"Love you," I call.

"Love you, too," he replies. "You major pain in my ass."

I carry the bag into the bedroom and leave it against the wall next to the closet. It takes about ten seconds, which leaves me approximately an entire hour to worry about family dinner and officially meeting Linus.

Leo is in the kitchen, opening drawers and taking out pots and pans and whatever else he needs to make whatever fancy food he's decided on. He really is serious about this. He's serious about Linus, too.

I have to make this work. Surely I can act like a normal person doing normal people things for a couple of hours or for however long family dinners last. If Leo wants a family dinner, then we'll have a family dinner. I will make nice with his boyfriend and apologize for being such an ass the first time we met. I will eat whatever ridiculous food Leo puts in front of me without complaint.

Well, I'll at least apologize to Linus.

But if I'm going to hold up my end of the family dinner promise, there is one thing I need to do first.

As going out the front door would raise questions, I sneak into the bathroom and climb out through the window and onto the fire escape. My surgical scar wishes I had used the door, but I manage. I make it down to the street and walk around the block to The Thieves' Den.

The Saturday night crowd is still in its early stages, but there are two people who aren't me sitting in my booth. Another sign Leo is serious about tonight. I try to stop staring at them as I belly up to the bar to wait for Robbie.

"You scared the shit outta us, you know," he says when he comes over.

"I'm sorry," I say. "I didn't mean to."

"You better not do it again."

"I don't intend to."

"Ain't much of a promise, Mags."

"Best I can do, Rob."

He nods. "What are you doing here anyway? Boss said you wouldn't be in tonight."

"Clearly." I glance toward my booth. "I hope they tip better than I do."

Robbie laughs. "Everyone tips better than you do. What do you want?"

"Wine."

"You don't drink wine."

"No, but Leo and his plus one do," I say. "It's family dinner night, and I'm supposed to bring wine, but I don't know what they like. I'm guessing you do."

"Family dinner?"

I shrug. "It's new."

Robbie nods. He goes into the back and soon returns with a wine bottle. He sets it in front of me. "If the boss asks, you didn't get this from me."

I salute him. "Thanks, Rob."

I take the bottle and walk out of the bar. Linus is walking right toward me. I freeze. He's wearing pants that aren't jeans and a blazer over a cashmere sweater. Why does he look so nice? Are we supposed to dress up? Shit. Is family dinner a formal event? There Linus is, looking like he's straight out of a fashion magazine for Cambridge yuppies or something, and I'm standing here wearing the same yoga pants I've had on for two days because I can mostly get them on by myself and the waistband is gentle enough for my stupid surgical scar.

He's getting closer. Should I say something? Will he recognize me? I'm sure I wasn't his immediate focus the night we met. He might not remember what I look like.

He slows when he sees me and stops. "Skye?"

Or maybe he will. "Linus," I say.

"Linus? Not Jesus?"

"Well, Leo's not here, so…" I shrug.

Linus smiles. "You two really are siblings."

His gaze drops to the bottle in my hand.

"I didn't steal this," I blurt. "Oh. Well. Technically, I guess I did, but…" I sigh. Yeah. This is going well. "I'm really sorry about the way we met. It was an asshole thing to do, and I'm an asshole—I really am—but the circumstances—"

"Leo told me," Linus says. "Not the details, of course, but he told me."

"Oh. Okay," I say. "I, uh…Yeah, the circumstances that night were pretty wild and aren't likely to be repeated—at least I hope to hell not—but you should know that I am a walking natural disaster, a raging, out-of-control garbage fire who will continuously make you want to tear your hair out and strangle me with it, and I'm sorry for that. It won't seem like it, but I am.

"But as long as you're with Leo, that will be your reality because I'm not going anywhere," I continue. "I would. I would just disappear into the dead of night, never to be heard from again, but if I did that…he would never stop looking for me. Never. And this great life he has built here—this really *amazing* life—would go away. He deserves a great life, so I'm not going to ruin this one. Not intentionally, anyway, but you know"—I point to myself—"garbage fire with a serious track record for destruction, so it could still happen regardless of my intentions.

"Anyway, I just thought you should know or be warned or whatever. I hope it's something you can live with because Leo's worth it. He's more than worth it. He's…" I shake my head. "You won't find anyone better than him anywhere, and if you are lucky enough to be loved by him…It's worth it. He's worth it. And I hope you agree."

Linus looks at me. Is he preparing to bolt? To turn around and run away because I'm such a damn freak? How am I going to tell Leo I screwed things up for him already?

"Are you done?" Linus asks.

"I think so."

He nods. "Good. My turn."

I brace myself. "Okay."

"I love Leo. Not like. Love. I love him," Linus says. "And the way he tells it, I wouldn't be able to love him if it hadn't been for you, so as much as I may want to strangle you from time to time, I won't. Not with my hair or my hands or anything else. Unless you actually do that whole 'disappearing in the dead of night' thing. Then I will track you down, and if you're not already dead, I will kill you for making the love of my life worry about you. Got it?"

I nod. "Got it."

"Good."

I wait a moment, but he doesn't say anything else. "Is that it?"

"Yes."

"That was a lot shorter than my thing."

"It was."

"You got to the point much quicker."

"I did."

"Is he really the love of your life?"

"Yes."

"All right, then," I say. "Let's go to dinner."

As convincing Linus to go back up the fire escape is unlikely, we use the proper entrance to the building and walk up to Leo's apartment. I'm reaching for the door knob before I realize the problem with my plan.

I look at Linus. "Do you have a key?"

"You don't?"

"Not on me." I gesture to my outfit. "No pockets. Or any idea where the key actually is at this moment. My apartment, probably, but possibly melted in a mysterious factory fire that I definitely did not start. Anyway, do you have a key?"

Linus smiles and reaches into his pocket. He pulls out a set of keys and sorts through them. He has a key. Leo gave him a key. I really can't screw this up.

Linus inserts the key and opens the door, but the chain prevents it from opening fully.

"The chain is on," he says. "Why is the chain on?"

"Oh, Leo's just afraid that either the mob or the FBI will be coming for me."

"The…what?"

"Don't worry about it," I say. "Have any dental floss?"

"Uh…no."

I nod. "Worth a try." I hand him the wine bottle and rattle the door. "Hey, Leo! Get over here and let us in!"

I hear Leo stop whatever he's doing and walk toward us. He glances through the crack, his face creased with confusion, before he closes the door and slides the chain, and then reopens it.

"What are you doing out here? How did you…" He looks over his shoulder, then back at me. "You went out the bathroom window."

I shrug as I walk inside the apartment. Linus follows.

"You have a broken arm," Leo says.

"Wrist."

Leo's lips form a thin line. "You have a broken wrist," he says through clenched teeth.

"I also have an unbroken one."

"You were shot," Leo says.

"You were shot?" Linus asks.

I glance at him. "Grazed."

Leo points to my side. "You have a *stab* wound."

"You were stabbed?" Linus asks.

"Only a little," I tell him.

"Skye!" Leo exclaims.

"What?"

He grabs the still-open door and shakes it before closing it. "I have a *door*."

"And I have issues. What's your point?" I take the wine out of Linus's hands and hold it out. "Look! I brought wine."

"Looks like Linus brought wine."

"He was just holding it for me while I got your attention because I have a broken wrist, you know," I say. "I brought the wine."

"You mean you stole the wine from my bar."

"That is also true, yes."

Linus laughs. "You two are going to be fun." He walks past us and heads for the kitchen. "What's for dinner?"

55

LEO MAKES MACARONI AND CHEESE for dinner. It's the real stuff—no packets of orange powder to be found here—baked in the oven with a buttery breadcrumb topping. Even I have to admit that it's pretty damn delicious, and easy enough for me to eat with my non-dominate hand without looking too much like an uncoordinated weirdo.

Which is good because there's so much other weird to be found around this table. I don't know what family dinners are supposed to be like, but this one is just plain awkward.

Probably because there are three of us. One couple, and then one tagalong who has no one or nothing else in their life, so they sit at the table across from the couple and try to smile and act as though they're not some kind of voyeuristic freak. Maybe that's easier to accomplish for people who aren't me. Maybe that's something that will grow easier over time.

I guess I have to hope so because I like Linus, and I like him and Leo together, and if Leo wants family dinners, then Leo will get family dinners. Even if I have to be the third wheel. Which I will be, because that's not likely to change anytime soon. Or ever.

But despite the awkwardness, it's nice to see Leo have something good, something normal. We sure as hell didn't grow up with much that could be considered either of those things. If one of us was going to manage it, I'm glad it was him. I'm glad he met Linus wherever it was they met—at the bakery or the grocery store or on the T, maybe—and that they had enough of a spark to want to see each other again and keep seeing each other.

I literally ran into Ryan on the street one night because men with guns were trying to kill me, then I lied about who I was for days because his job is to arrest people like me. Not exactly the stuff dreams are made of. We couldn't be more wrong for one another if we tried.

Doesn't seem to stop me from missing him, though. Whatever that's all about. I'm sure it'll fade with time.

I hope.

When dinner comes to an end, the guys clear the table and clean up in the kitchen while I am sent to sit on the couch like a child in time-out. I watch them work around each other, exchanging smiles and glances and touches. An elbow graze, a hand on the small of their back. They're good together. I smile to see it, to know it without doubt, but it also reconfirms what I already know.

I cannot stay here indefinitely.

After Linus leaves for the night, Leo secures the door behind him and then joins me on the couch.

"So...family dinner?" he says. "A success?"

I have no idea. I have nothing with which to compare it. But there was no screaming, crying, or murder of any kind, so it certainly could have been worse.

"Food and fun was had by all," I answer.

Leo's gaze narrows slightly. Apparently, my response didn't hit the appropriate amount of enthusiasm.

"You okay?" he says. "Are you hurting?"

In more ways than one. I sigh. "Why didn't you ever tell me about Linus?"

"What?"

"Were you ever going to tell me about him? I mean, if I hadn't walked in—"

"Barged in."

"—on you," I continue, "would I *ever* have met him?"

"Skye—"

"He was the adult stuff, right? The adult stuff you told me I'd have no interest in?"

Leo slumps against the couch. "Yeah."

"Why would you think that? I do plenty of adult stuff, you know."

"I do know. With FBI agents, even."

"One agent. One time," I say. "Fine, twice. Well, technically more than that, but—"

"Wait. Twice?" Leo sits up. "You told me it wouldn't happen again."

"And clearly I was lying," I say. "But so were you. About a lot more for a lot longer."

"It wasn't a lie so much as a—"

"A lie of omission is still a lie, and we don't lie to each other," I say. "At least we didn't used to."

Leo sighs. "I didn't think you'd approve."

I shake my head. What the hell is he talking about? "Of...Linus?"

"Of me letting Linus in. Of me letting *anyone* in," Leo says. "It's been just you and me for so long that I thought maybe—"

"I wouldn't want you to be happy?"

Leo hesitates. His mouth opens and closes a couple of times but no sound comes out.

"When you put it like that," he says finally, "it sounds pretty bad."

"Yeah."

"Is it better or worse than you bursting in—"

"Walking in."

"—to my bedroom to announce that you were going on a suicide mission to rescue a kidnapped FBI agent?" Leo says. "Not to mention stealing my favorite hoodie in the process."

I guess he has me there. "Worse," I say. "Way worse. Just…so much worse."

Leo smiles. "Are you sure? It was a *really* nice hoodie."

"Yeah." I sigh again. My body hurts. Perhaps climbing out of a bathroom window and down a fire escape this soon after surgery was a bad idea. "I do want you to be happy."

"I know."

"Linus makes you happy? Like, really happy? Like, you…love him?"

"Yeah. I do. I really do."

I nod. "Then don't fuck it up."

Don't let me *fuck it up*, I want to add. My eyes water, a combination of pain both physical and emotional. Leo sees it—hell, it can probably be seen from space—and frowns.

"How much pain are you in right now?" he asks. "Before you answer, you should consider that if you want to maintain whatever moral high ground you have right now, you should tell me the truth."

Moral high ground. Yeah, I have so much of that. I roll my eyes. "I may be in a little pain."

"If you're admitting it, it's more than a little," Leo says. "I'll get your meds."

He hurries back to the kitchen and quickly returns with a glass of water and the prescription bottle Nurse Ratched gave me on my way out. After placing the water on the coffee table, Leo opens the bottle and shakes out two pills. He hands them over, and I pop them in my mouth and wash them down with the water. Leo watches me so intensely that I wonder if I'm now supposed to prove to him that I did, in fact, swallow the meds instead of cheeking them, but he only takes the water and pill bottle back to the kitchen.

When he returns, he still looks concerned. "It was too much, wasn't it? What was I thinking? You just got out of the hospital. I shouldn't have—"

"Leo, it's fine. Really. I'm just tired. I just need sleep."

"Promise?"

"We don't lie to each other," I say. "Remember?"

"Okay." He nods. "Then let's get you into bed."

I want to tell him that I can get myself into bed, but instead I let him help me off the couch and into the bedroom.

"Do you want to change into something else?" he asks, picking up the tote bag I never unpacked. He carries it over to his dresser and sets it on top. "Pajamas or something?"

I sit on the bed and toe off my slip-on shoes. "I'm already wearing pajamas."

He glances at my outfit. "Different pajamas?"

"I'm good. I can sleep in this. Are you sure you don't want me to take the couch?"

"I'm sure. Stop asking." Leo opens his bottom dresser drawer and pulls out a pair of flannel pajama pants. He closes the drawer and looks at me. "It's temporary, Skye. Okay? Tomorrow, we'll start looking for a two-bedroom. Then neither of us will have to sleep on the couch."

I smile because it's expected. Because I owe him that.

"Sounds good," I say for the same reason.

Leo smiles, too. "I'm really glad you're here."

"In this apartment, or on this earth?"

"Both," he says. "You need anything else?"

I shake my head. "I'm good."

"Okay." Leo walks toward the door. "Yell, if that changes."

"Hey," I say before he leaves, "thanks for taking care of me."

He stops and tosses the pajama pants over his shoulder. "It's what we do. Right?"

"Yeah," I say. "It's what we do."

He pulls the door closed but leaves it partially open. Turning off the light, I lie on my back and look at the ceiling while listening to Leo get ready for bed.

A two-bedroom apartment. Won't that be nice. I'm sure Linus will cherish the opportunity to be the third wheel in his own relationship. What person wouldn't?

This is my fault. I scared Leo. A lot. Too much, clearly. This is a knee-jerk reaction to that fear. I will have to tread carefully. He's never liked me being in danger—of course he hasn't—but this…I pushed things too far. Leo may not have come out of this with broken bones or stab wounds, but he still needs time to recover. I get that. But as much as I do love him, and as reluctant as I am to hurt him in any way, I'll need to move on eventually.

One of us needs to consider Leo's love life, and it would seem that someone's going to be me.

It's okay, though. I can hang here in the meantime. I'll need time to execute my new life plan. Not to mention coming up with a new life plan.

I could always set up shop at The Rebel Fly. Take over Jay's booth and pick up where he left off. Clients wouldn't need to know they're hiring me. You need a thief? I can find you a thief.

Except…should I do that? Would that be doing something good? I mean, I'm good at it, but maybe it would be too hard on Leo now. And it's definitely not what Lew had in mind when he gave me that envelope.

You can help us without helping us, he said. Which sounds great, but I still don't know what that means. Stupid Lew, running around, acting like he's a federally funded Riddler or some shit. He couldn't have just said what he meant? Like I would feel cheated if I didn't work it out on my own?

When Leo starts snoring, I look back toward the door. I won't be getting any more thinking done tonight. At least not here. I could try sleeping, but there's way too much going on in my head for that. Maybe a walk will help.

I get out of bed. I can't get my shoes back on, so I slide my feet into Leo's slippers and walk to the bedroom door. Attempting to go out through the living room is too much of a risk with my warden sleeping right there. I'll have to use the fire escape instead. I make my way to the bathroom. Leo doesn't wake up, so I climb out the window and head into the night.

56

IT'S LATE, I HAVE NO money, and I'm also wearing slippers, so I walk into The Thieves' Den where I'm bound to be served regardless of what I may or may not have on me.

Someone is in my booth. A different person than before, this one is sitting all alone, with his back to the entire establishment. Couldn't he have picked a different booth in which to be a sad loner? I glare at the back of his head as I choose an open seat at the bar. Robbie makes his way over.

"Twice in one night," he says.

"Lucky you."

"How was family dinner?"

"It made Leo happy."

Robbie nods. "You drinking?"

"Please."

Robbie jerks his head toward my booth. "Go sit. I'll bring it over."

"Are you blind? There's someone already over there."

"Yeah, but..." Robbie shrugs. "I think maybe you won't mind so much."

What? Why? I look at the back of the man's head. It isn't...is it?

It is. I spent a lot of time staring at the back of that head in a surveillance van. So much time that I should now be embarrassed that I didn't recognize it before. Shit. I really should have stayed in bed.

"But if you want," Robbie says, "I'll throw him out on his ass."

I glance toward the exit. He doesn't know I'm here. I could make a break for it.

"Maggie?" Robbie says. "You want me to throw him out?"

I shake my head. "How long has he been here?"

"A couple hours, maybe. Ordered a whiskey, but I don't think he's even touched it yet."

"Good whiskey?"

"Tullamore."

"Not bad." I stand and walk over to the booth and sit down across from Ryan. "Of all the gin joints in all the world."

Ryan looks up. "What are you doing here?"

"This is my bar. And my booth," I say as Robbie sets a glass on the table. "And my drink. Thanks, Rob."

He nods and backs toward the bar to keep an eye on us. Or me, at least. I smile.

Ryan turns his head slightly to the right. "He gonna throw me out?"

"Only if I ask him to."

"Are you going to ask him to?"

"Depends why you're here," I say. "Isn't there some cop bar closer to home?"

"Several." Ryan nods toward my wrist. "Lew told me they discharged you."

I move my wrist into my lap. "Yeah."

"You okay?"

"Okay enough." I move my drink closer. "Did you come here to ask if I'm okay?"

"No. They wouldn't have discharged you if you weren't okay enough."

"Then why?"

I don't know what I'm hoping to hear. That he misses me? That he misses me at least as much as I'm missing him?

Ryan shrugs. "I was thinking about you. Because El called, and because..." He shakes his head. "I didn't think you'd be here."

"Why?"

"Well, because of..." Ryan gestures to me. "That."

I roll my eyes. "It was a minor stabbing."

"It needed surgery."

"Minor surgery."

Ryan's eyes seem sad for a moment. Then he jerks his head toward the bar. "Also, your bodyguard over there told me you weren't coming in."

"Go easy on him. I really wasn't supposed to come in tonight. He didn't mean to lie to a federal agent."

"Lie to a federal agent?"

"That's a crime, you know."

"Yeah."

Ryan picks up his glass and sips some whiskey. Hasn't touched it in two hours. I sit down and, two minutes later, he starts drinking. Definitely a good sign.

He puts the glass down. "So, why are you here if you're not supposed to be?"

I pick up my drink and sample it. It's a very strong double. Possibly a triple.

"I decided to take a walk to clear my head."

"Why? What's on your mind?"

Is he serious? Is there something he's hoping to hear? Am I just projecting? This is what I get for sneaking out of the house. And then not going back when I had the chance.

"Did Lew tell you what we talked about at the hospital?" I ask.

Ryan shakes his head. "Just that you were...okay enough."

Interesting. Or maybe not. Ryan did pass on the case. He passed on *me*. Maybe he doesn't care what Lew and I talked about.

"Are you going to tell me what you talked about?" Ryan asks.

"I don't know if I should."

"Why?"

"There are a lot of reasons," I say. "Aren't there?"

"I suppose there are," Ryan says. After a moment, he adds, "Maybe we could be friends."

I laugh. Probably a little too much. "You got a lot of thief friends, do you?"

"No." He traces the rim of his glass with his finger. "We could be just two strangers who strike up a conversation at a bar one night."

"I'm not in the habit of telling strangers...well, anything, really."

"I remember, *Tess*."

"My name's not Tess," I say. "I think you have me confused with someone else."

"Guess I do. What is your name?"

I shake my head. "No names. Let's just be...two ships passing in the night or something like that."

"Gotta call you something."

"You really don't."

Ryan looks at me, his eyes seeming sad again. Regret? For passing me on, maybe? For saving me from the murderous gunmen in the first place? Probably that one. That was the night his life went off the rails, after all.

"Passing ships," he says finally. "So, what's a nice girl like you doing in a place like this?"

"Are you suggesting this isn't a nice place?"

"Depends how much the bartender likes you, I think."

"That's a fair observation," I say. "I'm here because I'm wrestling with some big life decisions and I think better with alcohol."

"No one thinks better with alcohol."

"You're only saying that because you haven't had enough to drink yet."

"How do you know how much I've had to drink?"

I shrug. "I hear things."

Ryan nods. "What are you trying to decide?"

"What to do, where to live—"

"Where to live," Ryan interrupts. "Are you moving?"

"Yeah, I need to…" I sigh. "Yeah. I'm moving. I'm staying with a friend right now, but I won't be there long."

Ryan's gaze drifts upward. When he looks back at me, he seems…relieved. Is he glad to know I'm not sleeping on the streets? Glad to know where to find me?

"Why's that?" he asks.

"Maybe I like being alone," I say.

"Do you?"

Yes. No. I don't know. I pick up my glass and have another drink.

Ryan tilts his head. "What did you and Lew talk about?"

So much for passing ships. I put my glass down. "He suggested I help…you."

"Me?"

"The FBI."

"How?"

"Without helping you." I shrug. "Whatever that means."

"Help us without helping us," Ryan says.

"Yeah. I don't suppose you know what the hell he was talking about."

He sighs. "Maybe he—"

"I'm not going to be your CI or anything like that."

Ryan laughs and picks up his whiskey. "I don't want you to be my CI."

"Good. Because I won't."

"Glad we got that settled."

"Me, too."

We both drink this time.

"I don't think Lew meant that anyway," I say then. "He seemed pretty adamant I give up my life of crime."

"You don't think you should?" Ryan asks.

He's trying to sound detached. The way a stranger might when engaging in meaningless conversation with another stranger in a bar to pass the time. Inside this man are two wolves. One really hates me. The other is trying not to hate me. Not sure why, though. That fight was over a long time ago.

"I don't know what I think," I say. "I used to know. Like, everything. I mean, not *everything*, everything, but you know what I mean. I knew who I was. I knew what I was doing, and I was good at it. Really good. I didn't spend sleepless nights wondering about…things." I shake my head. "And then you came along and fucked it all up."

"Me? Not the gray ghost?"

"No. Sure, that guy's an asshole, but that was just business. You, though…That wasn't business. That was…" I shrug. "I don't know what that was."

"Yeah. I know what you mean." Ryan finishes his whiskey. "You're very chatty tonight."

"Am I?"

"Yeah. Why?" He leans in, his expression somehow more serious than before. "You okay? What's wrong with you?"

I scoff. "That's rude. I mean, a lot's wrong with me, but still…rude."

"Sorry about that. Are you on pain meds?"

"What?"

"When they discharged you from the hospital, did they send you home with painkillers?"

"Yeah."

"Did you take any tonight?"

"Yeah."

"And you've been drinking?"

"Yeah."

"Jesus," Ryan says.

"Oh, he went home."

Ryan turns around and waves his arm in the air. Robbie comes over to the booth, wiping his hands on a towel.

"Can you call Leo and have him bring her home?" Ryan says.

Robbie glances at me. I shrug. I don't know what Ryan's problem is.

"You forgot about the pain meds," Ryan says.

Robbie's eyes widen a little. He points at me. "Not cool."

As he walks away, I look at Ryan. "Did you just get me in trouble with the bartender? *That's* not cool."

"I'm sure he'll forgive you eventually," Ryan says. "Do me a favor, okay? Stay here and wait for Leo."

"Where are you going?"

"Home," Ryan says. "I'm going home."

"See you next time?"

"There won't be a next time. Not for us."

"Passing ships."

"Something like that."

"We'll always have Skyreach."

Ryan smiles. "You're fun when you're high."

"I'm fun all the time."

"I don't doubt it," he says. "Tell me you'll stay here and wait for Leo."

"I will stay here and wait for Leo."

"You won't wander off or disappear through any windows or cracks in the floor?"

I lean over to look at the floor. "If a crack in the floor is big enough for me to slip through, we have bigger problems than—"

"Just…stay here. Okay?"

I look at him. "Okay."

He slides out of the booth and stands.

"You okay getting home on your own?" I ask.

"Yeah. I can manage it."

He lightly taps the table with his fingertips before nodding and walking away.

A little while later, Leo comes through the front doors wearing pajama bottoms and a sweatshirt from Northeastern.

That must belong to Linus. It's not like either Leo or I went to college.

"I am going to nail that window shut," Leo says when he reaches me.

"That's a fire hazard."

"What are you even doing here?"

I sigh. "Making things worse. What else?"

"Well, we all have our talents," Leo says. "Come on, let's get you to bed."

57

IT HAS BEEN TEN DAYS since my last FBI encounter.

I celebrate the achievement by covering for Leo at The Thieves' Den so he and Linus can have a proper date night. It's a lot less fun to be at a bar when you're serving drinks rather than consuming them, but it's a small price to pay considering everything Leo has done for me.

Even if I'm spending entirely too much time looking at my booth and remembering that last FBI encounter.

This is where attachments lead you. Staring at a stupid booth and thinking about the one who got away. The one you let go. The one who let you go.

I remember thinking—hoping—that it would get easier. It doesn't seem to be happening yet. But I've made it ten whole days now. I will make it ten more. And ten more after that. Eventually, I'll forget. Or move on. Or whatever it is people do.

"I gotta piss," Robbie says. "You good on your own?"

I look away from the booth. "What?"

"I gotta piss," he repeats. "You good to hold down the fort for a minute?"

"Yeah," I say. "Take your time."

He walks away, leaving me alone behind the bar. I hand out menus and pour a couple of pints for a pair of new arrivals before wiping down an empty section with a damp cloth. It's already perfectly clean, but I could use the distraction. Anything to keep my mind from going where I would rather it not go. Again.

"Should've known I'd find you here," a familiar voice says.

I look up to see Jonas standing in front of me. It has been zero days since my last FBI encounter.

"Whatever happened," I say, "I didn't do it."

He sets a paper bag on the bar. "Funny."

I lean in. "You know, as nice as it was for your mom to pack you a lunch, we do serve food here."

"It's not food, and I'm not staying." Jonas nods at the bag. "Just dropping that off for you."

"What is it?"

"Not what."

What the hell does that…I stand straight. Shit. I point to the bag. "Is that…Jay?"

"Yeah. Per your request." Jonas backs up. "No offense, but I sincerely hope this is the last time I ever see you."

"None taken," I murmur as he walks away.

At the end of the night, I take Jay to Leo's apartment. I'm not sure there's ever a *good* time to get the ashes of your childhood exploiter, but at least Jonas picked a night when I have the place to myself. Now I won't have to explain to Leo why those ashes are in his house instead of being dumped in a gutter where I'm sure he would say they belong.

And maybe he would be right. Maybe they do belong there. Maybe they'll end up there one day.

Not tonight, though.

I set the bag on the counter while I secure the door behind me. Then I look at what I have brought home.

A paper bag. I'm not sure what I was expecting, but it wasn't this. They put him in an honest-to-goodness paper bag. And not even a big one. It looks like what you wrap your forty in so everyone can pretend you're not carrying an open container on a public street. But instead of cheap alcohol, it's a person.

What's left of one, anyway.

I open the bag and look at the silver container inside.

An urn. That's the proper word. It's a proper urn, too, all shiny and silver and not the cardboard box I was expecting the state to use for the unclaimed cremated remains of a John Doe. Did Lew arrange for an upgrade? That seems like something he would do. Smug jackass. Always doing stupid, thoughtful things, thinking it'll make a difference.

Which it doesn't.

Why would it?

I put the urn on the coffee table and go fetch the Ketel One from the kitchen. I take it back to the living room and sit on the couch, holding the bottle close to my chest as I look at that goddamn urn. Tears prick at my eyes as I open the vodka. It makes no sense—I should not care about this—but my body doesn't seem to give a shit about what may or may not make sense. Doesn't seem like there's really anything to do about it except give in.

At least for the night.

"You were a real asshole. You know that?" I say to the urn. I salute it with the bottle. "Thanks for everything."

When the vodka's gone, I leave the urn on the coffee table and take my drunk ass to Leo's bed where I lie awake and look at the ceiling. What am I going to do with Jay now? I can't leave him on the coffee table, and I don't exactly have any space that's actually mine in this apartment. Maybe I could take him to Revere and dump his ashes on the beach or in the ocean or something. Not that he was really a beach guy. Or an ocean guy. No, he was a barfly through and through. Which I suppose means there's really only one place for him. Here's hoping Angie agrees.

Late the next morning, I put the urn back in the bag and head to The Rebel Fly, arriving just as Angie is unlocking the door. She holds it open for me and I walk inside.

"The fuck you doing here this early?" she asks, going back behind the bar. "I didn't think you came out when the sun was up."

I set the bag in front of her.

"What's that?" Angie asks.

"Not what," I say. "Who."

She doesn't get it as quickly as I did, but she didn't know Jay was dead until just now. She opens the bag and removes the urn.

"Fucking vacation," she says. "You told me he was on a fucking vacation."

"Thought it sounded nicer than the truth."

"Yeah? What is the truth?"

I shake my head. "You don't want to know."

"Well, shit." She looks at the urn again. "He was a real fucking asshole."

"Yeah."

"I'm gonna miss the shit outta him."

"Yeah," I say. "Me, too."

Angie gets two glasses and puts them on the bar next to the urn. She then gets a bottle of Bushmills and opens it. She pours a generous amount into each glass, then sets the bottle aside.

She raises her glass. "To a real asshole."

I pick up my glass and gently knock it against hers. Angie downs her entire drink in one impressive swallow. I take a much smaller sip.

Angie puts down her glass. "What are you gonna do with him?"

"Dunno. It's not like he cared about anyplace other than here or the dog track, and the dog track's closed," I say. "Maybe you could give him a place of honor behind the bar."

"That why you brought him here? To get rid of him?"

"No. You noticed he was missing. You cared enough to ask," I say. "I'm pretty sure you and I are the only people on the planet who care that he's…"

"On vacation?"

I smile. "Sightseeing and sunbathing and shit."

Angie smiles, too. She glances back at the mirrored wall and the three rows of watered-down alcohol in front of it. She turns and starts rearranging the bottles on the middle shelf.

"We're not the only ones, you know," she says as she works. "Those kids are gonna notice, too."

I frown. "What kids?"

"His kids." Angie looks at me over her shoulder. "Jesus Christ, Maggie. You should know. You were one of them."

"He was still doing that?"

Angie goes back to rearranging. "Of course he was still doing that. Did you think you were the last?"

I didn't think about it at all. I always assumed I wasn't the only thief who worked with him, but I never did consider from where those other thieves came. I didn't care. Surviving took all the energy I had. There wasn't room for anything else.

You never stopped trying to survive, Leo told me. It still sounds stupid, but maybe there's something to it. Maybe if I had stopped, I would have known. Maybe if I had stopped, things would be different.

So many things.

Angie finishes with the bottles and turns around. She picks up the urn and looks at it. "Shit," she says. "Those fucking kids. Jimmy wasn't much, but he was something. Who do they get now?"

Help us without helping us. I think I get it now.

I pick up my glass and drink the rest of my whiskey.

"Me," I say. "They get me."

58

I AM AN EXPERT—OR pretty close to one—at cracking safes and picking locks. I have the grip strength of an Olympic rock climber—if those are even a thing—and I can hold my own in a fight—most fights, anyway—but I am an utter disaster when it comes to creating aesthetically pleasing foam designs in a cup of coffee.

Lacey looks at my latest attempt. "Hmm. Well…it's coming along."

She sounds like she regrets having hired me and possibly like she regrets knowing Nia at all because now she's stuck with me. And until I find something else—which is much easier said than done, given my complete lack of experience that doesn't involve lock picking or safecracking—I'm stuck with this because unofficially adopting a group of homeless kids isn't exactly the cheapest endeavor in the world.

Not that they've let me do a whole lot. It's not surprising. They don't trust me yet. They don't trust people they don't know, and they don't know me. They don't know how well I can relate to their situation. Or how well I can understand their reluctance to trust anyone because I wouldn't have, either, when I was their age or in their shoes. It's only been a couple of months, though. They'll get there. And when they do, I will be ready.

Behind us, the door chime goes off, indicating a customer has entered. I hope they want nothing more elaborate than black coffee in a to-go cup.

"Okay," Lacey says, moving my failed coffee art to the side. "You take the order. I will fill it."

Sounds fine by me. I nod and step up to the register.

"Welcome to Jitters," I say, looking at the customer. "What can I…"

Lew. It's Lew, his face now free of puffiness and bruises. Which makes sense. It's been two damn months since I've seen him. A German shepherd sits on his left, tail thumping enthusiastically.

"Hi, Skye," Lew says.

Lacey sidles up on my right. "Hey, handsome. Long time no see."

Lew smiles at her. "You talking to me or the dog?"

"Rufus, of course." She leans toward the dog and says in a baby voice, "Yes, you are, Rufus. You are so handsome, aren't you?"

Rufus responds with a high-pitched yip. He breaks his sit and prances around until Lew tells him to stop.

"Thanks for that," he says to Lacey.

She shrugs. "You want the usual?"

"Make Nia's a decaf."

Lacey makes a face. "At her request or yours?"

"Mine. And the doctor's."

"Fair enough. But tell her I did so under protest."

"Will do." Lew reaches for his wallet and puts a fifty on the counter.

"That's too much," Lacey protests.

"No, it isn't." Lew nods toward me. "Mind if I borrow your cashier for a quick chat?"

Lacey looks at the total lack of customers waiting and shakes her head. "She's all yours."

As Lacey moves off, Lew looks at me and jerks his head toward the tables. I suppose after everything, I at least owe him a conversation.

I sigh. "Fine."

I walk around the counter and follow Lew and Rufus to a corner table by the window. I select the chair that lets me keep my back to the wall. Lew sits across from me. Rufus lays at his feet.

I fold my arms across my chest. "You just have to lie about everything, don't you? You can't help yourself."

"What are you talking about?"

"You said I'd never see you again."

"That was before you took a job at my wife's favorite coffee place."

"So you came all the way to Boston just for coffee?"

"Visiting the in-laws. Nia wanted to get one last trip in before the baby."

I nod. "And what are *you* doing *here*?"

Lew points his thumb over his shoulder. "Getting coffee."

"And?"

"Visiting you."

"To what end?"

"Don't know yet."

"You G-men aren't big on knowing things, are you?"

"We prefer it, actually, but we don't always get what we want, do we?"

That's the understatement of the century. "No, we don't," I say. "Tell me what you want."

"I want you to come to dinner tonight."

"Dinner? Where? At your in-laws' house?"

Lew nods.

I laugh. "You want me to have dinner with a fed *and* a police chief?"

"And a few non-law-enforcement types."

"Any other criminals?"

Lew shrugs. "Nia's overly fond of breaking and entering."

"Thanks, but I'll pass. After everything I put you through, the last place I should be is at your family dinner," I say. "And even if I hadn't put you through anything, I still wouldn't go to the chief of police's house for any reason."

"Just keep your hands off the silver and it'll be fine."

Jackass. "Funny guy." I glance toward the counter. What is their usual order, and why is it taking Lacey so long to prepare it? "Why do you really want me to go to dinner?"

"The Kellys would like to thank you for what you did to save my life."

"And what do they think about what I did to endanger your life?"

Lew smiles. "They want you to come."

"They don't know me."

"They know Nia likes you. They know I like you. They know Rufus likes you."

I look at Rufus. His tongue's hanging out of his mouth. "His approval opens a lot of doors, huh?"

"You have no idea," Lew says. "So? Will you come?"

"Skye!" Lacey calls.

Both Lew and I look at the counter. A modest line of customers has formed.

"Say yes, Skye," Lew says as I stand.

"I'll think about it."

Lew pulls a folded piece of paper from his jacket pocket and holds it out. "Six o'clock."

Taking the paper, I stuff it into my pocket and go back to work.

59

AS SOON AS I GET home, I stop to empty my pockets onto the kitchen counter before getting into the shower to scrub off the smell of coffee as best I can. I'm not positive, but I'm pretty sure it makes no difference. I am now doomed to smell like a Starbucks for the remainder of my days. The price of an honest day's labor, I suppose.

After the shower, I go into the kitchen to survey my dinner options. Leo keeps the fridge stocked with easy-to-reheat meals, but using the microwave and utensils feels like entirely too much work, so I take a box of cereal out of the cupboard and set it on the counter. The piece of paper Lew gave me earlier catches my eye. I pick it up and unfold it. An address for someplace in Chestnut Hill. Figures. I glance at the time on my phone. If I leave now, and if the trains are running remotely on schedule, I could be there pretty close to six o'clock.

Except that would be crazy. Even if Lew wasn't an FBI agent and his father-in-law wasn't a cop, it would still be crazy for me to show up there. Hello, family of strangers. Please feed me. That would be even worse than being the third wheel at family dinners with Leo and Linus. I don't know who attends Nia's family dinners, but I have to imagine half the room would want to arrest me on sight and principle alone, and all of them would just be waiting for me to steal something.

Keep your hands off the silver, and it'll be fine, Lew said.

He really is a jackass.

But he is a jackass to whom I owe a pretty substantial debt. I suppose trekking all the way out to the suburbs isn't too much to ask. Maybe I should just get it over with.

I text Leo that I'm heading out for a few hours and leave the address on the counter in case I don't come back. Then I go catch a train to Chestnut Hill.

I end up standing in front of a modest ranch-style home. So this is where Nia's family lives. What would it have been like to grow up in a house in the suburbs? What would it have been like to have an unmovable constant like that? How would I have been different?

I knock on the front door. A dog starts barking immediately. At least I know I have the right address.

A moment later, a gorgeous blond woman opens the door.

"Hi," she says. "Can I help you?"

Oh, I should not have done this. I swallow. "I, uh—"

"Wait—are you Skye?"

I hate that they all know my name. I nod.

"I'm Susannah. Come on in."

She slides to the left so I can enter. Too late to turn back now. I walk inside, wait for her to close the door, then allow her to lead the way to a loud and heated argument. Are they perhaps debating the merits of inviting a certain criminal to their family dinner?

"Are you crazy?" Nia exclaims. "No, never mind. I already know the answer because you're obviously *certifiable* if you think—"

"You're all crazy," Susannah announces as she walks into the room. "The Yankees will win the pennant because your beloved Sox got nothin'."

The room sinks into silence. The heated argument was about baseball? I look from one face to the other. Nia is the only person I know. She's sitting on a couch, Rufus at her feet. I recognize her father, however, from the news. There's another guy in the room who bears such a strong resemblance to Nia and her father that I assume he's Colin. He's bouncing a toddler on his knees, a beautiful, blond, blue-eyed boy. Clearly Susannah's son.

"Traitor!" Nia points to her brother. "You, my friend, have married a traitor." She looks at the child next. "Your mommy's a big, fat traitor. I'm sorry you had to find out this way, but it's better that you know now."

Susannah rolls her eyes. "I'm not a traitor. I just really hate baseball."

Nia and Colin fake heart attacks. The boy laughs as though he's never seen anything funnier in his short life.

"By the way," Susannah says, "Skye's here, so maybe you should try to pretend to be normal."

Everyone now looks at me. Oh, I hate this so much.

"You came. Good," Nia says. "Forgive me for not getting up, but everyone here has decided I am too helpless to do anything so crazy."

"I do believe the employed phrase was 'take it easy'," Susannah says. "But you got the crazy part right enough."

Nia flips her off. "That's Susannah, my sister-in-law and tormentor-in-chief." She jerks her thumb to the right. "This is my brother, Colin, and their spawn—"

"Son," Colin interjects.

"—Liam." Nia then gestures to her father. "And my dad, Patrick. Everyone, this is Skye."

I nod to Colin before looking at Chief Kelly. "Thank you for inviting me."

He doesn't react. His expression isn't unfriendly, but it doesn't exactly scream warm welcome, either.

"Dad," Nia says.

He looks at his daughter. It takes a moment, but his love of her conquers his distrust of me. He looks back at me. "You're most welcome."

"You can come in, you know," Susannah says then. "Their bark is much worse than their bite."

Because going deeper into a cop's home is always a good idea. Still, I force myself forward. I glance at the windows to my left. Which would be the faster way out of here? Those windows or the front door? Probably the door.

"Still no Llewellyn?" a new voice asks.

I look to my right to see a short, slightly plump, older woman wiping her hands on a dish towel. Mrs. Kelly, I presume. Chief Kelly stands to kiss her cheek.

She gently pushes Chief Kelly back as she focuses on me. This is a woman you do not cross.

"Who is this?" she asks, but I'm guessing she knows exactly who I am.

"This is Skye," Nia says. "Skye, this is my mother, Nancy."

Mrs. Kelly smiles at me. Her expression is warmer than her husband's but still reserved. Why did I do this? Why did Nia and Lew want me to come here? Payback for all the misery?

"Hello, Skye," Mrs. Kelly says. "I'm pleased you could join us."

It's not the most insincere thing I've ever heard, but...close. I nod. "Thank you for having me."

Mrs. Kelly turns to her daughter. "Have you heard from Llewellyn? Is he close?"

"He knows dinner's at six, Mom. He'll be here." Nia looks at me and mouths, *Relax*.

Easier said than done. I just walked willingly into the lions' den. I used to be smarter than this.

Mrs. Kelly looks at Chief Kelly. "Come help me in the kitchen?" she asks, and he nods and walks out of the room. She turns to follow but adds, "Lavinia, please text your husband and find out how much longer he'll be."

"Oh my God, he'll be here," Nia groans as her mother leaves.

"Your ne'er-do-well husband is holding up dinner," Colin says, shaking his head. "I knew I never liked that guy."

"Don't be a dick, Colin," Nia says, and Colin laughs.

Susannah doesn't. She removes Liam from his father's arms. "You've already taught my son to say 'shit', Vinnie. Maybe 'dick' can wait until he's older."

Nia waves her off. "Everyone loves foul-mouthed little kids."

Susannah walks away. "Not everyone."

"Ick, ick, ick!" Liam exclaims as they leave the room.

Colin chuckles under his breath. He stands, kisses the top of Nia's head, and follows his family out. Nia looks at me.

"Lavinia? Vinnie?" I say. "How many aliases do you have?"

"Well, Tess-Maggie-Skye, I'll show you mine, if you show me yours." Nia gestures to the now-empty room. "Are you going to sit down or just stand there all night?"

"I was actually thinking about making a run for it."

"Don't do that."

I sit next to her. Rufus creeps closer to sniff my legs. Which does not terrify me. At all.

"You shouldn't have forced me on them," I say.

"They're not tense about you," she says. Off my look, she concedes, "They're not *only* tense about you."

"No? Why? Who else did you invite to dinner? The Boston Strangler?"

"Well, I asked, but he was busy, so I had to settle for—"

"Me," Ryan says.

The sound of his voice immediately makes me feel…things. Cold. Hot. Everything in between. I lift my head to see him standing with Lew in the living room.

Well…fuck.

60

"YOU'RE LATE," NIA SAYS, AS though I am not dying at her side. "Mom's pissed."

"I'll make it up to her," Lew says.

From the corner of my eye, I see him come into the room to greet Nia and an excited German shepherd, but the bulk of my focus is on Ryan. Quiet, yet-to-move Ryan.

I look at Nia. What the hell was she thinking? Was this the plan the entire time? Was Lew in on it, too?

"I know. The trickery," she says. "I feel just sick about it. Of course, that could just be the pregnancy."

"Nia—"

"Look, here's the deal." She leans toward me. "Sad Sack over there is driving me crazy, and I'm afraid that if you two don't figure out some way to be together that he's going to end up living in my basement. I already have one baby on the way. I don't need a second."

"Jesus, Nia," Ryan mutters.

She looks at him. "You know it's true." She turns back to me. "So, do me a favor and work something out, okay? Again, not for you, but for me."

I gape at her. There is something seriously wrong with this woman.

"Hey, sweets," Lew says. His facial expression is harder to read, but I think he's trying not to laugh. Love is most definitely blind. "Why don't we give them some privacy."

"If you two work it out, you can stay for dinner," Nia says as Lew helps her to her feet. "If not, I cordially invite you to piss off."

"Lavinia!" Mrs. Kelly calls.

"Sorry," Nia calls back. She looks over her shoulder at us. "I'm not sorry. I mean it."

She, Lew, and Rufus disappear into another room. Their voices are muffled, but it sounds like Mrs. Kelly is scolding Nia for being rude. What is their plan now? Just sit around the dining room table and listen to us have an awkward conversation about our doomed relationship?

"What are you doing here?" Ryan asks.

Being tricked, apparently. I look at him. He hasn't moved.

"I was invited," I say. "But I wouldn't have come if I had known…" I shake my head and stand. "It doesn't matter. I'll go."

Ryan continues to stand in my way. "Why did you come?"

Good question. "Because they asked," I say. "What are you doing here? Nia inviting you to dinner wasn't a red flag?"

"El asks me to join them whenever they're in town. Mrs. Kelly keeps Nia from throwing too much food at me."

I have no idea if that's a joke. Knowing Nia, it could go either way. I nod. "Is Jonas coming, too?"

"He skips family dinner night. He's not exactly Mrs. Kelly's favorite person."

I get that. I gesture to the hallway behind Ryan. "If you move, I'll go. You can tell them…Tell them whatever you want."

Ryan still doesn't move. I attempt to go around him, but he blocks my way. What is he doing?

"Let me go," I say.

"I already did."

"Then do it again."

"I don't want to."

"It doesn't matter what you want. It doesn't matter what I want, either."

Ryan steps forward, the look in his eyes making my stomach clench. Shit, that's intense. It definitely doesn't make me want to do things to him on Nia's mother's couch that Nia's mother wouldn't appreciate.

"Why not?" he asks. "What do you want, Skye?"

To be literally anywhere else in the entire universe. "You know why, Ryan." I point to him. "Cop." I point to myself. "Robber."

"You don't like guns."

"What?"

Ryan points to himself. "Cop." He points to me. "Burglar."

I nod. "Get caught with a gun, and it's a lot worse."

"Yeah."

"Does that make it okay? Me, being a burglar and not a robber, I mean."

It doesn't. Of course it doesn't. He hesitates, which tells me he damn well knows it, too.

He shakes his head. "You're not doing that anymore."

How the hell does he know that? Is he watching me? Having someone else watch me? Is the goddamn FBI keeping tabs on me? I don't care how much I want to jump this guy. I don't like that. At all.

I step back. "Are you spying on me?"

"No. Of course not."

"Is the FBI spying on me?"

"No."

"Then how do you know what I'm doing or not doing?"

He doesn't know. The doubt is in his eyes. In the tick of his jaw. He wants to believe, but he's not *sure*. He could never be sure. And that's the problem. Or, at least, one of them.

"You're not doing that anymore," he says, emphasizing it like he can manifest it into truth. "You're just trying to…I don't know. Scare me."

"If that's all it takes to scare you, you should really consider a career change," I say. "Now, if that's all—"

"That's not all," Ryan says. "Don't go."

"Don't do this," I counter. "This is nothing. It can't be anything else."

"Why?"

"Well, for one, it's crazy."

"I know."

"It doesn't make any sense whatsoever."

"I know that, too. Okay? I know," Ryan says. "I know we are fucking *doomed* before we start, but I still can't get clear of this. Of you. Of us."

I know exactly what he means. Not that I will admit it. "You probably shouldn't swear in here. I'm guessing Mrs. Kelly doesn't like it."

"Mrs. Kelly raised Nia. It's nothing she hasn't heard before," Ryan says. "Stop trying to run away from me and…just *talk* to me."

"Why?" I ask. "What will be said that hasn't already been said? What deep truth do you think will be revealed that will make this"—I gesture between us—"possible?"

"I want to try," he says. "I want to see what we can be."

Oh. That's new. I can't breathe.

"Maybe…" He shakes his head. "Maybe we really can't be anything. Maybe it will never work. But what if it could?"

"Pretty big 'what if'."

"Maybe."

"Probably."

Ryan nods. "Probably, but…I still want to know for sure. I want to try. What I don't know is if you want to try, too."

I do. I do want to try. I don't, however, want to lose. And there does seem to be an awful lot to lose here. For both of us.

"I'm a mess," I say.

He shrugs. "So am I. So is everyone."

"I'm a bigger mess. And a criminal."

"Reformed."

"For the moment, maybe, but what if that changes?"

"Why would it change?"

"Because I am a mess. And a criminal," I say. "Haven't you been listening?"

"No. No, I haven't," he says. "Because whenever I am with you, whenever I am close to you, all I can think about is how badly I want to kiss you."

I wouldn't mind kissing him, either. I look at his lips and lick my own before putting a little more distance between us. "So your plan is to...what? Base our entire relationship on sex?"

"It's a place to start."

"Not a good one!"

"There are worse ideas."

"Are there?"

"Not trying," Ryan says. "And out of everything I have heard you say today, I haven't heard you say you don't want to try."

That's not true, is it? Maybe it is true. If we were anyone else, we probably would have already done...whatever it is people do. Whatever couples do. Take leisurely walks in the park. Go to the movies. Have brunch. Double date with Leo and Linus. And those things are...intriguing. Is that enough, though? It might be, if we were anyone else...but we're not. We're just not.

"If I say that—if I say I don't want to try—you'll let me go?" I ask.

Ryan's shoulders droop. He suddenly looks every bit the sad sack Nia claimed he was.

He nods. "Yes. I will let you go."

He doesn't add anything about making him believe it. Not that it would matter. I am a liar. A good one. He isn't. I could make him believe it, too. Maybe that would be the kind thing to do.

Because I am a liar. And he isn't.

But. There's always a goddamn but.

I fold my arms across my chest. "What if it doesn't work out?"

His shoulders straighten. I have given him hope. However small.

"Then it doesn't work out," he says.

"What if it doesn't work out because I rob a bank?"

"You're going to rob a bank?"

I shrug. "I get bored sometimes."

Ryan smiles. "Well, then, I suppose I'll have to arrest you."

I scoff. "You'd have to catch me first."

"Yes, I would."

"I wouldn't make it easy for you."

He steps toward me. "I would expect nothing less."

I don't move away. "It'll never work out, you know."

"I'm sure you're right." Ryan takes another step. "We'll just have to enjoy it while we can."

I nod. "Get while the getting's good."

"Does that mean you're in?"

Oh, this will be an absolute disaster...but what's life without risk?

I grab his jacket with both hands and back him out of the living room and into the hallway. When he comes up against a wall, I kiss him. His hands find my waist as he deepens the kiss. We're on the fast track to escalating to the point where Ryan would probably have to arrest himself. Because somewhere in this house is a foul-mouthed toddler. And the rest of that toddler's law enforcement family. Maybe Ryan has forgotten that, but I haven't.

I pull back and put up my hand to keep him where he is.

"Saturday night," I say.

"What's Saturday night?"

I shrug and walk toward the front door. "Figure it out."

"Skye?"

I look at him over my shoulder and smile. "Catch me if you can."

About the Author

M.J. Fifield is a semi-functional bundle of anxiety with a totally unrelated addiction to Dr Pepper, an absolutely necessary stockpile of purple pens and notebooks, and a completely healthy and normal obsession with medieval weaponry.

She writes because she loves it, publishes if she must, and markets wholly against her will. When she isn't thinking deep thoughts about grammar or devising ways to make her characters miserable, she's…Yeah. She's never *not* doing that. Never mind.

M.J. lives with her family in Florida. Visit her online at mjfifield.com.

www.ingramcontent.com/pod-product-compliance
Lightning Source LLC
LaVergne TN
LVHW010636110826
845149LV00014B/2847

* 9 7 9 8 9 9 5 4 1 3 7 0 7 *